A NEW SENSATION

"Another superstition attached to the lights that I failed to mention"—his voice was a husky murmur, spilling over her with caressing force—"is what happens to the people who witness this magical display."

"What happens?" Her own voice had a breathy sound.

"Supposedly . . . they do things they wouldn't normally do." Cody turned her toward him.

"Yes." It was a choked little sound.

When his mouth came down upon hers, she was moving to meet it. The sexual chemistry between them was volatile, producing sensations as fiery and brilliant as any she had witnessed in the sky. . . .

from "Northern Magic"

<u>BOOK YOUR PLACE ON OUR WEBSITE</u> <u>AND MAKE THE</u> <u>READING CONNECTION!</u>

We've created a customized website just for our very special readers, where you can get the inside scoop on everything that's going on with Zebra, Pinnacle and Kensington books.

When you come online, you'll have the exciting opportunity to:

- View covers of upcoming books

- Read sample chapters

- Learn about our future publishing schedule (listed by publication month *and author*)

- Find out when your favorite authors will be visiting a city near you

- Search for and order backlist books from our online catalog

- Check out author bios and background information

- Send e-mail to your favorite authors

- Meet the Kensington staff online

- Join us in weekly chats with authors, readers and other guests

- Get writing guidelines

- AND MUCH MORE!

Visit our website at
http://www.kensingtonbooks.com

JANET DAILEY

Let's Be Jolly!

ZEBRA BOOKS
KENSINGTON PUBLISHING CORP.
http://www.kensingtonbooks.com

Contents

NORTHERN MAGIC

Chapter One

As her flight descended beneath the gray clouds over Anchorage, Shannon Hayes strained to look through the plane's scratched window. A dark wall of mountains loomed close to the city, their peaks lost in the cloud cover. Below, she saw a scattering of homes and an interweaving of roads; and in the distance, rectangular gray buildings disappearing into the sky's low ceiling.

Alaska's largest city wasn't all that big. Shannon was a little surprised, having expected to see a busy metropolis something more like Houston, Texas, her own hometown. But the thought didn't last long—it was almost instantly overpowered by the excitement of seeing her destination at last.

Her brown eyes were shining as she leaned back in her seat. A smile hovered at the corners of her mouth in anticipation of the joy she would find at journey's end. She touched the engagement ring on her left hand, rubbing the square-cut diamond as if it were a talisman. The gray gloom outside the aircraft's window could not dampen her eagerness.

She heard the thud of the wheels on the airport runway, followed within seconds by the reversing thrust of the jet engines to slow their landing. It had the opposite effect on her pulse, which picked up tempo and beat faster.

Shannon smoothed her chestnut hair with one hand, though she had brushed it into a sexy tousle only minutes ago. She had touched up her makeup as well, knowing that Rick cared a little too much about how she looked. He was proud to claim ownership—his word, and it irked her a little—of a dark-haired, dark-eyed, totally gorgeous babe. Also his words. She hoped he would still think of her that way. Being totally gorgeous just wasn't possible after a five-hour flight.

It had been long and lonely months since she'd seen him. She remembered how much she'd cried at the airport the day Rick left for Alaska, the promises they'd made to each other, and the desperate quality that marked their kisses. He'd written now and then, called a few times, e-mailed her when he could get to a computer, but none of that had filled the emptiness of their separation.

More than one of her girlfriends had told her to forget him and move on, but Shannon couldn't. He was working as a bush pilot, she knew that much. She didn't expect him to be sitting by the phone waiting for her to call—he was out in the wilderness somewhere. Admiring the most glorious scenery on earth. By himself.

At least that was what she assumed. Did being a pilot mean that he never had to be accountable for his time or say he was sorry for making her wait and wonder?

Rick had promised that the minute he had a secure job and a place for them to live he'd send for her. Neither had anticipated that it would take so long. She'd last heard from him more than a month ago, at the end of July, a phone-card call that she'd missed.

Rick had left a voice-mail number that he said would be activated by the end of August. It was better than nothing but still . . . Shannon couldn't help worrying.

Then a FedEx envelope arrived on the first of September. It had contained a good old-fashioned paper ticket to Anchorage and nothing more—no letter, no note—but the ticket was one way. The message was loud and clear: Rick wanted her with him.

Her hidden fear that he might have stopped loving her was banished, and Shannon was on her way to his arms.

She had been ready to go all along and it had taken her no more than a week to make arrangements to move and pack all her things—some to take with her and the rest to be shipped. Her parents would be flying in on the coming weekend for the wedding. Of course, they were convinced she and Rick were both crazy.

Which was understandable, she thought. Leaving the warm Gulf Coast of Texas for the frigid climate of Alaska might seem crazy to a lot of people. But Shannon had been drawn to Rick's adventurous personality since the day they'd met. He'd wanted to experience life on America's last frontier, and to a certain extent, she shared his feelings. But she was realistic enough to know it wasn't going to be paradise.

Whatever. Here she was, in Alaska at last. Heeding the call of the wild, as her parents wryly referred to it. They'd tried to discourage her, but had given up a while ago. After all, she and Rick had been engaged for more than a year now. It wasn't like marriage was something she was rushing into.

She was only seconds away from the great reunion. The thought made her smile a little nervously. When the seat belt sign was turned off, Shannon tugged her shoulder bag from underneath the seat in front of her and collected her blue parka and carry-on from the overhead bin. Arms full, she joined the line of disembarking passengers.

Despite her burden, her steps were light and quick as she left the plane through the airliner tunnel. She scanned the small crowd waiting beyond the gate area, looking for Rick's tall, lanky frame and that familiar shock of sandy blond hair. She was oblivious to the interested glances she received from the men as she skipped over the faces of strangers in search of Rick.

So where was he? Her steps slowed. She was accidentally jostled from behind by another passenger and moved out of the line to look around again for Rick. The brown radiance that had lighted her eyes now held a glitter of confusion. He was nowhere in sight.

Shannon lingered in the corridor outside of the arrival gate until all the passengers were off the plane and had either been met or continued to the baggage-claim section of the terminal. But Rick never came.

When the airline notified her last night that her flight would leave and arrive later than the time listed on the ticket, she had left word on Rick's voice-mail number and e-mailed him, too, but she had no way of knowing whether he'd gotten either message.

Of course, the flight number was on the ticket, which he had bought. Wouldn't he have checked the arrival time before going to the airport?

Evidently not. She looked around once more. Maybe he had assumed they would meet at the baggage claim. She moved to follow the other passengers there. She would have to pick up her checked suitcases no matter what. She got a better grip on the parka and carry-on she was holding and walked on.

But he wasn't at the baggage claim either. Or parked outside in the loading zone. A line of cars, SUVs and trucks picked up passengers and drove away one by one, but there was no sign of Rick.

Surrounded by her suitcases and feeling a little foolish, Shannon stood beneath the terminal overhang and stared through the drizzle at the grayness cast over everything by the clouds.

Trying not to fret over his failure to meet her, she found excuses to explain why he wasn't there. Maybe he was working and couldn't get away to meet her. She shook her head. He still could have had her paged. But maybe she hadn't heard the page. Hey, he was expecting her. He had *sent* for her.

With a determined thrust to her chin, Shannon decided on a plan of action. There had obviously been a mix-up somewhere, so there was no point in waiting at the airport any longer. She waved to a waiting taxicab. The driver stepped out, running an appreciative glance over her while maintaining a respectful attitude. He wasn't much older than Shannon, dressed in a windbreaker, its collar turned up against the drizzle.

"Sorry." He smiled at her. "I saw you standing there, but I thought you were waiting for someone."

"I was, but . . . I guess he couldn't come to pick me up for some unknown reason." She voiced the excuse she had been making over and over in her head.

"Oh. Maybe something happened," the young cabdriver suggested. "Not anything bad," he added quickly. "Just, you know, a flat tire or something like that."

That hadn't occurred to Shannon but hearing the cabdriver say it reassured her. "That must be it. No point standing around here—let's go."

The cabdriver popped the trunk open.

"I have to check the address." She nodded to him to load her luggage into the trunk and slid into the backseat, opening her shoulder bag to look for Rick's last letter with his Anchorage address.

The driver climbed behind the wheel and half turned to glance at her.

"Where to?"

"Northern Lights Boulevard," Shannon replied, certain of the street. Then she found the letter and gave him the address of Rick's apartment. Their future home, she thought. How strange that sounded.

As they drove away from the terminal building and the row of commercial hangars, the cabdriver glanced into the rearview mirror at Shannon's reflection. "This your first trip to Alaska?"

"Yes." Her gaze strayed out the window, her concern over Rick lessening to the point where she could take in her new surroundings. "It's much greener than I expected." She observed the lawns in front of the houses and the grassy verges of the road. The blue parka was heavy on her lap, and the cableknit sweater she was wearing over her lavender silk blouse actually felt a little hot. "It's a lot warmer than I expected it to be in September."

"You had visions of an ice-encrusted city, huh?" The driver chuckled softly.

"Well"—her laugh was low and slightly embarrassed—"I don't think I'm going to need the long johns in my suitcase for a while." Her smile deepened at the sight of flowers blooming in the gardens they passed.

"The climate here is milder than you might think. Anchorage weather is really pretty good, but it gets a hell of a lot colder in the interior around Fairbanks," he admitted.

"Are you from here?" Shannon asked.

"I'm a native Alaskan." There was pride in the admission, a pride that was quickly tempered with humor. "Three years ago I went down to the Lower 48 to visit some relatives in California, but I came back—which shows you how stupid I am."

Shannon laughed, as she was supposed to do. She knew instinctively that his friendliness was natural and not just an attempt to flirt with her. "I doubt that."

"It's kinda late in the season for tourists. You visiting? Or are you planning to move up?"

"I'm moving to Anchorage." Her tone was decisive.

"Do you have people here? Friends?" the driver asked curiously.

"My fiancé," Shannon replied, and glimpsed the disappointment that flickered across the man's reflection in the rearview mirror.

"I see," he murmured as he turned off the thoroughfare onto a main cross street. "What does he do?"

"He's a pilot," she explained.

"Who isn't around here?" The cabdriver laughed. "Sometimes I think there are more planes than cars. Flying is the only way to reach a lot of places in Alaska. Does he work for one of the big airlines?"

"No. He has a job with a private charter service." She sighed inwardly. Flying commercial jets had been Rick's ambition once—until he'd found out more about opportunities for pilots in the Alaskan wilderness and anything else just seemed too tame.

"That's good. Year-round jobs aren't that easy to come by in Alaska, no matter what you hear."

He slowed the taxi and stopped in front of a nondescript, two-story building painted beige. "This is it."

It didn't look like much. Shannon wondered if Rick was here or out struggling to fix a flat on a freeway somewhere. Well, it wasn't as if she could sit in the cab and wait to find out. She gathered her things together.

When Shannon paid the fare and added a tip, the cabdriver pocketed it and thanked her. "I'll carry your luggage inside for you."

Leaving the cab, she walked to the central entrance and opened the door. Rick's apartment number was on the door opposite the one marked MANAGER. She had a feeling he wasn't here—and she'd be seriously annoyed if he was—but she knocked on the door anyway, just on the off chance. There was no immediate answer. Hoping the manager would let her into the apartment to wait for Rick, Shannon turned away just as the door opened a crack.

She swung swiftly around with a smile of happy surprise. It was instantly wiped away by the sight of the badly dressed, whiskered man peering out the door. He gave her a bleary-eyed stare, raking her up and down.

"Whatever you're selling, honey, I'm not buying," he declared and slammed the door shut.

The cabdriver came in with her suitcases as Shannon recovered from her shock at seeing a total stranger—no, make that a total slob, who was unbelievably obnoxious to boot—in Rick's apartment. Obviously there was no logical explanation for the man's presence and he sure wouldn't be Rick's choice for a roommate.

Maybe her dear fiancé had moved to another apartment without telling her. Maybe the slob knew where Rick was. Either way, Shannon was steamed.

She knocked again. This time the door was jerked open but the stoop-shouldered man stood up a little straighter when she tried to look inside the apartment.

"G'wan," he said impatiently. "I work nights. I don't like being woke up in the middle of the afternoon. Go knock on someone's else's door."

"I'm-looking-for-Rick-Farris!" She rushed the words out, because she had the feeling he was going to slam the door on her again.

"Never heard of him." The door started to close.

"But this is his apartment," Shannon protested.

"Hey, I don't know what your game is." He eyed her with exasperation. "But this here is *my* apartment. The name is Jack Morrow and there ain't nobody living here but me."

"There must be some mistake." She rummaged frantically through her shoulder bag for Rick's letter.

"If there is, you're the one who made it," he retorted. He looked at the cabdriver, who scowled at him, then softened his tone a little. "Check with the manager. Maybe the guy you're looking for moved upstairs or something. Ask him, okay? Now I need my beauty sleep."

The door had already closed by the time Shannon found Rick's letter. She double-checked the envelope, but she was already sure that the address of the apartment was the same. Confused, she turned and found herself facing the cabdriver, who had piled her luggage in the middle of the hall. He was wearing a sympathetic expression.

"You might as well check with the manager," he said. "Your boyfriend could've changed apartments or found a cheaper place to live."

"I suppose." Shannon, growing more and more annoyed, thought again that Rick should have let her know. So much for their romantic reunion. So far, this one was a minor nightmare. But she didn't exactly want to complain out loud—there was a limit to how much she was going to confide in a cabdriver, however friendly.

"I'll wait for you . . . just in case," he volunteered.

"Thank you," she murmured and crossed the entryway to the manager's door, keeping Rick's letter in hand. She knocked twice and heard shuffling steps approach.

An older man of retirement age opened the door and peered at her over the top of his reading glasses. He spied her suitcases in the hall and darted a sharp look at her.

"My name is Shannon Hayes—" she began.

"Sorry," he interrupted, making his own guess as to why she was there. "No vacancies at the moment. I could put your name on the waiting list, but there's already four ahead of you."

"No, you don't understand. I'm looking for Rick Farris. I'm his fiancée," Shannon attempted again to explain.

The apartment manager harrumphed. "So he ran out on you, too. Well, if you find him, tell him he owes me a week's rent. When he pays it, I'll give him back the stuff he left."

An icy chill ran up her spine. "Rick isn't here?"

"I thought that was what I just said." The old man cocked his head to one side.

"Didn't he leave a forwarding address?" A sensation of alarm was beginning to grow. None of this sounded like Rick. Maybe something worse than a flat tire had happened to him. She felt suddenly guilty for not considering that possibility and gave the manager a worried look.

"No, he didn't," the manager replied. "He didn't even give me notice that he was leaving. But I saw him going out with a suitcase, just two days before the rent was due. 'Course he told me that he'd be back in time to take care of it, but I never saw hide nor hair of him after that." The manager shook his head, indicating by the gesture that it was an old story. "I hafta admit he fooled me. And he seemed a real likable fella. I waited a week before I rented the place to someone else."

"Do you mean Rick hasn't been here for two weeks?" Shannon asked, realization dawning. "Then he couldn't have received the messages I left telling him when I would arrive."

"He didn't have a phone in the apartment, as far as I

know, miss. Guess he had one of them cellular ones, but it wasn't in with his things."

"What did Rick leave?" she asked. "May I see?"

The manager hesitated. "You can see, but I can't let you take anything," he said at last, and stepped out of the doorway to let her enter his apartment. "I packed it all in a couple of boxes. He rented a furnished unit, so there wasn't much."

Shannon walked in and looked around without saying a word.

He motioned toward the two boxes sitting in the corner of his living room. "Nothing of value in 'em. If he doesn't come back for this stuff pretty soon, it's going to the attic where it'll be out of my way."

She crouched down to unfold the flaps of one box. Mostly it contained odds and ends and a few clothes—everyday shirts and worn jeans. In the second she found a gold-framed photograph of herself, the one she had signed. *With all my love.* Her fingers tightened on it.

"Rick wouldn't have left this behind," she whispered to herself. But there was nothing wrong with the manager's hearing. A look of pity was on his face when she looked up. "That day you saw him with the suitcase—did he say where he was going?"

"Nope." He shook his head. "And I didn't ask. At the time I didn't think it was any of my business."

"This isn't like Rick." Again, Shannon said it mostly to herself.

The old man shrugged. "People change."

"No." She wouldn't accept that argument. She set the framed photo back in the box and stood up. "There's a reason for this. I don't know what it is, but I'm going to find out . . . somehow."

"Good luck to you," was the skeptical encouragement from the manager.

"Thank you." Shannon opened the flap of her shoulder bag and reached inside for her leather wallet. "How much does Rick owe you? I'll pay for it and take his things with me."

The manager drew back. "I don't want to be taking your money, miss."

"It's all right. Rick and I are going to be married." With a sad little smile, she held up her left hand to show him the diamond engagement ring.

He hesitated, then grudgingly named an amount, as if it went against his grain to take money from a woman for a man's debt. While he wrote out a receipt at a small desk for the money she'd paid him, Shannon picked up one of the boxes and carried it into the building's entryway, where the cabdriver stood watch over her suitcases.

"Did you find out anything?" he asked quietly.

She shook her head, chestnut hair brushing her shoulders. "There's another box inside. Would you mind carrying it out?"

"Be happy to," he assured her, and entered the manager's apartment as the old man walked out to give Shannon her receipt.

"If you hear from Rick, or if he stops by, would you tell him I'm staying at—" She stopped and glanced at the cabdriver and the box he had in his arms. She hadn't thought about a hotel but that would have to be her next move. "I need a hotel in Anchorage, a well-known place that's centrally located."

"The Westward is good." He deliberated for a moment. "And there's Captain Cook's . . . and the Sheffield House."

Shannon chose the first. "I'll be staying at the Westward."

"I'll tell him," the manager promised, but his doubtful expression said much more.

When she left the building to carry the box to the taxi, the cloud cover seemed to be hanging lower, darkening everything. A fine mist hung in the air, replacing the earlier drizzle. The damp chill seemed to penetrate to her bones. So many unexplained things had happened, her anxiety increased from the weight of them. One question kept echoing in her mind: *Where was Rick?*

The cabdriver took the box from her and stowed it in the trunk, then helped her into the rear seat. "You wait here while I get the rest," he instructed.

Sitting alone in silence, Shannon tried very hard not to imagine the worst. Just because Rick wasn't at the apartment didn't necessarily mean that he had been injured or become ill. There were probably several explanations—even if she couldn't think of a single one. She didn't know where he was but that didn't mean he was missing.

Yet nothing that had happened made sense. She was confused and—she had to admit it—more than a little frightened.

"Do you want me to take you to the Westward?" The driver slipped behind the wheel and closed the door.

"Yes, please."

He turned in his seat and noticed how tightly her hands were clasped together in her lap. "There probably isn't anything to be upset about. When you finally see him, you'll probably laugh about this wild-goose chase."

"Probably," Shannon agreed, and managed a brief smile at the gentle assurance.

Facing front again, he turned the key in the ignition, and paused before putting the car into gear. "It's possible that he might be trying to reach you. If he didn't get your message, he doesn't necessarily know you're here," the cabbie reminded her. "Is there someone you can call in Texas to see if he's been trying to contact you?"

"Yes." She'd call her parents the instant she reached the hotel. Then she realized she hadn't told the cab-driver where she was from. "How did you know I'm from Texas?"

A wide grin split his face. "Kinda hard to mistake that drawl," he explained. "We get a lot of Texans up here, what with the ongoing oil development and things like that."

Her tense mouth relaxed in a natural smile. "I should have guessed." Coming from Houston, she did-n't think she had much of a twang, but she guessed people everywhere else thought otherwise. Her smile faded as the cab pulled onto the street. The cabbie's comment served to remind her that she was in unfamiliar territory. The city was strange to her. She knew no one here except Rick, and she didn't know where he was.

The traffic became heavier near the center of Anchorage, demanding more of the driver's attention. He pointed out some of the landmarks. Shannon looked, but she was too preoccupied with her own concerns to have much interest in the sights around her.

At the hotel entrance a porter stepped out to take her luggage into the lobby. After she'd paid the driver and tipped him well, he gave her a card with his phone number written on it. "My name is Andy," he told her. "If you need some help locating your boyfriend, give me a call. I'll do what I can."

"Thank you." She was touched by his offer. "Like you said, it's probably a misunderstanding."

He nodded and waved good-bye. She turned to cross the expansive lobby, where she registered and was given the key cards to a room on the fifth floor. She left most of the luggage for the bellhop to bring up, and went di-rectly to the phone to call her parents.

Her mother answered after several rings. "Hello?"

"It's me—Shannon."

"I've been wondering about you! Are you in Alaska? How was the flight? I bet you're frozen solid." There was hardly a break between sentences as her mother rattled on. "You should have taken warmer clothes. Do you want me to overnight you some extra sweaters and socks, rather than wait until your father and I come up this weekend?"

"No. The weather is fine, Mom," Shannon assured her, then felt that statement needed some qualification. "It's no different from Houston in the winter—gray, drizzling and cool."

"Are you sure?" her mother asked skeptically. "Velma Jo and Fred were in Anchorage two years ago and said they practically froze to death."

"I promise you I'm not freezing." She took a deep breath, preparing herself to ask if Rick had called, and her mother took advantage of the scant second of silence.

"How was the plane trip? What is it—three or four hours' time difference? I never can figure those things out. How jet-lagged are you, Shannon? Traveling is tiring enough without going through those zones and whatnot."

"Yes, I . . ." She realized at that moment just how tired she was. She'd been too worried about Rick to notice.

Her mother's voice grew muffled. "I'm talking to Shannon. She's calling from Alaska," she said to someone else in the room.

"Who is that, Mom?" Shannon was struck by the absurd thought that it might be Rick. What if he had taken it into his head to fly to Texas and accompany her personally on the long flight here?

"It's your father. He wants to say hello." The receiver

was obviously passed to her father, because Shannon heard his voice a second later.

"Hi, honey, how are you?"

"I'm fine, Dad."

"How's my future son-in-law? I suppose he's there with you."

Which meant he wasn't there in Texas—not that she had really thought he would be. With a sinking heart she realized that it also meant Rick hadn't called her parents' home. There was no message for her.

"Actually . . . he isn't here," she admitted, trying not to let her concern seep into her voice.

"Oh?" It was a pregnant sound. "Didn't he meet you at the airport?"

"No. He didn't get my messages about the flight delays," Shannon explained, at least partially. She considered confiding in her father, until it occurred to her that he was too far away to help. Besides, there was no reason to needlessly alarm her parents. "Rick is . . . out of town right now."

"How soon will he be back?" Her father had barely asked the question when his voice became muffled; obviously, he was explaining the situation to her mother.

"I'm not sure," she answered. "I haven't talked to Rick yet." Which was the truth.

"Whoever he's working for knows when he'll come back, doesn't he?"

A ray of hope shone. "I'm going to call and find out." Why hadn't she thought of contacting Rick's employer before? He would know Rick's whereabouts, his new address, everything. "I just wanted to let you and Mom know I arrived safely."

Chapter Two

Another five minutes went by before the conversation with her parents finally came to a close. Afterward Shannon ransacked her large purse again in search of the letter from Rick, which contained the name of his employer. She found it—Steele Air. Flipping open the telephone book, she ran her finger down the column of S's and stopped when she found Steele Air. She picked up the receiver and dialed the number.

On the sixth ring a man answered, "Steele Air. No matter where you wanta go, we'll take you there." There was a rasping edge to the male voice that hinted at his age.

Shannon smiled at the slogan so proudly recited. "I'd like to speak to Rick Farris, please."

There was a pause. "Who?"

"Rick Farris," she repeated, and added, "He's a pilot."

"Who ain't?" was the retort, but a reply wasn't expected. A hand was cupped over the receiver on the other end of the line, muffling the words of the man who spoke to someone else. A second later the same rasping voice returned to the line. "No one here by that name."

"Wait a minute," Shannon said quickly, in case the man intended to hang up. "Do you have a phone number where I could reach him?"

There was another lengthy pause. "We don't have his phone number."

"Can you tell me how I might contact him?" she persisted.

"Miss, I really don't know." The voice sounded indifferent and dryly amused.

"How do you get hold of him?" There had to be some way.

"Why would we want to?"

"He works for you," she replied, and began to wonder if she wasn't being given the runaround as a kind of joke.

"What?" The man sounded startled. "What did you say his name was?"

"Rick Farris."

"We don't have any pilots working for us by that name. You probably want one of the other charter outfits," came the patient yet gruff reply.

"No." Shannon glanced at Rick's letter again. It plainly read Steele Air. "This is Steele Air, isn't it?"

"Yes, but there's no Rick Farris here," he stated, very positively.

It finally sank in that he meant it. "Thank you," she murmured, and heard the click of the phone being hung up. Slowly she replaced the receiver on the cradle.

Tiny lines creased her forehead as she picked up Rick's letter and began reading it through again word by word. It was filled with information Rick had gleaned about the owner and operator of the service, a man named Cody Steele. Nowhere did it say that Rick had been hired, yet the implication was strong.

Her frustration mounted. The letter was a month old, but it was the only clue she had. Someone with Steele Air had to know something about Rick. If not the man who'd answered the phone, then someone else.

Shannon started to reach for the telephone to call back, then changed her mind and scribbled down the address of Steele Air on the back of the letter's envelope. Grabbing her purse, she slipped the leather strap over her shoulder and dropped the room key card inside.

Five minutes later she was in the hotel lobby downstairs, requesting a taxi. One responded immediately to the call. As she crawled inside and gave the driver the address at Merrill Field, Shannon was almost sorry she hadn't asked for the young driver named Andy, for moral support.

Instead of taking her to the Anchorage International Airport, where she had arrived by jet, the cab drove to another airfield closer to the heart of the city. Shannon couldn't recall ever seeing so many small planes in one place in all her life. They passed row after row of hangars, with single- and twin-engine aircrafts parked inside or tied down on the concrete aprons outside. There was a multitude of aviation companies, so many that the names began to run together in her mind.

When the cab turned and stopped in front of one of the hangars and its attached office, Shannon stared at the sign across the front that read STEELE AIR. It was a full minute before realization sank in that she had reached her destination. Except for the sign, there was nothing to distinguish this outfit from any of the other flying services.

With the fare paid, she stepped out of the cab into

the misting rain. After a second's hesitation she walked toward the door of the concrete-block building that adjoined the metal hangar. Her boots made small splashes in the gathering puddles of water, ripples ringing out from her footsteps.

Entering the building, she paused inside the door to wipe her high-heeled boots on the bristled mat—a consideration others hadn't observed, judging by the muddy tracks on the tiled floor. Her entrance brought the conversation in the small office area to a halt.

The long room that ran the length of the building looked much more like a waiting area than an actual office. Aeronautical charts were tacked on the walls along with photographs, plaques and a bulletin board crowded with cards, advertisements and notes scribbled on torn slips of paper. There was a desk, its metal sides scratched and dented, that held a computer and printer, neither particularly new. The swivel chair behind it was vacant and showed signs of wear.

The coffee table was littered with aviation magazines and—yuck—an overflowing ashtray that smelled awful. One of the men sitting on the green couch was using the table for a footstool, his feet propped on top of it. Another older man was leaning forward, braced with his arms on his thighs, while a third man sat in a cushioned chair covered with dark gold vinyl straight out of *That '70s Show*.

In the corner of the room near the couch, a large coffeemaker emitting a gasping, fill-me-up noise sat atop a table surrounded by cups in assorted shapes and sizes, as well as a stack of disposable cups, and a couple of community spoons. There was also a container of sugar and a powdered cream substitute, something Shannon considered about as tasty as sink cleanser and never, ever put in her coffee.

She told herself not to make a face. This was clearly a male space, decorated in classic Palazzo de Testosterone style with thrift store furniture by guys who were totally indifferent to cleanliness.

Two doors opened into the long room. One of them was ajar, giving Shannon a glimpse of another room that more closely resembled an office than this one.

All three of the men were staring at her with open speculation. Shannon had the impression that it wasn't every day a female invaded their domain. The older man in the red plaid flannel shirt finally straightened to his feet. Age had thickened his middle somewhat without taking away from his muscled physique. His tanned face was craggy but pleasant, for some reason reminding Shannon of a stuffed teddy bear. His dark hair was graying, giving him a grizzled look, but there was a gentle quality in his blue eyes.

"Can I help you, miss?" he inquired in a gruff voice that Shannon instantly recognized. This was the same man she had spoken to on the telephone.

"Yes. My name is Shannon Hayes. I talked to you a little while ago—I was asking about a pilot named Rick Farris," she explained, and noticed the man's eyebrow shoot up.

"Right. I remember. Like I told you, miss, we don't have anybody here by that name." He repeated his previous answer with a show of patience.

"I know you did, but—" She paused to reach inside her purse for Rick's letter. "I just flew into Anchorage this afternoon. I'm trying to locate Rick. He's my fiancé. I received this letter from him indicating that he planned to go to work here for a man named—" She got the letter out to recheck the name. "Cody Steele. I understand he's the owner, is that right?"

"Half right. Cody and I are partners," he rasped out

the correction. "It doesn't really matter what he wrote you, miss. I'd know if we had anybody working for us by that name—and we don't."

"I'm sure you would know if Rick was working for you," Shannon agreed with that. "I was wondering if you might know where he is. Evidently Rick talked to this Cody Steele. Is he in? Could I speak to him?"

"I don't know what good it will do you," he shrugged. "Cody probably won't remember any more about this fella than I do." He saw that she was going to insist on finding that out for herself, and gave her a resigned look. "But you can ask him."

Turning, he walked to the door standing ajar and pushed it open. Shannon had a glimpse of a lean, dark-haired man poring over papers on his desk, who glanced up at the interruption.

"Yes?" The weary edge to the man's voice seemed to demand a good explanation for the disturbance.

"Remember that phone call I got a few minutes ago, Cody?" the older man said. "Well, the lady is here—a cheechako. She wants to talk to you."

Shannon heard a sound like a long sigh, then the creak of a swivel chair being rocked back. The man in the office was lost from her view, blocked by the older and broader figure in the doorway.

"Send her in," was the reply.

The older man stepped out of the way and motioned her inside the office. "He'll see you."

As she walked in, the first thing she noted was how neat and orderly the office was compared to the outer room. Then her attention centered on the man behind the desk. He was rubbing a hand over his eyes, a gesture indicative of the tiredness she'd sensed before. The rubbing motion carried his hand to the back of his neck in an effort to ease its stiff muscles.

At that moment his glance fell on her, and a stillness

held him in that position for the span of several seconds. Pitch-black hair framed his lean, sun-hardened features. His eyes were a shade of blue too light for his complexion, which gave an unusual intensity to his gaze. Shannon felt it penetrating her, probing with steady insistence.

In the blink of an eye he seemed to shrug off the tiredness and take on an air of macho vitality. There was a definite boldness in the way he looked at her as he swung to his feet, all six-plus feet of him. Working at the desk, he had appeared to be in his late thirties, but Shannon was revising the estimate backward now. He seemed younger, although still interestingly mature and experienced.

Something about him heightened her senses. *Okay, so what?* she asked silently. She was simply responding to him because he was an attractive man. A very attractive man. Basic biology. A natural reaction that didn't bother her.

"I'm Cody Steele." He extended his hand to her in greeting. The action stretched the heavy knitted pullover sweater across the breadth of his shoulders, its dark charcoal color blending with khaki-gray slacks. *You really need to stop thinking like a catalog,* she told herself. *Even if he does look like a male model.*

"Shannon Hayes." She shook his hand, liking the firmness of his grip.

His all-encompassing gaze had made a thorough inspection of her, and he seemed to like what he saw. She doubted if his measuring look had missed anything, yet there had been nothing offensive about it. Some men could undress her with their eyes and make her feel dirty and ashamed; and others, like Cody Steele, could look and make her feel proud of being a woman. She didn't understand the reason for the difference, but it existed.

"Please sit down, Ms. Hayes." His voice had a husky

pitch to it that was pleasing to the ear. He motioned toward a captain's chair in front of his desk.

"Thanks." She sat, feeling a little prim and proper, while he continued to stand behind the desk.

"Would you like a cup of coffee?" he offered.

Until that moment Shannon hadn't felt the need for any kind of stimulation, caffeine or otherwise. Now it sounded good. "Yes, please."

"Cream? Sugar?"

"Sugar," she said. "I'll skip the cleanser."

"What?" He looked baffled for a moment and then he smiled. "Oh, you mean the non-dairy creamer. Hey, it keeps. But it is weird stuff, I have to admit. Probably a petroleum by-product."

A plain white cup was sitting on his desk. He picked it up and walked to the door standing ajar to the outer room. Cody Steele paused in its frame. "Dad? Ms. Hayes would like a cup of coffee . . . with sugar. I'll have one, too."

Dad? Recognition dawned in her eyes when the older man in the red plaid shirt took the empty cup from Cody's hand and disappeared in the direction of the coffeemaker. They were father and son—and partners.

There was a resemblance, although Cody Steele's features weren't nearly as craggy as his father's, and he was taller and slimmer.

As Cody Steele turned to walk back to the desk while his father brought the coffee, his glance fell on the envelope Shannon was holding. The corners of his mouth lifted into a half smile, but there was a certain professionalism to his expression, veiling his male interest in her. At the desk he stopped to set a hip on the edge of it, one leg bent at the knee, and faced her.

"How can I help you?" he inquired.

"I'm trying to locate a pilot named Rick Farris. I got

this letter from him nearly a month ago." Shannon indicated the envelope in her hand. "From what he wrote, I had the impression he was employed by you."

"I believe my father already told you that we don't have anyone flying for us by that name." He exhibited the same patience his father had displayed toward her inquiry.

"Yes, I know," she admitted. "But Rick must have applied for a position with you. He wouldn't have written what he did if he hadn't had some contact with you."

A question glinted in his light blue eyes, a gleam of curiosity showing, but his father appeared then with the coffee, momentarily interrupting the conversation. Cody Steele waited until the cups had been set on the desk top.

"Offhand I don't recall the name, but I've talked to a lot of people in the past month or so, clients and pilots." There was an expressive lift of his wide shoulders that admitted the possibility he had spoken to Rick. "Do you mind my asking why you want to find him? Is he a relative?"

"He's her fiancé," his father answered for Shannon, and there seemed to be a warning in the look he gave Cody Steele, as if instructing him to behave himself.

She saw a flash of indulgent humor in Cody's light blue eyes, although it quickly disappeared when they rested on Shannon again. His gaze swung to the letter and envelope in her hand.

"What about the return address on the letter?" he asked.

"I went to the apartment," she admitted. "The manager hasn't seen him in two weeks. Rick left one day and didn't come back." Shannon tried to sound matter-of-fact, but she heard a note of apprehension creep into her voice.

Cody Steele looked away, letting his attention focus

on the cup of coffee he had picked up and allowing her the opportunity to get a grip. When he spoke, it was to his father. "Close the door on your way out, Dad."

His father cast a disapproving glance over his shoulder, but shut the door as he left. Shannon was in control of her nerves when she met the blue eyes again.

"Perhaps if you described your . . . fiancé to me," Cody Steele suggested.

"He's about your height, with sandy hair and hazel eyes." She reached inside her purse for her wallet, where she kept a picture of Rick. Removing the photograph from its plastic sleeve, she passed it to Cody.

He studied it, then flicked a considering glance at her. "His flying experience?" His dark brows drew together in a thoughtful frown.

"He's fully qualified. He has all his ratings." Before she could continue, he nodded his head.

"You know, I do remember talking to him." He returned the photo. "He had been an instructor for six months prior to coming here."

"Yes, that's right." She smiled, relief showing in the faint dimples in her cheeks.

"You're from Texas," Cody guessed. "Your . . . fiancé was, too, as I recall."

"Yes." Her smile widened. There was a responding glint of humor in his eyes. It intensified the inherent boldness that marked him.

"Don't worry. We Alaskans don't brag about how big the state is. We just pride ourselves on being unique."

The sparkle of wicked amusement was deliberately obvious. Then he added, more seriously, "I remember that your fiancé stopped by to ask about flying with us, but we couldn't use him. I wish I could be of more help than that."

"Did he indicate where he could be reached?" Shannon persisted. "Or where he might be working?"

"He might have, but to tell you the truth, I didn't bother to keep his address. Our business is mainly cross-country charters. I mean, he was qualified, as you said, but he had no experience flying in Alaska, so I wasn't interested."

She was slightly stunned by Cody's blunt words. Worse, she seemed to be faced with another dead end. As if sensing her dazed reaction, Cody handed her the cup of coffee. She sipped at the sugary liquid, then sighed deeply.

"I don't know where to go from here," she murmured in confusion. "How can I find him?"

"I suppose you could start calling other flying services." But his tone didn't sound too promising. "Maybe he's given up and gone home. It's possible you wasted your time coming all the way up here."

"Rick knew I was coming." She shook her head, refusing to believe the obvious implication. "He was expecting me, so he wouldn't have left, not without letting me know. I talked to my parents in Houston just a little while ago. They haven't heard from him."

"How long have you been engaged?"

She didn't see the point of that question, but she answered it anyway. "A year."

"And how long has Rick been here in Alaska?"

"Six months. Why?" And why was this guy getting so personal all of a sudden, she wondered.

"You haven't seen him in six months. And you obviously haven't heard from him since you received that letter a month ago. Maybe he's had a change of heart," Cody reasoned.

"No. That isn't possible." Shannon denied that suggestion emphatically.

"Why?" He sounded curious more than anything else.

"Because two weeks ago he sent me a one-way plane

ticket to Anchorage. Before he left Houston we agreed that as soon as he found a permanent job and a place for us to live he would send for me." She returned his steady look. "Rick hasn't changed his mind. He just wouldn't do that."

"That doesn't explain why he moved two weeks ago without letting you know," he reminded her.

"I'm . . . not sure that he moved." Shannon finally voiced the concern that had been on her mind since she'd left Rick's former apartment building. "He left some of his things in his apartment, some clothes and other things, including my picture. If he was moving to another place, why didn't he take his stuff?"

He raised an eyebrow at the question and avoided her look as he sipped at his coffee. "He said nothing to his landlord?"

"Just that he'd be back in a couple of days—before the rent was due." Worry gnawed at her. She tried to reason it away. "I keep telling myself that it has to be a mix-up. Maybe Rick actually doesn't know I'm here in Alaska. Now I don't know where he is or where he's working. If he moved, he would've let me know his new address, because he knew I was coming any day."

"There's probably a simple reason." He shrugged to indicate his lack of concern. "Maybe he sent you his new address and the letter was lost in the mail. Things like that happen."

"That's true." That hadn't occurred to Shannon, and she breathed a little easier at the thought. "Of course, he could've e-mailed it, too."

"Maybe a spam filter ate it."

"Yeah, right. I mean, maybe not. I think I'm coming up with too many excuses," she said dejectedly. "And none of them solve the problem of how I'm going to find him."

"Where are you staying?" He half turned to pick up a pen and find a clean slip of paper.

"At the Westward." She watched him jot down the information.

"Why don't you let me check a few places, ask some questions," he suggested. "I'll let you know what I find out, if anything."

"I would be grateful, Mr. Steele." Her smile was small but warmly sincere.

"I'm counting on that, Texas," he replied with a grin. "If you don't mind the nickname. And the name is Cody."

"I don't mind the nickname. I'm proud to be from the Cowpie State."

"Is that what real Texans call it?" He grinned even wider.

"No, and you'd better not. Unless you want to be the last man standing after a barroom brawl. Anyway, thank you . . . Cody." It was strange how easily she spoke his name, as if she had known him for a long time.

There was a loud knock at the door. "Yes?" Cody turned his head in that direction.

The door opened and Cody's father appeared. "I was just checking to see if you wanted some more coffee." His sharp gaze darted from his son to Shannon, bright with suspicion and revealing surprise that there seemed to be no reason for it.

"Not for me," Cody replied, and glanced at her.

"No, thank you," she refused, and slipped the strap of her purse over her shoulder. "I've taken enough of your time. I'd better be leaving."

"It's still raining out there," his father said.

"May I use your phone to call a cab?" Shannon rose to her feet.

Cody straightened from the desk to stand beside her. She was conscious of the warm male smell of him, elusive yet stimulating. Even with the added height of her boots, the top of her head still only reached his chin. At close quarters she was even more conscious of his sexual attractiveness. She told herself again that it was just good old biology and had nothing to do with the way she felt about Rick.

"There's no need for you to call a cab," Cody stated. "I have an appointment downtown. You're welcome to ride with me."

"Thank you. I—" Shannon didn't have a chance to finish the sentence.

"What appointment?" his father wanted to know. "You didn't mention anything to me about it. Who do you have to see?"

"I'm going to see Darryl Akers at the bank." Cody appeared to shrug away the importance of his meeting.

"If you're going to the bank, I'd better come along with you," his father stated. "I'll get my coat."

"There's no reason for you to come with me." But Cody was talking to an empty doorway. He shrugged for Shannon's benefit anyway. Then a gleam of amusement lightened his blue eyes.

"Parents," he mocked affectionately. "They never listen."

"True." The corners of her mouth deepened with a contained smile, and he noticed. His gaze lingered for a pulse beat on the curve of her lower lip.

"How about that ride, Texas?" he asked.

"Yes." She nodded, the chestnut length of her hair sweeping her shoulders.

"My car's parked just outside." He almost let the flat of his hand rest on the small of her back in a gentlemanly gesture, then thought better of it. But she wouldn't have minded if he'd followed through. There was a masculine ease to his actions that had a familiar quality, much too natural to raise any objection from Shannon.

His father was zipping the front of a light jacket as they entered the outer office. He reached the door ahead of them and held it open for Shannon, then led the way toward a late-model car parked in front of the building. He reached it first and opened the rear door, stepping aside so Shannon could slide in.

Cody forestalled her. "She can sit in the front seat," he prompted his father, a thin edge of irritation creeping into his voice.

"I'd look pretty silly sitting in the backseat all by myself after we leave her at the hotel, now, wouldn't I?" his father reasoned.

"You could always move up," Cody replied.

"What's the point in getting in, then getting out and getting in again?" his father argued, being deliberately difficult.

Shannon settled the pointless disagreement. "I don't mind sitting in the backseat." She moved to take her place in the back.

"There, you see?" Cody's father beamed in triumph that he'd got his way. "She may be a cheechako, but she's not dumb. She has better sense than to stand around arguing about where she's going to sit when it's raining."

Cody made no reply as he saw Shannon safely inside, but his blue eyes were very expressive of his feelings when they met her glance. He was both irritated and amused by his father's maneuvering. Although she didn't understand the reason behind it, Cody obviously did.

When both men were in the car, Shannon asked, "What does cheechako mean?" It was the second time his father had used the term to describe her.

"It refers to a greenhorn or a tenderfoot," Cody explained. "Usually applied to anyone from the outside."

"Outside?" she questioned.

"Anyplace outside of Alaska."

It was a short drive to the hotel. His father began a monologue that lasted until they arrived, eliminating any exchange of conversation during the ride. Before Shannon climbed out of the car, Cody turned to look back over the seat.

"I'll be in touch later to let you know what I've found out," he said.

"All right." She stepped out of the car.

"Found out about what?" his father wanted to know as she shut the rear door. He continued his demand to find out what Cody was talking about, but she didn't actually hear the questions. She waved her thanks for the ride and noticed the tinge of exasperation in Cody's features at his father's incessant prying. Smiling to herself, she walked to the revolving entrance doors to the hotel.

The smile faded when she reached her hotel room. The boxes containing Rick's belongings were sitting beside her luggage. The sight of them started her wondering again where Rick was. Kneeling beside the boxes, she began going through them, looking for any clue—no matter how trivial—that might tell her something.

Chapter Three

Shannon found nothing in the boxes, not even a matchbook cover that might tell her of a restaurant or bar that Rick hung out at in Anchorage. Damn and double damn. She would have been happy to find a strip club souvenir, if that was what had been going on. Maybe he'd blown all his money on good times and bad girls. As Cody had said, things happened. If Rick had been generous with the fives and tens . . . the thought made her sigh heavily. With the boxes repacked and stored in the hotel closet, she unpacked her suitcases.

Her wedding outfit was a white tailored suit with a ruffled silk blouse of the palest blue and shoes to match. A white hat with a half veil was her mother's— something borrowed. Shannon's father had given her an antique brooch that had belonged to his mother, which was to be her something old.

As she smoothed the lapel of the white jacket, Shannon wondered if there would be a wedding on Saturday. So far she was a bride without a groom. She jumped at the sound of the telephone ringing, her heart catapulting into her throat. Was it Rick?

She nearly tripped over an empty suitcase in her haste to reach the telephone on the bedside table. "Hello?" Her voice was eager and expectant, anticipating Rick on the other end.

"Hi, Texas," a husky male voice responded, but it wasn't Rick. "Have you had dinner yet?"

Pausing, she tried to contain her disappointment, but some of it slipped through. "Hello, Cody. No, I haven't. I've been unpacking and . . ." Suddenly she remembered why he was calling. "Have you found out anything about Rick?"

"Not exactly," he replied.

Which was a definite no. "What did you find out?"

"Mostly I found out where he isn't. I'll tell you all about it over dinner," he said.

"All right. I—" Shannon stopped as she realized she had just accepted Cody Steele's invitation. She hardly knew the man.

"I'll meet you at the restaurant on the top floor of the hotel in . . . twenty minutes."

There was a click on the line as the connection was broken, before she could decide whether she should meet him or not. She chewed at her lower lip, considering the alternatives. Since he had suggested dining at the hotel, where she would have eaten anyway, it didn't seem to make much difference. It was simply a matter of having company or eating alone. Shannon decided that she preferred company.

Twenty minutes didn't give her much time. Rather than completely changing clothes, she took off her cableknit pullover to wear just the blouse and skirt. She slipped off her boots in favor of high heels. The addition of an amethyst pendant and earrings completed the change as she brushed her hair into the sexy tousle she'd done only a few hours ago on the plane. What the hell. She didn't have to look like a nun just because Rick had gone AWOL.

When she stepped into the elevator and pushed the button for the restaurant on the top floor, Shannon had five minutes to spare. The top floor of the hotel contained a restaurant and lounge. Its glassed walls provided a view of downtown Anchorage and the harbor of Cook Inlet. Leaving the elevator, Shannon paused at the entrance to the restaurant and lounge to look around for Cody.

He was sitting at the bar. When he saw her, he set down his glass of soda and rose to join her at the archway. She noticed he'd changed clothes since she'd last seen him that afternoon. In place of the sweater and slacks, he was wearing a navy tweed jacket and navy slacks but no tie. His white dress shirt was open at the throat, exposing the tanned hollow at its base. The lazy charm of his half smile and the admiring light in his blue eyes reached out to draw her into the spell of his sensual presence. Shannon didn't feel threatened by it—just amused.

"You're right on time," Cody stated with half-mocking approval. "Thanks. I hate cooling my heels on an empty stomach."

"Interesting mixed metaphor."

He grinned. "Sorry. Are you hungry?"

"I honestly haven't thought about it," she admitted. "Too many other things on my mind, I guess." Namely, locating Rick.

"When did you eat last?"

"This morning on the plane."

"Take my word for it, you're hungry," he stated, and turned to face the hostess as she approached them.

"Two for dinner?" she inquired.

"Yes," Cody affirmed. "We'd like a table by the window, please."

"One moment, please." The woman paused to check the seating-and-reservation chart before showing them to a table.

A gruffly accusing voice came from behind them. "There you are, Cody. I've been looking all over for you." They both turned simultaneously to be confronted by Cody's father. "I recognized your car in the lot across the street and wondered what it was doing there."

"Now you know." There was an underlying hardness to Cody's reply that politely and respectfully suggested his father should get lost.

But the older man stubbornly ignored the broad hint. "I thought I'd check to see what you wanted for dinner tonight before I stopped at the market." Then he shifted his attention to Shannon. "Have you found your fiancé yet?"

It was an odd question, she thought, as if Rick were just waiting somewhere on a park bench for her to walk by. "Not yet." She shook her head as a twinge of uncertainty quivered through her at Rick's unexplained disappearance.

An arm curved itself along the back of her waist, asserting possession. Cody's arm. There was a measure of reassurance in the firm warmth of its pressure. Shannon lifted her gaze to Cody's profile, more smoothly chiseled than his father's craggy features.

"Shannon and I are having dinner tonight, so you can fix what you like," Cody informed him.

"If that's the case, I'd better join the two of you," his father declared. Shannon felt Cody stiffen in resistance, the line of his jaw hardening.

"Dad—" He attempted a protest but wasn't permitted to finish it.

"People might get the wrong impression if they find out you're having dinner with her when she's engaged to somebody else," his father explained his reasoning. "I don't want them to think you're trying to steal a sweet little thing away from her fiancé."

Except that Shannon knew no one in Alaska who would care one way or another. She suspected that the old man was just lonely. And stubborn. And more judgmental than he ought to be.

Cody's chest rose in a deep breath, which he expelled as a sigh. His glance sliced to the hostess. "Change that to a table for three," he requested grimly.

Concealing a smile, Shannon followed the hostess to a table set for four by the window. It was possible that Cody's father didn't exactly trust his son to behave properly with her and he seemed determined to make sure that Cody did. It was both touching and amusing to have her reputation so staunchly protected. Shannon wasn't sure whether the elder Steele believed females were too weak to know their own minds or whether he believed Cody was irresistible.

After Cody had seated her in the chair closest to the window, he took the one beside her, facing his father across the table. She pretended not to notice the exchange of warring glances as she studied the view out the window. Clouds continued to blanket the sky, but it had stopped raining, the visibility improving.

"The ceiling has lifted some," Cody remarked, winking at Shannon. "Aeronautical term, sorry."

"I'm familiar with it. My father turns on the Weather Channel every morning and afternoon. Don't ever get him started on the difference between a cold front and a storm system."

"Hey, I can explain it," said the older Steele. "I love the Weather Channel."

Shannon smiled faintly. Why was that not a surprise?

"Anyway, you can see farther than you could earlier today," Cody went on.

"That bay is Cook Inlet, isn't it?" Shannon guessed.

"That's right," Mr. Steele answered. "Sometimes there's as much as a twenty-nine-foot difference in the tides."

Shannon looked suitably impressed, then looked out at the range of mountains rising inland to wall in the city. The gathering shadows of twilight made them indistinct. Streetlights were blinking on against the coming nightfall.

"On a clear day you can see the twin peaks of Mount McKinley, roughly a hundred and fifty miles north," Cody told her. "It's the highest mountain on the continent. At twenty-thousand-plus feet, it's the third highest in the world. Aconcagua in Argentina is the second highest, and there's a hill called Everest over in the Himalayas that *claims* to be the highest."

Catching the mocking emphasis on the word, she glanced at the man seated next to her. The gleam of dancing amusement sharpened the blue of his eyes, his rough-cut features softened for a moment. It was impossible not to be drawn into his light mood.

"It only claims to be?" Amused, she questioned his choice of words, a sparkle in her brown eyes.

"It cheats," Cody replied, the corners of his mouth deepening without an actual smile showing.

Shannon raised an eyebrow. "How does it do that?"

"Very easily." He folded his hands and gave her a know-it-all look. "It rises from a plateau that's already at fourteen thousand feet, which gives it a head start. The land at the base of McKinley has an elevation of some three thousand feet and the mountain rises seventeen thousand feet from there. Now, if we just discount the fact that Mount Aconcagua exists, then Alaska rightfully has the highest mountain in the world," he concluded.

Shannon laughed. "But you're not bragging," she countered.

"Texas, we don't brag," Cody chided, a smile slowly widening his mouth, warmly mocking and captivating in its effect.

With difficulty Shannon broke contact with his gaze when the waitress stopped at their table. "Would any of you care for cocktails before dinner?" she inquired.

"Nothing for me, thank you," Shannon refused, and opened the menu lying in front of her.

Neither Cody nor his father ordered a drink. The waitress left to give them a few minutes to peruse the menu and returned later to take their order. On Cody's recommendation, Shannon chose the broiled salmon with cream of celery soup as a starter. Both men opted for steak and salad.

As she passed the menu back to the waitress, Shannon was aware that Cody had casually stretched his right arm across the top of her chair back. There wasn't any actual physical contact, but his father eyed the move with obvious disapproval.

"That's a beautiful engagement ring, Shannon. Okay if I call you Shannon? I guess we've gotten to first names by now."

Another jab that was meant for his son. Shannon and Cody exchanged a glance without the older man seeing it. He reached across the table and lifted her left hand as if to make a closer inspection of the ring, shooting a meaningful look at Cody, who had leaned back in his chair. "Did you notice it, Cody?" he asked pointedly.

"Yes, Dad. As a matter of fact, I did," Cody admitted with a mildly sardonic smile.

"Yes, sir, it's a beautiful ring," his father repeated as he released her hand.

Shannon was baffled by the way his father kept hinting to Cody that she wasn't available. But it was kind of funny and it didn't seem to bother Cody all that much. "Thank you, Mr. Steele," she responded.

"Call me Noah. Everyone does," he insisted. "When's the wedding?"

"Saturday. At least, that's what we had planned." She quickly qualified her initial answer. Concern for Rick sobered her expression as her questioning glance swung to Cody. "What did you find out today? About Rick?"

He lowered his arm to the table, absently straightening the silverware. "I found out where he isn't."

"What do you mean?" she asked.

"He isn't a patient at any of the local hospitals—or in jail." His unemotional tone caused Shannon to stiffen in recognition of a possibility she had been afraid to consider. His side glance caught her movement, and he went on to explain. "There was a chance that he could have become ill or been in an accident, but no one by that name, or anyone fitting his description, has been admitted to the hospital in the past three weeks. The police have no record on him, either."

"I should be relieved to know he probably isn't sick or hurt," she murmured with a troubled sigh. "But where to look next . . . I wish I knew."

"Well, don't assume the worst. Good thing that Cody's narrowed it down some." Noah Steele seemed to be insisting that she should be reassured by what little they did know.

"Yes." She gave Cody a thankful look and he nodded in silent response. "Anyway, I hope Rick's all right. It's just that I'm no closer to finding him than I was before." Her voice was weighted with the frustration and confusion she felt.

"You haven't had much time to look, either," Cody

reminded her calmly. "You only arrived in Anchorage this afternoon."

"It seems much longer." She grimaced wryly.

"You must be exhausted after all that traveling," Noah Steele declared in sympathy. "You need a good night's rest, so don't let Cody keep you up till all hours talking after dinner."

Sounded like he wasn't sticking around forever, Shannon thought. If he was anything like her own dad—and he was, in a lot of funny ways—the older Steele was headed for a post-dinner snooze in a Barca-lounger.

"I have no intention of keeping her up late tonight." Even when he was irritated with his father, there was a strong thread of respect and affection in Cody's voice, Shannon noticed.

"I should hope not," his father returned. "You belong in bed yourself." Then he explained to Shannon. "Cody just got back this afternoon from flying freight to Dutch Harbor in the Aleutians. Hell of a trip. In his line of work, he has to be alert, which means he needs plenty of rest. FAA regs mandate downtime for commercial pilots but I have to lean on this guy myself."

She recalled how tired Cody had seemed at the Steele Air office, although it was difficult to detect any weariness in him now. There was a resiliency about his strength, a whipcord durability that encouraged others to depend on him—the way she was doing.

"Your concern is touching, Dad," Cody murmured dryly, and paused as the waitress arrived with their first course. When it was served he sat up straighter, letting his glance touch Shannon with its light intensity. "It's amazing how food and sleep can improve a person's outlook. The situation won't seem so bad in the morning."

"Probably not," she agreed as she thoughtfully stirred her soup. "I have one definite clue. Rick has a job"—she was careful not to say *had*—"otherwise he wouldn't have sent me that plane ticket. Tomorrow I'll start calling all the flying companies until I find the one where he's employed." She paused, a tiny frown of confusion making faint lines on her forehead. "Why did Rick have such a hard time finding a job when he's so well qualified?"

"His lack of experience," Cody replied.

His father elaborated. "Conditions here aren't what he's used to on the outside. Anchorage, Fairbanks, Juneau—all have fully equipped, modern airports, good as any you'll find in the smaller states. But once you're out in the bush, your airstrip might turn out to be a sandbar along some river. And no radar or global positioning system is going to find it for you."

"Yeah, well, GPS doesn't hurt," Cody murmured.

His father waved away the statement with his fork. "It's as good as the person using it. From the air it's hard to tell one river and mountain from another, especially in the spring, when creeks become rivers. I've been a bush pilot for thirty-five years and there have been times when I've been lost. If you make a mistake in this country, you don't often get a chance to make another one. It's no place for a cheechako."

"I'm beginning to understand," she murmured. Which was true. She had a much clearer idea of why Alaska had appealed to Rick. It still had the challenge and excitement of a new frontier—and genuine danger.

Her glance strayed to Cody, reassessing him. Rick's letter had been filled with glowing praise for this man's ability. Behind that reckless smile and those bold eyes there was a swift, calculating mind, always weighing odds and chances and making split-second decisions. If he ever took chances, they were deliberate ones—with all factors taken into consideration beforehand.

"Now take Cody here," Noah Steele continued. "He's been flying since his legs were long enough to reach the rudder pedals. It's nothing for a boy to learn to fly before he learns to drive a car out here. Half the roads in Alaska don't go anywhere, leastwise rarely to the place you want to go. I taught Cody everything he knows. There's some would argue, but he's the best in the business as far as I'm concerned."

"You understand he's a little biased," Cody said dryly.

"Yeah, I am, but facts are facts." Noah defended his claim. "I've seen a lot of hotshot pilots in my day—air force jet jockeys and commercial pilots. When they're redlining a plane they're in a cold sweat."

"Want an explanation?" Cody asked her with a wink.

"Sure."

"Anything below or above the maximum and minimum recommended by the aircraft manufacturer as safe operating limits is referred to as redline."

"Believe me, Shannon, Cody knows the limits of his aircraft," his father assured her. "He pushes it to that point and no further. That's why he's sitting here tonight when some others didn't make it. He knows what he's doing every minute."

Noah stopped abruptly, as if just realizing he'd said something profound. He eyed his son sharply, then glanced at Shannon. "I shouldn't have rattled on like that. You'll just have to chalk it up to paternal pride. I know you aren't interested in hearing about Cody now when you're so anxious about your fiancé."

She sensed his underlying regret that he'd bragged about his son, perhaps raising her estimation of Cody over that of Rick. He had included himself at the table to keep the two of them apart more than anything else, she realized.

"But I'm interested in what it takes to be a bush pilot," she insisted. "After all, it's what Rick wanted to do, so I should know something about it." Noah Steele looked relieved by her reply, satisfied that he was off the hook. "I have to confess I don't know very much about Alaska."

"Except that it's bigger than Texas." Cody couldn't resist the friendly jab.

"I've heard that rumor." An answering smile played with the corners of her mouth.

"If you take Alaska at its widest point," his father spoke up, "and put one end in Maine, the other end would reach to San Diego."

She looked at him in faint astonishment. "Are you serious?"

"The Aleutian chain of islands alone is more than a thousand miles long," Noah pointed out. "This is the only state with four time zones. Oughta give you some idea of its size."

"Big. Bigger. Biggest," Cody said with a smile. "It's a guy thing."

"It's a fact," his father insisted. "I'm not exaggerating."

"I'm impressed," Shannon said, and meant it.

"People on the outside have a lot of misconceptions about Alaska," Noah remarked. "Generally they associate the name with blizzards, Eskimos and sled dogs."

"Not to mention the 'Texas tea' that was found at a little place called Prudhoe Bay on the North Slope," Cody said. "Are we boring you, Shannon? If you don't know about Alaskan oil, development thereof, environmental controversy relating to, my dad will fill you in."

"Goddamn tree huggers and moose lovers," his father growled.

"Thanks for the cogent analysis," Cody said.

"Don't get snotty with me." The older man looked insulted.

Shannon squelched a smile. "I'd heard rumors to the effect that you'd found a little crude," she countered, aware that it was a vast understatement but eager to defuse the tension.

"I still haven't made up my mind whether that was a good thing or not for Alaska," Cody's father declared in a more contemplative tone. "But I can't stand people from out of state telling us how to do things up here."

There was a break in the conversation as the waitress served their entrées. Afterward Noah resumed his discussion of the changes that had come about in Alaska since the oil discovery decades ago and the subsequent construction of the Trans-Alaska pipeline. A few interested questions from Shannon encouraged the garrulous man to expound his opinions. He explored the topic through the meal, finally lagging over the second cup of coffee.

During a moment of quiet, Shannon was caught stifling a yawn with her hand. "Told you so. Damn jet lag finally got you, little girl," Noah Steele announced. "It's time you were calling it a night."

"It's early yet." Her watch indicated that, but it was set for the Anchorage time zone. Her system hadn't made the adjustment yet.

"Dad's right." Cody surprised his father with his agreement, and pushed his chair away from the table to stand and assist Shannon. "It's time you turned in." His hand cupped her elbow, firm in its grip. "I'll see you to your room," he stated. There was a complacent gleam in his eyes when he met his father's startled look. "Take care of the check, will you, Dad? I'll meet you downstairs in the lobby."

Before his father could protest, Cody was guiding

Shannon away from the table. Her sideways look noticed the smile that lurked at the edges of his mouth. Cody glanced down at her, and the suggestion of a smile became more evident.

"What self-respecting man would want his father with him when he walked a beautiful woman to her door?" Cody asked in defense of his maneuvering to be alone with her. He was great at humoring his overbearing father, that was for sure. She was beginning to realize that Cody rarely treated anything too seriously—at least not on the surface.

"Just don't forget that I'm engaged," she replied.

He winced and made a funny face. "Please don't remind me." He punched the button for the elevator, and a set of doors obligingly opened, without making them wait. Once they were inside, the doors closed and Cody pushed her floor number.

"Your father is a fountain of information," she began.

"That's a tactful way to put it."

"He really is, though," she said as they began their descent. "Anyway, I like him a lot."

"So do I, but don't tell him that." He grinned. "Besides the fact that he's my father, he's also the best pilot I've ever known."

"Does he still fly?"

"He was grounded this spring—couldn't pass his medical," Cody explained with a sigh. "He hasn't quite figured out what to do with himself yet, which is why he tends to get himself involved in matters that don't concern him."

Like tonight, when he'd appointed himself as her chaperone, Shannon thought. The elevator stopped on her floor. Cody's hand was at the back of her waist, providing unobtrusive guidance as they started down the hotel corridor.

"He's become my self-appointed guardian, determined to keep me out of trouble." His glance moved over her face. "It's difficult to tell him to butt out of my personal life without hurting his feelings."

"I imagine it would be. It can't be easy for either of you," she sympathized.

"Don't feel sorry for him. He's as cagey as a wolf and five times as smart," Cody assured her.

She paused in front of the door to her hotel room to extract the key card from her purse, and looked up at him through the sweep of her lashes. "Like father, like son?" she guessed.

There was a hint of a smile, but Cody didn't respond as he took the key card from her, stuck it into the slot and unlocked the door, pushing it open. He looked inside briefly and turned to her. "Okay. No bad guys. Go on in."

He put the key card into her left palm and held onto her hand, turning it over to study the diamond ring on her finger. His attention drew Shannon's gaze to it.

"You're really going to marry this guy when you find him?" His remark seemed to challenge her.

Her head moved in a nod as she stared at the ring Rick had placed on her finger. "My parents were going to fly here this weekend for the wedding, but we may not be able to make arrangements in time. It's possible we'll have to postpone the ceremony until next Saturday," she conceded.

She caught her breath when his hand cupped her cheek and jaw, forcing Shannon to lift her chin and look at him. The disturbing intensity of his gaze held her attention while his thumb rubbed her cheekbone in an absent caress.

"You say it's been six months since you've seen him?"

"Yes," Shannon admitted, aware of the quickening rush of blood through her veins.

His thumb slid down to trace the outline of her lips while his light blue eyes studied the action. "Hmm," he mused. "For six months these lips haven't been kissed. That's a crime."

His head bent to bring his mouth against them. A sense of loyalty to Rick kept Shannon motionless beneath the warm pressure as his mouth moved over her lips with sensual ease. The kiss made no demand for a response, but she realized that six months of abstinence had made her hungry for the touch of a man, not just that of her fiancé. She was enjoying the feel of Cody's mouth against hers, the male smell of him making her feel warm all over.

If he had wanted to, Cody could have overcome her passivity and aroused a response, but he pulled slowly away. Shannon believed he was just being polite, but she wasn't sure. She should have felt relieved that he hadn't taken advantage of the fact that they were alone in the hallway, but instead she felt vaguely disappointed.

Satisfaction glinted in his look when he surveyed her upturned face. "Don't mention this to Dad, will you?" he said.

"Like I would," she said indignantly.

"Well, I'm just making sure. If he found out about this innocent little kiss, he'd probably take a belt to me. Or give me a lecture. I'm not sure which is worse."

Basically, he was dismissing the kiss as unimportant, which was the way she had decided to regard it. So why was that so annoying? Was it ego? The desire to conquer even if she wasn't interested in the victory? It troubled her that she wasn't able to take a casual kiss casually at all.

"No problem. I can keep a secret," she said, smiling in an attempt to make a joke of it.

"Good." He seemed pleased with her answer. "It's

been a long day. Get some rest, okay? It's time I was heading downstairs—before Dad shows up with a shotgun."

"Thanks for dinner," she remembered to say as he moved away from the door. "And tell your dad I thanked him, too."

"I'll be sure to pass the message on," he promised with a saluting wave.

Inside her room, Shannon leaned against the closed door, thinking that this was crazy. If Cody had kissed her with passion, she would have been outraged. Now, because it was a friendly, innocent kiss, she was wondering what was wrong with her. *He respected me and I'm wishing he hadn't.*

"Oh, Rick," she sighed, and looked at her ring. "Where are you?" she whispered, suddenly desperately needing to see him again.

Chapter Four

By mid-afternoon of the following day, the clouds had blown away and the sun had come out to shine its warmth on the city. A corduroy jacket was all Shannon needed to keep warm as she wandered aimlessly through the downtown business district.

Well, not quite aimlessly. She had brought her digital camera, a professional-grade one that had been her graduation gift from her parents. Exactly what she was going to do with all the images she'd taken so far, she wasn't sure, but her college photography teacher had told her she had a knack for a unique shot and a rapport with her subjects that might enable her to turn pro some day.

Alaska, with its stunning vistas and local characters, might prove to be a gold mine in more ways than one. Rick had thought so. It occurred to her, suddenly on her own for the first time in a long while, that he'd never given a lot of consideration to what she might want to do. But once Rick was found, they could talk about all that. And he was going to be found. Shannon didn't even want to think about any other possibilities.

She stopped at a well-known landmark, an air distance marker topped by a silhouette of a backpacker and looked at the signs below denoting the distance to major cities all over the world. Even though she was walking down a street that didn't look a whole lot different from any other in the U.S., Anchorage was still thousands of miles from everywhere. But the vast Alaska backcountry stretched thousands of miles farther. Rick had to be out there somewhere.

She'd been on the telephone all morning and most of the afternoon, calling charter and flying services to see if Rick was employed there. Some recalled that he had applied for a job, most had no recollection of him at all, and none of them had him listed on their payroll.

A sense of defeat had driven her out of the room to walk off some of her frustration. She kept searching the faces of the people on the off chance that by some miracle she'd find Rick among them. She paused at a crosswalk and glanced around to get her bearings. Across the street was her hotel. She'd come full circle. There was no place else for her to go.

Crossing the street, she entered the hotel through the revolving doors. As she walked through the lobby, she thought she heard someone call her name and stopped to look over her shoulder. Her mouth curved into a smile that didn't lighten the defeated dullness of her eyes.

"Hello, Mr. Steele," she greeted the older man, and half turned as he approached. "I didn't expect to see you today."

"Noah," he corrected.

"Okay, Noah. Is Cody with you?" She glanced around in search of his dark-haired son.

"No, he's busy," Noah explained, and Shannon felt a slight letdown at the answer. "I had some free time, so I thought I'd stop by to see if you had any luck finding your boyfriend."

"No." She shook her head, the corners of her mouth drooping. "I called every company in the telephone book. A couple of them remember talking to him, but Rick isn't working for any of them." Her shoulders lifted in an expressive shrug. "I just don't know what to do next."

"Let me buy you a cup of coffee." He winked as if he knew the remedy. "Nothing is ever as bad as it seems."

"That's what I keep telling myself," she sighed, and let herself be led to the coffee shop off the hotel lobby. "At this point I'm open to any suggestion."

"Two coffees," Noah Steele ordered as the uniformed waitress brought glasses of ice water to their table. He waited until she returned with a pot of coffee and the two brown mugs were filled before he responded to her earlier statement. "Maybe you should go to the police and file a missing-persons report on him."

"I've been thinking about that." She measured a spoonful of sugar into her coffee and stirred. "Except that I don't know that Rick is missing. I just don't know where he is. I'd feel pretty foolish if it turned out to be a false alarm."

In her side vision she caught a glimpse of a tall figure entering the coffee shop. When the man started walking toward their table, she turned her head to cast a curious glance in his direction. Recognizing Cody, she sent a startled look at his father.

"I thought you said Cody wasn't with you," she said.

A fleeting expression of guilt crossed his features when he looked around to see his son approaching them. "No, he didn't come with me," Noah Steele insisted.

"Hello, Shannon." Cody smiled at her, then turned a speculative look on his father. "Dad, this is a surprise. What are you doing here?"

"I thought I'd stop by to see Shannon and find out whether she'd had any luck locating her fiancé." His expression was almost too bland. "After all, she doesn't know a soul here, so it can't be easy on her, being alone with no one to turn to for help."

"Strange," Cody murmured, tipping his head to one side. "Those words sound very familiar. I believe I expressed a similar thought about an hour ago when you asked me what my plans were tonight."

A redness crept up his father's neck, and Shannon realized Noah had known all along that Cody intended to see her today. That's why he'd arranged to be there first, so Cody would be the one intruding this time. The only problem was that Cody had exposed his father's hand and revealed his intention.

"Why don't you sit down and have a cup of coffee with us?" his father invited.

"Why, thank you," Cody mocked the invitation, pulling an empty chair away from the next table. "Did you have any luck, Texas?"

"No. I called everyone. I don't know where to go from here," she repeated her earlier frustration.

"Maybe he got a job doing something besides flying," Noah Steele suggested.

"No." Shannon was positive about that. "He would have come home before he'd done that. Wherever he's working, you can be sure it's associated with flying. He wouldn't have settled for anything less than that."

"There are any number of companies that have their own fleet of planes." Cody filled an empty cup with coffee from the insulated pot on the table, his remark raising her hopes and offering her another avenue to pursue in her search for Rick. "He could have hired on as a copilot or navigator for one of them, to gain some experience in this kind of country."

"Say, now that's an idea!" his father declared, showing genuine approval of the suggestion. "Wade Rafferty is a good go-to guy. Why don't you check with him?"

Shannon glanced from one to the other, wondering if she should be nosy. She kept her tone casual and asked, "Who's Wade Rafferty?" The name meant nothing to her, and certainly not in connection with Rick.

"Wade is Cody's fishing buddy," Noah Steele replied, as if that explained everything.

"He heads up the Alaskan operation of a petroleum company with interests in the pipeline," Cody said. "He could find out if your fiancé is flying for any of the oil companies. And then there are the extreme-sports charter pilots. We get every dumb-ass daredevil in the world coming up here and they pay big money to anyone who'll fly them into inaccessible areas. Wade knows some of those guys. He'll check around."

"Would he?" She was almost holding her breath.

"If Cody asked him, I'm sure he'd do it as a personal favor," his father insisted.

"I believe he would," Cody verified his father's statement. Her anxiously eager expression seemed to ask what he was waiting for. He studied her face, looking at her with resignation. Then with a little push he shoved himself away from the table and straightened from his chair. "I'll call him right now."

"Thank you." Her glowing smile of gratitude caught his attention. His light eyes looked intently at her, as if trying to understand the depth of her emotion. For a brief second he uncovered something. Shannon didn't have a chance to identify the feeling deep inside before some inner mechanism shut it out of her conscious mind, but it left her a little shaken.

"Are you sure you want me to find your fiancé, Texas?" It was a low question, quietly issued.

Before she could clear her muddled thoughts to assure him that she did, Cody's father jumped in. "Why did you ask a thing like that? Of course she wants him found! She's going to marry him, for heaven's sake!"

Cody gave a nearly invisible shrug as he relented in his demand for an answer from her. "I'll phone Wade and get the search in motion on his end," he said, excusing himself.

His long, deceptively lazy stride carried him quickly out of her sight toward the public phones in the hotel lobby. Shannon sipped her sweetened coffee with a preoccupied air, her thoughts full of Cody and his question, which shouldn't have disturbed her.

As if reading her mind, his father spoke up. "Don't you let Cody put doubts in your mind."

"He isn't," she said quickly, and almost convinced herself.

"That's a relief." Noah sat back in his chair, relaxing a little. "Once that boy makes up his mind that he wants something, he has the devil's own way of getting it. I have my hands full just keeping him in line sometimes."

"Are you hinting that Cody wants me?" There was a thread of amusement in her voice.

Noah Steele looked uncomfortable, then bluntly admitted, "Hey, he's attracted to you. I saw it in his face when you walked into the office the other day. I don't want you getting the wrong idea about Cody. He wouldn't make a move unless he had a signal from you that you wouldn't object."

Shannon couldn't think of a thing to say for a moment. It would be easy to call Noah Steele interfering, but maybe it was just protective instincts working overtime. How could she tell him politely to back off? He seemed to hear only what he wanted to hear.

He coughed a little self-consciously. "I don't normally get involved in my son's private life. It's just that with your fiancé missing and all, you're in a vulnerable position."

"I think I can take care of myself," she suggested gently but firmly.

"Maybe so." He conceded that point somewhat grudgingly. "But it seems to me that since your fiancé isn't here, somebody should be looking after you for him. Once we find the guy, if Cody wants to make a play to win you away from him, then it would all be fair and square."

There was something two-fisted and comically old-fashioned about that manly little speech, but she didn't want to laugh. Noah meant well. Still, it sounded like guys in Alaska divvied up the available women the way they would divvy up a catch of salmon or a case of good whiskey.

If she had to guess, the state's famously skewed male-to-female ratio probably had something to do with it. She was just going to have to get used to the chest-thumping and roaring, that was all. "I appreciate what you're saying, Mr. Steele. But I hardly know your son—and he barely knows me." Shannon resisted the way he was taking it all so seriously.

Noah gave a determined shake of his head, dismissing her argument. "You can know a person for twenty years and not know him any better than a stranger on the street. Or you can meet a stranger and twenty minutes later feel as though you've known him all your life. Time doesn't count that much."

Shannon was forced to agree. Within minutes after meeting Cody, there had been a purely instinctive feeling that she had known him a long time. It was not something that could be explained. But the subject was shunted aside when she saw Cody approaching the table.

Before she could ask whether he had been able to reach his friend, Cody was relaying the results of his phone call.

"I talked to Wade and he's going to run through the employee files on his computer." Cody sat down in the chair he had left earlier. "He suggested we stop by his house around seven this evening. He may have some answers for us by then." His glance stayed with Shannon, not straying to his father.

"That would be nice," Noah said enthusiastically. "I haven't seen little Molly in almost a month. I'll bet she's grown an inch."

"Molly is Wade's and Maggie's daughter. She's two months old," Cody explained for Shannon's benefit.

"Yeah," his father agreed, and elaborated on the explanation. "Molly is Cody's goddaughter."

"Really." Her interested glance ran back to Cody and the glinting blue of his eyes.

"Do you have trouble picturing me as a family man?" It was a low question, with a suggestion of intimacy in its tone.

After only a second's consideration, Shannon shook her head. "No." She was sort of surprised to discover that she didn't have any difficulty visualizing him with children. Cody had a boyish streak that showed in his grin. He'd definitely be the kind of dad who had fun with his kids, and his strong self-discipline would come in handy for the tough stuff.

"That's good," he murmured.

There was something in his look that sent a hot warmth through her veins. Shannon attempted to change the subject. "You must have known Wade Rafferty and his wife for a long time."

"Wade and I got acquainted about six years ago when he first came to Alaska." Amusement glittered in his eyes; he was aware of her ploy.

"Almost seven," his father corrected, and Shannon was relieved to have him take part in the conversation again. "We haven't known Maggie, his wife, that long, of course."

"Have they recently married?" she asked.

"You could say that," Noah Steele agreed with a broad hint that there was a great deal more to the story. "You see, they were divorced when Wade moved up here. He went back to Seattle about a year . . . year and a half ago. It got complicated. Um, Wade was engaged to Belinda Hale, the daughter of the president of his firm. He'd gone back to break the news to his son, Mike, and get married. He got married all right, but to his first wife, Maggie." He paused, a grim expression dominating his rough features. "It was too bad about Belinda."

"We won't go into that now, Dad." Beneath Cody's casual statement there seemed to be a warning.

His father flashed a look at Shannon and shifted uneasily in his chair. "Yeah, I'm talking out of turn," he admitted.

Shannon concluded that Cody didn't feel his father should be gossiping about his friend's personal affairs, and let the intriguing reference to Belinda Hale go without comment. After all, it had nothing to do with her.

"Where would you like to have dinner tonight, Texas?" Cody asked.

She took a breath, remembering the big meal she'd had the night before, and knew she wasn't hungry enough to eat that much again. "I don't have much of an appetite tonight." She shrugged her indifference to food.

"I'm sure you could eat a sandwich," Cody asserted. "There's an excellent deli up the street."

"We'll eat there," his father stated. "This time Cody can pick up the check."

In spite of herself, Shannon laughed at Noah's insistence that he wasn't going to be stuck with paying for their meals a second night in a row. A surge of gratitude followed at the way this father-and-son pair were keeping her spirits up. Alone, she would have worried herself sick about Rick, but the Steeles kept the gloomy shadows at bay.

"Okay, you've talked me into it," she agreed, the soft laughter staying in her voice.

Leaving the coffee shop together, they paused at the cashier's while Noah paid for the coffee. Then it was outside into the crispness of an Alaskan autumn. With a Steele on either side of her to guide her to their destination, Shannon started up the street. At an intersection she spied a word included in a store sign, and remembered how often she'd seen it.

"I've been meaning to ask," she began, "what's a cache? So far I've seen shops called a fur cache, a book cache and a jewelry cache."

"'Cache' is an Alaskan term." Cody pronounced it "cash." "It's like a shed, but it's up on poles to keep animals from reaching it. Caches used to be everywhere in rural areas for food storage, and you still see them here and there. Kind of a symbol of Alaska."

"I can see why," Shannon replied. "It's unique."

"Alaska prides itself on being unique," he reminded her with a twinkling glance.

"But you don't brag about being big," she teased him back.

"No, we leave the bragging to that small state down south called Texas." He softened the remark with a smile. His needling was all in the name of good fun.

Shannon had picked up on that right away. She laughed softly. The comparison of their home states was becoming a private joke between them—something personal and warm.

"Here we are," Noah announced, and stepped forward to open the door to the delicatessen for Shannon.

A hostess showed them to a booth and left them menus. Shannon ordered a roast beef sandwich on a sourdough bun, believing that she was ordering in proportion to her appetite. When it was served, she realized she had been mistaken. Between the bun halves there was a mound of sliced beef, and the bun occupied nearly the entire plate.

"I can't possibly eat all of this," she protested. "There's enough for three people here."

"You Texas chicks just pick at your food," Cody chided.

"That's right," she agreed on a laughing note, "Big hair is one thing but a big butt is another. Who needs the calories?" She added wickedly, "Of course, Alaskans get to burn them up keeping warm in arctic nights."

"I can think of better ways to keep warm," he countered suggestively, and Shannon decided against pursuing that line of banter.

Picking up half of the sandwich, she reverted to her original statement. "I'm not going to be able to eat all of this."

"Do the best you can," Noah advised. "You need to keep up your strength. We can't have you wasting away to nothing before your wedding day."

As she bit into her sandwich, she was conscious of Cody glancing at the diamond ring on her finger. She wasn't sure whether it was his father's remark or the sight of her engagement ring that caused him to fall silent, but he didn't say much while they ate. She managed to eat half of the sandwich and nibble around the edges of the second half before her stomach protested that it was full and refused to tolerate another bite. As she leaned against the slatted boards forming the booth's backrest, she noticed that Cody also had left some of his sandwich uneaten.

"You didn't have much of an appetite, either, did you?" she observed.

He flashed her a remote blue glance to acknowledge the remark, but didn't directly respond to it. Instead he glanced at his watch. "It's nearly seven. Wade's expecting us." He reached for the bill the waitress had left on the table and slid out of the booth.

His father quickly wiped at his mouth with a napkin and followed suit. "Where did you park your car, Cody?" he asked, as he politely helped Shannon out of the booth.

"Across the street from the hotel, near your pickup," Cody answered, and took out his wallet to pay for their meal.

"Good. I'll ride with you and Shannon. When you bring her back to the hotel later on this evening, I can pick up my truck then. That way we can save the gas it would take to drive two vehicles," Noah declared, satisfied that his solution was both logical and practical. Cody offered no objection, but Shannon sighed inwardly. She was beginning to get seriously annoyed by the older man's constant hovering.

After leaving the delicatessen, they backtracked their route to the hotel and crossed the street to the parking lot where Cody had left his car. In the business district of Anchorage, neatly painted homes often shared the same block with commercial buildings, but he drove them to a residential area overlooking the bay. The side street he took ended in a cul-de-sac with rustic two-story houses, heavily beamed and sided with stained wood. He parked in the driveway of one and shut off the engine.

"What a beautiful home," Shannon remarked.

Cody directed a half smile at her as he opened his car door. "Not everyone in Alaska lives in a log cabin or an igloo."

It was almost a relief to have him tease her again about her preconceived notions of Alaska. He'd been much too preoccupied since their evening meal. She had begun to wonder if something was wrong.

Noah opened the front passenger door and extended a hand to help her as she stepped out of the car. "You'll like the Raffertys," he assured her with gruff gentleness. "They're a nice family."

A sidewalk curved from the driveway to the front door. Following Cody, Shannon walked ahead of his father to the sheltered stairs of the entry and waited while Cody pushed the button for the doorbell.

The door was opened by a young boy of about twelve with dark hair and eyes and a sprinkling of freckles across the bridge of his nose. He was holding a fussing baby against his shoulder.

"Hiya, Cody." His voice was in the midst of changing octaves as he greeted Cody with easy familiarity.

"Hi, Mike. How are you?"

"Okay, I guess. Come on in. Dad's on the phone and Mom's in the kitchen rescuing a cake from the oven. She forgot to set the timer, so it might be kinda chewy and gooey."

"Chewy and gooey sounds good to me." Cody stepped to one side to let Shannon enter the house ahead of him. Once she and his father were inside the tiled foyer, he introduced her. "Mike, I'd like you to meet Shannon Hayes. This is Mike Rafferty and his baby sister, Molly."

"Pleased to meet you, Miss Hayes," Mike nodded. His sister began squirming fretfully in his arms.

"I'll hold her," Cody volunteered, and relieved the boy of his wiggling burden without a trace of awkwardness. "How have you been, Molly?" Cody asked, as if he expected an answer. The baby's dark eyes opened wide in an attempt to focus on the face of the man holding her.

"You'd better take this, Cody." Mike passed him a small towel. "She spits up a lot. It really makes your clothes smell if it gets on them." His nose wrinkled in distaste.

"What do you think of my goddaughter, Texas?" Cody asked with a trace of pride.

"She's beautiful." She marveled at the thick mass of curling black hair on the baby's head.

"Molly has her daddy's coloring—black hair and black eyes," Cody remarked absently.

"Yeah, but she's got my mom's temper," Mike declared. "When she gets mad, you can hear her screaming a block away. She's spoiled already."

A woman's voice came from the living room, laughing and warm. "And look who's spoiling her! Every time she whimpers, Mike is there to pick her up!"

Shannon turned to watch the petite redhead approach them. "Hello, Cody, Noah. It's good to see you again." Her green eyes looked curiously at Shannon. "I'm Maggie Rafferty."

"Shannon Hayes," Shannon volunteered.

"Welcome to Alaska," Maggie responded warmly, then let her smile encompass the others. "Well, make yourselves comfortable. Wade knows you're here, so he should be out directly."

A natural stone fireplace dominated the cozy room with its paneled walls and beamed ceiling. Comfortable overstuffed furniture was clustered about the hearth, spaced close for intimate conversations. A thick carpet softened their footsteps. As Shannon sat down on the opposite end of the sofa from Cody, a tall, dark-haired man entered the room from a branching hallway, his broad, muscular frame enhanced by a ribbed sweater.

There was a rush of exchanged greetings, and Shannon was introduced to Wade Rafferty. Then there was a moment of calm as Wade joined his red-haired wife on the sofa, a twin to the one on which Cody and Shannon were seated. She watched his arm circle Maggie's shoulders in a natural, loving gesture of closeness that momentarily made her forget the question she wanted to ask about Rick. The quiet was broken by the baby in Cody's arms as she began a fussing cry.

"I'll take her." Mike was quick to reach for his little sister. "She probably wants a bottle or something."

As he lifted her out of Cody's arms and started to carry her from the room, Maggie Rafferty spoke up. "Don't let her go to sleep yet, Mike."

"Molly takes after her mother," Wade explained, gesturing at his wife. "She has absolutely no respect for time. She has her days and nights mixed up and expects everyone to march to the beat of her drum." Then he smiled at the others. "If I want Maggie to be ready on time for anything, I have to set all the clocks in the house ahead one hour."

"Wade Rafferty, that isn't true!" Maggie declared with mock outrage.

"All right," he conceded. "I only set them a half an hour ahead."

"That is true," Maggie admitted with a laugh. Cody shifted his position on the sofa, stretching his arm along the backrest behind Shannon. Her glance swung to him and met the silent assurance of his gaze. His hand touched her shoulder but only briefly.

"I know Shannon is anxious, so I'll ask the question

for her, Wade," he said. "Did you come up with any leads on her fiancé?"

There was a slight pause as Wade's coal-dark gaze rested on her. "Nothing, I'm afraid," he admitted.

"Not a thing?" Shannon echoed softly, and felt the warm clasp of Cody's hand on her shoulder in quiet comfort, a measure of his strength flowing into her.

"No." Wade shook his head. "I checked the employee files for flight crews and the ground crews. No one by the name of Farris, though. But I'm poking around in the databases of our consortium companies, just in case. I have access to most of their files. Heck, I wish I had more information for you, Shannon. Just give me time. I can check the flight rosters of other companies with the new program I just installed."

"Is that legal?" Cody asked.

"Hey, you gave me the software."

"Oh, right."

She swallowed her disappointment and managed to smile. "I'm really grateful that you took the trouble to check."

"It wasn't any trouble," he assured her, then attempted to lighten the atmosphere. "Now would you mind telling me how you managed to get hooked up with this devil from out of the blue?" he asked, indicating Cody.

"From Rick's last letter, I had the impression he was working for Cody," she explained, thinking that Wade's description of his friend was accurate. For starters, the wicked gleam in Cody's blue eyes. The sexy way he walked. The cockiness. And a few other really good things. She told herself to snap out of it.

"Anyway," she continued, "when Rick wasn't at the airport to meet me and his landlord claimed he'd moved out of his apartment, I went to Steele Air, thinking I would find Rick there."

"Only he wasn't working for us," Cody carried the explanation further. "I couldn't turn away a damsel in distress without offering some assistance. I didn't want her to have the impression that Alaska was a cold, unfeeling place."

"The fact that she was a total babe had no bearing on your decision, of course" Wade said with a taunting grin. "And all alone in a land where babes are few and far between."

"Hey," Maggie began indignantly.

"Honey, you know you're a babe," Wade said. "That's why I married you." He gave her a nuzzling kiss on the ear and she wriggled with pleasure.

"Shannon's engaged, by the way. Don't forget that," Noah inserted, drawing a laugh from the others, all except Wade Rafferty. A thoughtful frown creased his forehead, his gaze narrowing slightly.

"I haven't, Dad," Cody said, and eyed Shannon with lazy intensity. "Although I admit there are times when I'd like to overlook that small detail."

"Do you have a photo of your fiancé I could borrow for a couple of days?" Wade asked. "I'll scan it and give it back as soon as I can."

"Yes, I do." She opened her purse and rummaged through the contents for her billfold. Extracting Rick's picture from its clear plastic sleeve, she handed it to Wade.

"Rick Farris—you said that was his name?" He studied the photo closely.

"Yes," she confirmed, and watched him attentively. She sensed an undercurrent in his attitude that she didn't quite understand.

Then he was smiling and the impression was gone. "I'll return this pronto." He slipped the snapshot into his shirt pocket and turned to his wife, deftly changing the subject. "How about some coffee, Maggie?"

"Coffee and cake, fresh from the oven—your favorite, Cody," Maggie stated as she rose from the sofa. "Streusel topping. I scraped off the overcooked part."

"Sounds good," he said with a nod.

"Would you like some help?" Shannon offered.

"No, I can manage. Thank you," Maggie refused.

A brief silence settled on the room after she'd left. Noah leaned forward in his chair, putting himself in the conversation. "Any word about your boss and his daughter?"

"No." Wade reached for a mint from the candy bowl on the coffee table between the twin sofas. He put it into his mouth and moved it into his cheek, where it made a hamsterish bulge. "Just quit smoking." He grinned at Shannon. "I can't believe how many of these I eat a day." He crunched it up with a thoughtful expression. "Anyway, Noah, they've officially called off the air search, although pilots flying in the area are still keeping an eye out."

"What happened?" A faint frown lined Shannon's forehead as she divided her glance between the two men.

"We don't know," Wade replied. "The board chairman of my company and his daughter left for a long weekend to fly to a remote fishing camp. The plane never arrived at their destination. We think it went down but no one got a signal. State-of-the-art GPS system on board but that doesn't mean it didn't malfunction."

"I'm sorry," she murmured awkwardly.

"Henderson was the pilot, wasn't he?" Noah asked. When Wade confirmed that with a nod, he shook his grizzled head. "Damned good man. He knew more tricks than Houdini to keep a plane in the air. You can be sure it wasn't pilot error. I remember the time—"

"Don't go back in history, Dad," Cody interrupted with a wry grimace. "Your memory isn't that reliable."

"My memory is as good as the day you were born," his father protested.

There was laughter in the glance he slid to Shannon. "Do you see what I mean? He's already wrong. I was born at midnight, not during the day."

"Dang it, Cody! Quit twisting what I say," Noah declared in irritation.

"Are you two arguing already?" Maggie appeared with a tray of refreshments. "I haven't been gone five minutes."

The appearance of streusel cake and coffee put the group into a more congenial mood. The conversation segued to other topics and the atmosphere became more relaxed as the shadows of worry were banished to the far corners of the room.

Later, when Shannon offered to help clear the dishes, Maggie accepted. "What's it like to live in Alaska?" she asked as she followed the slim redhead into the kitchen.

"It's an adventure." The tone of Maggie's voice indicated that was an understatement. "Especially when you leave the city and go into the country. You certainly don't run to the corner store every other day. The isolation is harder on the women in the outlying towns and the backcountry than for those of us in Anchorage or Fairbanks. I don't suppose you've had much time to go sightseeing since you've arrived."

"No, I haven't," Shannon admitted.

"Because of his job, Wade spends a lot of time in Valdez. By the way, be sure to pronounce it Val-*deez* or the natives get snotty," Maggie advised with a smile. "Even with the pipeline terminus there, it's safe to say it's still off the beaten path. But before Molly was born,

I used to go there with Wade a lot. Now it's a big jump-ing-off place for extreme athletes, ice-climbers, heli-skiers, people like that. Maniacs." She took the dishes from Shannon and stacked them in the sink. "I mean, mani-acs with money. They spend a lot to get up here."

"Rick said the north was America's last frontier," Shannon said.

"It's all that and more."

When they returned to the living room, the men were deep in a heavy conversation. Shannon caught Wade Rafferty's last statement, "I hope I'm wrong," be-fore the discussion was abruptly halted by their ap-proach. Cody's expression was troubled and grim, but it vanished the instant he met her look, to be replaced by a quick smile.

"Sorry. We got into state politics," he said to explain the serious atmosphere.

"I hope you settled all the burning issues," Maggie smiled.

"Naturally," Wade replied.

It was nearly an hour later when Cody suggested that they leave. And it was another fifteen minutes before they actually made it to the door. Wade walked them to the car.

"I'll be in touch as soon as I have some definite an-swers," he promised.

Although the statement was more or less directed at Cody, Shannon thanked him. "I appreciate the time you're taking."

"My pleasure," he assured her, and waved as Cody re-versed the car out of the driveway.

For a change, Noah Steele wasn't very talkative dur-ing the drive back to the hotel. Shannon was fine with that. Her own father was nowhere near as inquisitive as the older Steele. The only subject discussed at any length was her impression of the Raffertys, which was a positive one.

Cody stopped next to the entrance to the parking lot first to let his father out. Before Noah climbed out, he started to ask, "Are you going to—"

"I'll be home directly, Dad," Cody interrupted him.

"Okay." The older man stepped out and closed the rear passenger door.

Parking the car around the corner in front of the hotel, Cody got out to see Shannon safely to her room. Little was said during the ride up in the elevator or while walking down the hallway to her room. Shannon unlocked the door and turned to thank him for an enjoyable evening, but the intensity of his gaze distracted her.

"Is something wrong?" She frowned.

He leaned an arm against the door frame, a corner of his mouth lifting grimly. "Yes, something is wrong. Me. I'm wrong." Cody said. His gaze possessively swept her upturned face to linger on her lips. "What I'm thinking is wrong." He looked lower, taking in the curved length of her body in a suggestive way. Her pulse raced. "What I'm wanting is wrong."

She was unnerved by his frankly sexual gaze, so blatantly demanding. "Cody, I don't . . . I mean . . . just back off. Okay?"

A nerve leaped along his jaw, exposing the raw edges of his desire, before the muscles relaxed and he smiled. "Okay. But tell me something. Do you believe in intuition, Texas, even when there aren't any facts to support it?"

The question puzzled her. Already on guard, she answered warily, "Sometimes."

"So do I. And my intuition tells me that the time will come when what I'm thinking and what I'm wanting will be right—for both of us." He leaned down to brush her lips with a feather-warm kiss. "Good night, Texas." He pushed away from the door frame, leaving her free to enter the room. "I'm a patient man. All things come to he who waits."

Chapter Five

The next morning Shannon was sitting beside the phone debating whether she should call her parents and tell them about Rick's apparent disappearance. The situation seemed completely unreal. Saturday was approaching—her wedding day. It seemed hard to believe . . . impossible, in fact. But she couldn't postpone the call much longer.

A knock at her door allowed Shannon to shelve the decision for the moment.

"Who is it?" she called.

"Cody!" was the partially muffled answer.

Sliding the bolt away, she slipped the safety chain free and opened the door. "Good morning?" Her greeting held a question; she wondered what had brought him to the hotel at this hour.

"Hiya." He stood in the hallway with his hands thrust into the pockets of his flight jacket. A lazy smile slanted the strong line of his mouth. "I believe I owe you an apology for some of the things I said last night. I was out of line."

"It's forgotten." But she felt a twinge of regret that he

hadn't meant them. Her mixed feelings really were becoming confusing.

"Last night I guess I just wasn't looking forward to going home and sleeping alone in a double bed," he explained with a shrug of his shoulders. "Who wants that?"

The man got right to the point, didn't he? Damn it. She found it all too easy to visualize herself in his arms, shaped to his length spoon-fashion.

"Uh, no one, I guess," she agreed, but uneasily.

"I hope you don't have anything on your agenda this morning." Cody abruptly switched the subject. "I've decided that you've been cooped up in this hotel long enough. It's time you saw something of Alaska up close."

"But . . . don't you have to work?"

"That's one of the privileges of owning a business. You can take a day off whenever it suits you." When she continued to hesitate, Cody reasoned, "What would you do if you didn't go with me?"

"I . . ." Her hand opened in an empty gesture.

"Nothing," he answered for her. "You need the break. Get your purse and a jacket."

It took her only a few seconds to collect both and join him in the hallway. "Where are we going?" she asked as they entered the elevator.

"I thought we'd take a drive out to Matanuska Valley."

"I don't know any more than I did before." She laughed, because the name held no significance for her.

"You will," Cody promised.

In the car Cody took the highway that angled north from the city. The sky was predominantly blue, with gray white clouds lingering on the ridges of the Chugach Mountains. Homes began to thin out, the settlement giving way to an encroaching forest of trees dressed in the autumn colors of gold and rust. When they passed a highway sign that advised MOOSE CROSSING—NEXT TEN MILES, Shannon turned to Cody with a disbelieving look.

"Moose crossing?" she said. "Are there that many? What do they do when they're moosing around?"

He laughed. "They like to browse on the young willow shoots that grow along the highway. You usually see them early in the morning or around sunset. A full-grown moose can weigh around a thousand pounds, so it's no joke if you hit one."

"Guess not." The chance that she might catch a glimpse of one of the giants of the wild kept her peering into the undergrowth even though it was midmorning. The homes she saw scattered along the highway were frequently constructed out of logs.

Miles slipped away as they traveled inland. The sight of a whole mountainside cloaked in shimmering gold leaves made her catch her breath in awe. But she hadn't forgotten to bring along her camera and she captured shot after shot of nature in all its spectacular glory.

"What kind of trees are those? Aspens?" she questioned Cody, not believing she could be right.

"The gold ones? Yes."

Her head moved from side to side in awed disbelief. "I've been to the Rocky Mountains in the fall, where you often see a clump of golden aspens against a backdrop of pine. It's the other way around here. A clump of pine trees with a whole mountainside of aspens."

"Impressive, isn't it?"

"That's an understatement," Shannon declared on a fervent note, and turned to look at him. Her gaze was distracted by the glimpse of a plowed field beyond him. "Do they farm around here?" Farms did not fit her image of Alaska—so far nothing had matched her pre-conceived notion of Alaska.

"Okay, this is going to sound like a geography text-book, but I'd say Matanuska Valley is the center of Alaska's agriculture."

"What do they grow?"

"Oats, wheat, barley, some vegetables." He named off the crops, then added, "We'll stop at one of the pro-duce markets near Palmer."

Her glance swept the valley to the left of the highway. "I suppose they raise a lot of cattle."

"Not as much as you would expect. There isn't a high nutrient value in the native grasses. Most of the big cat-tle operations are located on Kodiak Island," he ex-plained. "Matanuska Valley was settled during the Depression when much of the midwestern United States was stricken with drought. The federal govern-ment provided transportation for some two hundred families to come here and gave them land to develop and farm."

"I didn't know that." A brief look of chagrin spread across her features. "I'm beginning to realize there are a lot of things I don't know about Alaska. I should have been reading up on my history."

"Alaska has to be seen to be believed."

"I'm discovering that," Shannon agreed.

They drove through several small communities. The conversation between them subsided, leaving Shannon free to photograph the continually changing scenery that surrounded them. Mountains, valleys, wilderness, farms, log cabins, modern homes, rivers, lakes, ribbon-slim waterfalls splashing silver down the rock face of a mountain, marshy lowlands dotted with wading birds—every curve in the road brought something new to see, sometimes at a better angle and sometimes just a tanta-lizing glimpse.

Outside of Palmer, Cody slowed the car and turned off the highway where a sign indicated a farmers' market. Two cars were parked in front of a shed with a sign that read OPEN. He stopped the car beside the other two and turned off the engine.

"Come on." He smiled. "We'll continue your education inside."

Shannon had a feeling she was about to learn more than she'd ever wanted to know about Alaskan produce. Flashback to elementary school, she thought with a smile she didn't let him see. She remembered coloring in small potatoes on a photocopied map of Idaho and little ears of corn for Iowa as she climbed out and walked to the front of the car, where Cody waited for her. Together they walked to the shed's door, his hand resting lightly on the curve of her waist.

Amazement registered in her expression within seconds after she stepped inside. She stared at the long tables with their picked-over selection of vegetables. Those that remained were so huge she doubted they were real. She walked over to a cabbage that weighed at least fifty pounds and touched a leaf.

"It's real," she murmured aloud, and lifted her rounded gaze to Cody. "What a monster. Is it a mutant? How did it grow so big?"

"That isn't big," he said as he critically studied the cabbage. "In fact, it's on the puny side."

"You're kidding!"

Cody only grinned. "Don't cabbages grow this big in Texas?"

"You brought me here deliberately," she accused without anger, wising up to his game, "so you could brag about how big everything is in Alaska."

"I don't have to brag, Texas. Alaska does it for herself."

She had to laugh, unable to dispute the accuracy of

his remark. "You're going to have to explain to me how this cabbage grew so big," she insisted.

"It's pretty simple. Just a little bit of northern magic," Cody said. "This is the land of the midnight sun. The secret is almost twenty hours of light during the day."

"I hadn't thought about that. Does that much sunlight make everything grow like this?"

"It makes everything grow, but it doesn't always produce," he admitted. "Corn, for instance; the stalks and leaves are tall and healthy, but the ears are small and unformed."

"Why?"

"Alaskan summers have no night, only a kind of twilight. In order for corn to produce ears, you have to put it to bed—cover it the same way you cover a bird's cage, with cloth or a paper sack. Commercially, that isn't practical, although sometimes families with home gardens do it," he explained.

"Oh, so that's it." Shannon turned back to view the cabbage again, still marveling at its size. "What a shock it must have been the first time someone planted a cabbage here and it grew into something like this." She took her camera out of her bag and motioned Cody over to the cabbage. "Stand next to it. They're not going to believe this back home."

Cody put a big hand on the monster vegetable. "This okay? What do you want me to do?"

"Smile at it—the cabbage, I mean."

"Smile at it? I'll look like an idiot." He smiled at her instead.

"Great shot. Thanks." She laughed and put her camera away, still finding it all a little incredible.

After they toured the small marketplace, they drove into Palmer and had lunch at the small café located inside the equally small hotel on the main street. Shannon was surprised at how hungry she was, devouring every bite of food on her plate. They returned to Anchorage at a leisurely pace, arriving back at her hotel in the early afternoon.

Suggesting coffee, Cody accompanied her into the hotel. "I think I'll check at the desk first, just to see if there are any messages for me," Shannon stated. As she started to cross the lobby, she recognized a couple standing in the center lobby.

"Cody, look! There's Wade and Maggie." When she looked back to him, she was surprised to find that he didn't seem pleased to see his friends. A thought occurred to her. "Do you suppose they found out something about Rick?"

"I don't know." He didn't venture an opinion as his hand applied pressure to the back of her waist, guiding her forward. "They've seen us. Let's go over and say hello."

She was almost afraid to hope Wade Rafferty had learned something about Rick's whereabouts. Crossing the lobby with Cody's hand firmly on her waist, she forced a smile to her lips.

"Hello. We didn't expect to see you here this afternoon," she said, and glanced expectantly from one to the other, waiting for an explanation that would answer the looming question of what had brought them to the hotel.

Wade flicked a brief look at Cody, and Shannon felt his hand tighten its grip. When his enigmatic gaze returned to her, she was puzzled by its remoteness. "Last night when I told you your fiancé wasn't working for us, I was wrong. His records were in a temp file that took me a while to pull up. Anyway, I happened to show his photo to a couple of our mechanics on the flight line; they recognized him. They thought his name was Nick."

She had been bracing herself for another dead end. It was just beginning to hit her that she had finally found out where Rick was working. "I can't believe it!" she burst out on a happy note of relief. "Where is he? Where's Rick?"

"Steady, Texas," Cody's voice cautioned on an ominously low note.

"Cody's right," Wade said. "I'm afraid I don't have good news."

"What do you mean?" Alarm flashed across her face as Shannon suddenly became aware of the quiet sympathy and concern in Maggie's expression. "Is Rick all right? Has he been hurt?"

"He was flying copilot on the plane that carried Jackson Hale, our board chairman. There isn't any easy way to say this, Shannon." Wade's voice was heavy with regret. "The plane was reported missing more than two weeks ago, presumed lost with everyone aboard."

She stared. They were saying Rick's plane had crashed, implying that he was dead. It was in their faces. A tremor of disbelief started, gathering momentum.

"There must be a mistake," she murmured in vague protest. "Maybe it wasn't Rick."

Wade returned Rick's photograph, placing it in her nerveless fingers. "The ground crew identified him as the copilot. Henderson, our chief pilot, had hired him only the day before. We're not sure whether the lack of an employment record was an oversight or if Henderson had it with his papers aboard the plane. Without it we weren't able to notify his next of kin. I'm sorry, Shannon. I'm truly sorry," he said grimly.

Her eyes blurred as she tried to look at the photograph in her hand. "No." It was a strangled sound of denial. She refused to accept that any of this was true.

"Come on." Cody's hand tightened around her waist, his voice brisk and commanding. "Let's go someplace less public than this lobby."

Shannon heard him, but she was barely conscious of

being swept along to the elevators. Insulated by a numbed kind of shock, she kept hearing fragments of Wade's voice, phrases out of context: "presumed lost . . . flying copilot . . . next of kin . . . missing . . . sorry, sorry, sorry. . . ."

"Where's the key card to your room, Shannon?" Cody was asking, his voice coming from some far-off place. "Do you have it?"

His request penetrated her consciousness, but she lacked coordination as she fumbled with the flap of her shoulder bag. Cody slipped the strap off her shoulder and handed her purse to someone else, his arm remaining around her in silent support.

"See if you can find her key card, Maggie," he ordered.

She was absently aware of a door being opened. She was half walked and half carried into the room. Images danced in her mind of an airplane flying into a cloud and never coming out, swallowed by the vastness of the Alaska sky. She closed her eyes tightly, trying to shut out the vision.

"Wade, call room service and order up some black coffee with plenty of sugar," Cody ordered as he pushed her into a chair.

Her eyes opened and saw only his lean, strong-jawed face. There was the glitter of unshed tears in their blue depths. A reluctant sadness was in his features, stamped with resignation.

"You weren't at all surprised when Wade told me." Her voice was hoarse, but the haze was dissipating, clearing her head. "You knew . . . or guessed before he told me."

"Yes," Cody admitted.

"How long? How long have you known?" She felt betrayed by this man she had thought she could trust.

"I found out this afternoon, a few minutes ago, when

I saw Wade in the lobby waiting for us. I suspected last night, *after* talking to Wade." He stressed the qualifying verb. "After talking to you, Wade realized that your fiancé could have been the unidentified copilot. That's why he wanted the photo."

"You knew—you suspected, but you didn't tell me," Shannon accused. "I had a right to know."

"Maybe you did. But I didn't see the point of your losing a night's sleep when we weren't even sure Rick was on that plane," he retorted with a trace of anger. "I don't regret it and I'm not going to apologize."

"I won't thank you for it, either!" she flared.

"I never asked for your thanks," he countered with equal force. A heavy sigh broke from him as Cody lowered his head and rubbed his forehead. "I'm sorry, Texas. I shouldn't have yelled at you." The anger of regret made his voice husky and rough. "I only wanted to make things a little easier."

There was a knock at the door and Wade quietly announced, "Room service is here with the coffee."

Cody moved away to answer the door. Shannon watched his wide-shouldered frame with blurring eyes. A little late, she realized he had kept the suspicions from her in an effort to spare her additional anguish. Maggie knelt beside her chair and covered Shannon's clasped hands with her own.

"Cody was only thinking of you, Shannon," she murmured.

"I know." She bit at her lips, curving them in a rueful line. "I wasn't thinking."

"That's supposed to be my excuse," Maggie said softly. "I'm always saying the first thing that comes to mind. Wade calls it being truthfully rude." Her expression grew serious. "Will you be all right, Shannon? We have an extra bedroom. You're more than welcome to stay with us tonight."

"Thank you, but—" She was interrupted by Cody as he stopped beside her chair and offered her a cup of hot, sweet coffee.

"Drink it." The determined set of his chin and the unyielding insistence of his gaze advised Shannon that he would somehow make her drink it if she refused.

"I know. It's supposed to be good for someone in shock," she murmured, and obediently sipped it. Even that small taste had a reviving effect, steeling her against the hopelessness that pressed on the edges of her mind. After the initial shock of Wade's news had eased, Shannon had already begun to fight back. The coffee just added strength.

"Is there someone we could call?" Wade asked. "Anyone we should notify?"

"No." Shannon paused between sips of coffee. "I have to call my parents. They were going to fly here for the wedding on Saturday. They can contact Rick's uncle in Houston, the only relative he has."

"Come home with us," Maggie repeated her invitation. "I don't like the idea of your being here alone."

"Honestly, I'll be all right," she assured them. "There's no need for you to stay."

"Are you sure?" Wade persisted, eyeing her skeptically.

"Yes." She lowered her chin for a fraction of a second, then lifted it with renewed determination. "I know how busy you must be—how many other demands you have on your time. Thank you for coming over to tell me personally about . . . Rick."

Shannon refused to use any of their words like "lost" or "missing." She accepted the fact that the plane Rick had been co-piloting hadn't reached its destination; she even accepted the possibility that it had crashed. But that didn't mean Rick was dead. People had survived plane crashes before.

"If there is any way we can help, please call us." The sincerity in Maggie's green eyes reassured Shannon that it was not an idle offer.

"Thank you." A wan smile touched her mouth.

"I'll look after her," Cody stated, a protective hand on her shoulder as he stood beside her chair.

"Let us know if there's anything we can do." Wade directed his statement to Cody while he and Maggie got ready to go. "There's some information the company will need, but we can get that later."

While Cody walked them to the door, Shannon remained in the armchair. Both hands were around the coffee cup. She lifted it to her mouth, draining the heavily sugared liquid. The three paused in the doorway, talking among themselves, but she wasn't interested in listening to their conversation. Pushing to her feet, she set the empty cup on a table and walked to the hotel window.

A mountain range thrust its ridge against the horizon. Her gaze scanned its rugged contours. Somewhere, far beyond those mountains, the plane had gone down—Rick's plane. She'd had a glimpse of the vastness of Alaska this morning—the Great Land, the brochures called it. Finding Rick in all that hugeness was going to be a monumental task, but she refused to consider that it was impossible. She hadn't come all this way just to catch the next plane home.

A pair of hands closed over her shoulders. She knew they belonged to Cody even though she hadn't heard Wade and Maggie leave or the door close. She had felt the firm pressure of his touch often enough in the past few days to recognize it. The gentle kneading of her shoulders eased the raw tension in her nerves. She relaxed against the solid support of his tall frame, letting her head rest on the hard wall of his chest.

"What's out there, Cody?" There was a poignant soft-ness to her question. "Beyond those mountains?"

"A valley, another range of mountains, a valley, mountains, and so on, and so on," he answered with a trace of grim acceptance.

Her breath caught in her throat at his answer, an af-firmation of the overwhelming distance into which Rick had vanished. The pressure of his hands turned her around, away from the window and into his arms. Their strength enfolded her in silent comfort. Shannon wound her arms around his middle, her cheek pressed against his chest. The solid beat of his heart was reas-suring. She felt his mouth moving over her chestnut hair, the stirring warmth of his breath.

"This isn't the way I wanted it to turn out, Shannon." His voice was a low, gentle rumble. "Winning by default is not my idea of fair competition. I know it hurts, but it will fade in time. It always hurts to lose somebody you care about."

He was talking as if Rick were dead. Lifting her head from his chest, she tipped it back to frown at him. "Just because the plane went down doesn't mean Rick was killed."

His hand lightly stroked her cheek, brushing a strand of hair behind her ear. It stayed to cup the side of her face while he bent his head to lower his mouth onto hers, warm and alive. Her lips clung to his a frac-tion of a second after the brief kiss ended, responding to the life force it conveyed.

"You have to be realistic, Shannon," Cody insisted quietly.

"I am. You don't know for sure that Rick is dead—that any of them are dead," she reasoned.

Patience softened the expression on his strongly male features. "The plane has been missing for more than two weeks," he reasoned with her. "They haven't found a trace of the wreckage. There were no signal fires, nothing. If anyone survived the crash, it's doubtful he'd be alive now."

"Doubtful." She used his word to argue her case. "It's doubtful, but it's possible."

His mouth thinned in irritation. "You're twisting things to make them say what you want to hear. Don't do it. It's only going to make it harder." The hand around her waist continued to mold the lower half of her body against him, the muscled columns of his legs providing support.

"You can believe what you like, but he isn't dead. I would know it if he were." Shannon refused to be swayed from her belief by any of his arguments, no matter how valid they appeared on the surface. "He's out there somewhere, alive. I'll find him myself if I have to."

The anger of exasperation tightened his features as Cody grew impatient with her. "Right. I don't think so. There are thousands of acres of wilderness out there."

"I don't care," she flashed. "I won't give up."

With an effort Cody gathered control of his temper and tried once again to reason with her. "I don't think you understand how long they've been looking for that plane or how many aircraft took part in the search. Jackson Hale wasn't an ordinary fisherman. He was an important executive for a Fortune 500 company. Cost was no object—not in money, time, equipment, men, nothing!"

The glacial blue of his gaze was chilling. Shannon recoiled from it, her hands pushing at his waist. His grip shifted to her shoulders, his fingers digging into the bones as Cody let her step back but kept her in his reach.

"I don't care how hard anyone else has looked," she declared.

"I suppose you plan to go out there by yourself and

find him." His jaw was tightly clenched, ridging the muscles. "Would you mind telling me just how you propose to accomplish that?"

She faltered at his challenge, realizing she had been unconsciously counting on his support. "I wasn't exactly planning to do it alone. . . ." Her brown eyes made a silent appeal for his assistance.

His gaze narrowed on that look. "I didn't think you were," he said curtly, his implication obvious.

"I wasn't going to ask you to do it for nothing." She was stung by his failure to offer his help. "I have some money saved." She didn't bother to explain that it was money set aside to buy things for the new home she'd planned to share with Rick. "I'll pay to charter your airplane."

"It isn't the money." He ground out the words angrily. "I don't want it."

"Then what is it?" Shannon demanded impatiently.

A low groan came from deep inside his throat. "Surely you've guessed by now, Texas." He hauled her roughly to him, bringing her within inches of his mouth. "Why should I help you find him when I want you for myself?"

"You're crazy—oh!"

He took possession of her lips, his arms encircling her, sympathy turned to passion he didn't seem able to control. Overpowered by emotions that could find release no other way, Shannon let him, comforted by his kiss and the strong arms that held her close.

Sheer possession didn't satisfy him. A subtle change began and spread. His mouth eased and began to urge, coax and demand more from her than passive acceptance. A response trembled inside her, hesitant and unsure. The supple caress of his hands only strengthened her arousal.

Never before had she desired a man's touch so

much—the touch of a man experienced in the ways to please a woman. She realized that as his nibbling mouth drew a moan from her throat.

"I can make you forget him." His husky voice vibrated against the sensitive skin of her neck.

In a cold breath of sanity, Shannon discovered that he could. She was appalled by this weakness in herself. She twisted her head away from him.

"But I don't want to forget Rick," she insisted tightly, and strained to break the hold of his encircling arms. "If you won't help me find him, I'll hire someone else."

Cody had tasted her response. "Convince me that I should help you."

Earlier he had given her the reason. Shannon repeated it to him now. "Do you really want to win by default?"

His stillness was a visible thing, complete immobility for the space of a heartbeat. Then he was releasing her and pivoting away. Long, impatient strides carried him across the room to the door.

His name trembled on the tip of Shannon's tongue. She longed to call him back, to have the seductive strength of his arms around her again and to feel the excitement of his kiss.

But she stayed silent, not even daring to ask herself how much of her need was dictated by a dread of being alone.

Chapter Six

The phone call to her parents had to be the most difficult one Shannon had ever made. Without Cody's support, she nearly accepted her father's offer to fly to Anchorage to be with her. In the end she refused. Her mother attempted to persuade her to come home, but Shannon had already resolved to stay until she had exhausted every possibility of finding Rick.

Yet it was hard to know where to begin. She paced the hotel room, trying to decide on a plan of action and still hoping that Cody would relent and come to her aid. As the afternoon turned to dusk, then night, she began to accept that Cody seemed to feel he was under no obligation to help her.

A sudden knock on her door brought a rush of hope. She hurried to answer it, sure it would be Cody. But when she opened the door it was his father who was standing in the hallway. He craned his neck to peer beyond her into the room.

"Isn't Cody here?" he asked.

"No." She wasn't able to conceal her disappointment. "I haven't seen him since this afternoon. He left without saying where he was going or . . . if he'd be back."

A frown of concern added to the lines on his forehead as Noah Steele chewed his lower lip thoughtfully. "I haven't heard a word from him since this morning. That isn't like him. I talked to Wade." He paused, then glanced apologetically at Shannon. "I was sorry to hear about your fiancé. It's a terrible thing to find out after coming all this way."

"Rick isn't dead," she stated with absolute determination.

His eyes widened in surprise. "He isn't? But I thought Wade said—"

"It doesn't matter what Wade said," she interrupted, dismissing the conclusions reached by others. "Rick isn't dead. I would know if he were."

He studied her closely before answering. When he did, it was with a smile. "My mother always knew when there was something wrong and I was sick or in trouble. It was just some sixth sense she had that defied logic."

This was the first positive response she'd had. "Then you understand why I have to try to find him. I seem to be the only one who believes they're still alive."

"Sure, I understand." He nodded.

"Mr. Steele . . . Noah," she corrected, "will you help me?" She saw his hesitation and guessed the reason for it. "I've already asked Cody. I even offered to pay him, but he refused me."

"He refused? I would have been ashamed of him if he'd taken money for helping you." He looked indignant and puzzled. "But why did he refuse to help?"

"He thought it was pointless, basically." Which was partly the truth.

"Maybe it is, but he should have kept his opinion to

himself and helped you anyway. Believe me, I'll give him a piece of my mind the next time I see him," he said, looking angry.

"Will you help me, Noah? I don't know where to start," Shannon admitted.

"Of course I will," he assured her.

"Good." She sighed in relief. "Come in so we can decide what to do first."

Pushing the door open wider to admit him, she pivoted to return to the center of the hotel room. After a second's hesitation he followed her inside.

"The first thing we need to do is check with the flight service and get a copy of the flight plan they filed," Noah began.

"Never mind, Dad." Cody's voice inserted itself in the conversation. Shannon whirled around to see him framed in the open doorway. There was a hard set to his features and a wintry-blue frost to his gaze. "I've already done that."

"Cody?" His father recovered first. "What are you doing here? We weren't expecting you."

His brisk strides carried him into the room—very emotionless, very professional. "I also have copies of the search grids, weather reports from both the pilots in the vicinity and the bureau on the day the plane disappeared, and a lot of other data that might be helpful." He stopped short of Shannon, taking a challenging stance.

"Have you . . . changed your mind?" The answer seemed fairly obvious, yet she had to ask.

"Shannon told me that you weren't going to help her," Noah explained in some confusion.

"I'm going to help her." A crack appeared in the emotionless mask of his features. Shannon caught a glimmer of that warm sparkle she usually saw in his eyes. His mouth quirked along a familiar line. "I've never been second best in my life. You might as well know that I'm used to coming in first."

Her smile was slow in forming. "I guessed that." His message was loud and clear. He still wanted her for himself. He would help her find Rick, but he was equally determined that after he did, it would be winner take all.

Once she would have said that was impossible. She had believed the six months' separation from Rick would ultimately strengthen their marriage. After knowing Cody these few short days, she had doubts—small ones, little questions, vague uncertainties. Her faith in the emotion she felt for Rick was just a little shaken.

But none of those doubts stopped her from being glad that Cody had come back. As long as he was there, she had the feeling everything was going to be all right. She couldn't explain it—any more than she could explain why she was so certain Rick was alive.

"When do we start?" she asked.

"Tomorrow. I'll be by to pick you up at seven in the morning," Cody answered. "Bring along what clothes you'll need for two or three days, but pack light. The hotel will store your excess luggage. Do you have a winter coat, a heavy parka, something warm?"

"Yes, I have a parka, long underwear, the works." Her smile broadened to show the dimples in her cheeks. "My mother insisted I bring it all along. I think she was under the impression that Alaska never thawed out."

"Bring the parka; you might need that. But the long underwear can stay in mothballs for a couple more weeks." The amused edges of his mouth deepened with shared humor.

"Where are you going?" his father wanted to know.

"We're going to refly the route listed on their flight plan, and improvise after that."

"In that case, I'm going with you," Noah stated.

"Dad." Cody's voice was heavy with patient reasoning as he turned his head to eye his father. "One of us has to stay here to keep the business going. We can't both be gone."

"You said yourself that it would be only a couple of days. Sy Turner can look after things. It can't be much of a business if it falls apart when the two of us are gone for a few days," he challenged. "Besides, Shannon asked if I'd help her look for her fiancé, and I said I would. I can't go back on my word."

"I did ask him," she admitted when Cody's glance slid to her. "You walked out and I . . ." She shrugged vaguely. "I didn't think you were coming back."

His gaze moved to linger on her mouth and vividly remind her of the driving possession of his kiss, so sensually demanding yet persuasive. That odd tremor started again, reminding her that he was capable of disturbing her much more deeply than she had imagined.

"You should have known better," was all the comment he made.

His astute father was conscious of the subtle undercurrents that charged their innocent exchange, eyeing them both. "Even if Shannon hadn't specifically asked me, I'd be going along anyway," he stated. "That way there's two of us with wilderness search-and-rescue experience. Shannon has no idea what she's getting into."

"You could be right, Dad." Cody's agreement caught Noah off balance. He obviously expected his son to be contrary.

"You can argue all you like, Cody, but I'm coming with you," he replied automatically.

Cody was patient, smiling. "Dad, I agreed that you should come."

"You did?" He faltered an instant, then recovered. "That's sensible of you."

Even though she kept silent during the brief discussion, Shannon concurred. She accepted the wisdom of having Noah along since she knew absolutely nothing about search-and-rescue. And having the older man along would keep things from getting too crazy between her and Cody. That passionate kiss had altered her relationship with him for good. They couldn't pretend it hadn't happened.

The knowledge of it would always be there, running through their glances, their words, the most innocent touch. They needed the presence of a third person to act as a buffer. Shannon knew it and so did Cody.

The weight of his glance was on her, reading her thoughts but passing no comment. "Can you be ready by seven in the morning?" he asked instead.

"Yes." Somehow, although it meant a lot of packing and sorting and organizing all the loose ends.

"Dad will pick you up at the main entrance. Wear pants and flat boots, something comfortable and warm," Cody advised.

"Yes." It was an all-encompassing agreement to his suggestions.

"Ready, Dad?" Cody questioned. "We have a lot of things to do, too, before tomorrow morning."

"Right." He nodded with a show of authority, then had to hurry to catch up with Cody, who was already walking to the door. "See you in the morning."

"Yes." Shannon followed to close the door after them. "Good night," she said to both of them.

From Cody she received a slanting smile of acknowledgment while his father responded, "Good night—and be sure to lock the door."

"I will," she promised.

Once they were out of sight in the hallway, she closed the door and slipped the bolt and safety chain in place. For an instant she paused, realizing that the eagerness she felt within had nothing to do with finding Rick. It sobered her enough to focus her mind on the task at hand.

As ordered, Shannon had packed light, taking only the essentials she'd need for three days and storing the rest of her things at the hotel. Dressed in fur-lined boots, a pair of forest green corduroy jeans and a bulky cream-colored sweater, she was ready and waiting precisely at seven o'clock the next morning in the hotel lobby.

Noah Steele picked her up. "Cody is waiting for us at the plane, getting it all checked out so we can leave as soon as we get there."

They had traveled several blocks before she realized it wasn't the route to Merrill Field. "Aren't we going the wrong way to the airport?" she asked hesitantly.

"We aren't going to the airport, leastwise not that airport," Noah replied. "We're going to use the float-plane."

"Oh." Her concern subsided as she settled back in the passenger seat and looked out the window at the scattered clouds in the sky.

As though bothered by her silence, Noah stole several glances at her. "The weather forecast says it will be clear by mid-morning, so we should have good weather," he told her, then launched into a lecture about flying. "With your fiancé's plane being missing and all, it's natural for you to be a little nervous about going up. Here in Alaska we average a light plane crash practically every day of the year. Those are kinda scary statistics."

"The number is higher in Texas." She had learned a lot of facts about flying from Rick, and a few depressing statistics. For one, the population of Texas was considerably more than Alaska's, which meant the risk was higher here.

"What those statistics don't tell you," Noah continued, not paying any attention to her comment, "is about the pilot flying the plane. Bush pilots have quite a reputation. It sounds romantic and exciting to these young kids. Before the ink is dry on their pilot's licenses, they're up here to become bush pilots. Just like your Rick. They don't know the weather, the terrain or their plane, and they wind up taking foolish chances with all three. But they aren't the only ones."

Pausing, he glanced over to see if she was listening. She was, mostly because she was confused. She thought he had intended to assure her how safe it was to fly, but he seemed to be trying to shake her confidence.

"There aren't many *old*, experienced bush pilots." He stressed the word old. "Even if they're born and raised here, somewhere along the line they find themselves in a situation where they feel they have to live up to their reputation of getting through no matter what. They take off when the weather's bad or won't turn back when they hit a storm front, or keep going even when they're low on gas. They'd rather crash than have someone question their manhood by doubting their bravery."

"That's stupid and dangerous," Shannon responded with a frown.

"Yep," he nodded. "But Cody ain't like that. He's the best damned bush pilot flying today. He knows it and he doesn't feel that he has to prove it. So you don't have to worry about flying with him. You're as safe as if you were in your momma's arms."

So that was what all this had been leading up to. Shannon smiled to herself. The message was loud and clear: he was assuring her of the competency of their pilot, because pilots crashed planes. Only rarely was it the other way around.

"Thank you, Noah. I do feel better," she said, and he seemed satisfied that he had succeeded in his self-appointed task.

When they arrived at the lake, one of several in the Anchorage area, the plane was fueled and preflighted, ready to go. All the gear was aboard, with the exception of the suitcase Shannon had brought. Noah passed it to Cody so it could be stowed in the luggage compartment.

"Do you want to ride in the front seat, Texas?" Cody asked.

"Sure."

It was a peculiar sensation to climb into a plane that was bobbing on the water like a boat. It was a single-engine craft with pontoons instead of landing gear. Shannon buckled herself into the right seat while Noah settled himself in the seat behind her.

Climbing into the pilot's seat, Cody buckled his seatbelt and went through the final checklist. The engine throbbed with power, overcoming the drag of the water. The floatplane was a new experience for Shannon. As he taxied away from the shore and turned the plane into the wind, Cody steadily opened the throttle to full power. The sensation of moving over water gradually decreased until the aircraft was smoothly skimming the surface and lifting off in a steady climb.

Takeoffs always gave Shannon a little rush of exhilaration. No longer earthbound, she was flying free. She glanced at Cody to see if he shared the sensation, the glitter of excitement in her brown eyes.

The smoke-colored lenses of his sunglasses shaded his eyes but didn't hide them. Shannon could see him meet her glance. A brief smile curved his mouth as if in response before he returned his attention to the business of flying. The sunglasses were a necessary protection, shielding his eyes from the glare of the sun, which could blind him to other aircraft in the vicinity.

She was discovering how many little pieces of information she had picked up from Rick, small things that allowed her to recognize the competence of this pilot. Surreptitiously she studied the man behind the metal-framed sunglasses, the chiseled strength in his profile and the sheen of his hair, which was black as pitch. He was calm and alert, with an air of proficiency. Shannon was conscious of feeling absolutely secure with Cody at the controls. It was a powerful feeling, strong and pulsing through her.

He looked briefly at her face and then back to the front. "I activated our flight plan," Cody said, referring to the radio communication he had just completed. "They made a stop in Valdez, so we will, too. We can stretch our legs and grab a cup of coffee."

Shannon nodded her agreement with the suggestion. They headed east where the Chugach Mountains stood. The city of Anchorage spilled onto their sides, pinning houses on their slopes. But civilization was left quickly behind and Shannon was mesmerized by the vastness that was Alaska. It was the green and gold of white spruce and aspen, the blue of the sky and sparkling water; it was wild and raw, majestic and limitless.

She pulled out her camera and set the lens to a wide angle, hoping to capture some of the beauty she saw. It would be a while before she could download the photographs and really look at them.

As the plane crossed the neck of Kenai Peninsula, the island-dotted waters of Prince William Sound glittered in the morning sunlight. The Gulf of Alaska lay beyond. There was a predominance of white on the mountains that crowded the sound. This was the snow Shannon had expected to see in Alaska.

"Snow." She pointed it out to Cody.

He glanced at her and shook his head. "You're half right."

Then Noah leaned forward, sticking his head between the seats. "Why don't you fly by the Columbia so Shannon can see it?"

"I planned on it," Cody answered, then explained to Shannon what they were talking about. "We're coming up on the Columbia Glacier. It's literally a river of solid ice, but it's shrinking like all the glaciers. Used to be four hundred fifty-odd square miles, about the size of Los Angeles."

Through the smoke gray lenses of his sunglasses, Shannon saw the gleam in his light-colored eyes. "But you're not bragging," she said with a knowing smile.

"What with global warming, we might not have bragging rights much longer."

He shook his head in a rueful way that touched her. She was glad he took a few things seriously, even if it wasn't things like fidelity and commitment. After last night she wasn't able to regard their relationship as strictly platonic. She had been aroused by Cody's advances, more so than was comfortable for her peace of mind. And she had become concerned that they might not be able to just be together in the easy way they had at first. But the bond between them hadn't been damaged, and she was glad.

As they approached the glacial formation, Shannon was able to see the course of the giant white ribbon of ice, pushing its way through the mountain forests toward the sea. When they reached its point of terminus, her breath ran from her.

"It's so blue." She turned to Cody in surprise, because the sheer-faced glacier had a definite sky blue coast rising hundreds of feet up from the water.

"It looks even more blue on a cloudy day. The ice is like a prism, refracting the light," he explained, and banked the plane so that she could have a better look. "Do you notice the color of the water?"

It was a dirty gray, littered with huge chunks of ice that had broken off the glacier. The ice chunks seemed unimpressive until she noticed an excursion boat weaving its way through them and realized that many of them were full-fledged icebergs.

"The water is called glacier milk because of the silt, debris and powdered rock it carries." He made a steeper bank and pointed. "We have some harbor seals down there, sunning on the ice."

"I see them," Shannon confirmed, spying the dark specks on the ice floes.

"Often there are whales in the area, but I don't see any this morning," Cody said. "I can make a three-sixty if you want to see more of the glacier."

Shannon hesitated for only an instant. No matter how fascinated she was by the massive river of ice, this wasn't a sightseeing expedition. "No, let's go on to Valdez," she replied.

"We're on our way." He smoothly leveled the plane and resumed his original course and speed.

Leaving the glacier area behind, they flew on. This bird's-eye view of the country from the aircraft window began to widen Shannon's perspective of the situation. She hadn't appreciated what Cody meant when he tried to warn her that finding the wreckage of Rick's plane was next to impossible. There were hundreds of miles of emptiness out there, and a gnawing sense of futility grew inside her. She silently struggled with it as she gazed out the window at the awesome reaches of wilderness.

"The Valdez Narrows are just ahead." Cody nodded to the front. "The authorities allow only one oil tanker to pass through the straits at a time. It's always accompanied by two tugs just in case it loses steerage. Only two tankers are permitted in the port itself at any one time. I'm sure you've heard of the disastrous oil spill in the 1970s. Took the area years to recover. The Arctic environment is fragile."

He had begun his descent, and the nose-down position of the plane gave Shannon a clear view of the narrow passage of water leading into the harbor. Mountain slopes formed the walls of the strait, less than a mile wide. Shannon waited expectantly for her first glimpse of the port city of Valdez.

Mountains formed a chain around the harbor, a dramatic setting with rugged peaks in the foreground in every direction. The huge oil-storage tanks were clustered along the southern side of the harbor behind a containment dike, as well as the many buildings housing the offices and shops of the operations center. But Shannon didn't see anything she would call a city.

"Where is Valdez?" she asked.

"That's it on the left." He reached down to adjust the trim of the aircraft.

"That?" She gave him a skeptical look.

"Yeah. Why? Is something wrong?" Cody allowed his glance to touch her once, busy with his landing preparations.

Her shrug was uncertain. "I thought it would be much bigger since it's the terminal for the Alaska pipeline. I guess I was expecting to see Houston, Texas."

Cody smiled in understanding. "Nope. Not even close. Check your seat belt," he advised as they started their landing approach to the harbor.

Once they were on the water and taxiing toward

shore, Noah leaned forward again. "The tidal wave that followed the Good Friday earthquake in 1964 destroyed or damaged practically every building in Valdez. What you see here isn't the original townsite. They moved the town four miles to this location and rebuilt it. The location was chosen for the terminus of the pipeline because this harbor is one of the northernmost ice-free ports in this hemisphere."

"What happened to the old townsite?"

"They leveled it off. There's nothing left of it now," Noah explained, and settled back into his seat.

Their stop in Valdez was brief. They stayed long enough to stretch their legs, have some coffee and refuel. Then they were taking off again, this time heading north across the alpine summits of the Chugach Mountains. They flew over Keystone Canyon with its spectacular rock formations and crystal-bright waterfalls.

Shortly afterward Shannon had her first glimpse of the pipeline. From the air it was a silver thread bumping over hillocks and running straight on flatter land, then disappearing underground to reappear farther along. There was an endless variety of things to see and photograph—more glaciers, spruce forests, tundra and meadows above the tree line. Lakes were sprinkled around the terrain like fat raindrops. Everywhere there seemed to be the sparkle of water. As they flew over a lake in a sylvan setting, Shannon couldn't help remarking on its untouched beauty.

"One of the states in the lower forty-eight is known as the land of ten thousand lakes," Cody remarked.

"Yes, that's Minnesota," Shannon said.

"I thought you should know that Alaska doesn't have ten thousand lakes." Cody paused deliberately. "At the last count, we had more than three million, in round figures. Mind you, I'm not bragging."

"No, of course not." She laughed.

As her gaze swung to the front again, she noticed what appeared to be a massive white cloud bank looming on the horizon. "Look. Is that a storm front?"

"That's the Wrangell Mountains," Cody informed her, dropping his voice into a sonorous bass for effect. "A range unparalleled in sheer magnificence and grandeur. Got anything like that where you come from?"

"No. They're spectacular. And thanks for the tour of Alaska's natural wonders. You make a great guide, Cody."

He grinned. "Enjoying yourself?"

Noah harrumphed. "She's looking for her guy. She's not supposed to be enjoying herself."

Chapter Seven

The glacier-clad mountains were a wilderness of forests, lakes and rivers. They were all she could see in any direction, and the plane had penetrated only the outer edge of the massive range, which encompassed an area of some six thousand square miles. Fifty miles back, Cody had informed her that they were passing the last known spot where there had been confirmed contact with Rick's plane. It had gone down somewhere out here. But where? Her eyes strained in their search of the rugged terrain below.

From the rear passenger seat, Noah spoke up. "Is something wrong, son?"

The quick, serious tone of the man's question brought Shannon's attention to the cockpit of the private plane. Cody's expression was cool and steady, but she sensed a heightened alertness. His attention never left the instrument panel as he replied to his father in a calm, very matter-of-fact voice.

"We're losing oil pressure. I'm going to set her down in that lake over there." He indicated the body of water a mile to their left, then cast a look at Shannon and smiled in quiet assurance. "Don't worry. This is just a precaution. We may not even have a problem."

She nodded her understanding and tried to ignore her sense of uneasiness. There was no change in the rhythmic power of the engine, which supported Cody's feeling that the plane's performance had not been affected—at least, not yet. She listened while he radioed their approximate position and an advisory of their situation. When his transmission was acknowledged, he sideslipped the plane to achieve a rapid and controlled loss of altitude.

It wasn't an emergency situation, and Cody was landing to make sure it didn't become one. Somebody knew where they were and why. Shannon kept thinking that it hadn't been that way for Rick. Whatever had gone wrong, either there hadn't been time for a distress call or else it had never been received.

They landed smoothly and without incident. "I noticed a log cabin tucked back in the woods," Noah said when Cody adjusted the throttle to taxi. "It was over on the north side just as we were setting down."

Following his father's directions, Cody taxied the plane back to the general area Noah had described. Shannon spied the cabin and pointed it out to Cody. He taxied the plane to the very edge of the graveled shoreline.

"Looks like it's deserted," Noah observed as the engine was switched off. "If anybody were living there, he'd be out here to find out what we wanted."

The primitive cabin built of logs was small, roughly ten foot square. Nothing stirred as they climbed out of the plane. There was a cache near the cabin, elevated high off the ground on legs and accessible by a homemade ladder. "Okay, we're set. Might as well take a look around," Cody said when the aircraft was secure.

"It's probably all locked up." It seemed reasonable to Shannon, since it had obviously been abandoned.

"If it is, it wasn't an Alaskan who owned it," Noah stated. "It's customary to leave a cabin open and stocked for anyone in need who might come along."

The wooden door had swelled, but it opened with a hard shove from Cody's shoulder. The owner of the cabin had observed the Alaskan custom. The single room had a packed dirt floor and a low ceiling. Firewood was stacked in a corner along with shavings for kindling, and matches in a waterproof box. In addition to a barrel stove, there was a crudely made table and chair and a bunk bed. Sacks of flour, powdered milk and sugar had been stored off the floor in labeled metal containers to keep out rodents and ants. A kerosene lamp was full and equipped with a new wick.

"There are probably dried beef and vegetables in the cache," Cody surmised. "At least if we're stuck here for long we won't starve." He turned toward the door and clamped a hand on his father's shoulder. "Come on, Dad. Let's go figure out what's causing that pressure drop."

"Can I help?" Shannon asked.

"Not unless you like to get greasy. No, you might as well relax and enjoy the scenery," Cody advised.

Shannon followed them back to the plane, partially beached on the lakeshore, and watched them work on it for a while. Eventually she tired of that. The lakeshore beckoned her to explore it, so she dug out her camera and began to stroll along its edge, not intending to wander out of sight of the plane.

The air smelled incredibly fresh and pure, tangy with the scent of pines. Birches and willows grew abundantly along the lake. The distinctive mound of a beaver dam led her on to take a closer look. On a fallen timber she took up watch and after a half hour's wait was rewarded with the sight of a large beaver swimming toward its home. She got a clear shot of its whiskery face rising out of the ripples, looking right at her.

By sheer chance she sighted a giant moose grazing on the opposite side of the lake. Even at that distance she could tell that the spread of his antlered rack was wider than she could stretch both arms. She considered returning to the clearing around the cabin, then curiosity changed her mind and she walked on to see what was beyond the next bend in the shoreline.

Before she had gone three feet, she thought she heard someone shouting. She stopped to listen. "Shannon!" It was Cody. The imperative tone of his voice turned her around.

"I'm coming!" she shouted in answer, and hurried to retrace her route.

But she had gone farther than she'd realized, and she was out of breath by the time she spotted the plane. She had just slowed down to catch her breath when she saw Cody striding toward her.

"Don't you know better than to wander off like that?" He sounded impatient and angry.

"Sorry," she said breathlessly. "I didn't realize I had gone so far." Then she noticed the revolver in his hand. Her winded laugh was confused. "What were you going to do? Find me and bring me back at gunpoint?"

"This is bear country, Texas." He tucked the revolver inside his waistband. "You could have met up with a giant grizz for all I knew."

"You mean a grizzly bear?" she repeated with a trace of apprehension. "You don't really believe there are any close by, do you?"

"I don't know how close one might be right now," Cody admitted, and waved a hand at a tree several feet from where she was standing. "But I do know the claw marks on that tree aren't more than a couple of days old." As she turned to look at the white scratches on the tree's trunk, scratches higher than her head, he explained, "That's the way they mark their territory. So don't go wandering off anymore."

"I won't." It was a fervent promise; his warning not one that needed to be repeated. She glanced at the plane and saw Noah working on the engine. "How's it going?"

"I think we've located the problem."

"Can it be fixed?" Here they were, out in the middle of nowhere, and Shannon didn't want to think about the possibility that it couldn't be repaired.

"Dad can jerry-rig anything, but it might take a while," Cody replied with confident patience. "That's why I was looking for you. I thought I'd see if you wanted to light that stove and fix us something to eat."

"Sure," she agreed. "Flour, sugar, powdered milk . . . who could ask for anything more? Fair warning: I don't cook. I nuke. But I'll try."

He grinned. "We're not that picky. And besides, Dad and I are covered with engine oil, so I volunteered you for the job. Check the cache, but be careful of the ladder."

She clambered up it rung by rung, eager to see what the previous inhabitant had left. Cookies would be nice, she thought. Was it asking too much to expect chocolate chip cookies in the wilderness? Apparently so. The cache held a treasure trove of stuff but no cookies. Besides rice, beans, Crisco, dried butter substitute, powdered eggs, dried vegetables and beef, Shannon found sleeping bags, long johns, mukluks, mittens and candles. There wasn't any coffee, but she did find a can of tea.

Lighting the wood-burning barrel stove turned out to be a case of trial and error. Then she had to haul water from the lake and wait for it to boil on the stove top in order to wash the frying pans and dishes she found.

It was well into the afternoon before she had a meal on the table. It wouldn't have won any cooking prizes, but the men ate it with gusto. Under the circumstances everyone agreed politely that the food was, well, filling. "No dessert," she announced. "Sorry about that."

"No problem, Texas. Thanks for pulling KP duty. We weren't expecting dessert." When they had finished, they took their tea outside to drink it. Somehow the fresh air added to its strong flavor.

"We aren't going to get the plane fixed before nightfall," Cody stated. "I'm not that familiar with this area to feel confident flying at night. You might as well plan on spending the night here."

"In other words, start cooking supper now so it will be ready by dark." Shannon wasn't going to forget how long it had taken her to fix a simple lunch in these primitive conditions.

"Something like that," Cody agreed with a hungry-man grin.

"Aren't you glad I came along?" Noah demanded. "Now you have someone who not only can fix your plane but also can be a chaperone tonight to keep everything respectable."

Oh, great, Shannon thought. The last time she'd been chaperoned was at her senior prom. The idea of being chaperoned in the wilderness was pretty funny.

"Dad"—Cody eyed him with bemused affection—"do you really want me to answer that question?"

"I don't," Shannon declared.

"Whatever you say, Texas." The expression in his eyes changed, heavy with meaning. She felt the tripping of her pulse. "I promise to be good, even when my dad isn't around."

She tried to make light of his remark. "You're just a sore loser."

"Wouldn't you be?" he countered. "Tonight we're going to sleep in the same room . . . with Dad."

Noah frowned in gruff disapproval. "Cody, you shouldn't be talking like that to her. It's her fiancé we're out here to find."

"Right," Cody agreed thoughtfully. "I guess that slipped my mind."

"You just remember that," Noah stated with an insistent nod.

There was a responding quirk of his mouth, but no reply. Shannon fully understood that Cody planned to pursue her in his own way regardless of the ring on her finger. She told herself that no matter what he'd said before they began this search-and-rescue mission, he must believe that Rick was still alive. If he thought otherwise, he wouldn't be chasing her.

Recognizing that, she also recognized that she was finding a disturbing thrill in the chase. As she noticed how closely he was watching her, she wondered if he could see that. Then she saw the gleam of satisfaction in the light blue depths, and knew he had.

Draining the last of his tea from the metal cup, Cody handed it to her, then turned to his father. "Let's get back to work."

As the two men walked to the plane, Shannon carried the cups into the cabin and began the task of cleaning the dishes. She had started the evening meal when she heard the drone of an approaching airplane. It was an alien sound in this wilderness. Frowning, she walked to the door of the cabin and watched as it swooped low to circle the cabin.

Cody signaled something to the plane. The message was acknowledged with a wag of its wings before it flew off.

"What did he want?" Shannon called.

"He was checking to see if we needed any assistance," Cody replied. "I signaled that we had everything under control."

"Do you?"

"Yeah, if we can figure out how to put it back together," he grinned.

She was smiling as she reentered the cabin. Cody had an irresistible sense of humor to go with his reckless smile and bold eyes, but what made him so formidable was his swift, keen intelligence. And it was all wrapped up in a handsome package. Absently she fingered her engagement ring, conscious only of a vague discontent. She shrugged the feeling away and went back to her work.

Either Shannon discovered the knack of cooking on the woodstove or else luck was on her side, because dinner turned out near perfect. The skillet biscuits were a little too brown on the bottom, but the vegetable-beef stew was delicious. So was the rice pudding with dried raisins.

By the light of the kerosene lamp, she washed the dishes while Cody dried them. The humdrum domesticity of the task didn't defuse the sexual vibe between them, but Noah harrumphed from time to time in a dadly way to make sure both were aware of his presence in the cabin. It didn't seem to matter. The steadiness of Cody's bold look didn't need any words to get his message across and succeeded with unnerving ease.

When the dishes were finished and everything was put back where they'd found it, Cody suggested, "Let's go outside and sit on the porch. It's a beautiful night."

Shannon had already noticed the brilliance of the stars in the sky outside the window. The call of the quiet Alaskan night beckoned to her. She was tempted to agree, but the temptation was more than the beauty of the night. Looking at Cody, she knew what else was tempting her.

"No, thanks." She tried to sound very casual about it. "It's been a long day and I'm kind of tired."

"You're right." Noah was quick to agree with her decision. "We should all turn in early. Morning's gonna be here before we know it."

"Absolutely." Cody's dry voice seemed to mock both of them.

"You can sleep in that bunk bed, Shannon," Noah instructed with a wave of his hand. "Cody and I will rough it on the floor."

"Okay," Shannon nodded.

"You sure your old bones can take sleeping on the floor, Dad?" Cody challenged, a wicked glint in his eyes. "Maybe you should take the bunk and let me and Texas have the floor."

"Don't you go worrying about my bones." Noah quickly rejected the idea, but not before Shannon's heart had done a little somersault at the implication behind Cody's words.

If they had both slept on the floor, he would have arranged it so that they weren't sleeping apart. Yet he knew perfectly well his father would never go along with the suggestion. It had been a clever ploy to keep her awareness of him aroused. Just for a minute, her imagination ran away with itself as she imagined what it would be like to sleep curled against his strong body. She made the mistake of looking at him and knew he'd instantly read in her eyes what she was thinking. She turned away.

"Now you've done it," Noah accused his son. "You've embarrassed her."

"Did I, Texas?" His tone indicated that he knew embarrassment wasn't her reaction.

"No." Shannon had to make him understand that

she knew his game and wasn't going to play it. At least not by his macho rules. "And I don't think you were trying to."

Cody glanced at his father. "Aw, shucks. I think she's getting wise to me, Dad."

"It's about time." Noah showed his impatience with his son's behavior. "Cody and I will step outside while you get yourself ready for bed," Noah told her. "You just give us a shout when it's all right to come in."

"Or if you need any help," Cody smirked.

"Guess what. I can't fix a plane, but I figured out buttons and zippers a while ago," Shannon replied dryly. "My hand-eye coordination is pretty good."

"Glad to hear it," he murmured.

"Give it a rest, huh?" his father said with disgust. "You sound like that English spy guy."

"James Bond?" Cody asked.

"No. Austin Powers." His father ushered him out the door with a show of irritation, while Shannon laughed.

Opening the suitcase Noah had brought up from the plane earlier that evening, she took out the few things she would need that night. The long-sleeved flannel nightgown reached down to the floor and buttoned all the way to the neck. It was just about as modest and unsexy as a nightgown could get. Shannon smiled when she considered Cody's probable reaction to it.

Leaving her socks on so her feet would stay warm, she climbed inside the sleeping bag spread over the bunk. She lay there for a few minutes, listening to the low murmur of voices coming from the outside.

"Okay!" she called finally. "You can come in now!"

Only one set of footsteps crossed the wood floor of the porch to the door. Shannon recognized the shuffling tread as Noah's. A little frown of disappointment creased her forehead as the door opened and the older man entered alone. He paused before closing the door and looked outside.

"Don't stay out too late, Cody," he addressed his unseen son with paternal concern. "You need your rest the same as we do."

"I won't," came the promise, and Shannon heard the dry affection and amusement in Cody's voice. "Good night, Dad." Then louder, "Good night, Texas. Sweet dreams."

"Good night," she called back, and snuggled a little deeper into the sleeping bag.

Her mouth curved slightly from an inner contentment she couldn't define. After Noah had settled into his sleeping bag on the floor, Shannon listened to the gentle night sounds for a while. She closed her eyes, not expecting to fall asleep until after Cody had turned in for the night. Yet at some point she drifted off.

A persistent hand nudged her shoulder to awaken her. She stirred, frowning a sleepy protest, and turned her head to this inconsiderate person disturbing her sleep. In the darkness of the cabin, all she could make out was a black form bent close to the bunk.

"What . . . ?" Her sleep-husky voice was low but a masculine finger on her lips told her to keep still.

"Ssh." Her tiredness vanished when Cody's voice whispered, "Put your parka on and come outside. There's something I want to show you."

Without giving her a chance to refuse or disagree, his dark shape stole away from the bunk and glided silently to the door. She sat up as he slipped outside. Despite all the very good reasons why she shouldn't go, her curiosity was aroused.

Taking care not to make any noise that might wake Noah, Shannon crawled out of the sleeping bag, thrashing and kicking out of its folds, hampered by the long nightgown. It wasn't easy trying to find her things in the dark. She had to move slowly and cautiously. With her shoes on and her parka over the flannel nightgown, she tiptoed to the door and stepped onto the porch.

It was lighter outside than she'd expected. She easily saw Cody standing a few feet from the cabin. He turned as she hesitated by the door.

"Come here." He motioned her to his side, his voice still pitched low.

Uncertainly she moved to him. "What is it?"

His gleaming blue eyes held her gaze for a long moment, setting off alarm bells of warning. "I know the stars are supposed to be big and bright in the heart of Texas. But I wanted to show you the magic of an Alaskan night."

Holy cow. The huskiness in his voice, the unexpected intimacy of the moment, her own reaction to his nearness—all conspired against her common sense. She definitely felt the magic and it seemed to be happening inside her. With difficulty she looked away from him toward the night sky and found the source of light brightening the darkness.

Her lungs filled with a slow breath of incredible delight as she stared at the shimmering curtain of blue-and-green light swirling about the heavens. It seemed to dance to some silent music.

Not taking her gaze from it for fear it would disappear, she murmured to Cody, "The northern lights?"

"Yes," Cody confirmed. "Aurora borealis—a symphony of light."

She was awestruck. She remembered looking into a kaleidoscope as a child, amazed by the changing patterns and colors of light, but that had been a poor imitation of the wonders nature could perform. The ever moving curtain seemed to be made of flashing jewels—emerald, jade, sapphire, turquoise—all with the brilliance of diamonds. It whirled about the sky with abandon, writhing and twisting, fading, then blossoming again. It seemed to pulse and throb with a life of its own.

"Are you impressed?" Cody murmured. He was very close to her, and Shannon wondered when he had put his arm around her shoulders. Until that moment she had been too enraptured by the dazzling display to notice.

"Very," she assured him, and leaned a little closer.

"Some people claim you can actually hear the lights," he said.

Shannon paused to listen. A little tingle ran along her nerve ends when she heard a swishing sound. It was very faint, soft and varying in its rhythm with the dancing lights. Her eyes were rounded when she looked at Cody.

"I can hear them," she insisted in a whisper.

She could see him smile. "That's the wind whispering through the pine needles."

"No, it isn't." She was positive it came from the lights.

"Whatever you're hearing, scientists claim it doesn't come from the lights," Cody explained without attempting to argue the point.

"What causes the northern lights?" Shannon was enchanted with the dipping, swirling banner of changing color.

"It has something to do with the earth's magnetic field at the North Pole and the solar winds from the sun, which cause a kind of friction." He smiled at her. "It's all very scientific, but theory spoils the illusion of magic."

"Yes," she agreed.

A streak of green light separated itself from the pulsating curtain and seemed to stab at the earth. Shannon gasped at the unexpected change in its dance. Then the entire wave of light appeared to come closer to the ground.

"Maybe it heard us talking," Cody murmured.

"What?" Shannon didn't understand that remark.

"One of the legends of the light is that it will come closer if you talk to it or whistle." He eyed her with a challenging blue gleam. "Why don't you try it?"

Pursing her lips, she whistled softly. There was an almost immediate reaction from the dazzling blue-green curtain. It hovered, then seemed to dip earthward.

An eerie thrill ran down Shannon's spine and she tried whistling again. The aurora writhed, seeming to come nearer, then darted away.

"Wrong note, maybe," Cody suggested with an indulgent glance.

"It seemed to respond, though, didn't it?" she said, a little awed.

"But we'll never know if it would have done the same thing if you hadn't whistled," he pointed out.

The iridescent haze began to fade, the brilliant glow becoming dimmer. Shannon held her breath, hoping it would come back, but it was melting and dissolving into the blackness of the night. Tipping her head, she looked at Cody.

"Will it come back?" she whispered.

"I'm afraid the show is over," he replied gently.

The smile on his mouth began to fade as he looked at her. Shannon felt the pulse start to beat loudly in her throat at the disturbing intensity of his gaze. "Another superstition attached to the lights that I failed to mention"—his voice was a husky murmur, spilling over her with caressing force—"is what happens to the people who witness this magical display."

"What happens?" Her own voice had a breathy sound.

"Supposedly . . . they do things they wouldn't normally do." His intent gaze was touching each feature of her face. His arms were slowly turning her toward him. "It must be more than legend because I told myself I wouldn't do this again, not until that ring was off your finger."

"Yes." It was a choked little sound.

When his mouth came down upon hers, she was moving to meet it. The sexual chemistry between them was volatile, producing sensations as fiery and brilliant as any she had witnessed in the sky. His hands moved inside her bulky parka, encircling her waist and moving lower, over her hips. He pressed her to his hard male length.

Desire seared through her, melting her into the glorious oblivion of his embrace. Her lips parted to discover the fulfillment of his devouring kiss. Nothing else existed in this moment. It belonged only to the two of them.

All Shannon wanted was to get closer to him. She strained to satisfy that need. Cody dragged his mouth across her cheek to her neck, roughly nuzzling the vein that pulsed there. His roaming hands became tangled in the loose folds of her flannel nightgown as it defied his attempts to cup the fullness of her breasts in his palms.

"My God, what are you wearing?" he muttered.

A brief, giddy laugh broke from her throat. "My nightgown. It's the granny kind," she murmured.

Cody sighed and drew in a deep breath, resting his forehead against hers. At some point her hands had slipped inside his jacket to spread themselves across his chest. She could feel the thundering of his heart.

"Tell me that you still want Rick." His voice was heavy and rough in its demand. "When we find him—"

"So you do think it's possible."

"Damn it—yes. But you have to tell me whether you'll still care about him. Can you . . . after this? You want me as badly as I want you. Admit it."

The diamond ring on her finger suddenly weighed a ton. She had forgotten and she didn't thank Cody for reminding her. There had been such beauty in the moment—and now it was destroyed by guilt. She breathed in a choked sob of protest.

His grip tightened, his fingers digging into the sides of her waist as if he wanted to shake her. "Admit it," he demanded again. "It's me you want, not him. Your body has already told me. Now I want you to say it."

"Yes." It was a thin sound, an admission even as she pushed away from the temptation of his embrace. She kept her chin lowered, not wanting him to see the anguish and torment in her face.

"You aren't going to marry him," he stated.

"Yes, I am." That's why she had come all this way to Alaska. There wasn't any other reason for her to be here. She loved Rick and there wasn't any way she could be sure she had stopped loving him.

Cody's stillness was charged with powerful emotion until he spoke. "You can't mean it."

Shannon lifted her head, the aftershocks of his kisses still trembling through her. She was surprised she could act so calm.

"I do mean it," she insisted. "You don't marry a man because of the way he makes your body feel. You marry him because of what's in your heart."

"And you're saying that you still love him?" He was obviously forcing himself to be calm.

"Yes," Shannon whispered. "As soon as I find him, we'll be married." It seemed that she had to say the words to convince herself. Looking at Cody, it was all she could do not to yield to the love she knew she would find in his arms.

He released her with a sharp sigh of resignation. "Then I'll find him for you. I'll find him. But don't invite me to the wedding."

Chapter Eight

The next morning Cody barely addressed five words to her. When he looked at her, which wasn't very often, his eyes were blank. There was no warmth, no laughing glint, no sexual chemistry to enthrall her. Shannon had never felt so confused. Nonetheless, she had to keep Rick foremost in her mind, and if that cost her Cody's friendship, so be it. Getting distracted by a moody, self-absorbed man with a one-track mind wasn't part of the plan. Okay, that was a harsh judgment of his character and he was helping her, but if she had to be objective . . . Anyway, she was just as harsh on herself, knowing that her mind seemed to be on the identical track.

There wasn't any way to hide the strain between them. Noah noticed it immediately. All through breakfast and while they were loading the plane to take off, his glance kept darting from one to the other in an effort to catch some word or phrase that would tell him what had gone wrong.

Dispirited and sleep-deprived, Shannon chose to sit in the rear seat of the aircraft, letting Noah take the copilot's seat next to Cody. As he taxied onto the lake for takeoff, she stared out the window, blind to the incredible scenery her eyes beheld.

Once they were airborne, she leaned her head against the back of her seat and closed her eyes, covering them with her hand. The steady drone of the engine filled her hearing. She was only half conscious of Cody communicating with someone on the plane's radio.

Noah's sudden whoop of glee startled her into alertness. Her hand came down as her eyes snapped open. She stared at the older man, who had turned to look at her with a wide grin on his face.

"Did you hear that, Shannon?" he asked in unabashed excitement. "Glory be! I thought it was a waste of time!"

"Hear what?" She leaned forward, a bewildered frown on her forehead as she tried to figure out what he was talking about.

"They made it!" he declared.

At that moment Cody put the plane into a steep banking turn, veering onto a new course at a forty-five-degree angle to the one they'd been flying. Shannon's stomach rolled with the pressure of the gravity force before the plane leveled off.

"Who made it? What are you talking about?" she finally responded to Noah's statement.

It was Cody who leaned back to answer, partially turning his head without actually looking at her. "They're alive," he clarified the statement in a flat voice. "Rick is alive. They walked out of the mountains. We just got word that they stumbled into a fishing camp this morning."

For a full second the news didn't register. It seemed impossible to believe, even though she had never doubted for a minute that Rick was alive. It was a case of hearing someone else say the words instead of her.

Relief flooded through her, leaving her suddenly weak. "He's alive," she repeated, although too softly for the men in the front to hear her. She waited for the uplifting tide of joy, but it didn't come. There was just an emptiness—a loss of purpose. She didn't have to look for Rick anymore. He'd been found.

"We're heading for the fishing camp now," Cody stated, raising his hard voice to ensure it was heard above the engine.

"Are they—is he all right?" She finally managed to ask a question.

"The transmission was a little garbled," he told her. "But none of them could be too badly hurt if they were able to walk out of the mountains."

True enough, Shannon realized, and leaned back in her seat. She caught herself twisting the diamond ring on her finger, trying to ease its constricting band as if it had become too tight and glanced down at her hand.

"Great news, huh?" Noah's voice prompted her to look up. "You said all along that he was alive."

"Yes." She forced a smile, then suddenly found feeling glad wasn't so difficult after all. "It's wonderful!"

Shannon was simply relieved that she was actually happy. She turned her gaze out the window with new interest. Somewhere up ahead Rick was waiting for her. Once she saw him again, everything would be the way it was before. Just keep telling yourself that, she thought.

If her glance strayed too often to the man with pitch-black hair flying the plane—if her heart was aching with silent longing—Shannon could ignore it. Her earlier irritation with his behavior vanished in a flash. All she felt for Cody was a mixture of physical attraction, gratitude for his help and friendship. It was Rick she loved. It was Rick she was going to marry. She'd said so often enough.

Almost two hours later the plane began to descend,

aiming for a lake winking in the morning sunlight. An eagerness began to build within Shannon. She made sure her seat belt was fastened tightly long before it was necessary. Automatically she braced herself when the seaplane bumped onto the lake's glistening surface.

Her gaze searched the painted log cabins clustered close to the shoreline. Other seaplanes were moored near the camp, as well as fishing boats. She scanned the figures of the people but didn't recognize Rick's lanky frame among those walking about the cabin area.

Cody taxied the plane toward the shore. Just before the metal pontoon scraped the graveled bottom of the lake, he cut the engine, which had already been reduced to a slow speed. In a matter of a few minutes Cody was offering her a hand to help her out of the rear seat.

The cool impartiality of his touch chilled her. Her glance briefly met his hard gaze and bounced away. His heady masculinity hadn't dimmed. Its powerful force was simply no longer directed at her. But she continued to be affected by it.

With solid ground beneath her feet, Shannon waited uncertainly for Cody and his father to join her before starting toward the cabins. Noah lagged behind, fussing with the securing ropes. Shannon sensed the impatience rippling through Cody.

"Come on, Dad," he finally said.

When Noah started forward, Cody turned. His glance fell on Shannon. There was a twist of ironic amusement to his mouth as he studied her.

"What are you worried about?" he said softly. "They're safe. And just in time, too. Winter comes early around here, you know."

"I thought about that."

"This is the big moment, Texas. You should be eager and radiant."

Her chin lifted a notch higher. "I will be," she insisted, "when I see Rick."

"Then let's go," he said, and motioned her to lead the way. "We'll probably find him at the office. That seems to be the hub of activity around here."

Her scanning glance located the cabin with the shingle hanging outside, the word "office" printed on it. She hurried toward the cabin, aware that she was driven more by Cody's urging than by her own.

When she opened the door, there was a hum of voices. The small room was crowded with people, most of them standing and all talking at the same time. Someone made way to let her enter the room.

Shannon wasn't sure whether she saw Rick first or he saw her. All of a sudden he was in front of her—as tall and lanky as she remembered, his sandy hair matted and dirty. That was about all the impression she had time to absorb.

"Shannon!" he cried in surprised disbelief.

"Oh, Rick," she gasped his name.

His arms lifted to reach out for her. Some inexorable force seemed to join the two of them. The minute she felt the familiar comfort of his arms, she seemed to relax. Rick was all right. It was suddenly all right to cry.

He must have felt the dampness of her cheek against his skin, because he cupped a hand under her chin and lifted it. "What is this?" Rick chided, and wiped away a tear with a forefinger. "Tears?"

"Yes," she admitted, smiling at him.

Now she could see the cuts and abrasions on one side of his face, the weariness in his red-rimmed eyes. He seemed to lack the wild-man enthusiasm and lust for adventure that she remembered so well. Rick had gone through an ordeal and it had marked him, Shannon realized. There was a subtle difference to him that she hadn't expected.

"You must have been through hell," he murmured sympathetically. "I kept thinking about you flying in here. I wasn't sure if you'd come—if you had used the ticket I sent you."

"I did. I tried to let you know when I would arrive, but we never connected. No one seemed to know where you were or where you were working." The whole thing seemed to have happened a long time ago—to some other person.

"I knew you'd be worried half out of your mind," Rick said with a grimace.

"But what about you?" Shannon drew back to look at him. "Are you okay? Were you hurt?"

"I'm fine," Rick assured her. "Some cuts and bruises, a pulled muscle or two, but I'm okay." He didn't seem to want to talk about the crash or its aftermath. "How did you get here?"

"Cody brought me." She wasn't able to meet Rick's look.

Shannon half turned to find Cody. He and Noah were standing only a few feet away. His light blue eyes seemed to pierce her before they flicked beyond her to Rick.

"Cody Steele." Rick's voice held recognition and vague confusion. It carried to Cody and he stepped forward. Rick turned Shannon to his side and reached out to shake hands with Cody. "Thanks for bringing her here."

"Your fiancée is a very persuasive woman," Cody said. "Did she tell you that she got me out searching for you—or the wreckage of your plane?"

"No, she didn't." Rick glanced at her in surprise. "I wrote you about him, didn't I?"

"Yes." She nodded.

"He's the best damned bush pilot there is," Rick declared, not shy about voicing his admiration.

"That's for sure." Noah was quick to agree with Rick's assessment.

A serious look stole across Rick's face. "I wish you had been along—although I don't know if it would have changed anything."

"You were lucky," Cody said.

"Yeah." Rick nodded wearily, then attempted to joke. "As the old saying goes, it's a good landing if you can walk away from it." He shrugged, trying to make light of the experience. "In this case we crawled, but I guess it still qualifies as a good landing."

"What happened?" Cody asked.

"There was a storm." Rick shook his head as if he weren't too clear about the events. "Before we knew it we were lost. Then we lost power. There was a leak in the oil line, we discovered afterward. I don't see how Henderson kept it in the air as long as he did."

"He's a regular Houdini," Noah declared.

"Let's go over there, Shannon, so I can introduce you to him," Rick suggested, directing her toward another circle of people. "I want you to meet Mr. Hale . . . and his daughter, too," he added, faltering a little.

The pilot was a burly man with silver hair. Rick made the introductions, but Shannon wasn't allowed to do more than acknowledge them. Henderson was being attended by a physician who had been flown in to examine the survivors of the plane crash and supply whatever medical aid they needed. The pilot had suffered a dislocated shoulder in the crash and had some nasty cuts on his forehead that needed stitches.

Then Rick guided her to the father-daughter pair. Jackson Hale didn't make Shannon think of an oil company executive. He looked like an outdoorsman, with a ragged beard covering his cheeks and jaw.

He picked up on the glance Shannon gave it and

rubbed the grizzled whiskers on his chin. "It's new," he explained. "Needs a trim, huh? I don't want to forget what a narrow escape I had, so I've decided not to shave it off." Then he glanced at Rick. "Is she the fiancée you were always talking about?"

"Yes," Rick admitted, and Shannon realized that he had simply introduced her by name without explaining her relationship to him.

"He's a hell of a guy," Jackson Hale said to her. "I hope you know that."

"I do." She smiled and happened to look up—straight into Cody's eyes. The blue of his eyes was polar; their lightness had crystals of ice in them.

Jackson Hale was talking again. "Rick kept me going when I was ready to quit. He was determined we were going to get out of those mountains. Looking at you, I can see why." He smiled.

"Thank you," she murmured in response to his compliment.

Noah got his two cents in, as usual. "I guess they're two of a kind. Shannon kept insisting her fiancé was alive even when everybody else had given you all up for dead. She twisted Cody's arm until he agreed to come looking for you."

"I'm going to be upset if I don't get an invitation to your wedding," Jackson Hale warned Rick. "She was flying up here to marry you, wasn't she?"

"Yes." Rick nodded stiffly, an uneven smile on his mouth. "Of course, there have been a few delays along the way."

"And a few more to come, I imagine," Shannon said. It was obvious that after all Rick had been through, they wouldn't rush right out and get married.

"Where are you staying?" the oil company chairman asked. "In Anchorage, I mean?"

"At the Westward," she replied.

Rick frowned. "Why didn't you stay at my apartment?"

"I hate to tell you this, but your apartment has been rented to new tenants," she informed him with a gentle smile. "Um, your rent was past due, and when you didn't show up, the manager packed your things and let it out to someone else."

"He what?" Then Rick sighed. "I guess he didn't know, either."

"No. I stored your things at the hotel with mine," Shannon added.

"Rick, have you introduced your fiancée to my daughter?" Jackson Hale asked, as if just realizing himself that the silent young woman sitting on the floor beside his chair hadn't joined in the conversation.

"I'm not sure if I did," Rick murmured uncertainly.

His daughter had been so unobtrusive that Shannon had barely noticed her at all. She studied her now, noting the triangular rips in the expensive blouse and the red scratches on an otherwise flawless complexion. The blonde's hair was disheveled, a bramble caught in one curl. The evidence of physical exhaustion was in her posture, her body loose and tired.

"Belinda, I'd like you to meet Rick's fiancée, Shannon Hayes," her father introduced them, covering the unintentional slight.

"How do you do?" The blond girl's voice was weary and the hand she extended was chapped and rough.

"It's my pleasure," Shannon returned, and leaned down to shake her hand so Belinda wouldn't have to get up.

"Let me get you a chair to sit on, Belinda," Rick volunteered, and started to move away.

"Don't bother, Rick," she called him back, smiling

stiffly. "I've gotten used to sitting on hard things—whether it's the ground or the floor."

"Yes." Her father laughed. "This is one princess who has learned to sleep on the pea."

Outside there was the whirring noise of a helicopter. It drowned out all the conversation in the room, bringing it to a standstill. Dust kicked up by the whirling blades billowed outside the windows as the helicopter landed at the camp. When the noise died to just the chop-chop of the blades, Jackson Hale smiled.

"The company said they were sending a jet copter to pick us up," he said. "I guess that's it." He laid an affectionate hand on his daughter's shoulder. "We'll be leaving for Anchorage in another twenty minutes. How does that sound?"

"Wonderful." There was little feeling in her voice, but Shannon guessed that Belinda was too tired to be very enthusiastic.

"You'll fly back with us, won't you, Shannon?" Jackson asked.

"I don't know." She glanced uncertainly at Cody.

His mouth slanted in an oh-so-polite smile. "You don't want to leave Rick, do you?"

That uncalled-for remark irked her—a lot. Shannon turned back to Jackson Hale. "If you think there's room—" she began.

"Of course there's room," he interrupted. "If there isn't, we'll leave somebody else behind."

Cody moved, crossing the short distance between them at a leisurely pace. Yet the air seemed to crackle with sexual tension when he stopped beside her. Shannon held her breath, sensing the impatience that seemed to burn inside him.

"Since you're flying back with them, Dad and I will shove off," he stated, his light eyes watching her every flicker of movement.

"Yeah," Noah said. "I'll see that your bag gets put on the chopper."

"Thanks, guys. For everything. And especially for helping Shannon," Rick said, standing at her side, yet not touching her or claiming her with a possessive arm.

"Don't worry, Rick." Cody gave him an automatic smile. "Thanks aren't needed. As it turns out, I did it for nothing." Shannon didn't have an opportunity to move or offer resistance as his hands closed on her upper arms, holding her still. "Good-bye, Texas."

His eyes locked with hers while she was still trying to guess his intentions. Incredibly, he seemed to be on the verge of kissing her—right in front of Rick and everybody and she shrank back. All too quickly he was holding her at arm's length. Then he brought her partway back, bending his head to murmur in her ear.

"Go ahead and marry him, Shannon," he said huskily. "And forget me—if you can."

Tears stung her eyes as Shannon glared at him and wriggled out of his light grip. Cody slanted a challenging look at Rick, then walked out.

"You take care of her," Noah admonished Rick, then shuffled hurriedly after his son.

Rick studied her with a curious frown. "What the hell was that all about?" he asked her.

Shannon didn't want to answer.

Chapter Nine

Night was falling outside the windows of Shannon's hotel in Anchorage. Rick had taken a room there as well, but at the moment he was in hers, stretched out on the couch with his head resting on her lap. They had dined together earlier at the restaurant on the top floor where Cody had met her that first night in Alaska.

Shannon had talked to Rick about him—but not about the intimate moments or the way she had responded so ardently to his kisses. She had made her relationship with Cody sound lighthearted and full of fun, relating the way he had teased her about Texas and how staunchly Noah had looked after her reputation. They had both laughed over it, although there had been a faintly hollow ring to hers.

Somehow they had talked all around the real issue—each other and their future plans. Even when they phoned her parents after dinner, they had both avoided giving a specific date for their postponed wedding.

"Did I tell you?" Rick looked up at her while her fingers absently stroked his sandy hair. "Mr. Hale says I have a job flying for his company for as long as I want."

"That's wonderful." Shannon smiled.

"When I crawled out of the wreckage," Rick sighed, "all I could think was, one, I was alive and, two, I'd blown it. Big time. Hey, my first gig as a bush pilot—well, okay, copilot—and we crash the goddamned plane with the top man of the company on board. Now it sounds funny, but at the time . . ." His head moved to the side in a show of hopelessness.

"I can guess," she murmured, but inwardly she was thinking that if she were on a couch with Cody they probably wouldn't be talking. "What was it like—finding your way out, I mean?"

"Frustrating." There was a lot of feeling in that one word. "Every time we went around another bend, we saw another mountain. There wasn't a sign of another living soul."

"The pilot must have been in a lot of pain with that dislocated shoulder," Shannon remembered.

"Henderson never complained." Rick paused and stared at the ceiling, seeming to look beyond it. "I wasn't too impressed with Belinda when I first met her on the flight. I thought she was daddy's darling and spoiled rotten, too." A faint smile curved his mouth. "But I wish you could have seen her. After she stopped fussing about her hair and the bugs and the food, she turned out to be a real trouper."

Belinda again, Shannon thought. It seemed that every time Rick took a breath he was mentioning her name. Was she being too touchy? She didn't think so. There was no resentment—nothing that resembled jealousy. Maybe it was just a simple observation.

"She seemed nice." Actually, Shannon hadn't formed any real impression of the blonde. There hadn't been an opportunity to talk to her on the flight to

Anchorage. The noise of the helicopter precluded any conversation except with the person sitting next to her, which had been Rick.

"She's terrific." Rick was more positive in his reply. Then he had to smother a yawn with his hand. "Sorry"—he smiled in apology at her—"that wasn't any reflection on present company." He pushed himself into a sitting position. "I'm really bushed, Shannon. Can we make it an early night?"

"Of course," she assured him.

As she stood up to walk him to the door, he took her hand. "You are one terrific chick, you know." He kissed her lightly. "I meant to tell you that before."

"You are one terrific guy," she countered. "My hero." *No*, she thought, feeling a flash of weird guilt for being honest with herself. *Belinda's hero.* "And I meant to tell you that before."

When he kissed her again, this time Rick took her in his arms. There was nothing demanding about the embrace. It was warm and comfortable. But she definitely saw no northern lights display. She told herself she didn't mind.

Slowly drawing back, Rick studied her with a peculiar intensity, as if seeing her for the first time. Shannon was a little confused.

"Good night," he murmured. "I'll call you in the morning."

"Sleep late," she urged. "The rest will do you good."

"Okay." Rick didn't need persuading. There was one more light kiss—a peck, really—then Rick was leaving her to walk to the door. Shannon watched him go, waving a hand when he looked back before entering the hotel corridor and closing the door.

Whether she liked the idea or not, she was mentally comparing Rick and Cody. The scales were starting to tip heavily in Cody's favor. Seeing Rick again and being with him had started to unmask some of the feelings she had tried to hide.

It was entirely possible that she didn't love Rick. She cared about him very much, but it wasn't the same. Shannon was slowly realizing that. Her teeth sank into her lower lip as she remembered she had told Cody that you married someone because of what you felt in your heart, not your body. Yet Cody got to her both ways.

She was troubled by the thought that she might never see him again. She did love him, she thought suddenly. Damn and double damn. How crazy was that? She hardly knew the guy. Maybe it was just a reaction triggered by her fears about Rick. Now that those fears had been laid to rest, she shouldn't feel anything for Cody . . . besides friendship.

But she did. And her feelings for him were a lot stronger, a lot more sexual than anything she'd ever experienced.

Nice welcome for Rick, she thought, ashamed of her indecision. She reminded herself that loyalty was a good thing—and then thought a little wildly that she didn't know which man to be loyal to. And she was the kind of person who believed in keeping promises, come hell or high water. Shannon couldn't even begin to think what she should do next.

But she knew instinctively that to marry Rick now would be the worst mistake she'd ever make in her life. *You don't marry one man when you're in love with another,* she told herself fiercely.

There was a light tap on the door. At first Shannon thought it was someone knocking at another door. Then the sound came again. A slight frown clouded her expression as she crossed the room to the door. It was probably Rick. An irrational hope sprang up. What if it was Cody?

Both guesses were wrong. When she opened the

door, Belinda Hale was standing in the hallway—a very different version from the tattered and weary Belinda Shannon had met at the fishing camp. She ran a hand through her blond mane in an affected way, trying a little too hard to ooze sophistication in what was probably a designer suit.

Shannon fought back a sneeze. Belinda was wearing a little too much perfume. Okay, she could understand that. Wandering in the wilderness would be tough for any fashion slave.

"If you're looking for Rick," Shannon guessed, "he just left a few minutes ago. He was going to his room."

"I know." It was a calm answer. "I waited in the fire stairs until he left because I wanted to talk to you. May I come in?" Belinda asked with absolute politeness.

A little stunned, Shannon stepped back to admit her. "Yes. Please do." There was a little flourish of formalities as each made sure the other was comfortably seated. "You said you wanted to speak to me?" Shannon prompted, her curiosity aroused and her intuition already working.

"Yes." Belinda primly crossed her legs. "You've probably already guessed why I'm here."

"I'm not sure, no." Shannon wasn't about to speculate. It might be too embarrassing if she were wrong.

"I'm in love with Rick." Belinda came straight to the point, not challenging or blunt in her tone, but speaking very calmly. "I'm sure you'll say—my father did, too—that it's because we went through so much together. It's totally sudden, I know, but it's really . . . real. And I just, like, know it was meant to be."

Beautiful but not bright, Shannon mused, not inclined to be kind to someone who was too blond to think straight. "Does . . . does he know this?"

"I told him, but he seemed to think I didn't know what I was saying, either." Belinda smiled. There was an indulgent quality in her tone, as if Rick needed to be humored. "What else could he say? He's engaged to you. My father's money and position don't help—not with Rick."

"Why are you telling me all this?" Shannon was a little amazed by the woman's audacity, although she admired it in a really weird way.

The announcement didn't upset her—obviously not, when she'd already made up her mind that it was Cody she loved instead of Rick. She had every intention of returning the engagement ring to Rick in the morning. All the same, it seemed the better part of wisdom to keep her mouth shut and let her rival do the talking.

"You didn't know me before the plane crash, Shannon, but I've done a lot of growing up in a very short time."

"Really." Shannon was baffled by that non-explanation but what could she do besides wait for the rest? If there was a rest . . . yes, here it came. Belinda was leaning forward with a confidential air.

The blonde flipped her hair back over one shoulder and went on. "Once I thought I knew how to handle every adult situation. I was extremely adult. I was engaged to a man who possessed all the qualities I wanted in a husband. Unfortunately, he was still in love with his ex-wife. At the time I insisted it was better that we discovered that before we were married. We went our separate ways—and they were remarried."

"I see," Shannon murmured when Belinda paused, but she didn't really see at all.

"It was only after I met Rick that I discovered I hadn't been in love with . . . my previous fiancé. I didn't even know what life was all about," she stated.

"And now you do." It seemed the logical conclusion to that remark, Shannon thought.

"I think you have a fair idea of my background—the

type of family and home life I've known," Belinda went on. "So I'm sure you won't be surprised to hear me say that virtually everything I've ever wanted has been handed to me. I've never had to struggle for anything . . . until the plane crash. That's when I learned how to fight for what I wanted."

"And you are here because you're in love with Rick." She began to realize where the entire conversation had been leading.

"Yes. He's engaged to you, so by all rights I should keep my hands off him. Once I would have—even if I loved him. But not anymore." Belinda paused slightly. "I came tonight to tell you that I intend to fight to take Rick away from you."

Wow, she must watch a lot of soap operas, Shannon thought with amazement. Belinda Hale seemed to be channeling *The Young and The Restless, The Bold and The Beautiful,* and *Beverly Hills Confidential* all at once. "I don't think it'll be much of a fight." Shannon was going to explain her own personal decision.

"He doesn't love you. He hasn't accepted that yet, but he doesn't love you," Belinda insisted.

"It will make it easier if he doesn't because I don't love him."

She finally had her visitor's attention. "But you're engaged to him." Belinda frowned.

"Not for long," Shannon replied. "I decided to give back the ring. Things have changed. I've changed. So has Rick. I noticed it tonight."

"Are you sure?" The very calm, very controlled Belinda was suddenly flustered. "You aren't just saying that?"

"If I had any hesitation before, it was because I didn't want to hurt Rick," Shannon explained. "I care about him a lot, and I want him to be happy, but I don't love him."

A soft sigh came from Belinda. Shannon watched her relax, only now seeing how tense she had been—a coiled spring inside despite the smooth facade.

"I don't know what to say," Belinda murmured—and Shannon guessed that was a new experience.

"I do." She smiled. "Good luck. And I hope you invite me to the wedding."

"I will," the other woman promised, her eyes sparkling with tears as she stood up. Shannon knew she wouldn't actually cry—what, and ruin her makeup?

Belinda hesitated. "Will you tell Rick that I came to see you?"

Shannon thought about it a minute, then nodded. "Yes, I believe I will. It might be just what it takes to convince him."

"Thank you." She looked radiant and even more beautiful—if that were possible. "You're really very nice, Shannon." She smoothed her hair as she stood up. "I can see why Rick wanted to marry you."

"Being nice isn't the same as being in love," she replied. "And that's something I just learned, too."

After Belinda had left the room, Shannon felt immeasurably better about her decision to break the engagement. Even if things didn't work out between Rick and Belinda, it was still the right thing to do.

And there was Cody. As soon as she gave the ring back to Rick, she'd call Cody. Thinking about it brought a huge smile to her face.

It was late in the morning when Rick called to suggest they have breakfast together—or lunch if Shannon had already eaten. She let her acceptance of the invitation be implied and asked him to come by her room.

Breaking their engagement was a personal thing, and she didn't want to do it in a public restaurant or over the phone. After Shannon had ended her brief conversation with him, she called room service to send up some coffee. It and Rick arrived at the same time.

"What is this?" he asked with a questioning glance. "I thought we were going down to the coffee shop."

"I wanted to talk to you first," she explained, and poured them each a cup. "You look rested this morning," Shannon said, handing him one.

He'd recovered fast. Probably in Belinda's arms, she thought, with only the slightest flicker of jealousy. Female reflex, she told herself. Even if you don't want him, you don't want anybody else to want him, just in case you change your mind and get desperate and want him back. She told herself not to be irrational and looked closely at Rick. The weariness was gone from his face and his tall, lanky frame seemed to be bursting with energy. Shannon could see a lot of the old Rick in him, but the subtle changes were still there.

"I slept like a log," he admitted, and folded his long-boned body onto the couch. He took a sip of the coffee. "Ahh, that hits the spot," he declared, and sent a quizzical glance at her. "What did you want to talk to me about?"

"I had a visitor last night after you left," Shannon began.

"Who?" Rick lifted a brow. "Cody?"

His guess startled her. "No," she said quickly. "What made you think he would come?"

"From what you said last night"—Rick studied the coffee in his cup rather than look at her—"I gathered he was interested in you. He is, isn't he?"

"Yes. Or at least he acts as if he is." Last night she had realized that Cody had never said he loved her. Of course, he might not have wanted to while Rick's ring was on her finger. "With Cody it's hard to tell when to take him seriously."

"I suppose so." His answer wasn't really an agreement. "Who was here last night, then?"

"Belinda Hale," Shannon answered.

Rick's head jerked up. A hint of guilt swept across his expression before he squelched it. "Why did she come to see you?"

"She's in love with you, Rick," Shannon said, tipping her head slightly to one side. "But you know that, don't you?"

"I know what she's told me." He was upset and trying to contain it. "I probably should have explained what happened out there. You have a right to know. I kissed her a few times and—" Rick paused, reddening and looking foolish.

And really, really unattractive. "You don't need to explain," Shannon interrupted.

"I do," Rick insisted. "There were times when it seemed we were Adam and Eve out there. I know that isn't an excuse, but—"

"Oh, please. Don't get biblical. You fooled around. People do. No one ever seems to get struck by divine lightning."

"Uh, well, we sort of did. You know that incredible feeling when—but maybe you don't, Shannon."

"Actually, I do," she said tartly, and watched him hesitate. "A lot has happened to both of us since you gave me this ring. We've changed. I don't think either of us feels the same. Am I right?"

"I . . ." He didn't finish the sentence as he looked at her with deep regret. "The last thing I want to do is hurt you, Shannon. You came all this way to Alaska to marry me. And now you have to go back and . . ."

"I'm not going back right away," she told him.

"You're not afraid to face your parents, are you?"

"It isn't that."

"Shannon, I'll help you explain if you want me to. Blame it all on me."

She shook her head. "I don't need to do that, and I don't want to. But I think it's time I was on my own for a while. I mean, I love my parents, but Alaska is an amazing place. I'm here. Might as well make the most of it. I have enough money to stay through Christmas. Then I'll think about going back to Texas. Don't worry about me."

"You sure?"

She nodded. It was definitely over and he didn't love her. Even though he hadn't said it, she knew it. She twisted the ring off her finger and handed it to him, smiling gently.

"I just don't love you the way I should, Rick," she declared when he hesitated at taking the ring. "And it has nothing to do with you and Belinda. If you want to blame someone, Cody is the most likely candidate. He made me see that if I really loved you, I wouldn't have been attracted to him."

"Are you absolutely sure?" Rick didn't want any doubts.

"Yes. I'd already made up my mind to give this back to you last night before Belinda came," she admitted. "But I was concerned about the way you would take it. The things she told me just made the decision an easier one."

Finally, he took the ring from her and studied the play of rainbow light on the square-cut diamond. With a shake of his head, Rick looked at her, affection warming his eyes.

"Shannon, I don't know what to say," he murmured.

"Hey, that's Belinda's line," she remembered with a dimpling smile. "But she really does love you. Why don't you call her?"

"It would never work." He ran a hand through his straw-colored hair. "I'm nothing but a flight jockey. She's the boss's daughter."

"So what? She wants you," Shannon said lightly. "Finish your coffee and call her. She's probably dying to hear from you."

Chapter Ten

The cab pulled up in front of the hangar at Merrill Field and stopped. There was light in Shannon's eyes as she read the sign, STEELE AIR, atop the attached concrete block building that served as an office.

For three days she had been trying to talk to Cody, but he was always out—off somewhere on a charter. She'd left messages for him to phone her, but he hadn't called. Twice she had almost told Noah about her broken engagement, but she wanted to make the announcement to Cody herself. She was determined to see him, which was why she had come to the charter service. She was prepared to haunt the place if necessary.

Paying the cabby, she stepped out of the taxi and walked toward the door. The sun was shining on the Chugach Mountains surrounding Anchorage. A few powder-puff clouds were in the sky and the autumn air was brisk.

Although nervous, she was comforted by memories of the first time she'd gone there. She even paused to wipe her high-heeled boots on the bristled mat outside the door, just as she had done the last time.

Inside it was just the way she remembered it: magazines scattered around, the coffee table littered with used throwaway cups that hadn't been thrown away, and a couple of weary pilots sprawled on the couch. Except this time the swivel chair behind the desk wasn't empty. Noah was sitting in it. He pushed to his feet when he saw her. She couldn't help noticing that the door to Cody's office was closed.

"Well, if you aren't a sight for sore eyes!" Noah declared, and came around the desk to greet her.

"Hello, Noah. It's good to see you again." She smiled warmly.

"What are you doin' here?" he asked in his familiar raspy voice. "I figured you'd be busy with your wedding plans and findin' yourselves a place to live."

"I came to see Cody. Is he in?" She glanced toward the door, then noticed Noah shift uncomfortably.

"He's in," he admitted. "But he ain't been himself lately. He's been snapping at just about everybody—including me," he added with a wounded look. "I don't think it would be a good idea if you saw him just now. He just got back from a long flight and he's kinda tired and extra cranky."

"I'll take my chances." Nothing was going to stop her from seeing him. It was there in the determined lift of her chin.

Noah shook his head, doubting the wisdom of her decision. "I'll tell him you're here," he said, and moved in his shuffling gait toward the closed door. "But the mood he's in, he just might throw you out. I keep tellin' him it's bad for business, but he won't listen to me."

Shannon followed and paused behind him when Noah knocked twice on the door. Cody's voice was muffled, but the door didn't shut out its harshness.

"What is it?" he demanded from the private office.

Noah sent her a grimacing look, then turned the

doorknob, opening the door a crack. "You got a visitor, Cody." All she could see was a corner of the desk in the room.

"Who?" Impatience laced through the question.

Before Noah could answer, Shannon laid a hand on his arm, then shouldered her way past him and pushed the door the rest of the way open to enter the room. Cody was seated behind the desk, his sun-bronzed features set in uncompromising lines. His expression didn't change when he saw her, but she felt his light eyes rake over her figure and saw his mouth tighten.

"What do you want?" Cody looked away, not bothering to rise to greet her when she walked in. He focused all his attention on the report on his computer screen.

"I've been trying to reach you." She heard the click of the latch as Noah closed the door behind her. "You never returned any of my calls."

"I've been busy," he countered, without looking up her way. "I have a company to run. The work piled up while I was gone."

He certainly wasn't making it easy for her. "I never did have a chance to thank you for all you did for me." Shannon realized how much of his time he had devoted to her—and to finding Rick.

His dark head lifted, the light blue of his eyes centering on her. "So now you've thanked me," Cody stated. "If there's nothing else, I have even more work to do. I can't spare any time for idle chitchat."

A little thread of anger ran through her nerves. "I came to tell you that Rick and I—" But he didn't give her a chance to complete the sentence.

"I told you I didn't want an invitation to your wedding. I don't even want to know when it is!" Cody snapped, a cold rage darkening his features.

"There isn't going to be a wedding!" Shannon flashed. "That's what I came to tell you." She showed him her bare left hand. There was a slight indentation where the heavy ring had circled the fourth finger but that was all.

Cody made no move toward her, his gaze inspecting her hand, then lifting to her face. "When did this happen?"

"Three days ago," she answered, and waited for some sign to show it mattered to him—a hint of pleasure or satisfaction. "You were right. I didn't love him."

"It damn well took you long enough to find out," he grumbled in irritation.

He didn't seem pleased at all. Shannon gathered up her pride, standing stiffly. "That's what I came to tell you. And to say thanks for your help."

"What will you do now?" Cody shot the question at her. "I suppose you're flying back to Texas now that the engagement is off."

"No." She hesitated, not ready to tell him that she'd been thinking of staying, even though she'd blurted out her hasty plans to Rick. She'd hoped . . . oh, hell. Maybe it was best to go home, after all. "I thought I'd make reservations to leave this weekend." Her fingers tightened on her shoulder bag. "So I guess this is good-bye as well." She turned to walk to the door, tears burning her eyes.

"Like hell it is!" Long strides carried him around the desk after her; he caught her before she reached the door, his arms turning her around. "You aren't going anywhere, Texas!"

After the cold shoulder he'd given her, Shannon wasn't about to melt into his arms even if that was what she wanted to do. "Why should I stay here?" she challenged.

That lazy light came back to his bold eyes. "Because you love me." His hand cupped her cheek, his fingers stroking her hair. The warmth of his touch spread across her skin. "That's really why you came here today, isn't it?"

"I never said that." She tried to resist the desire to respond, to remain passive under his spell, but awareness of him was shooting through her.

"No," Cody agreed. "You've denied it every time I've tried to convince you that it's true. You had to put us both through all this useless bullshit."

"How romantic."

"I'll show you romantic, Shannon."

He lowered his head toward her, Shannon instinctively lifted hers to meet his descending mouth halfway. His kiss staked its possession of her as his arm circled her waist to draw her against his body. Her hands slid around his strong shoulders and into the virile thickness of his hair. Happiness flamed inside her, burning away the last remnants of resistance.

Her shoulder purse got in the way, and Cody slipped it off her, bringing her arm momentarily down to her side before she returned it to his neck. He gave the purse a little toss so that it landed with a thump on the floor nearby.

"My camera!" she squeaked.

"I'll buy you a new camera. Ten new cameras. Just quit jerking my chain, okay? Is that too much to ask? Damn it, Shannon, can I kiss you now?"

He didn't give her a chance to answer. In another second, his arms were molding her to his hard length, shaping her soft curves to his masculine contours.

His passion deepened and burned, showing her one of the many sides of love. She reeled under the glorious force of it, wanting to love him completely and forever.

Neither of them heard the door open. They weren't aware of any intrusion until his father issued an astonished, "Cody! What are you doing?" There was a rasp of reproval in the question and then Noah quickly shut the door so no one in the outer office could see their embrace.

Cody's arms tightened, not allowing even a discreet distance to come between them when he lifted his head, a deliciously sexy half smile touching his mouth as he looked at her. Shannon was dazzled by the light blazing in his eyes.

"I'm kissing the bride, Dad," he replied, and the breath she'd taken became caught in her throat at his answer.

"Well, you shouldn't be doing it like that," his father admonished. "A person could get the wrong idea. Why, if her fiancé had seen that, I wouldn't blame him if he punched you out."

"You're looking at her fiancé, Dad," Cody stated, and his smile deepened at her radiant smile.

"I don't remember your asking me," Shannon murmured.

"A small oversight," he shot back. "If you want to be technical, I don't remember that you accepted."

"Would somebody mind telling me what's going on here?" Noah demanded in exasperation. "How can she marry you when she's engaged to someone else?"

Considering the role Noah had played, Shannon thought it only fair to explain the situation to her future father-in-law. "I'm not engaged to Rick anymore." She waved her left hand airily. "I gave the ring back to him."

"Now mine will go there," Cody stated. "You can't keep us apart anymore, Dad."

"Well, if this don't beat all!" Noah exclaimed, and came forward, extending a gnarled hand to Shannon. "Congratulations. I didn't think this boy of mine would ever settle down. I hoped it would be a gal like you. Problem is, there aren't very many gals like you."

"She's the only one," Cody said softly.

Shannon patted his arm, silently asking him to relax his hold on her so she could accept his father's congratulations. "You've been wonderful to me, Noah. I haven't thanked you for that."

"Yeah? I thought I was being a pain in the butt. I really was trying to be, you know."

"I didn't notice," Cody said wryly.

"You never did pay a whole lot of attention to your old man." He clapped Cody hard on the shoulder. "But I think you inherited some of my brains. Your late mother, God rest her sweet soul, would approve of this girl. And, Shannon, you can thank me by giving me some grandkids," he replied with a knowing wink. "How big a family are you planning? I'd sure like to have a granddaughter and a grandson."

"Dad, would you mind if I married her before you started planning our family?" Cody requested.

"Whoa," Shannon said. "Whoa. Whoaaa, nelly. We are going to get to know each other first. I believe in long engagements."

"You do?" Cody burst out laughing and Shannon punched him in the arm. He didn't even flinch.

"When are you going to marry her? When's the wedding?" Noah asked. "I'm gonna have to buy me a new suit for the occasion."

"We'll be married just as soon as Shannon's parents can fly up here," Cody stated, then glanced at Shannon and added, almost as an afterthought, "All right?"

"Yes," she assured him, love shining from her eyes. "I mean, I think so. They might try to have me committed to a loony bin."

"You over twenty-one?" Noah asked.

"That's what it says on my driver's license."

"Then don't worry about it, girl. We'll explain everything to your folks."

"No, Dad. I'll explain everything."

"No, I will," Shannon said.

"Wow, is this our first family fight?" Cody said, laughing again. "This is going to be really, really interesting."

"Looks that way." Noah folded his arms over his chest and smiled broadly at them.

With an effort Cody dragged his glance from her face. "Dad, will you get out of here? I'd like to be alone with my future wife, if you don't mind."

"Well, just see to it that you behave yourself," Noah said. "Wink, wink."

"Go," Cody ordered with dry amusement.

"I'm going, I'm going," Noah muttered, and shuffled to the door.

When they were alone again, Cody gathered her back into his arms, nuzzling her cheek and the hollow of her ear. She felt him shudder.

"Do you have any idea what I've been through these past few days?" he murmured thickly. "I thought you were really going to marry him."

"Well, I thought so, too," she admitted. "But I guess I had to see Rick again to know that I didn't love him—not the way I thought I did. He's nice and I like him, but it's you I want to marry."

"I've been waiting to hear that since the first time you walked in that door," Cody declared.

She drew back to study his face. "How's that again? Explain."

"I don't know how I knew." His fingers traced the curve of her cheek and paused near her lips, underlining their softness. "But the minute you walked through that door, I knew you were the girl I'd been waiting for. It was a rude discovery to find out you were wearing another man's ring on your finger. It complicated the situation."

"So did your father," Shannon smiled.

"Yes." Laughter danced in his eyes and he chuckled. "No use telling him what to do. Alaskans are independent by nature, and he's bossier than most. He's bound to do more than his share of meddling. "

"I like him." She knew Noah's interference was always motivated by the best of intentions. "And I like Alaska. And I love you."

Cody kissed her hard. "I love you, too, Shannon. More than you know. And I always knew that Alaska and Texas would make an unbeatable combination," he declared, and covered her lips again to prove it.

Three months later . . .

A howling blizzard was doing its best to deliver a white Christmas to Anchorage. But it didn't matter to Shannon. She and Cody were safely ensconced in a warm living room, setting up their first Christmas tree. The dangerous weather had kept Noah at home, happy to hang out with his poker buddies, chowing down on salty snacks and getting toasted on whiskey sours, and half listening to episodes of *M*A*S*H* on DVD, with enough bonus features and interviews to keep them occupied until New Year's Eve.

Still paying for the wedding, Cody and Shannon had decided to give everyone a few good gifts and let it go at that. Buying his father the complete set of his all-time favorite show had been Cody's idea. And he'd made him open the gift-wrapped box before Christmas Eve, just to give them a little break. Shannon had knitted her father-in-law a pair of socks, which he promised with tears in his eyes never to wear, they were that nice. And she'd framed the photograph of Cody with the cabbage, which Noah had hung up immediately, proud and pleased.

"Hey, it's tipping," Cody said from somewhere deep inside the scratchy needles.

She pulled apart the branches and looked at him. "So straighten it."

"I think the trunk is crooked."

Shannon shrugged. "Then there's nothing we can do."

"I can think of something."

"Oh, no. Not that," Shannon said. "Can't do that in a tree."

He grinned and reached out for her with one hand, keeping the other on the trunk to steady it. "We could start with a kiss."

She leaned in through the fragrant branches and kissed him, hard. Off balance, Cody toppled and took the tree, and her, down with him.

"You're trouble, you know that, Texas?" he laughed.

"Yeah, I know." She scrambled backward on all fours, brushing pine needles from her hair. He followed, letting the tree lie where it had fallen.

"Merry Christmas anyway." And he kissed her again.

BRIDE OF THE DELTA QUEEN

Chapter One

Selena's fingers curled around the post supporting the balcony overhead, and her hazel eyes sparkled as she surveyed the narrow, bricked street. Being on her own in the Vieux Carré, the French Quarter of New Orleans, was just plain amazing—and it was everything she'd expected. Quaint. Crazy. Packed with people. A definite plus for someone whose favorite sport was people watching. She loved it all, even the tourist traps. Selena looked around at the old brick buildings decorated with ornate balconies of iron lace and sighed with satisfaction.

After almost two full days of sightseeing, Selena Merrick still hadn't become accustomed to the wonder of it, even though she'd planned this vacation for a couple of years. Not that everything had gone according to her plan. Her best friend, Robin Michaels, was supposed to come along but had canceled her reservations at the last minute owing to a family crisis.

It had never crossed Selena's mind to cancel the trip or postpone it because of Robin. As she looked down the picturesque streets, a faint smile curved her lips.

She was perfectly happy on her own. She could tour the Quarter at her own pace, see as much or as little as she wanted without consulting anyone else. There were times when Robin, good friend or not, could be a soppingly wet blanket.

On the opposite side of the street, a white lace balcony caught the rays of the setting sun, the painted ironwork reflecting the gold tint. This silent reminder of passing time snapped Selena out of her reverie, and she let go of the balcony post to move on.

Threading her way through the stream of fellow tourists, she crossed the street and walked toward her hotel. The sunlight warmed her shoulders, bared by the halter sundress in a springlike apricot print. The closeness of the air, heavy with humidity, made Selena think of summer instead of the last week of April. It tightened the natural wave of her light auburn hair, much to her annoyance, and made her skin feel sticky. She would definitely need to shower before changing for dinner. And blow-dry her beginning-to-frizz hair into submission, she thought.

A sidewalk café bar, crowded with customers, added to the congestion of pedestrian traffic on the narrow street. A passerby accidentally jostled Selena, knocking her sideways into one of the wrought-iron chairs and its occupant.

"Sorry," Selena said, offering a quick, smiling apology to the man she had bumped. Her glance caught the movement of crisp black hair as the man nodded in acceptance of her apology. She changed direction, skirting the edge of the tables that had been set on the sidewalk.

She paid no attention to the men grouped around the next table. Their loud talk and raucous laughter blended in with the street sounds. But she hadn't escaped their notice, with her gleaming bare shoulders and copper hair.

As she came closer, one of the men rose and staggered into her path, checking her steps. Selena smiled briefly in apology, unaware that he had deliberately blocked her way, and paused to wait for a break in the steady stream of tourists to walk around him.

"Why don't you join us for a drink, Red?" His voice was slurred. Uh-oh. He seemed like a happy drunk, but he was still a drunk.

Selena cast a sweeping look over the group of men, noting the conventioneers' badges on the pockets of their jackets. Hello-my-name-is-and-I'm-from . . . she didn't bother to read their names. Whatever podunk town they were from, they were obviously having a great time whooping it up in the wild and wicked city of New Orleans. They were undoubtedly respectable businessmen, but she had no intention of joining them.

"No thanks," she said.

An empty chair was offered to her. "Come on, honey, sit down with us," another voice spoke up.

She simply shook her head.

"Aw, come on, Red," the first man cajoled. "Have a drink with us and later I'll buy you dinner," he promised with an expansive wave of his hand.

Selena smiled and shook her head again, not expecting trouble. It was broad daylight and the streets and sidewalks were crowded with people. She was about to make some excuse and a fast escape when the first man bent his head toward her in an attitude that suggested secrecy. But he didn't lower the volume of his voice.

"You can call a couple of your friends for the guys and we'll really do up the town."

At first Selena was astonished. "My friends?" she echoed, before suddenly realizing that they thought she was a native of New Orleans instead of a tourist like themselves.

"You know," a third voice chimed in to prompt her, his voice loud enough for everyone to hear. "Your, uh, colleagues. Ladies of the evening like yourself. I like blondes," he proclaimed.

Ohhhh-kay. They had taken her for a hooker. They were not only drunk, they weren't very bright. In fact, they reminded her of some of the totally clueless older men in her father's congregation. She debated telling them that she was a minister's daughter, but she knew they were too far gone to care.

Graying, paunchy men who were well past middle age had a way of turning into randy frat boys after the first drink or two, even though these guys seemed harmless enough.

Next thought: should she tell them what she really did for a living? As a freelance journalist, she was always on the lookout for story ideas, and her current predicament had the makings of a cute it-really-happened-to-me article. She might be able to sell it to a major magazine if she could spin it just right.

"Whaddya say, baby? Wanna light my fire?"

How subtle. How suave. How much they deserved to be taken down a peg in print. Selena took a deep breath and lowered her voice, just in case a cop was listening. "Nothing doing. I don't think you can afford me."

Her response set them back in their chairs, except for the one who was still standing beside her. He swayed a little, looking at her with awe.

"How much?" he asked softly, holding his breath.

Selena whispered the first sum that came to her mind. The man's mouth opened and closed several times, and Selena's lips twitched in an effort to control her laughter at the whole ludicrous situation. Maybe she wouldn't write an article on this after all. *Glamour* wouldn't run a feature story on a dumbstruck old coot who looked like he was catching flies. Time to forget her mad impulse and move on.

"Bye, boys," she said airily.

As she turned to slip into the throng of tourists, her attention was caught by a pair of dark eyes assessing her with amused coolness. They belonged to the man seated alone at the next table, the one she had accidentally bumped into. Selena recognized the ebony black hair, and noticed something speculative in the arch of his eyebrow. Well, he could think what he liked. She wasn't going to see him again.

Unfortunately, as far as Selena was concerned, the old coot chose that moment to recover his voice when his pals asked, "How much?" and replied breathlessly, "One thousand!"

And the dark eyebrow lifted a fraction of an inch higher. Selena's stomach muscles constricted. A slowly spreading warmth started to fire her skin as she escaped into the concealing stream of pedestrians. Pretending to be an expensive hooker for a bunch of old men was one thing, but knowing that a really cute guy had overheard her was embarrassing.

She walked away as fast as she could without actually running, and within a couple of minutes she arrived at her hotel. In the interim, she managed to shake her feeling of foolishness as she replayed the incident in her memory, turning it into a tale to tell her friends when she returned from the vacation. They would think it was a hoot, laugh, and then forget all about it.

She slipped inside the elevator and inspected herself in its silvered mirrors as it rose. There were only six floors in the old-fashioned hotel, and she didn't have much time to study her reflection.

Why had the men believed she was a high-priced

streetwalker anyway? Was it the color of her hair? They were definitely from a generation that associated the color with scarlet women, to use a quaint old phrase.

She ran a hand through her hair. Between the humidity, which increased its tendency to wave, and the occasional breeze that had sneaked down the narrow streets, her shoulder-length style was tousled to the max.

Sighing, Selena dismissed the color of her hair as the cause. Perhaps it was the bold gleam in her green-flecked eyes, but it had always been there, shining through long, sun-kissed lashes.

Her father, the Reverend Andrew James Merrick, had often accused her of embracing life too passionately. Of course, he never meant it in the lustful sense of the word. He was referring to her lack of fear. His darling daughter had an inclination to rush in where angels feared to tread, he had always said.

But not where men were concerned. Even though her little charade might lead a certain gorgeous black-haired guy to think otherwise. No, she had never been impulsive when it came to dating and relationships.

She looked at herself once more in the mirror before the elevator reached her floor. There was nothing outstanding about the rest of her features. She had a girl-next-door face, pretty but not breathtaking or anything like that. Except for her lips. A friend had once described them as full and sensuous, but Selena hadn't paid too much attention to the remark. Looking at them now, shining with gloss, she had to admit that her mouth was nicely shaped and possibly inviting.

The elevator stopped and the doors whooshed open. Yet another mirror, a full-length one, hung on the opposite wall, and she gave herself a final once-over, still trying to see if anything was different.

Maybe it was just being in a city like New Orleans,

she decided. The sultry climate made her walk more
slowly, with a sway to her hips. She tried out a fashion
model's pout in the mirror and fluttered her eyelashes.
Smirking at her reflection one last time, Selena turned
and looked down the hall to be sure no one was coming, then strutted to her room, swinging her bag.

Her friend Robin would have been appalled at the
reason Selena was so focused on her appearance. As far
as that went—Selena smiled to herself—her girlfriend
would have been appalled at the entire incident.

No, Robin would have been outraged by the mistake
in the first place and wouldn't have dreamed of perpet-
uating the impression, even as a joke. She probably
would've dumped the conventioneers' drinks over their
heads, itty-bitty paper umbrellas and all. The thought
made Selena want to laugh, but she decided it was just
as well that Robin hadn't been able to come along on
the trip. She couldn't exactly cut loose with a prissy girlfriend acting shocked all the time.

Later, as she finished dressing for dinner, she re-
tracted the last thought. Selena hated eating alone in a
public place, and as for going out to a club by herself,
forget it. As it was, she knew she would draw a lot of curious glances by herself in the restaurant. The usual as-
sumptions were bound to be made and she could just
imagine the sotto voce remarks. She was waiting for a
hot date. She had been stood up. She was looking for
fun.

To tell the truth, she was. New Orleans was practically the live entertainment capital of the universe. Jazz,
zydeco, rock, Delta blues and Louisiana soul, Southern
hip-hop, retro bluegrass and progressive country, and
alternative whatever—name it, New Orleans had it,
judging by some of the posters and advertisements
Selena had seen on the famed Bourbon Street. She
would have liked to experience the nightlife, but deal-

ing with guys on the prowl, not to mention the drunks and the stoners, just seemed like too much trouble.

With her hair done up in a French braid, Selena smoothed the sides absently with her fingertips and reached for the delicately crocheted shawl that matched her flame-orange dress. It was an unusual shade and one that brought out the fiery lights in her hair. She draped the shawl around her shoulders and tied the ends in a loose knot.

Going out into the carpeted hotel hallway, she paused to make sure the key card was in her evening bag, a beaded treasure she had found in a resale shop. She closed the door and had barely taken two steps away from it when a door farther down the hallway opened and a man stepped out.

It took Selena about as long to recognize where she had seen him before as it took him to remember her. Black hair. A quizzical look. Handsome. It was him. Just her luck.

Her first sinking thought was, why had she chosen such a brilliantly colored dress to wear? Because you don't have any boring clothes, she reminded herself, adding a mental Note To Self: bring along something beige and baggy on her next trip. But it was too late now. Fighting the urge to scurry back into her room, Selena continued down the hallway. Her steps slowed as she crossed her fingers, hoping he would ignore her and continue on his way.

Not a chance. He stood waiting expectantly for her, those glinting dark eyes sweeping her from head to toe. The look branded her with the iron Selena herself had put in the fire.

"Hello, Red." His voice was low, and conveyed what she had seen in his eyes when she'd nearly landed in his lap at the sidewalk cafe: amused interest.

It seemed pointless to ignore him or pretend that

she didn't recognize him. Selena was positive that he knew she remembered him.

"Hello," she returned the greeting with what she hoped was a detached and disinterested smile.

Slipping his key card into his suit pocket, he stepped forward to meet her. Selena couldn't make up her mind whether she should walk past him or stop.

Her fleeting glimpse of him at the café had not prepared her for getting this close to him. Several inches taller than her five-foot-six frame, the man was powerfully built. He was wearing a suit that looked expensive, probably Armani. Selena, who considered herself a world-class shopper and had the credit card bills to prove it, didn't need to see the label. Okay, he had money. So what? She tipped up her chin and gave him a haughty look.

"Are you coming or going?" he asked, meeting her gaze with a slight smile.

In the glinting blackness of his eyes, Selena saw what he had left unsaid in his question. The very fact that they had met a second time in the hallway of the hotel indicated that she must have come from one of the rooms. And his silently suggestive look told her exactly what he was thinking.

Her anger boiled near the surface, but Selena determinedly cooled it. She had no one to blame but herself for what he was thinking.

At some point in his approach, she had stopped. It was a mistake, she realized, and one not easily corrected, since the breadth of his shoulders blocked her way.

"Going," she answered his question and made an attempt to pass him, hoping he would move out of her path.

He didn't budge an inch. "Where?"

Her father had often told her that the truth could

never hurt. Selena hoped he was right as she answered frankly, "To dinner."

Unknowingly, she was clutching her purse, knuckles white with the tenseness of her grip. His gaze slid to her hand, drawing her attention to her death hold on her funky little evening bag. Instantly she guessed how he interpreted that—he must think she was protecting her hard-earned payment for services rendered. She seethed with frustration.

"Did you work up an appetite?" The question was almost a taunt.

This time Selena didn't attempt to contain her anger, letting it blaze in her eyes. "Get lost. I don't have to answer that crude question." She started to push her way past him, all stiff and proud, wondering what the hell else she could say . . . *I'm not a hooker?* He would probably just laugh.

His large hand rested on the bareness of her arm to stop her. "That was crude," he acknowledged smoothly. "I had no business saying it to a lady of your caliber. I'm sorry."

Of your caliber. That phrase was even more annoying. If he had just left well enough alone and ended his sentence with the word *lady*, Selena might have been more willing to accept his apology.

Instead all she could manage was a freezing, "That's quite all right," that made a lie of her acceptance.

His dark gaze scanned her features, his own expression inscrutable. "Dining alone?"

He was making no attempt to hold her, but Selena found she couldn't move or pull her arm from the light touch of his sun-browned hand. Yet her muscles were rigidly resisting his nearness.

"Maybe," she answered noncommittally.

He seemed pleased. What an ego. It wasn't as if she had invited him to join her.

"How lucky can a guy get? I'm alone too." His right hand was thrust in his trouser pocket, holding his jacket open with studied casualness. "Care to join me?"

Be careful what you wish for, Selena thought with an inward sigh. So much for being perfectly happy alone. Only moments before leaving her room she'd hoped for company, and now the Fairy Godmother of Surprise Dates had suddenly granted her wish.

Selena knew instinctively that this man was very, very sure of himself. There was something in his dark eyes that made her a little nervous, something that said too hot to handle. Exactly the kind of man that she liked most. But . . . she had been impulsive enough for one day. She didn't have to say yes.

"No thank you." Her tone was cool.

But it seemed to pique his interest even as it deepened the dimpling grooves next to his mouth. "Why not?"

"Because I choose who I go out with," Selena retorted, wishing she could bring an end to this ridiculous meeting. Why wouldn't he let her pass?

"Just as you choose who you go to bed with?" he countered in a low voice.

"Exactly!" The word burst from her in an explosion of temper.

In the back of her mind, she had been wondering how she could convince him that she had only wanted to fool the suits who had mistaken her for a hooker, with an eye to turning the situation into a possible magazine article. But a red flash of anger made her feel that she owed him no explanation at all.

Something cynical flickered across his expression as one corner of his mouth slanted without humor. "I'm well aware there's a price for your time, Red. I'm prepared to pay it."

He pulled his right hand from his pants pocket and

took out folded bills. Then he tucked them into her cleavage. She froze, momentarily unable to move or speak. But at the brush of his fingers against her bare skin as his hand withdrew, the spell was broken.

Bending her head, she looked down at the green bills, aware of a distant sensation of degradation. Slowly she removed the money and lifted her gaze to his. "I'm surprised," she heard herself say evenly. "You don't seem like the type who would have to pay for his pleasure."

He cocked his head, his dark gaze sweeping over her. "Maybe I'm curious what 'pleasure' you have to offer that would be worth so much," he countered.

Something in his tone or his look, or maybe it was the sheer magnetism of his presence, warned Selena of the dangerous game she was playing. Her pulse accelerated in alarm.

"I don't happen to be selling right now," she rushed, and tried to force the money into his hand while pushing her way by him.

His hand closed around the fingers holding his money at the same moment that he took hold of her elbow. "You know, there's a better place for this discussion."

He was propelling her forward. Selena's initial, confused reaction was that he was going to direct her down the hallway to the lobby and restaurant. Her mouth was open to protest, her widened and slightly angry gaze on his strong face when he paused to reach in front of her. He opened a hotel room door, obviously his.

"This will be more private," he announced with a lazy, mocking glint in his eye.

Panic screamed through her nerve ends. This charade had gone too far, too fast. "Wait a minute—no!" But she was already through the door and it had closed behind her.

She pivoted, ready to bolt, but he was right there in her way although he kept his distance, regarding her with curiosity. She could feel her heart thumping against her ribs.

"Guess I didn't give you enough. Do you work for an escort service, or are you on your own? Whatever. Name your price. You're one of the most beautiful women I've ever seen."

Selena gaped at him. A compliment? Was that typical behavior for Armani-clad guys who enjoyed the company of, um, escorts? What was next, flowers and candy? Meeting his mom? *Glamour* might go for an article with an angle like that. *He Thought I Was A Hooker . . . Which Means An Orange Dress Is A Really Big Don't.*

He didn't make a move, for which she was infinitely grateful.

"Look," Selena took a shaky breath and swallowed, "this is all a mistake—"

The folded bills were still in her hand. He took them from her clenched fingers, added a few more from his pants pocket, then removed her evening bag from her other hand and slipped the money inside.

"You don't understand—my purse!" she squeaked when he gave it a toss to some point behind her. *Damn it, why am I thinking about a stupid little beaded purse?* she thought wildly. *What about me? What the hell is he going to do next?*

She started to turn but managed only a glance over her shoulder, enough to see her evening bag slide to a stop on top of a low dresser. The strong hands closing around the bare flesh of her upper arms kept her from turning around completely to retrieve it.

"It will be perfectly safe there," he assured her.

But she wasn't perfectly safe. That fact was driven sharply home to her as she felt his hands slide to the shawl, freeing the ends from the loose knot with the simplest of tugs. She clutched at the trailing ends, but they escaped her grasp as he let the shawl fall to the floor.

Selena would have stooped to pick it up, but his hands were on her arms, drawing her to his chest. Hunching her shoulders, she used her forearms to wedge a small space between them. His chest was like a solid wall, immovable.

"Don't!" She struggled, but it didn't seem to bother him.

His cheek and jaw were near her temple, the clean fragrance of his aftershave tickling her nose. His fingers were spread across the bareness of her spine, pressing her ever closer.

"Stop acting." His breath stirred the hair near her ear as he spoke.

"I'm not acting!" Selena flared, breathing in sharply when he began nuzzling the sensitive area of her neck below her earlobe. "Did it ever occur to you that the lady might not be willing?" she gasped, twisting her head toward her shoulder to stop his exploring mouth.

He merely laughed. "It's your profession to be willing."

"Well, I'm—" Her indignant protest was lost as she made the mistake of lifting her head to deliver the protest to his face. Immediately his mouth muffled the rest of her words.

Oh, my. Oh, mercy. The man could kiss. Startled, she surrendered to the sensation for a few incredible seconds before her brain returned to full functioning. Selena would have to give him a four-star rating on sensual skill alone. No, make that five stars. But she wasn't going to let him go further. She wrenched her head away from his mouth, drawing back, the storm of anger flashing green in her eyes.

Zebra Contemporary

NEW YORK TIMES BESTSELLER
JANET DAILEY
SHIFTING CALDER WIND

NEW YORK TIMES BESTSELLING AUTHOR
LISA JACKSON

LORI FOSTER
unexpected

PICTURE PERFECT
FERN MICHAELS

To start your membership, simply complete and return the Free Book Certificate. You'll receive your Introductory Shipment of FREE Zebra Contemporary Romances, you only pay $1.99 for shipping and handling. Then, each month you will receive the 4 newest Zebra Contemporary Romances. Each shipment will be yours to examine FREE for 10 days. If you decide to keep the books, you'll pay the preferred subscriber price (a savings of up to 30% off the cover price), plus shipping and handling. If you want us to stop sending books, just say the word… it's that simple.

FREE BOOK CERTIFICATE

Yes. Please send me FREE Zebra Contemporary romance novels. I only pay $1.99 for shipping and handling. I understand that each month thereafter I will be able to preview 4 brand-new Contemporary Romances FREE for 10 days. Then, if I should decide to keep them, I will pay the money-saving preferred subscriber's price (that's a savings of up to 30% off the retail price), plus shipping and handling. I understand I am under no obligation to purchase any books, as explained on this card.

Name _____

Address _____ Apt._____

City _____ State _____ Zip _____

Telephone (____) _____

Signature _____

(If under 18, parent or guardian must sign)

Thank You!

CNHL5A

Offer limited to one per household and not to current subscribers. Terms, offer and prices subject to change. Orders subject to acceptance by Zebra Contemporary Book Club. Offer Valid in the U.S. only.

PLACE
STAMP
HERE

llı.ıl..llluıllhıılhlı.lılılıth.lll.lıl..llıll..l
Zebra Contemporary Romance Book Club
Zebra Home Subscription Service, Inc.
P.O. Box 5214
Clifton , NJ 07015-5214

He raised one dark eyebrow and gave her a look that was heavy with desire. She was conscious of the large hand at the base of her spine, pressing her hips and legs to his long, muscular body. A fiery gleam lit up his dark eyes, and the look on his face was . . .

Hard to describe. But try. You're a writer, Selena thought, as if for a moment she was standing outside herself, watching the whole scene instead of being a part of it. He was . . . amused. Passionate. Confident. And she was . . . confused, even if she had enjoyed the kiss. Very much.

"Will you let me go?" she blazed in a temper born of sudden desperation, realizing belatedly that she had very little control over what was happening.

She pressed her hands against his shoulders and strained with all her might to break out of the steel trap of his embrace. All she succeeded in accomplishing was to arch the lower half of her body more fully against his.

Impatience hardened the firm set of his mouth. "Look, this game of hard-to-get might work with your older clients, but it doesn't impress me."

Her chin and jaw were captured by long fingers to hold her mouth still for his possession. Selena was helpless to prevent it, unable to move her head, and her hand and arms were pinned between the crush of their bodies.

Soon the long, deeply sensual kiss began to relax her. Being held in this man's arms was like nothing else she had ever experienced, and there was genuine tenderness in his touch, no matter who or what he thought she was. For a moment she allowed his roaming hands to mold her pliant body to his. The sensation of the kiss was threatening to become addictive.

When the fingers on her chin relaxed their hold, it took all of her willpower to slide her lips free of his kiss.

He permitted it, tipping her head back in order to explore the smooth column of her neck and the hollow of her throat.

The nibbling caresses spread molten warmth all through her. Then Selena felt the coolness of air against her back and realized with a start that her dress was being unzipped. Very slowly.

Oh no. A hot kiss was one thing, but sex with a total stranger? She didn't want to play in that park, not ever. At his tug on the fragile straps of her dress, she knew she was lost unless she did something quickly. Her next move would have to catch him off guard. Not too difficult, considering what he was thinking about.

Taking a deep breath for courage, she was filled with a strange combination of fear and exhilaration. His hand was on her shoulder now, pushing away one of the offending straps, her dress hanging loosely about her.

"If you tear the dress, it will be extra," she warned on a bold and breathless note.

For a split second, he didn't move, his mouth pressed against the curve of her neck. Selena was almost afraid to say more. Thick, jet-black hair brushed her jaw as he lifted his head, a complacent curve to his mouth.

There was space between them now, but his hands were still resting on her shoulders. Selena attempted an alluring, if tremulous, smile and raised her eyes to look at him. Gently and carefully, he slipped the spaghetti straps from her shoulders and the flame-orange dress fell around her ankles.

Her lashes fluttered once, but it was the only outward sign she gave of embarrassment. Inwardly she knew her knees were threatening to buckle, and it took all her nerve not to cover the scanty lace of her strapless bra with her hands.

She looked down at her panties when he did and had to smile. She had forgotten that she was wearing waist-high, discount-store, six-to-a-package briefs in a flowered print not exactly calculated to drive men wild with desire.

Keeping the smile fixed on her lips, she reached out for his hand as she stepped out of the dress, which lay around her ankles and unfortunately stepped out of one of her shoes, too.

She kicked the other one off as she led him farther into the room and away from the door. She stopped short of the bed, a fact the fathomless black eyes made note of while continuing to watch her with burning brightness.

Maybe he had a thing for waist-high discount-store briefs, she thought a little desperately. Then again, maybe he didn't—she glanced over her shoulder and caught him looking at her flowery butt with a wry grin. Releasing his hand, she reached for his jacket, sliding a hand along the lapel. "Shall I help you off with your clothes?" The huskiness of her voice was not entirely fake.

A dark brow briefly flickered upward. "I think I can manage," he assured her.

Shrugging, she turned away, relief washing through her. But he was still watching her as he peeled off his jacket. Selena wandered to the mirror, patting the escaping tendrils of copper hair back into place and keeping him in view in back of her reflection.

Then his shirt came off. Selena quivered at the sight of all that naked muscle, without an ounce of extra fat or the least little love handle in evidence. Quite a package, and sun-browned to a teak shade. All that male virility oozing from him was not a sensation to settle her already taut nerves.

When he unfastened his pants and stepped out of one leg, she bolted. There wasn't time to worry about shoes or her dress lying on the floor. She made a sweeping grab to retrieve her evening bag and darted to the door, ignoring his muffled curse.

For the first time in this misadventure, Selena felt luck was on her side. There was no one in the hallway, no one to see her racing to her hotel room in a pretty good bra but really awful underpants. She wasted a precious second fumbling for the key card in her purse then inserted it quickly in the slot and turned it.

Opening the door and slipping into her room, she darted one last glance down the hall just as he appeared, bare-chested and fastening his pants. He looked away from her, for which Selena said a prayerful, whispered thanks. She quickly and quietly closed the door.

Her knees buckled, and she leaned weakly against the door, taking deep, quaking breaths. Sounds that were somewhere between laughter and sobs came from her throat. Then she heard footsteps in the hall and sobered quickly into silence, but the footsteps gradually receded.

Gathering strength, she walked into the room to take the cotton robe from the foot of the bed and wrap it around her. The red-orange dress had been one of her favorites. It was gone for good now. Selena doubted that she would have worn it again even if she could have managed to bring it with her out of the room.

Her stomach growled, reminding her that she still hadn't had dinner. She shook her head, knowing there was no way she was going to risk bumping into that man again. She walked to the telephone and dialed room service. A deep, drawling voice answered and asked for her order.

"Steak, done medium well. Salad, with vinaigrette dressing. A glass of red wine. And the biggest damn piece of chocolate cake in the kitchen, please."

She could almost hear the grin on the other end of the line, but she didn't care. When life got weird, a major hit of chocolate fixed it.

Chapter Two

Determined not to be a prisoner in her room, Selena slipped out of the hotel early the next morning. She took precautions to keep from being recognized, donning huge sunglasses and tucking her hair under a floppy straw hat. She had checked herself in the elevator mirror before the doors slid open. Yikes—it was quite a look. Sort of a cross between *Breakfast at Tiffany's* and *Dukes of Hazzard*.

But her fear of meeting the man a third time vanished when she stepped outside the hotel into the sunlight of a spring Sunday.

There was no hesitation in her footsteps as she left the hotel entrance. She knew exactly where she was going—to the French market to pig out on beignets and chicory coffee. Her guidebook recommended a famous café and mentioned that it could be found blindfolded, the fresh beignets were that good.

Well, she was going to test that hypothesis. She was just about blind in sunglasses this dark. And the route she'd chosen was not the most direct, but the guidebook said it was picturesque. Selena doubted that there was any place in the French Quarter that was not picturesque. She looked over her sunglasses at the map and set off.

Wandering down a narrow street, she wondered again why it was called the French Quarter when all the architecture looked so Spanish. Not wanting to walk with her nose in a guidebook, she decided the name had to have come from the Creole French who had lived for generations in this section of New Orleans. Looking around, Selena felt almost as if she were in a foreign country.

Emerging from the shaded coolness of Pirates' Alley, she paused near the entrance of St. Louis Cathedral and marveled again at the fairy-tale turrets and steeples of the oldest cathedral in the United States.

As she crossed the street, she noticed the artists setting up their wares outside the iron fences surrounding Jackson Square and promised herself she would browse through it all after she had breakfast.

She took the shortcut through the square to the French market and quickly discovered that she wasn't the only one who had decided to pig out. The café was filled with hungry customers, and the aroma of freshly brewed coffee and beignets. Selena felt her appetite increasing as she looked for an empty table and chair.

The beignets, square-shaped doughnuts minus the hole and covered in powdered sugar, were still warm when they were served. She took a wake-up sip of the black coffee and immediately added a liberal amount of cream to weaken its potency. Chicory coffee was an acquired taste, she decided.

Later, wiping the powdered sugar from her lips and hands, she sipped at the cup the waiter had refilled, thinking that the coffee was pretty tasty after all. Some things just took a little getting used to. At least an authentic New Orleans breakfast was an experience that could be shared with the folks back home. Her unexpected rendezvous . . . well, no. She planned to keep that to herself.

She contemplated yesterday's encounter for several dreamy moments, well aware that she had found it exciting in a lot of ways. Not that she would ever want to be a call girl, of course . . . but playing the part of one with a sexy stranger had been almost liberating in a strange way.

Okay, enough, she told herself sternly. Shut up and stop fantasizing. Still, the memory of the way her man—that man, she corrected herself—had kissed her and the hot desire in his eyes made her feel warm all over.

To distract herself, Selena turned her attention to the little boy at a nearby table who was chattering to his mother. "Mom! Mom! I heard someone say the Delta Queen is in! Can we go look at her? Huh? Can we?"

The mother's reply was too low for Selena to understand, but the nod of her head and the boy's hoot of joy convinced her that it had been in the affirmative.

The Delta Queen was a famous old paddlewheeler, Selena knew that. Bored with the movies on TV, she had leafed through the tourist brochures in her room last night. Several times. Not at all what she wanted to do on one of her precious nights in New Orleans, but she hadn't felt like going out.

Wrapped in her bathrobe, she had admired the photos of the boat's magnificent interior and idly considered signing up for a day cruise. In fact, the more she'd thought about it, the more she'd wanted to take a week-long cruise up the mighty Mississippi, but later in the year. Much later, around December. Everything would be cheaper before the Mardi Gras crowds arrived, and Christmas in New Orleans sounded like a lot of fun.

If she could sell a freelance article to one of the

Southern lifestyle magazines—call it Creole Christmas or something like that and play up the traditional aspects of a Louisiana-style holiday—she could return to New Orleans for an all-expenses-paid trip. She'd racked her brain for a surefire pitch that would get her a decent advance.

Now, blinking in the bright sunlight despite her big sunglasses, Selena realized her chances were slim. Every freelance journalist in the country must have pitched that idea a thousand times over.

She set down her coffee cup, feeling a little depressed and a lot more awake, then looked around at the other tourists and the handsome waiter, who was showing new customers to another white-draped table. His tousled black hair reminded her of the sexy stranger, not that the waiter looked much like him otherwise. Still, it occurred to Selena that she could very easily run into the man right here. Right now.

Perhaps she ought to check out of the hotel and find someplace else to stay. She would rather not worry if she didn't have to, and skulking around in hats and sunglasses was hardly a solution.

She motioned for the check, and the waiter nodded, bringing it over a minute or two later. Selena dug in her tote bag for the money and tip, leaving both on the table. She unzipped a small pocket inside the tote to see if the folded bills the stranger had given her, which she had transferred from her evening bag, were still there.

Yup. Safe and sound. And she intended to return it all as soon as possible. She rose from the table with the tote bag over her shoulder.

The day had grown warmer. Selena dawdled on the way back to the hotel, window-shopping and people-watching to her heart's content. New Orleans was full of crazy characters, even at this hour of the morning. She tossed a few coins into the cap of a street musician playing the accordion for all he was worth and singing what sounded like a love song in plaintive Cajun French. Madame Belle Poitrine had done him wrong, it seemed.

Turning down a crooked street she thought she remembered, she made her way back to the hotel, entering through the wrought-iron portal and looking around for . . . him.

Fortunately, there was no him, only a gaggle of pale, sneakered ladies in unflattering khaki shorts. They were clustered around a guidebook that one of them held, flipping the pages.

"Do we want to do the Voodoo That You Do tour or go to the Bayou Belles Dance?" she said.

"We're not really dressed for dancing, Miriam," her companion replied, looking down sadly at her baggy attire.

"I vote for voodoo," said another. "Maybe I can buy a spell that will turn my husband into a sex machine."

"Good old Bob? Not likely. He'd rather go ice fishing. Don't forget, there's Cajun Cooking, too," said Miriam. Her friends made indecisive murmurs and flipped through more pages as Selena walked by the group, smiling.

Time to take care of business. Then she could check out. The simplest and least risky way of returning the money would be to slip it in an envelope under his door. She had put some of the hotel stationery inside her bag before leaving that morning, just in case she felt compelled to correspond with anyone, since she hadn't brought her laptop with her.

First things first: she had to find out if he was still in the hotel. Not that she had ever known his name. But she did know his room number.

Nodding to the desk clerk, who gave her a friendly smile, she walked to the courtesy phone in the lobby and dialed the room number. She let it ring four times, drawing in a deep breath when someone finally picked up.

An impatient and very male voice crackled into her ear. "Yes?"

It was him. She remembered that voice. She would probably always remember that voice. Commanding and low, it had thrilled her almost as much as his kiss— and his caresses. Just give him the money back, she told herself. Then run.

"Who is this?" he asked.

Ever so gently, Selena replaced the receiver in its cradle. If she returned the money now, she ran the risk of being caught slipping it under his door. She would have to wait until she saw him leave. But that brought up another problem. He would have to be just going out for a while, not carrying a suitcase and a garment bag and all that. How else would she know that he hadn't left the hotel for good?

Well, carrying or not carrying a suitcase didn't prove anything, of course. For all she knew, he was a cheating husband who didn't bother with stuff like that. She thought again of the risk she'd taken and mentally kicked herself.

Maybe the friendly desk clerk would let her know how long the man was staying if she gave him the room number.

Nope, not a good idea. The friendly desk clerk would probably take her for a call girl, too, if she asked a question like that about a man whose name she didn't know.

Time for Plan B, Selena thought. But she didn't have a Plan B. She glanced at a rack of tourist brochures and groaned inwardly at the thought of reading them all over again until the stranger ventured forth. She sighed. She would have to.

After putting the money into a hotel envelope and sealing it, she strolled to the rack and took several brochures, selecting some she hadn't read. She pulled the brim of her hat a little lower as she settled primly on a lobby sofa, pretending to read as she watched the other hotel guests come and go for a while.

One brochure that featured a well-written history of the Delta Queen actually did capture her interest. And there was a coupon for half off the fare for the upcoming Christmas cruise. Selena took it as a sign. She tore it out very carefully and tucked it into her tote. Good deal. She was definitely coming back, freelance article or no freelance article.

More minutes drifted by until Selena looked up again, realizing that she might very well have missed seeing her quarry. Hell. She wasn't about to sit here all day. There had to be another way of getting the envelope to him. It dawned on her that she could leave it at the desk.

She got up and crossed to the check-in area, bestowing a gracious smile upon the clerk.

"May I help you, miss?" he inquired, giving her a sweeping look of admiration that made her a little nervous.

"Would it be possible for me to leave a message for one of your other guests?" Selena fingered the envelope nervously.

"Of course. What room number, please?" he requested. Selena gave it to him. He frowned as he glanced at the computer screen. "I'm sorry, miss, but that room is vacant."

"Vacant? But—" she began.

"The gentleman checked out this morning," the clerk explained.

So she had missed him after all. Selena nibbled at the inside of her lower lip for a thoughtful second, then said, "I don't suppose you could give me his name and address? I could forward it to him."

"Now, we can't do that, miss. Our privacy policy doesn't permit us to give out that information."

"I see," she murmured and managed a smile. "Thank you." As she walked slowly away from the desk, she wondered what she was going to do with the money. She couldn't keep it. But now it was impossible to return it to him. That left only one choice—to give it away to a charitable institution where it would do some good.

Selena walked to the lobby pay phone and riffled through the city directory. If she could find a small organization, her donation was much more likely to be remembered, just in case she ever had to prove she'd actually made one.

She traced a fingertip down the columns of the yellow pages and stopped. There—the Society for the Preservation of Old New Orleans looked like a safe bet. She could check their bona fides online when she got home and send a money order in the amount that the stranger had given her to the address listed. Too bad there was no Society for the Preservation of Young Female Freelancers, she thought. A wistful smile tugged at the corners of her mouth.

Chapter Three

Eight months later, almost to the day, Selena came back to New Orleans. She headed down Poydras Street, feeling a little boxed in by the skyscrapers of the oil companies, hotels, and financial institutions; looking for the Delta Queen when she passed the Riverwalk Marketplace, decked out in honor of the season, and the concrete walkway running alongside the river.

She knew generally where the boat was docked. With the towering trade center building as a landmark, it was easy to walk to it. She shivered, not quite warm enough in her lightweight hooded jacket, and held her tote bag closer, wondering if she should take out a sweater and put it on. Louisiana was colder than she'd expected it to be in late December, but nothing like her home state of Iowa.

A sudden breeze tugged at her jacket hood as Selena turned right, moving past the silver-painted monolith called The Admiral. Farther down the dock, she could see a stirring of activity and walked toward it. Her view of the Delta Queen was blocked by other boats until she was almost upon it. At the first glimpse of the name painted on the black hull, she slowed her steps, letting her gaze run up the four-storied lady of the river.

Deckhands were moving around the forward deck, while uniformed porters carried luggage off the boat, followed by strolling, unhurried passengers. A few other spectators had gathered along the dock, some to meet disembarking passengers while others were there, like her, simply to see the Delta Queen.

At the head of a gangplank, a sign was posted that read SORRY, NO VISITORS AT THIS TIME. She knew the boat wouldn't leave the dock until tomorrow but she was glad she had come all the same. Selena touched the ticket in her pocket, bought and paid for, even though her freelance assignments had been few and far between that autumn. After her brief visit in April, she had been determined to visit New Orleans again, and her parents had given her the steamboat ticket as a Christmas present in advance.

It was to be her first holiday season away from home, but since they had encouraged her to enjoy herself thoroughly, she supposed her mom and dad weren't missing her too much. She'd been out and on her own for several years anyway, and if anyone missed her, it was her tabby cat, Pippin, who was probably shredding her best silk scarves in revenge, even though Robin had been persuaded to feed and pet him twice a day.

Selena had been boning up on the history of New Orleans in the intervening months, following the recommendations of the online friend she'd made at the Society for the Preservation of Old New Orleans, who had sent her a letter of thanks for her generous donation. She felt only the least little bit guilty for misleading the organization as to its source.

She wondered idly what had become of the black-haired stranger who had been willing to pay so much for an hour of her time. Not your time. Your body, she reminded herself. The thought made her blush even now, and she put it out of her mind.

Selena walked toward the stern. The polished teak handrails circling the top three decks and the black smokestack with its gold crown perched behind the pilothouse made her wish she could explore the interior. At the stern the red paddlewheel rested, not required to churn muddy water until the boat again left port.

One of the crew, a young woman, was repainting the Delta Queen's name on the large signboard above the paddlewheel. The gold whistles of the calliope gleamed in the morning sunlight.

Here and there, Selena caught glimpses of the boat's age, most of them artfully concealed with a fresh coat of paint, reminders that the legendary Delta Queen was the grand old lady of the riverboats.

"Like something out of the past, isn't it?" a voice said.

Startled, Selena turned, becoming aware only at that moment of the older woman standing near her. "Yes, it is," she agreed, recovering quickly to smile. "Somehow I never realized it was such a large ship."

"Boat," the woman corrected gently. "Any vessel that plies the river is a boat, no matter what her size."

"A large boat, then," Selena conceded, her smile widening.

"Yes," the woman nodded. "She accommodates one hundred and ninety-odd passengers and a crew of seventy-five," she added in a knowledgeable tone.

"You know a lot about the Delta Queen, don't you?" Selena commented, running a considering eye over the woman.

Almost as tall as Selena, she had dark hair except for silvered wings at the temples that gave her a distinguished air. There was a suggestion of crow's feet at the corners of her brown eyes, but otherwise her facial skin was relatively unlined. Selena guessed that the youthful appearance came in part from good bone structure—that was something that didn't change—and she figured the woman was in her late fifties or very early sixties.

She wore a close-fitting tailored suit with the ease of one accustomed to wearing custom-made clothes. Selena suspected that the woman had never been a beauty, even in her youth, but she decided that she had probably been attractive in the same strong sort of way that she was now.

"I am very familiar with the boat and her history," the woman answered.

"You're from New Orleans?" Selena was positive that there was something in the picture the woman was presenting that she wasn't seeing.

"Yes," was the brief reply, and then the woman's brown gaze was riveted on the steamboat.

Selena let her attention slide back to the boat, trying to disguise her sudden intense curiosity about the woman beside her. She couldn't stop herself from asking more questions. Her nose for news, as her parents referred to it, not entirely approvingly.

"Have you ever taken a trip on the Delta Queen?" Selena's intuition told her the woman didn't work for the company.

"Yes, I have . . . many times." There was the slightest pause in her words, the length of a heartbeat, leaving Selena with the impression that the woman had a catch in her voice.

With a sideways glance, she studied the woman again. Initially she saw the same image as before—an older woman, calm and composed and completely in control. Then Selena noticed the flaws.

A white linen handkerchief edged with lace was being twisted by agitated fingers. And the luminous quality of the woman's brown eyes was produced by a fine mist of tears. Too many times, members of her father's congregation had come to the parsonage, ostensibly for a friendly visit, only to have something in their behavior betray an inner turmoil, as this older woman was doing now.

Selena was not her father's daughter for nothing. "Excuse me, but . . . is something wrong?" Unconsciously she adopted the gentle, consoling tone she had so often heard her father use. She removed her sunglasses so the dark lenses would not shade the woman's reaction.

"I—" Instant denial formed on the woman's lips. As she caught sight of the compassion gleaming quietly in Selena's eyes, she checked the denouncement and turned away. "It's . . . nothing."

"I don't mean to be personal, but I can tell something is troubling you. Sometimes it helps to talk about it, even to a stranger." Selena noticed the faint quivering in the woman's chin.

"You're very astute." The reply was accompanied by a stiff smile. "Not many people your age would be concerned enough to even ask," she sighed.

"It's probably a case of environment and upbringing." Selena dismissed the idea that she was in any way special. "My father is a minister."

"Ah. That accounts for it." The woman glanced at her lace-edged handkerchief and nervously tried to smooth out the wrinkles she had twisted into it.

"My name is Selena Merrick." Selena offered her hand to the woman.

"Julia Barkley," the woman returned, clasping Selena's hand warmly but briefly. "Are you here on vacation?"

"Yes. I'm a freelance journalist. Not much money in it, but my time's my own."

"That's a blessing, dear. Time is something you never get back. Enjoy yourself while you're young."

"That's what my parents keep telling me. They gave me this trip for a Christmas present."

"I see," Julia said. "That's very kind of them. So they won't mind that you're not with them for the holidays."

Selena shook her head and smiled. "They're going to Florida. For the first time in I don't know how many years, my mother isn't going to bake twenty million Christmas cookies. Says she'd rather bake herself in the sun. With plenty of sunblock, of course."

"And where do your parents live, dear?"

"Iowa."

"Oh. Well, coming from the farmlands of the prairie, you probably don't mind the flatness of our delta land, do you?" the older woman asked, smiling.

"No," Selena agreed, "although we actually have more hills than you do. Do you live in New Orleans?"

"Actually my family's home is outside of New Orleans, but I keep a small apartment here so I can get away every once in a while to be on my own." Unconsciously the older woman stressed the words "get away."

Selena immediately guessed there were family problems at home, possibly a daughter-in-law that Julia Barkley wasn't able to get along with. That thought became sidetracked as she caught the woman staring again at the massive paddlewheeler in an attitude that could only be described as wistfully reminiscent.

"You have a special attachment to the Delta Queen, don't you?" Selena observed softly. "Because of something that happened to you."

The woman's tears were in definite evidence, welling diamond bright in her eyes, but there was a radiant happiness, too, about her expression. Her reddened lips curved into a faint smile.

"I met Leslie on that boat," she whispered absently.

"Your husband?"

"No." Julia Barkley blinked away her tears before glancing at Selena. "I'm not married. I'm the old maid of my family, literally," she tried to joke as Selena reacted with surprise. "That's why they think I'm being overly romantic and silly now. Women of my age aren't supposed to act the way I do."

"What do you mean?" Selena was thoroughly confused. Her guesses about the older woman and her family problems had obviously not been accurate.

"Do you believe in love at first sight, Selena?" she said, responding to Selena's question with another question, then added, "May I call you Selena?"

"Of course."

The older woman's face brightened. "Then call me Julia."

"Okay. Julia it is. Getting back to your first question"—Selena laughed—"I'm not exactly an expert. I've never been in love before. A few near brushes here and there, but never the real thing. I have no idea if it can happen the first time you meet."

"Believe me, my dear, it can. It did for me—with Leslie." Her gaze swung again to the boat, distant and vaguely dreamy.

"What happened?" Selena dared the question.

"He asked me to marry him." A mixture of pain and confusion seemed to flicker across the woman's smooth forehead. It was quickly masked with a polite smile as Julia Barkley turned to Selena. "I was on my way to church. Would you like to join me? Afterward, if you have no other plans, perhaps you'll have Sunday dinner with me at my apartment. Don't hesitate to say no if you'd rather not come. I quite understand."

"I would like to come," Selena accepted without hesitation.

Despite the wealth and status implied by her clothes and manner, Julia Barkley was a lonely woman, plagued at this moment by memories of a lost love. Selena sensed it as surely as if it had been put into words.

And Selena enjoyed people too much to even consider that a few hours in the older woman's company would prove boring. Besides, she had a long vacation ahead of her, so what did a few hours on a Sunday matter?

Just for a moment, she imagined she could hear her mother laughing and exclaiming, "Stray dogs and orphans couldn't find a better home than with you, Selena." Even at twenty-three, Selena had to admit she was sometimes too trusting of strangers.

But she couldn't imagine anything bad happening at church.

Which turned out to be, not suprisingly, Episcopalian. The congregants were well-dressed, well-bred, and generally subdued. Selena could barely make out the words of the sermon that the distinguished older man was giving from the pulpit and Julia seemed not to hear it at all. The altar and pews were decorated with elegant swags of Christmas greenery, tied with tasteful bows in maroon velvet.

At the conclusion of the service, a car was waiting outside for them, a previous arrangement made by Julia Barkley before she had left her apartment.

But Selena was a bit confused when the car stopped at the canopied entrance of a building complete with a doorman. It had all the earmarks of a hotel. When she stepped out of the car, her suspicions were confirmed by the name, Hotel Pontchartrain.

"The hotel has suites they let on a permanent basis," Julia explained as they entered the marble lobby.

Once they were on her floor, Julia opened the door

to a luxurious apartment filled with lovely old furniture. Some of the pieces Selena was sure were valuable antiques. Yet it was a very comfortable place, with a Christmas tree in one corner that stood perfectly upright, not too tall and not too short, covered with delicate glass ornaments, each one of a kind and clearly a family treasure.

Selena walked over for a closer look, touching a Czech glass bird with a streaming feathered tail. It quivered on its twig almost as if it were real, and Selena smiled.

Her hostess smiled back in a vaguely distracted way.

Julia, she noticed, was both charming and friendly, if at times a bit preoccupied. Their dinner, coq au vin prepared in advance by Julia, was simply but flawlessly cooked and served on very good china.

As Selena helped clear the dishes from the table, she noticed a bedroom door ajar in the hallway. Selena happened to glance inside and her eyebrows lifted curiously at the suitcases and clothes covering the bed.

"Are you going on a trip, Julia?" she questioned, not wanting to stay if her hostess had to pack.

Julia's hands trembled slightly as she set the china plates on the counter. "Do you know, I can't make up my mind?" The hiccupping sound that came from her throat was half laughter and half sob. "Isn't that silly?" She looked at Selena, tears gathering in her eyes again.

Not since they had left the wharf had Selena noticed any crack in the older woman's composure. Now it was there and widening.

"No, I don't think it's silly," Selena offered. She hesitated to probe, but she felt Julia wanted her to ask. "Were you planning to return home to your family?"

"No." Julia turned away to discreetly wipe the tears from her eyes and smooth a silvered wing of hair into the dark. "I have a passage booked on the Delta Queen tomorrow—to meet Leslie."

"Leslie?" Selena echoed, grateful the woman couldn't see her startled expression. For some reason she had thought Leslie was dead.

"Yes," she answered with a hesitant nod. "He's supposed to meet me in Natchez . . . where we're to be married."

"Really?" This time Selena couldn't mask her incredulity. Then she saw the woman's tightly clutched fingers and the frown of pain wrinkling her brow. "You are going, aren't you?"

"I don't know," Julia murmured uncertainly, shaking her head.

"But you said you loved him." It was Selena's turn to frown.

"I do," the older woman hastened to confirm, then sighed in frustration. "I don't know what's the matter with me. I'm as nervous and unsure of myself as a schoolgirl."

In a gesture of bewilderment, Selena ran her fingers through the auburn hair near her ear. "I think there's some point in all of this that I'm missing. You love Leslie and he wants to marry you, but there seems to be something that's holding you back. What is it, Julia?"

"My family," the woman admitted. "My brother thinks I'm crazy. He insists that Leslie is only interested in the family money and the doors the Barkley name can open for him. My sister, everyone, agrees with him."

"Have they met him?"

"Oh, yes, they've met him," Julia assured her, and Selena realized it had been a foolish question to ask. Of course, she would have introduced him to her family.

"Leslie and I met on the Delta Queen during its autumn cruise last year. We corresponded for a time. In one of the letters, he proposed to me."

Selena could well imagine that his letters were tied up in a pretty blue ribbon and secreted away in some safe place to be read over and over again. Julia was clearly a hopeless romantic.

"I was so deliriously happy," the older woman continued. "I invited him to New Orleans after the winter holidays to meet my relatives. It was—" Julia stopped, unable to finish the sentence.

"Disastrous?" Selena completed it for her.

"Totally." Julia sighed. "My brother, Hamilton, insisted there was too large a difference in our ages."

Selena gave an involuntary start of surprise. Was Leslie younger than Julia? It seemed unlikely at Julia's age—whether it was fifty-five or sixty—that her brother should protest about her marrying a man fifteen or twenty years older.

If he was that age, what would Julia's status and money mean to Leslie? If a man in his seventies proposed to a woman in her sixties, Selena felt he should be applauded instead of condemned.

"And the rest of my family," Julia continued, "believes that I'm foolish to take this romantic fling, as they call it, seriously. They absolutely forbid me to have anything more to do with him."

"They forbid you?" Selena repeated. Julia Barkley was old enough to behave or misbehave however she wanted. "You obviously didn't listen to them."

"No, though perhaps I should have," the woman murmured with a rueful twist of her mouth. "But I had to write to him and explain why I couldn't marry him. Initially I did refuse him," she added in quick explanation. "Then Leslie wrote me back, and I answered it. Before I knew it we were exchanging letters again. In one of his letters, he told me how much he loved me." There was a definite throb in Julia's voice as she added,

"And how much he wanted me to be his wife, a-and suggested that we elope. . . ."

"Now you can't decide whether you want to marry him or not," Selena concluded.

"Oh, I want to marry him. But my family . . ." Her voice trailed off, the tug-of-war still going on inside. She looked beseechingly at Selena. "What would you do?"

"Oh, my. Please don't put me on the spot like that, Julia," she declared. "I—I hardly know you, and I really couldn't say." It seemed impossible that a woman old enough to be her grandmother would be asking her for advice about love and marriage.

Selena reminded herself that Christmas could be, and often was, the loneliest season of the year for far too many people. Julia Barkley's confiding in her might seem inappropriate, but it was understandable. Her father had once preached a memorable sermon about the odd and unexpected ways in which the holidays made friends out of strangers.

"There isn't anyone else I can ask," the woman replied with a despairing shrug. "My family is dead set against Leslie. As you pointed out, you and I scarcely know each other, but you are impartial."

"You have to live your own life, Julia." Selena fell back on the advice her father had always given to her when she had sought him out. "Whatever decision you make will be the one you'll have to live with and not your family."

Julia murmured absently, "It's the things in life you don't do that you regret." She glanced at Selena and smiled. "That's what my nephew always says when my brother begins to lecture him about his questionable escapades."

"There's a great deal of truth in that," Selena agreed, thinking to herself that at least there was one member of the Barkley family who evidently didn't automatically obey the family's edict.

"Yes, and I would always regret it if I never saw Leslie again," Julia declared with a wistful sigh. "Especially since Christmas is almost here."

"I think you've just come up with your own solution." Selena smiled gently.

"I have?" Julia gave her a startled look.

"Take the trip and see Leslie again," Selena explained. "Maybe what you once felt for him won't be there anymore. You would still have time to back out before the marriage takes place."

"You're right. That's exactly what I will do!" The shadows left her brown eyes at last, leaving them clear and sparkling. "What would I have done without you, Selena?" Julia declared. "If I hadn't met you today—"

"You still would have made up your mind one way or another," Selena interrupted, unwilling to take any credit for prompting Julia.

"But you have helped me, more than you know. And I feel . . . I know in my heart that this decision is right."

"I'm glad," Selena said, and meant it.

"Dear, I am so happy." The words were no sooner out of her mouth than Julia's expression brightened as an idea flashed through her mind. "I shall buy a ticket for the cruise you're taking, and we'll travel together. You don't mind, do you, Selena?"

The question caught Selena completely by surprise. "I—" She couldn't seem to get any answer out.

"As crazy as it sounds, I've never traveled anywhere alone," Julia admitted with a self-deprecating laugh.

"Never?" echoed Selena, although she didn't know why she was astounded. Julia had obviously led an unusually sheltered life.

"Never. Sophie, my cousin, usually goes with me. She accompanied me on the cruise where I met Leslie."

"Well, then, maybe she—" Selena began.

"Could come along this time?" Julia finished the phrase and laughed, a throaty, amused sound. "I think not. She despised Leslie. I think she was jealous. Sophie is a few years younger than I am and much more attractive, but Leslie didn't look at her once on the cruise."

This was rapidly turning into a very odd little soap opera, but Selena found herself fascinated nonetheless. She had always had a weakness for the convoluted charm of really tacky soap operas, which she shared with her mother. In fact, it was unnecessary for Julia to explain that her cousin would violently oppose the elopement.

"I suppose it wouldn't be a good idea to have her go with you," Selena conceded.

"No. Not at all. But, oh, Selena, this was meant to be," Julia gushed. "You came to New Orleans at just the right time, and it's going to be wonderful."

Selena gulped. "Um, I hope so."

"As you know, the cruise takes eleven days, and we go up the Mississippi River for quite a ways. There's entertainment and Christmas caroling and holiday parties aboard, and dancing, and classes on Louisiana traditions. Wait until you see the bonfires on the levees at night!"

"I beg your pardon?" Selena only half-heard the long list of activities but the last one made her snap out of it. She couldn't imagine the matronly Julia dancing around a bonfire.

"It's an old Cajun custom. To light the way for Père Noel. Our Santa Claus."

"Oh," said Selena. "But how will you get a ticket? Don't you have to buy them months in advance?"

Julia's eyes widened. "Gracious! Here I am making all these plans and I don't even know if there's a room available." Julia jumped up and walked toward the telephone in the small sitting room. "I'll call to see."

"But it's Sunday," was the only protest Selena could offer in her astonishment. She felt as if she were caught in a whirlwind.

Julia tossed her a twinkling glance that made her look very young. "This is one time when it's an advantage to have Barkley for a surname." And she picked up the telephone receiver.

Later that afternoon in her hotel room, Selena wondered how in the world Julia had succeeded in persuading the Steamboatin' Company to sell her a last-minute ticket for the popular Christmas cruise.

Selena hadn't had the heart to say it wasn't a good idea, and there was no way she could change her own ticket to some other time. She consoled herself with the idea that there was a story in it somewhere. Whether it would turn out to be truth or fiction, she had no idea.

She was supposed to meet Julia at four o'clock the next afternoon at the riverboat terminal on the wharf. Glancing at her luggage, Selena was glad she had unpacked less than half of her clothes. It wouldn't take her long to get ready when it was time to get ready, which meant she would get to see more of New Orleans before she left. Flexibility had always been one of her key traits, she reminded herself. Plus a sense of adventure. A combination that definitely had a way of getting out of hand, she thought ruefully.

Chapter Four

Following Julia Barkley over the gangplank onto the boat, Selena felt a rush of excitement and nostalgia. If it wasn't for the orange Volkswagen with the black letters *STEAMER DELTA QUEEN* painted on its doors that was parked on the bow of the boat, she could have been stepping into another era.

Polished wood gleamed darkly in the wide stairwell leading to the second deck of the boat, where fellow passengers were milling around the large and gracious sitting room. Julia didn't pause to let Selena take in the furnishings but continued straight to the purser's office at the end of the room.

A tall, uniformed man was talking to one of the porters, but when his ever-roving gaze touched on Julia Barkley, a smile wreathed his face. With a quick word to the white-coated porter, he stepped forward to meet her, extending his hand.

"Miss Julia, it's good to have you aboard with us again," he declared with beaming sincerity. "I understand congratulations are in order." He winked, as he squeezed Julia's hand.

Selena smiled at the blush that colored the older woman's cheeks. It made her look very youthful and vulnerable and also very happy.

"Yes, they are, Douglas. Thank you," Julia said. "And it's good to be aboard the Delta Queen again. How is your father?"

"He's fine, Miss Julia, just fine." His blue eyes flicked their attention to Selena, then beyond her. "Where's your cousin, Miss Sophie? Isn't she with you?"

"No, not this time. She wasn't able to come. But Selena—Miss Merrick—is traveling with me." Julia turned to draw Selena forward. "Selena, this is the chief purser, Douglas Spender."

"We're pleased to have you aboard with us, Miss Merrick," he said as he shook her hand.

Selena had the distinct impression that he meant it and was not simply issuing polite words of welcome. In his mid-forties, he was a tall and slender man with brown hair and blue eyes. There was a pleasant drawl to his voice, and his Southern gallantry charmed her socks off. Selena decided that she liked him—and she even liked being addressed as Miss.

"I know I'm going to enjoy it." Her smile widened into dimples.

"This is your first cruise?" he inquired.

"Yes," Selena nodded.

"Well, we aim to please," he smiled. He clasped his hands in front of him in a gesture of decision. "I'm sure you'll want to see your cabins. Kevin"—he motioned to one of the porters—"would you show Miss Julia and Miss Merrick to their cabins?"

The man he summoned was not any older than Selena and definitely could be classified as cute. Things were looking up, Selena thought. She ventured a smile.

"Yes sir." Kevin smiled at both of them, his gaze lingering a fraction of a second longer on Selena's face. "This way, please, ladies." He led them through an opened door into the wide interior passageway leading to cabins on the same deck.

"You have your customary stateroom, Miss Julia," he said, pausing in front of a door numbered 109 to open it with a key before handing it to the older woman. "Your luggage is already inside. Is there anything else you'd like right now?"

"No, I don't believe so, Kevin." Julia smiled and glanced at Selena. "I'll meet you in the forward cabin in about twenty minutes."

"Fine," Selena agreed, then frowned in bewilderment after Julia had closed the door.

"Are you wondering where the forward cabin is?" the porter asked, grinning.

"Yes," she said, laughing with a trace of self-consciousness.

"You just left it," he explained. "It's the sitting room where you met Doug Spender, the chief purser."

"Thank you." She glanced over her shoulder, hoping to keep her bearings.

"Your cabin is 237, up on the texas deck, Miss Merrick. I'll take you there now," the porter said, reclaiming her attention.

She followed him as he led her down the passageway, smiling to herself.

"Where is the texas deck?" she asked.

"One floor up."

"I'm never going to get these terms straight," Selena said with a sigh.

"It's easy. You're on the cabin deck," he explained. "Front and back are forward and aft, or bow and stern. After a few days on board, they'll come naturally to you."

"I hope so," Selena murmured with a skeptical smile.

Should she tell him that he was dealing with a land-locked girl from Iowa?

He went right down the short hall toward an exit door leading to the outer passageway. There was also a door on the opposite side of the boat, Selena noticed.

As he turned to make certain she was behind him, the porter saw her glance at the other door. "We'll use this one," he said, pushing the door open. "Watch your step." He indicated the raised threshold over which Selena carefully stepped. "The odd-numbered cabins are on the port side of the boat," he said, explaining his reason for using this exit.

"Oh dear!" Selena laughed softly.

Walking only a half a step ahead of her, he turned his blond head to give her an understanding grin. "As you face the bow of the boat—the front—the port side is left and the starboard is right."

"Of course," she nodded, but the sparkle in her eyes said she would never remember, and the porter laughed, his gaze openly admiring. As they ascended the covered stairwell to the next deck, Selena said, "I know I'm being foolish because I'll probably forget your answer, but why is it called the texas deck?"

"It's texas deck with a small 't.' It's customary on a riverboat for the largest deck to be called the texas deck after the largest state, Texas. But with a small t. And that will be on the spelling test this afternoon."

Selena looked alarmed.

"Just kidding. No tests. A Christmas cruise is all about having fun."

"Well, okay. That's what I had in mind."

He winked. Selena wondered what made her say things like that and then reassured herself that female passengers probably flirted with the crew members all the time. Kevin didn't seem to be taking it too seriously.

"Right. Anyway, staterooms derived their names from the fact that they were named after states—the Kentucky Room, the Vermont Room, and so on."

"Fascinating," murmured Selena.

At the top of the stairs he stopped, producing a key from his pocket. "Your room, Miss Merrick," he announced and opened the door.

"Thank you." She added with a smile, "And thank you for the information, too."

"Definitely my pleasure," he declared and handed her the key.

With a nod to her, he turned to retrace his steps. Selena hesitated, then stepped over the raised threshold into her cabin.

A single chest of drawers stood against the wall just inside the door. Two single beds flanked the room. Her luggage was sitting on the floor at the foot of one of the beds, her garment bag hanging on a clothes rod in the corner. A full-length mirror covered the door leading to the bathroom. The room was compact and efficient and very comfortably adequate.

Unpacking only the clothes that had a tendency to wrinkle, Selena left the rest of it till later. She put on a touch of lip gloss and ran a brush over her copper hair. Slipping her room key into her bag, she left the cabin a few minutes ahead of the agreed time to find her way to the forward cabin lounge. She retraced the exact route the porter had taken and met Julia just as she was stepping out of her stateroom.

"Selena, come see what was waiting for me in my room," Julia exclaimed with delight.

Following Julia into her cabin, Selena stopped just inside the room. A dozen long-stemmed roses glowed velvet red from their crystal vase atop the dresser.

"They're beautiful, Julia," Selena smiled, knowing instinctively that the bouquet was what the older woman had wanted her to see.

"They're from Leslie, of course." There was extra warmth in her voice as she said his name. "Here's the card that came with them."

She handed Selena a small envelope, opened to reveal the card inside.

Selena read the personal message written on it silently and somewhat self-consciously. The words were simple but eloquently touching. *I love you, Julia. May I always and forever be—your Leslie.* Silently she handed it back to Julia. All the comments that came to her mind seemed inadequate and trite.

Julia read it again before slipping it back in its envelope. "It's moments like this that make me wonder why I have any doubts," she said with a sigh. Again Selena couldn't think of a suitable response and remained silent. As if pulling herself out of her reverie, Julia turned to Selena, fixing a bright smile on her face. "Have you done any exploring yet?"

"No, not yet," Selena admitted. "With the passengers and crew coming and going, it's pretty crowded and confusing."

"That's true. Well, there'll be plenty of time for you to discover every nook and corner of the boat before the cruise is over," Julia stated with a knowing gleam in her brown eyes. "Since the weather is so nice, shall we go up to the texas lounge? Perhaps there'll be a table free. We can relax and have a glass of sherry."

"Sounds fine," Selena agreed. She didn't much like the sticky sweetness of sherry, but she could always have something else.

In the interior passageway, Julia stopped to obtain their table assignment in the dining room from the head waiter before continuing, with Selena at her side, to the forward cabin lounge. Stopping abruptly just inside the lounge, Selena breathed in sharply at the sight of the grand staircase leading to the texas lounge.

"Wow."

"It takes your breath away, doesn't it?" Julia commented.

"Yes it does," Selena declared, admiring the gleaming wood columns that stood regally at the fanned-out base of the stairs.

Highly polished brass kickboards shimmered gold on the steps. The sweeping curve of the banister railings was inset with lacy scrolled wrought iron. An arched opening had been carved into the ceiling, where a gorgeous chandelier was suspended.

"It's like something out of *Gone with the Wind*," Selena said in a somewhat awestruck tone. "I feel like Rhett Butler is going to appear any minute and carry me up the stairs. I loved that scene."

"Don't we all," said Julia, dropping her ladylike demeanor for a few seconds and giving Selena a mischievous smile. She moved forward to ascend the stairs. "In her day, the Delta Queen was the epitome of luxury river travel. Her woodwork and paneling is all oak or mahogany. Of course, most of it's covered now with fire-retardant paint—Coast Guard regulations."

"It's a pity." Selena observed all the wood moldings and paneling that were painted a cream white.

"But a necessary compromise for passenger safety. I don't think it diminishes her charm."

"Not at all." Selena could already feel the gentle atmosphere warmly enveloping her.

The sensation was intensified as she reached the top of the grand staircase and entered the horseshoe-shaped texas lounge, windowed all around. The rich

luster of the wood was free of paint, its casual elegance
enhanced by thick carpet underfoot.

Furnished with small square tables and captain's
chairs, the room had a bar with tall stools in the center
of its horseshoe shape. Double doors on either side of
the room could be opened onto the outer deck, where
white wrought-iron tables and chairs were set.

As Selena and Julia walked toward one set of double
doors, a bartender leaned over the bar. "Hi, Miss Julie. I
heard you were aboard."

After an initial blank look, surprised recognition
flashed across the older woman's face. "Greg! I didn't
expect you to be here. I thought you were quitting to go
to college."

"I was." He ducked under the narrow opening cut
into the side of the bar and walked over to meet them.
"But I decided to work through the summer and sign
up for the fall semester."

"Be sure that you do," Julia insisted in a matronly
tone. "You need to complete your education."

His light brown eyes moved to Selena, studying her
intently. Despite his full mustache, Selena decided he
wasn't any older than she was, possibly a year or two
younger. He was good-looking, and there was something in his expression that said he knew it. Another
Southern charmer, she thought, with an engaging smile
and a slow, drawling way of talking.

"Is this your niece, Miss Julie?" he asked, his gaze
staying on Selena.

"No, Miss Merrick is a friend. Selena, this is Greg
Simpson, an incorrigible but likable young man," Julia
introduced them. "And the only one who gets to call
me Miss Julie instead of Miss Julia."

The minor distinction was almost lost on Selena, but
she got it as soon as Greg spoke.

"Miss Julie, you know you like it," he said teasingly,

and Selena guessed he was right, judging by the twinkle in Julia's otherwise stern expression.

"If I didn't know how hard you work in this job, I would say you waste too much time sweet-talking," Julia stated.

The bartender laughed off her reproof and smiled at Selena. "Anyway, Selena, welcome aboard the Delta Queen."

"Thank you," she said with a nod.

"The chief purser, Doug Spender, gave orders that your first sherry of the cruise was to be on him, Miss Julie," he announced, swinging his attention back to the older woman. "Would you like it on the outer deck?"

"Please," Julia agreed.

He turned to Selena. "And what would you like to drink? Doug said to include you."

Hesitating for a fraction of a second, she said, "What would you recommend?"

"How about a Sazerac? That's a famous New Orleans cocktail. Invented right here around 1830."

"What's in it?" asked Selena, looking a little dubious.

Greg grinned. "Good things."

Selena was willing to try something new but she hoped a Sazerac wouldn't turn out to be a famous headache in a glass. "Could you be more specific?"

"Sure," Greg said. "It's bourbon with a drop of bitters, sugar, a dash of Pernod and lemon peel."

Bourbon in the afternoon seemed kind of decadent . . . but she was on vacation. Well, when in Dixie, do as the Dixians do, she thought. "Okay. A Sazerac it is."

The women watched as Greg went back behind the bar, pouring a very good sherry for Julia and mixing up Selena's cocktail with a showman's flair. He handed the drinks over with a smile and a wink.

"There you go, ladies. And if there's anything else you need, just call me."

"Incorrigible!" Julia clucked reprovingly under her breath, but Selena noticed the indulgent gleam in the older woman's eye.

On the outer deck the air was seasonally cool with only an occasional breath of breeze. Seated in the wrought-iron deck chair, Selena enjoyed the warmth of the late-afternoon sun on her face. Her back was to the doors of the texas lounge as she faced the Mississippi River.

Julia wrapped her long paisley scarf around her neck with a dramatic flourish and buttoned up her coat, then took a few dainty sips of her sherry. "I'm glad it's not too chilly, dear. Did you know we had snow in New Orleans late last December? The first in fifty years. But it didn't last."

"I heard about that," Selena replied. "We got about three feet in Iowa. Most of it didn't melt until April."

Julia laughed. "Then aren't you glad you're here?"

"As a matter of fact, I really am. I propose a toast. To Christmas in New Orleans!"

They clinked glasses. More passengers were migrating toward the lounge, some of them spilling onto the deck where Selena and Julia sat. Their happy, laughing voices were in keeping with the bustling activity Selena was witnessing on the river.

A large oil tanker was moving slowly up the river while other ships, freighters mostly, were docked along the wharves. There seemed to be an almost constant stream of towboats pushing barges up or down the river. In the middle of all this activity, the ferryboat to Algiers was darting back and forth across the Mississippi.

Selena was absorbed by the river scene until she heard a sharply indrawn gasp from Julia and saw her dismayed expression.

"Julia, what's wrong?"

"It's my nephew. He's here." She bit at her lower lip, her gaze focused on something or someone beyond Selena. "I should have known my brother would send him to try to stop me!"

Selena really didn't want to be caught in the middle of a family dispute. She had already noticed how quickly Julia Barkley's mood could change, but had given her the benefit of the doubt, especially knowing how difficult the holidays could be for people. But a snoopy, judgmental nephew was not someone Selena wanted to meet.

"Ah . . . I'll leave so you can speak to him alone." She started to rise, but Julia lifted a hand to stop her.

"Please stay," she requested with a hint of panic in her low voice. "I'm afraid I'll need your moral support."

There didn't seem to be any way to refuse without appearing heartless. After the way Julia had befriended her, Selena knew she couldn't treat the older woman that way. But she promised herself she wouldn't become involved or take sides as she sat back in her chair, aware of the firm, steady strides approaching the table.

"Hello, Julia." At the sound of the male voice, a chill ran down Selena's spine.

It couldn't possibly be the same man who had propositioned her in the hallway of the hotel, her mind cried in disbelief. Her fingers closed around her cocktail glass, shock waves vibrating through her body.

"What a surprise to see you here, Chance." Julia's voice quavered.

Selena dared an upward glance at the man who had stopped at their table. Her look was returned by coal black eyes hard with recognition before he looked at the older woman seated opposite Selena. With an alacrity that surprised her, he assumed an expression of gentleness and patience.

"Is it a surprise, Julia?" There was affection in his mocking tone.

"How did you know where to find me?" The older woman sighed heavily.

Part of Selena wanted to bolt for safety, but she remained rooted to her chair. Staring fixedly at her glass, she was uncomfortably aware of the thoughts and opinions that were probably going through the man's mind. She tried to comfort herself with the knowledge that she had been trapped by an unfortunate set of circumstances, but it didn't lessen her trembling.

"I stopped by your apartment," he answered his aunt's question. "The girl at the desk told me you'd left on a trip. After that, it was simple deduction that brought me here."

"I suppose Hamilton sent you," Julia declared with a trace of resentment.

"Yes, he was hoping I would be able to persuade you not to do this," he admitted.

"He should mind his own business." Agitation quivered in Julia's reply, drawing Selena's gaze to the tears glistening in the liquid brown eyes.

"Dad is your brother. It's natural for him to be concerned about you and what you're doing with your life," was the calmly reasoning response. Selena sensed that he was choosing his words with care, not wanting family matters to be discussed in front of a stranger like her.

"But it is my life. And I want to do this; it's my right," Julia insisted, a betraying lack of conviction in the strong words.

"He doesn't want you to be hurt—none of us do. What you're doing is foolish, and it's only going to cause unnecessary anguish. Come home with me now, before it goes any further." His tone was persuasive. Even Selena could feel its pull. "I—"

"Chance," Julia interrupted to protest, "you know how I feel about Leslie."

"Julia—" Impatience flashed in his voice, and Selena looked up. His features were etched in grim lines.

"No," Julia stopped the rest of his sentence. "I know what you're going to say. I've heard it all before, and it isn't going to change the way I feel. Please, I'm going to do this," she appealed to him to understand. "Don't try to talk me out of it."

Covertly, Selena watched his reaction to the plea. At first there was a stubborn set to his strong jaw, his narrowed black gaze unrelenting.

Then suddenly his eyes smiled. There was no other way to describe the change in his expression. There was no movement of his mouth, nothing except his eyes crinkling at the corners.

"All right, I've tried. My duty to the family is done," he stated. "All that's left is to have a bon voyage drink with you and the young lady."

There was no smile in his eyes as his gaze swung to Selena. Only a faint challenge glittered through the black shutter he had pulled over them. It was his first formal acknowledgement of her existence, and Selena felt trapped. Every nerve end tautened into alertness.

"Where are my manners?" Julia exclaimed in embarrassed agitation, and she hurried to correct her omission of an introduction, one that Selena would rather have avoided. "Selena, this is my nephew, Chance Barkley. Chance, this is a new friend, Selena Merrick."

"How do you do, Mr. Barkley." The words sounded stilted and cold even to her own ears.

"Miss Merrick." He made a mocking half-bow to acknowledge her greeting, his gaze hard and glittering as it rested on her upturned face. Drawing an empty chair to the table, he directed his next remark to his aunt.

"She must be a very new friend of yours, since I don't recall ever seeing her with you."

There was the faintest emphasis on the last two words, but Selena heard it, as Chance Barkley had guessed she would.

"Oh, yes. As a matter of fact, we just met this weekend," Julia admitted.

The upward flick of his dark brow seemed to say, "You too?" Selena felt like squirming in her seat. It didn't help that he was aware of her discomfiture and was enjoying it.

"You must have a knack for making new friends easily." If it was possible for a man's voice to purr like a smug cat, his did.

The double-edged meaning was not lost on her. "I try, Mr. Barkley," she retorted in a voice riddled with fine tension.

"Call me Chance. You see"—his taunting smile returned—"already I feel as if I've met you before."

Selena's troubled, green-flecked eyes lowered their attention to the quirking line of his mouth, which was subtly drawn, very masculine, and provoked the memory of his potent kisses. Unnerved, she curled her fingers around the glass, ordering her hand not to tremble as she lifted it to her lips. A gulp of the strong cocktail didn't dull her senses, which leaped in alarm.

His glittering regard was distracted by the appearance of the bartender, Greg, at the table. "Would you like something to drink, sir?"

"Scotch. Chivas Regal on the rocks." Chance Barkley leaned back in his chair, relaxed and insolent, but Selena knew it was only a pose. Despite that lazy look he was giving her, he was just as alert as she was.

"Very good, sir," Greg said nodding. "And how about you, Miss Julie? Would you care for another sherry?"

"One is my limit, Greg," she replied primly.

"Yes, ma'am." He smiled and turned to Selena, a flirtatious look in his light brown eyes.

Chance Barkley seemed to notice it. A sardonic expression flashed across his chiseled male features.

"And you, Selena?" asked Greg.

She stared at the glass her fingers circled and the bourbon-soaked sugar that barely covered the bottom. "Nothing, Greg, thanks," she answered stiffly.

When the waiter left, Chance said, "I'm curious. How did the two of you meet?"

"Here," Julia answered. At his sharply questioning look, she laughed and explained, "We met on the dock. We'd both come to see the Delta Queen when she docked. We started talking, then one thing led to another, and I invited Selena to church and Sunday dinner."

"To church?"

He might as well have laughed aloud, she thought with annoyance, as his derisive gaze swung to her. Selena's chin lifted in defensive challenge.

Julia seemed not to notice the undercurrents of tension. "Yes, Selena is a minister's daughter."

"Really? I would never have guessed." His voice was bland, but the look in his eyes held a shadow of contempt. Selena burned slowly in helpless anger, unable to explain.

"We had a very enjoyable time together yesterday," Julia went on blithely. "And when I decided I was going to take this trip, I—"

"It was only yesterday that you decided to go on this trip?" Chance looked at his aunt with thoughtful contemplation.

"I d-did have a few doubts before then," Julia hesitated, glancing anxiously at Selena. "But it was entirely my own decision."

Selena winced inwardly. Julia wasn't a very good liar,

even though her statement was half true. Selena knew she had influenced the decision, however inadvertently, and Julia's assertion to the contrary held a false note. Selena saw the flash of doubt in his expression as Chance Barkley heard it too.

"In fact," Julia went on, as if to cover her previous words, "once I decided to go, I realized how lucky I was that Selena was coming too." At that harmless statement, Chance Barkley's gaze narrowed into black diamond chips slicing over Selena. "You know how I hate to travel alone, Chance." Julia smiled at Selena. "And Selena is such good company."

"Lucky for her that she can take off work at a moment's notice." His smiling comment didn't fool her, not with that sharp edge meant to remind her of his knowledge of her alleged profession.

"I came here on vacation," she retorted.

"We all need one now and again," Chance stated with an expressive shrug, the hard glint not leaving his eyes, "no matter what we do for a living."

Selena was just about to inform him of her true occupation, but Greg's arrival with Chance's drink checked the words. When he left, Selena decided it would be useless to tell him. Chance Barkley would simply assume that it was a story she had concocted to make herself appear respectable in Julia's eyes.

"Aren't you concerned that you might find this cruise boring, Selena?" Chance sipped at his drink, looking oh-so-nonchalant.

"I think it'll be interesting," Selena countered. "Why should it be boring?"

"Haven't you noticed?" He swirled the ice cubes in his glass, glancing at her over its top and making her aware of his powerfully handsome features. "The majority of your fellow passengers belong to my aunt's generation."

"That doesn't bother me, Mr. Barkley."

"Chance," he corrected.

"Chance." Her teeth grated as she uttered his name, pinning a cool smile on her mouth.

There was something coldly calculating in the look he returned that made her want to panic. She sensed a determination in his character that could border on ruthlessness if the situation warranted it.

But she couldn't gauge just how vengeful he felt over that incident in his hotel room and the cash she hadn't been able to return to him. If only she hadn't been so conscientious about mailing that money order in the same amount to a charity. She would be happy to hand it over to him right here, right now, and vindicate herself to some degree.

Of course, the last thing she wanted to do was explain to him what she had done and why she had done it—and she sure as hell didn't want to explain anything about the rest of her encounter with Chance in the hotel room to Julia.

The hoarse whistle of the steamboat blew a long and two shorts, hesitated, and repeated the sequence. At its cessation a monotone voice issued an announcement over the public-address system.

"All ashore that's going ashore. All aboard that's coming aboard."

"Oh dear," Julia murmured ruefully. "That means you have to leave, Chance."

"So it does," he agreed with a certain grimness. He downed most of his drink, setting the glass on the table as he pushed himself to his feet. He towered over Julia's chair. "There isn't anything I can say to persuade you to come home with me?"

"No." She shook her head in answer to his half- statement, half-question. "Don't be angry with me, Chance," she pleaded softly.

A warm and gentle smile softened the hard contours of his face, crinkling his eyes. "I'm not angry, Julia, never with you. You should know that."

"Perhaps," she conceded, with a wealth of affection gleaming in her brown eyes as she gazed up at him. "But it makes me feel better to hear you say it."

Bending down, he kissed her powdered cheek. Selena glimpsed the springing thickness of black hair curling around his collar. As Chance straightened, his gaze sought Selena. He nodded his head in her direction and walked away, disappearing into the interior of the texas lounge.

What had it been—a concession? Selena wondered. She was fully aware that she had been spared because she was with Julia. The boat would be leaving in a few minutes or he might have separated her from his aunt. And that might have been very humiliating and difficult.

"Chance is almost like a son to me," Julia remarked, pride and sadness mixing in her expression. "He used to call me his 'other mother.' He was always so protective when he was young. He still is, in his own way. It wasn't fair of Hamilton to send Chance to stop me."

"He did seem very fond of you." Selena knew her remark was inadequate, but none other came to mind.

"Yes, he's often said that his mother and I are the only women he needs in his life on a permanent basis." Julia sipped at her sherry, thoughtful and vaguely reminiscent. "Not that he has much time for a private life now that Hamilton has turned everything over to him except the stud farm. And Chance hasn't been content to just manage. He's had to build and expand, take risks and experiment. Never foolishly, you understand."

Selena nodded. She suddenly felt weak and nerveless. She finished the sugary dregs of her cocktail, hoping it would somehow fortify her. It didn't. She hadn't realized how much of a strain she had been under until this minute. Seeing Chance again so unexpectedly after all these months made her feel shaky and limp inside.

Assured by a nod that Selena was listening, Julia continued to talk. "Chance always holds on with one hand and reaches out to take what he wants with the other. Of course, he's always willing to pay the price. He doesn't expect to get it for free."

Selena paled at that—the words were coming too close to her own experience—but Julia didn't seem to notice.

"I've often wondered if his name had anything to do with the type of man he is. I suppose not, because his grandfather was very much like Chance, too—willing to take risks."

"I hope he's a good loser," Selena commented.

"Oh, he is," Julia insisted. "Before he makes a move, he weighs the odds. No matter how much he loses, Chance doesn't blink an eye, because he's already considered that possibility from the first. Unless he's been cheated. Then it's an entirely different matter."

Uh oh. Chance definitely believed she had cheated him. Selena's stomach fluttered. A series of wheezing discordant notes sounded from the stern of the riverboat, distracting Julia from her subject.

"Listen! They're going to start the calliope concert. Would you like to walk to the sundeck? There's also a welcome-aboard party in the aft cabin lounge, if you'd rather attend that," Julia suggested cheerily.

"Actually, Julia, I think I would prefer to go to my room. I'd like to shower and do some unpacking before dinner," Selena said with an unsteady smile.

"You go right ahead, honey. Dinner is at seven in the Orleans Room. We're seated at table 40."

The band had finished playing in the texas lounge, although the banjo player was plunking out a few notes

as Selena made her way around the bow of the boat to
the side of the texas deck where her cabin was located.
For a time, the banjo vied with the calliope, both playing festive songs of the season.

"O Come All Ye Faithful" sounded truly weird on a
banjo, Selena decided. But soon the texas lounge was
behind her, and all she heard was the calliope.

Pausing at the railing outside her cabin, she didn't feel
very festive. In the windows of the river terminal building where they were docked, she could see the reflection of the bundled-up passengers gathered on the top
deck listening to the musical steam whistles of the calliope. The short December day was drawing to a close,
and it was noticeably cooler now that the sun was going
down.

She pulled up her jacket hood, and her gaze strayed
to the spectators scattered along the dock below her.

A little girl waved to her and Selena smiled and
waved back, the smile soon fading to a faint curve. Her
gaze wandered the length of the dock forward to the
gangplank. There it was arrested by the tall, muscular
figure of Chance Barkley, standing with his hands
thrust in his pants pocket, talking with the security
guard on duty at the gangway.

As if he possessed an inner radar attuned to her,
Chance turned his head, seeming to look directly at
her. Shaken, Selena stared back, a fiery heat licking
through her veins.

A gambler of sorts, Julia had called him. Selena conceded that he had some of the necessary qualities: the
facile charm to trip the innocent, the unrelenting confidence to bluff his opponent, and the black shutters
that could keep any of his thoughts from being revealed in his eyes.

Perhaps most of all, Chance Barkley had a certain
aura of danger about him gained from taking risks, a

calculated recklessness that attracted. Combine that with his vital maleness and hard good looks and the end result was potent.

The dark head turned back to the guard, releasing Selena from his ensnaring gaze. She pivoted abruptly, searching through her purse for the cabin key. Her hand shook as she inserted it in the lock and opened the door.

Chapter Five

The shower had the necessary reviving effect on Selena, making her feel alive again and a lot more cheerful. Her skin tingled as she rubbed herself dry, wrapping up her wet hair in an improvised turban and the rest of herself in an outsized terry-cloth robe. How unglamorous, she thought when she looked in the mirror. Giant fuzzy bunny slippers would be all she needed to complete the effect.

Barefoot, she stepped into the main area of the cabin. With the louvered wood insets raised, she couldn't see out of the window. Walking over, she slid the shutter halfway down. Instead of looking out through the glass at the windowed terminal building, she saw a strip of brown river water.

She remembered what the chief purser had said and smiled to herself. Something about the mighty Mississippi being too thick to drink and too thin to plow, and how the catfish needed extra-long whiskers to find their way around in it.

It occurred to her that they ought to be leaving the

dock right about now, but there was no sensation of
movement at all. Then she listened and heard the
rhythmic thump of the engines, distantly, almost a vi-
bration instead of a sound.

She turned from the window after raising the louver
and walked to the chest of drawers. Her traveling alarm
clock said twenty minutes to seven, plenty of time to
dress before dinner. Picking up her hairdryer, she
plugged it in and began to dry her hair in sections, hoping it wouldn't frizz. It wasn't long before she was
brushing it, something she always found soothing. She
stroked the bristles through her hair until it was crack-
ling and glistening like burnished copper.

A sharp rap at her cabin door brought a puzzled
frown to her forehead. She hesitated, still holding the
hairbrush in her hand.

"Who is it?" she called, positive it wouldn't be Julia.

"The steward," came the response, partially muffled
by the door between them.

Setting her brush on the dresser, Selena glanced over
her shoulder to see if any of her luggage was missing. It
was all there. With a little shrug of bewilderment, she
reached for the door, unlocking the deadbolt and holding on to the knob to open the door.

In the next second, she stepped backward, instinctively avoiding the towering man who stood there. Her
startled cry ended the instant she recognized him. He
entered without an invitation and shut the door behind
him.

"I thought you left," she whispered, not at all happy
to see Chance Barkley.

"I think we have some unfinished business, you and
I." His voice was calm and low.

She clutched the lapels of her outsize robe together.
She was too surprised and angry to be afraid. She

stamped her bare foot and he only grinned, not seeming exactly intimidated. She might as well have been wearing giant fuzzy bunny slippers.

"No, we don't. Get out," she ordered in a hissing rush.

"I don't think I will," he said, defying her complacently and taking a step toward her.

Selena backed up. She grabbed for the hairbrush, clutching the smooth handle and brandishing it at him.

"Keep away from me!"

Chance came closer and looked at her curiously. "Hmm. Is that thing loaded? I don't think I've ever been threatened with a hairbrush." He plucked it from her fingers and set it back on the dresser. "Didn't your mother ever teach you to play nice, Red?" The low, taunting voice was smooth and complacent. "I'm sure you don't want to hurt me. And I don't want to hurt you."

"I want you out of here. What do I have to do, bash your head in? Oh!" Selena gasped with surprise as he came even closer and suddenly took her in his arms, crushing her soft shape to his length.

"You're a bloodthirsty little thief," he reproved mockingly.

"Let me go or I'll scream," she threatened, tilting her head back to glare at him. "I mean it!"

He shifted his position, easily capturing both of her wrists with one big hand. "We can't have that," he murmured.

And Selena realized he was ignoring her warning. Taking a quick breath, she opened her mouth to scream, but his free hand was at the back of her head, holding it still while he smothered her cry in a very, very interesting kiss. Furious with him and excited by his sensual skill at the same time, Selena resisted to some degree, muted cries and words of damnation coming from her throat, to be swallowed by his mouth.

This can't be happening, she thought desperately. Not again.

Powerless against his superior strength, she kicked at his shins with her bare feet, nearly breaking her toe. Ouch. That had clearly hurt her much more than it hurt him.

That discovery was quickly replaced by another as she moved backward, one as alarming as the first. The backs of her legs touched the bed and she lost her balance, though she was still in his arms and, worse yet, enjoying it.

With a balancing knee on the mattress, Chance took the opportunity to lower her to the bed. She took the initiative. As the solidness of the bed formed beneath her, he released her wrists.

Selena didn't question his reason, but took advantage of it to bring her arms around, spreading her hands against his chest before his weight came down on her.

He seemed content to let her stop him, stretching his length beside her, even slackening his hold a little.

With her lips throbbing from the excellent kiss, Selena tried to roll away from the tautly muscled man lying beside her, but his large hand covered her hipbone to bring her back. She realized with a start that that wasn't all his hand was doing. He let his fingers trail along one lapel of her robe as if he was about to fling it open.

"No, don't!" she gasped in panic.

"Such modesty, Red." His throaty voice laughed at her attempt to slap away his hands from her robe. "You act as though I haven't seen you in less. But I have. I remember that lace bra . . . and those flowered granny panties. Unforgettable."

Her mind was a whirl of embarrassment, anger, and some other feelings she didn't want to name. Her thoughts jumbled one on top of the other, making no sense. The only coherent thought that pierced her confusion was that Chance wasn't even supposed to be here.

"Why aren't you in New Orleans where you belong?" Selena accused breathlessly. "Don't you know the boat has left port?"

"Yes, I know." He was nibbling at her collarbone. Her face was turned against the pillow as she struggled to stop his roving hands. Her nerve ends were tingling where his firm mouth explored, his warm breath caressing her sensitive skin.

"You were off the boat. I saw you," she declared, wondering whether she wanted to resist him much longer. "How did you get back on?"

"I slipped aboard when no one was looking," Chance murmured against her skin.

"What?" Selena wasn't sure she had heard him right, what with the clamoring of her other senses.

She stopped trying to ward off his wayward hands. The priority had shifted to ending the arousal those male lips were causing. Her hands cupped his smoothly shaven jaw to push his face away from her neck.

Selena partially succeeded in lifting his head, her fingers slipping into the midnight black of his hair. The silky crispness of the thick strands curled around her fingers and against her palms, the feel of it incredibly sensual.

"I stowed away," drawled Chance, and began an intimate exploration of her face, the wing of her brow and the curving sweep of her lashes. "You'll have to hide me."

Her fluttering lashes opened at the last low statement, while her hands slipped to his shoulder, splayed and resisting. "I'll do no such thing!" she denied hotly. "I'll turn you over to the captain, and he'll put you ashore immediately. Failing that, I'll throw you overboard myself. Or ask one of the crew to do it."

"Really? Which one?" Lifting his head a few inches, he studied her lazily, mockery glinting in his jet dark eyes at the indignant flames flashing in hers. His hand raised to cup the underside of her jaw. "Are you working this boat?"

"Shut up! You know that's not—" But he didn't know it wasn't true. And she had a feeling that the more she tried to explain, the less sense she would make.

His thumb rubbed the point of her chin. There was something possessive in his action, as if he intended to claim her in some way. Selena could read his unspoken thought in his eyes and remained warily motionless.

"If you turned me over to the captain, Red, I'd simply have to tell him about you." He touched her trembling lips as he added, "And the money you stole from me."

Swallowing, Selena tightly insisted, "I didn't steal your money." Her lips moved against his thumb as she spoke. It was not an altogether unpleasant sensation.

His veiled look focused on her mouth, sending her pulse rocketing, while his thumb directed itself to a more thorough exploration of her lower lip. His expression was completely masked as his gaze flicked to the round alertness of her eyes.

"Am I supposed to regard the orange dress and shoes you left as equal to the value of the money you took?" he inquired in soft challenge. "Neither of them happen to be in my size or my color."

"That isn't what I meant," Selena protested.

"Then what did you mean?" His voice was as smooth

as polished steel. "I gave you the money—you took it. And I didn't get what I paid for. I don't like being conned, Red. Nobody cheats me and gets away with it."

"That was months ago," Selena began, sensing the anger behind his words, though she suspected it had more to do with being played for a fool. "I didn't mean to take your money." With an effort, she kept her voice calm and firm.

"Didn't you?" A black eyebrow arched in mocking skepticism as his thumb moved away from her mouth.

"Honestly, I didn't," she insisted with a trace of taut anger. "When I grabbed my purse, I'd forgotten you'd put the money in it. All I was interested in was my key card that was in it."

"Your key card? You had a room at the hotel?"

"Yes, I was staying there."

"How convenient for your clients," Chance drawled.

"I don't have any clients," Selena retorted in exasperation. "It was all a joke."

"Then why am I not laughing?" he countered.

"Because you took everything seriously," she explained earnestly, her brows drawing together in a slight frown.

"When money is involved, I'm always serious." Flat black eyes regarded her steadily and her own faltered under the look.

"Hey, it really was a mistake," she began nervously. "I'm—"

But Chance interrupted her. "I almost forgot. You're a minister's daughter."

"From Iowa," Selena tacked on helpfully.

Laughter rolled from his throat, rich and deep, as he threw his head back and relaxed his grip. At least it gave her a chance to wriggle free. She moved a little distance away from his body, but she didn't get up. His laugh died to a low chuckle, but amusement glinted brightly in his eyes, challenging her assertion.

"A minister's daughter from Iowa," he repeated. "Is that supposed to make your claim legitimate? Because you're from Iowa?"

He laughed softly again, infuriating Selena to the point where she wanted to whack him with the hairbrush. But he had placed it well out of her reach. "It happens to be the truth! And I don't give a damn whether you believe me or not!"

His eyes widened in pretend shock. "What would your father say if he heard such language?" he murmured reprovingly.

Selena gave a frustrated groan. "Why won't you listen to me? I tried to return the money to you."

"I'm sure you did." There was a slight trace of disbelief in his voice.

"I did," Selena snapped. "When I discovered it in my purse, I didn't know what to do. I was going to slip it under your door when you were out. I don't suppose you remember that phone call you got where there was nobody on the other end. It was me, calling to see if you were in your room."

"I don't. Anyway, how can you prove that when there was no one on the other end?" Chance continued to bait her.

"I guess I can't," she retorted. "You seem to be determined not to believe me."

"Okay, I'll give you the benefit of the doubt. If you called, you might have been trying to figure out a way to get back into my room to retrieve your dress and shoes," he pointed out.

"I wasn't," Selena denied his claim in an impatient burst. "As a matter of fact, I even tried to leave your money at the desk, but you'd already checked out."

"Why didn't you just return it in person instead of sneaking around?" His look was bland, unrevealing and unconvinced.

"Are you crazy?" she said scornfully. "And risk ending up like this—in bed with you?" Uncomfortably aware of her own reluctance to end the odd game they seemed to be playing, she tried to sit up, but his hand pressed her shoulders to the bed. "I ran out of your hotel room to avoid this!" she hissed.

His gaze narrowed thoughtfully as he weighed her words. "All right," he conceded. "Return my money and I'll forget the whole thing."

Selena paled, the anger flowing out of her with a rush. "I don't have it anymore," she said in a small voice.

She hadn't been aware of any softening in his expression until it hardened. "You don't have it anymore," he repeated her statement. "Well, like you said, it was months ago and it's not as if you were expecting to meet me here. I suppose I'm wasting my time by asking you what happened to it?"

"The desk clerk wouldn't give me your name or address so I couldn't mail you a money order for the same amount. And I wasn't about to send you a personal check with my personal information on it."

"But you thought it was okay to ask for mine," he pointed out.

"Only because— Oh, shut up! I'm so confused!" She picked up a pillow and hugged it to herself like a shield.

"But you're beautiful when you're confused," he mocked. "That red face. That faraway look, as you try to figure out just exactly what to say to a guy you ditched with his pants half off."

So she had hurt his pride. That was a much, much bigger deal to a man like this than the money, Selena had a feeling. She was silent for a few moments as she tried desperately to come up with a way to explain the dilemma she had been in. "Look, that money wasn't mine, so I couldn't keep it."

"Oh, no, a minister's daughter couldn't keep money that didn't rightfully belong to her," he agreed wryly. "So what did you do with it?"

"I gave it away." She couldn't tell whether he was believing any part of what she said. "To a charity."

A smile seemed to play with his mouth, the corners twitching. "Do you expect me to believe that?"

"It's the truth, I swear," Selena vowed.

"It seems to me," he said, pausing to watch his finger as it traced the sensitive cord on the side of her neck, "that we're back to where we started—with the money paid and the goods still to be delivered."

"Will you stop?" What he was implying was something she knew she actually desired, but she knew better than to give in to that desire. When it came right down to it, she didn't know Chance Barkley from Adam, and she didn't want to know him.

It was not as if she could ever bring him home to Mom and Dad. She could just imagine the introductions. *Hey, everybody, this is Chance. I met him in New Orleans when I was pretending to be a hooker and he believed me. Isn't that a hoot?* As far as they knew, she was a virgin and would remain a virgin until some lucky guy got her down the aisle, tossed her garter to the tallest bridegroom, drove her away to a honeymoon hotel, and removed her white satin gown using only his teeth.

But this was the Delta Queen, not a honeymoon hotel, and she had Chance's dotty maiden aunt to answer to. As romantic as Julia was, she would get the idea immediately if Selena decided to fool around with her dangerously handsome nephew. No, things had gone as far as they were going to go. But before she could say anything more to Chance, his mouth descended toward her. She turned her head to elude it.

"Don't!"

Winding some of her tousled red hair around his fingers, Chance tugged her back, capturing her lips with practiced ease. His other hand slipped inside the robe and stroked the bareness of her stomach, arousing a tumult of emotion that she was powerless to control. His seductive mastery was completely beyond her experience.

When he felt her trembling response, he lowered his head, seeking the hollow of her throat. Selena's resistance stiffened as she felt the bra strap slipping from her shoulder and the trailing tips of his fingers making their way to the exposed swell of her breast. She clawed at his hand, only to have it close firmly over the lacy cup of her brassiere.

"Don't do this, please," she pleaded.

"Why not?" His voice was husky and persuasive.

"Um, I'm not that kind of girl?"

"You're pretty funny." He followed the curve of her neck to her ear, nuzzling it, his warm breath arousing and stimulating. "Are you trying to convince me that you don't sell your favors despite what I overheard at the café?"

"I don't, no," Selena protested, fighting the breathlessness that had attacked her voice. "Those drunks thought that was what I did and I just went along with it. It was . . . it was just a little harmless fun, a joke. When I saw you later at the hotel, I didn't know what to do. One lie just led to another."

He moved, his mouth playing over her lips, teasing and tantalizing them into wanting his kiss.

"Isn't that a strange kind of joke for a minister's daughter to be playing?"

"I don't think you've known many ministers' children," she breathed tightly. "We tend to be more mischievous than other kids."

A swift, hard kiss effectively silenced her before Chance unexpectedly levered himself from her. Propped up by an elbow, he studied her flushed and shaken expression.

"Let's suppose I believe that. Now what?" he challenged.

"Do you believe me?" She searched his dark, unreadable features.

"I believe at least part of your story, although I find your tale about what happened to my money is a little hard to swallow," he returned.

"It's true," Selena rushed. "I have the stub for the money order at home. I could show it to you."

"Sure. Let's ask the captain to go left at the Des Moines River and you can go get it."

"Then I'll send it to you."

"That would involve giving you my name and address, and I'm not going to," Chance said firmly. "Besides, you probably spent it to pay for this cruise." His gaze narrowed. "Unless my aunt paid your passage."

"No, she didn't," she flashed, resenting his accusation. "This trip was a gift."

"From one of your, um, admirers?"

"No! I don't have any admirers!"

"Hard to believe," Chance taunted softly. "Well, however you came by the money for the fare, it'll be a good investment. Hoping for a high rate of return?"

"What are you talking about?" Selena frowned.

"I'm sure there are several rich old guys on board. Easy pickings."

"I'm not looking for a husband," she interrupted coldly.

"I wasn't talking about husbands, Selena."

She glared at him.

"But speaking of easy pickings, my aunt is a trusting, vulnerable woman," he concluded. "She's completely taken in by you. You know that, don't you?"

"I don't think I like what you're implying." A wary fire smoldered in her eyes as she shrugged. Her hair tumbled over her shoulders and she pushed it back.

"Not any more than I do," Chance stated. "But if you were planning to con any money out of her, on whatever pretext that red head of yours has dreamed up, you'd better forget it. Because, honey, I'm going to see to it that you don't get a penny."

Selena was indignant. "It was never my intention!"

"As if you would admit that it was," he jeered.

"You have some nerve!" Her voice trembled with the violence of her emotions. With a surge of strength, she pushed him away. "Get out of my cabin!"

As she sat up, Chance rolled over onto his back, folding his hands beneath his head. "But there is still the matter of where I'm going to spend the night, isn't there?" he asked, looking very much at home.

"Well, you certainly aren't going to stay here!" she snapped.

His gaze slid over the single bed and Selena already cramped against the wall. "No, it would be too crowded with both of us, but luckily you have a spare bed that's empty."

"I'd sooner have a snake in my room than you!" Selena blurted out, discovering she was treacherously close to tears. "So you can just get out and see if the Barkley name can work any wonders with the captain."

Laughter again rolled from his throat as he swung himself to his feet with an ease unexpected in a man of his size. His hand was in front of him, holding a key.

"What's that?" Selena eyed it warily, almost afraid

that he had somehow managed to obtain her cabin key from her purse.

"The key to my cabin," he informed her. "You see"—his confidence was clear in every line of his stance—"when I found you with Julia, I arranged for a passage on this cruise so I could keep an eye on you."

"Does Julia know?"

"Not yet. I wanted to find out what your game was first," he answered.

Resentment seethed in Selena. "Julia told me what an important and busy man you are. I suppose I should feel flattered that you canceled everything and came on this cruise because of me." She stiffened as another thought occurred to her. "Or is it entirely because of me?" At his silence, she pursued it. "You want to stop this thing with Leslie, don't you?"

"That's a personal, family matter and none of your business," Chance stated coldly.

"Then I'm right," Selena concluded. "How can you be so heartless? Julia is old enough to make her own decisions. Your family has no right to stand in the way of something that will bring her happiness."

In the short time she'd known Julia, Selena had picked up on the older woman's fragility, and she wasn't about to let her obnoxious beast of a nephew give her grief. In fact, she felt quite protective of Julia Barkley. And wildly attracted to the obnoxious beast, she had to admit. There was no figuring out those conflicting emotions, not right this minute. She looked forward to the time when she could curl up in this bed and be alone and think it all over.

Chance cleared his throat. "I have no intention of discussing it with you. And I suggest that you stay out of it." There was a unshakable calm in his tone.

"Is that right?" Although intimidated, Selena still defied him.

"Yes." His gaze glittered over her, implying amusement at her challenge. "Put some clothes on. Unless you intend to go to dinner like that?"

"I'll get dressed"—she paused pointedly, her lips tightening—"when you leave."

"You're only going to be putting clothes over what I've already seen." His eyes were crinkled, laughing at her again. "Is this what you're planning to wear?" Turning, he nodded to the pink flowered dress laid out on the other bed.

"It is," Selena acknowledged stiffly.

"Very pretty." Chance picked it up, fingering the material in a way that was oddly intimate, almost as if they had been lovers for a long time and were just getting dressed to go out to a party. "Although it isn't nearly as sexy as the orange one." He tossed the pink dress to her. "Put it on."

Glaring at him, Selena had the distinct impression that if she refused, he was quite capable of taking a hand in the procedure himself. This was one time, she decided, when discretion was the better part of valor. Clutching her robe tightly shut and holding the dress in front of her for added protection, she slid from the bed and retreated behind the closed door of the bathroom.

When she emerged from the bathroom several minutes later, fully clothed and with fresh makeup, Chance was standing at the window. He turned, running a practiced eye over her.

"Took you long enough," he observed, but without complaining.

"I had trouble with the zipper," Selena admitted, smoothing the obi sash at the waistline.

The dress was girly, in a simple retro style that she had seen on *Sex and the City,* from its slender band neck with its demure front slash to the artful seams that curved over her body to open into a full skirt. The delicately flowered print was in the softest pinks imaginable.

"I could have given you a hand," Chance stated, watching as she slipped her sheer-stockinged feet into her shoes.

"Yes, you're good at zippers," she retorted. "You got my dress off in record time back in April."

"Try me on bra hooks," he said smugly. "I once set an Olympic record for the one-handed removal of—"

She held up a hand. "Too much information. You can shut up now. I mean it."

"Shall we go?" Her purse was in the hand he extended to her.

Holding her tongue was an effort, since the urge was strong to tell him where she thought he should go, but her sense of self-preservation and her concern for Julia prevailed. Taking her purse and a pale pink cardigan for warmth in case the dining room was chilly, she walked to the door. As she reached to unlock it, his hand was there to turn the key and push the door open, his arm brushing her shoulder.

Selena stepped quickly over the raised threshold onto the outer deck. Anxious to escape the confining intimacy of the cabin, she nearly walked into the path of two other couples heading for the stairs.

Chance's hands were there, curving into the short sleeves covering her upper arms and pulling her back, and she tensed under his hold.

One of the men glanced from her to Chance to the cabin door swinging closed. He couldn't possibly know that she and Chance weren't really together, and she felt the growing pink of embarrassment warming her cheeks. The boat was not so large that at some point the man would discover they weren't.

As the two couples descended the stairs, Chance released Selena to move from behind her to her side. She averted her head, but not quickly enough to escape his observant gaze. She tried to hurry to the stairs, but his hand gripped her elbow to forestall her rush.

"Are you blushing?" he questioned, tipping his head down for a closer inspection.

"Yes." She muttered the admission under her breath.

"Why?" Chance sounded amused.

"Because I don't like the idea of those people seeing you come out of my cabin," she retorted. "They might get the wrong idea."

"Just as long as they believe that you're with me, I don't particularly care what other ideas they get," Chance stated.

"Well, I'm not with you!" Selena flashed.

"For the duration of this cruise, everyone is going to think you are," he informed her. "Because I'm going to keep you in my sight every waking minute."

"Is that right?" Her chin lifted in the beginnings of defiance.

His mouth curved into a smile, one that didn't reach his eyes, as she knew it would if it was genuine. "I suggest that you be glad I said every *waking* minute."

"If that's supposed to be a threat, I'm not frightened," she countered.

"Suit yourself." Chance shrugged, and released her elbow. "But you'd do well to remember all that I've said."

Selena turned up her nose at his advice and walked to the stairs, well aware that he was following her. And she was also aware that there was very little she could do about it, short of pushing him overboard, and she didn't have the strength for that.

Not until she had reached the cabin deck did Selena realize that she had no idea where the meals were served. She glanced around, hoping to see fellow passengers on their way to dinner so that she might follow them. There wasn't a soul in sight.

It grated to have to turn to Chance. "Do you know where the Orleans Room is located?" she requested stiffly.

The grooves on either side of his mouth deepened now as his lips tightened to conceal a smile. He seemed to know how much it irritated Selena to ask his assistance.

"I believe I do, yes," he drawled, and guided her to the area where the forward cabin lounge was located.

As Selena entered the lounge ahead of Chance, Julia saw her. "I was wondering where you were, Selena," she exclaimed. "I was about to go down without you." Then she saw the man following Selena. "Chance! What are you doing here?" Julia greeted him with surprise and delight, with none of the trepidation she had voiced at his appearance before the boat left the dock.

"I decided to come on the cruise with you," was his brief reply. He nodded to Selena, adding, "I found . . . Selena." He paused deliberately before using her given name while his gaze flicked to her red hair, reminding Selena of his nickname for her. "She was wandering about lost, and I volunteered to show her where the dining room was."

"Oh dear," Julia exclaimed in dismay. "I didn't tell you where it was located, did I?"

"It's all right," Selena assured her. "There was a map in the nightstand. But Chance has been . . ." She glared at him and finished her sentence through gritted teeth. "So helpful."

"Thank you for directing her here." Julia smiled at her nephew, then sighed happily. "I'm so glad you've come, Chance." She clasped one of his hands warmly between her own. "I very much wanted a member of my family at the wedding, and now you're here."

"Yes, I'm here," Chance agreed blandly. But Selena noticed the way his jaw hardened when Julia referred to her marriage to Leslie. She knew intuitively that if Chance had his way, the marriage would never take place. Obviously he was going to do everything in his power to stop it. Selena resented, on Julia's behalf, this desire to dominate.

Chapter Six

"Shall we go down to dinner?" Chance suggested, interrupting their preprandial conversation, clearly bored with Julia's romantic prattle and Selena's automatic replies.

Behind the grand staircase was a stairwell leading below. The identifying words *Orleans Room* were in plain sight. At the base of the stairs, double doors of cream white stood open in welcome, giving them a glimpse of the holiday decorations and the delicate lights that softly illuminated the room. The maitre d' stood just inside the doors, resplendent and distinguished in a well-cut black suit, and smiling a greeting as the trio descended the stairs.

"You and your companion have table 40 as usual, Miss Julia," the man announced with grave courtesy, before turning to Chance. "And your table, sir?"

From his suit pocket, Chance withdrew a round numbered disk indicating table 83. He handed it to the maitre d'.

Selena darted Chance a look through sweeping lashes. He caught and read the message written in her eyes, triumphant relief that she wouldn't have to suffer his presence at the dinner table.

"Your table is on the starboard side, sir," the maitre d' explained. "Your waiter will show you."

"This is my nephew, André," Julia spoke up. "Chance Barkley."

"Mr. Barkley," the man bowed slightly as he shook Chance's hand. "It's a pleasure to have you aboard." Then, to all three of them, he said, "Enjoy the buffet."

The tables of food ran the length of the room down its center, splitting the dining area in half. Most of the passengers had already helped themselves and were seated at their assigned tables. Filing behind Julia, Selena noted the spaciousness of the room. There was no suggestion of crowding, and the leisurely atmosphere invited her to take her time over the varied selection of New Orleans specialities and plainer fare for the unadventurous.

Selena was glad there were identifying signs for some of the entrées. She read them, trying to make up her mind. In general, when she wore an expensive dress, she ate things that matched it, just in case. Saved on dry cleaning.

She savored the delicious aroma of the gumbo for a moment. But she was pretty sure it involved okra. A lot of okra. Slippery stuff when boiled, and her least favorite vegetable. And the gumbo broth was a deep red. No.

She moved along to a platter of crawfish étouffée and another filled with shrimp remoulade, a giant bowl of red beans and rice, and a platter with muffuletta sandwiches piled high and dripping chopped-olive dressing. She decided on the shrimp.

Their waiter was at the end of the buffet to carry their plates to the table for four. An elderly couple were already occupying two of the chairs, and there was a friendly round of introductions as Selena and Julia joined them.

Selena couldn't remember the last time she had enjoyed such an unhurried meal. Against the middle of the far wall was a bandstand, complete with a grand piano. A man sat at the keyboard, softly playing a medley of show songs and popular Christmas tunes. Her gaze wandered to the opposite side of the room and glimpsed the satin blackness of the back of Chance's head, but he was too far away to disturb her serenity.

They went back to the buffet when the desserts were set out, choosing between the killer chocolate confections, traditional bread pudding with whiskey sauce, and pralines.

Their waiter, another college boy, appeared unobtrusively at the table, refilling Selena's coffee cup and whisking away her dessert plate. Selena relaxed in her chair to listen to the dreamily soothing piano music.

The arrival of night had darkened the windows. Water shimmered occasionally beyond the panes where the lights from the steamboat touched the river's surface.

Yet the sun-yellow walls of the dining room kept the mood mellow, enhanced by the glow of Tiffany lamps located on the walls between each of the green shuttered windows. The individual lights resembled a trio of palm fronds, their stalks secured with a gold bow, while crystal pendants were suspended from the tip of each golden spiked leaflet.

The hoarse whistle of the steamboat blasted a single long wail. In the distance came a long answering toot, low and deep, reverberating into the interior of the boat. Curious, Selena waited expectantly for something to happen.

Julia noticed her expression and smiled. "Our captain just signaled to another vessel coming down river that we would pass on the port side," she explained. "The other vessel, probably a towboat with barges, returned the signal. Two whistles would mean the starboard side."

"I see," Selena said. "It's amazing how much you know about this boat."

"It's written on the walls by the door." Julia pointed.

Selena turned slightly in her chair. On the wall to the left of the double doors was written ONE WHISTLE PORT. On the right it read TWO WHISTLES STARB'RD. The sign also signified which side was which.

"The vessel will be going by shortly," Julia added. "Would you like to go up for a better view?"

"I'll get the coats if you give me your key," Selena said with a smile. The other couple at their table had already left.

"Of course," the older woman acknowledged, folding her linen napkin and placing it on the table near her coffee cup.

When Selena returned, the table had been completely cleared and Julia was waiting, looking at her own reflection in the darkened window across the dining room with a dreamy expression. She started when Selena touched her shoulder gently.

"There you are, dear. I was just thinking . . . Oh, never mind." She trailed off and took her coat and dramatic scarf from Selena's arm. "Thank you for bringing my things. I expect it's quite cool outside by now."

They went up and chose spots along the rail, watching the massed barges and pushing towboat go past from where they stood in front of the forward cabin lounge. Selena had seen similar barges and towboats from the New Orleans dock, but it was a much more impressive sight from the moving steamboat as the two vessels met and glided slowly and silently past one another.

When the towboat was gone, there was only shadowing darkness on the great river that flowed past them. Julia shivered. "Shall we go in?"

"Yes. It's beautiful, but it is chilly." Selena held the door open for the older woman. She stepped in and found Chance standing nearby, holding an unlit slender cigar between his fingers. "Hello, ladies. I was just going to go outside to smoke."

"Show's over," Selena said. "The towboat passed. It was fun to watch."

"You'll get used to it." His perceptive gaze moved over her face, rosy pink from the cool December air. "In a few days, you won't even glance out the window when the pilot blows the whistle."

Selena didn't respond to his cynical observation, but she hoped he was wrong. Instead she remarked, "Delicious dinner, wasn't it? I hope you enjoyed your meal."

"I did. Did you?"

Selena managed only a nod before Julia broke in to ask, "Chance, do you recall what time the show in the Orleans Room is this evening?"

"Nine-fifteen, I believe," he answered.

"You are going, aren't you?" Julia directed the question to her nephew.

"I thought I would, yes."

"It should be very good," Julia remarked idly. "They have some excellent entertainers aboard. I know you'll enjoy it, Selena."

"Oh, but I'm not going." She had made up her mind the instant that she heard that Chance Barkley was.

"But it's your first night," Julia protested, while Chance smiled knowingly.

"Yes, I know, but it's been a full day, and I want to write to my parents. I promised them a day-by-day account of the trip. They're thinking of taking this cruise themselves next year." Selena felt her excuse was excellent, even if Chance did guess why she was making it. "There'll be other nights and other shows."

"I suppose so," Julia conceded gracefully.

"Excuse me. I noticed the gift shop was open, and I'd like to pick up a few postcards. Forgot my digital camera."

Chance gave her a yeah-right smirk that his aunt didn't see. but Selena was already moving away, making her escape while she could. "I'll see you in the morning, Julia. Good night."

There was an interesting assortment of souvenirs displayed on the gift shop counter and some Christmas trinkets, including a Cajun Santa Claus in a windup sleigh pulled by eight tiny alligators. Another customer got it going, and the mechanical alligators clattered across the counter, their little legs whirring in unison. Selena looked at it and laughed, but all she bought were a few postcards and an inexpensive flash camera.

An hour later, the first installment of the travelogue for her parents was written—to fulfill the excuse she had made—as well as one to her girlfriend Robin. Selena glanced at the turned-down covers of the bed, courtesy of a dinnertime visit by the maid, and knew she wasn't ready yet to sleep.

She hesitated, then put on the pink sweater and her jacket over that, and took the cabin key from her handbag. She stepped out of the door onto the outer deck. At first she was struck by the silence of the night, broken only by the rush of water cascading from the paddlewheel and the muffled throb of the engines.

Moving outward, she leaned against the teakwood handrail and stared at the glow of light from New Orleans. Rising above it was a full moon, looking like a gigantic sugar cookie. Selena shook her head, wondering why she was thinking about cookies when she'd just had dessert. The moonlight on the rippling water below made a striking effect.

"It's beautiful," she murmured aloud.

"Yes, it is."

Selena turned with a start as Chance separated himself from the shadows and moved to the railing. "Why don't you quit spying on me?" she demanded and pivoted back to stare at the river.

Chance ignored her question, seeming to indicate that he didn't believe it warranted an answer, and remarked, "You didn't mention that you were going to take a romantic stroll around the deck."

"I just wanted some fresh air before I turned in," she replied, and immediately wished she hadn't offered an explanation. It was none of his business. "What are you doing out here? I thought you were going to the show." Her sideways glance found him nonchalantly leaning against the railing.

"I wanted some fresh air." He used her excuse deliberately, Selena thought, to mock her somehow.

"Go and find it somewhere else," she retorted. Being alone with him made her awfully nervous.

"Have any suggestions?" Chance sounded amused.

Selena felt an unreasoning irritation, and it got the better of her. "Why don't you try the bottom of the river?"

Silence followed. In the stillness she had an inexplicable urge to retract her words, to make peace whatever the cost.

When Chance did speak, it was in a voice that reminded her of velvet. "Do you really want to be on deck alone—under that moon?" Her gaze slid to the full moon, bathing her with the serenity of its light and catching her in its romantic spell. "It seems to say, 'for lovers only,' doesn't it?" His voice sounded dangerously close.

When Selena turned, she turned into him. Her hands, raised as if to ward him off, brushed against his jacket. The moonlight half-shadowed his compelling features, but she could see that his eyes, black as midnight, fathomless and shimmering, were focused on her lips. Everything seemed to come to a standstill . . . her heart, her breath, her thoughts.

His hands settled lightly on her shoulders as his head bent lower. She knew what he was going to do, but Chance had kissed her so many times before, it seemed natural. At the warm touch of his mouth she responded, hesitantly at first, then with increasing ease. She let his shaping hands mold her to him, his oak-strong solidity something she could lean on.

The pressure of his kiss relaxed, although his firm male lips continued sensually playing with hers, their warm breath mingling. "I've wanted you, Red, ever since I saw you again at the hotel," Chance murmured against her mouth.

The use of her nickname snapped her out of her reverie, making her aware of the danger in his embrace. This was not an innocently romantic kiss in the moonlight, not with Chance Barkley as a participant. Why had she let herself be caught up in all the talk about the moon and lovers?

She twisted out of his arms. "You're still making the same mistake about me," she accused with a catch in her voice.

His head was drawn back, a hint of arrogance in his look. "Am I?"

"Yes, you are." Chance made no effort to stop her as she stepped away, well aware that her own foolishness had given him cause to think that way. "I'm going to my cabin," she announced, adding a definite, "Alone," when he started to follow her.

His mouth quirked. "A gentleman always sees a lady to her door."

"You aren't a gentleman," Selena retorted.

His eyes said *and you aren't a lady,* but they had already crossed the few feet to her cabin. Selena tried to ignore him as she inserted the key into the lock. When she started to pull the door open, his hand was there to stop it.

"Don't you think I should check to make sure there aren't any unwanted visitors in your room?" he asked mockingly.

"Like who?"

"Spiders, mice . . . and other critters that might have slipped aboard."

"Oh, you mean rats," Selena suggested with a cloyingly sweet smile, and ducked under his arm to slip inside the door.

She heard his soft chuckles as she closed it behind her. She waited just inside until she heard his footsteps moving away from her cabin.

After changing into her nightclothes, she switched off the light and crawled between the covers of her bed. A couple walked by her door, passengers murmuring a greeting to someone. There was a tightness in her chest as she heard Chance's familiar voice respond.

He was still outside her cabin, somewhere close. She rolled onto her side, punching her pillow with the unladylike wish that it was his face. But that wasn't really what she wished, and she knew it.

Morning brought renewed zest and a firm resolve that she wasn't going to let Chance Barkley get under her skin—or anywhere else.

Her clothing was casual for the day of cruising up

the river. The cashmere sweater was a natural beige that didn't wash her out— Okay, it did, but her carefully applied makeup took care of that. Anyway, just being out on the water seemed to put pink in her cheeks and a glow in her eyes. Natural linen pants matched the top, and if she never sat down, they wouldn't wrinkle. Sometimes she wondered why she had a taste for high-maintenance clothes.

Breakfast was being served in the Orleans Room, and Selena skipped lightly down the stairs, the brilliant sunlight shining outside reflected in her bright eyes.

Inside the entrance she stopped dead. Chance was sitting at her table, sipping a cup of coffee. When he saw her poised inside the doorway, he rose and pulled out a chair for her.

Selena moved to the table, her good mood vanishing in a rush of irritation. "What are you doing here?" she demanded.

He continued to stand beside the chair, waiting for her to be seated. "I arranged to have my table changed," he explained with a wicked glint in his eyes. "The headwaiter understood that I would prefer to sit with my aunt."

She wanted to turn and stalk from the room, but that would give him too much satisfaction. Ignoring the chair he held out for her, she chose one that seated her opposite him.

The long, narrow menu card was leaning against the crystal vase of Christmas greens and holly sprigs in the center of the table. Selena picked it up and forced herself to concentrate on the selections, ignoring Chance as he took his chair.

"Are you ready to order?" Danny, their waiter, asked as he appeared at the table.

"Selena?" Chance directed the inquiry to her.

"I haven't decided. You go ahead."

He hesitated, then ordered a full breakfast. The waiter turned to Selena. "Have you made up your mind, miss?"

"I think I'll just have orange juice and a sweet roll," she stated, replacing the menu. She had decided to skip the messy beignets, not wanting to chat with her nemesis if she had powdered sugar on her face. No reason to give him an excuse to laugh at her, was there? "And coffee."

When the waiter left for the kitchen, Selena felt Chance's gaze center on her. "I expected an Iowa girl like you would eat a hearty breakfast," he commented.

"Did you?" Coolly, Selena lifted her gaze to meet his. "But then you've consistently misjudged me, haven't you?"

Chance made no reply, his gaze narrowing briefly. Silence reigned through the morning meal, with Selena finishing hers while he was still chasing a little sausage around the plate. It seemed determined to elude him. She identified, totally. She gave him an icy smile and excused herself from the table, leaving him there alone.

Later she saw him on deck, but he made no attempt to approach her, although she noticed that he kept her in sight. Soon his presence lost the ability to annoy as she became caught up in the spell of the Mississippi River.

The Delta Queen steamed up the river with majestic slowness, a stately, old-fashioned lady taking a leisurely paddle up the Mississippi. Levees, emerald green with thick grasses, paralleled the river's winding course as it sometimes seemed to attempt to twist back into itself.

Bare-branched trees and lush shrubs forested the banks. Cottonwoods, bald cypresses, patchy-barked sycamores—an almost endless variety—grew there to baffle and break up the raging current when the river went out of its banks at flood stage. Through breaks in the trees, there were glimpses over the levees of sprawling flatlands, cotton and sugar plantations.

A trio of egrets perched on a fallen tree near the river's edge, and a deer grazing in a grassy glade flicked his white tail before bounding into the trees. The river itself was a dirty brown, rushing full between its banks, creating eddies and then destroying them. Logs and tree branches were swept helplessly in its current, along with other debris now and then. The river was showing a face that had changed little since the days when steamboats ruled its waters and Mark Twain described its lure.

But there were other faces: buoys marked the channel, and industry spilled onto its banks. Vast chemical plants and refineries with their complex network of intertwining pipes and towering stacks rose above the levees. Water towers and church steeples marked towns that were hidden from view.

Except for the Crescent City of New Orleans, nowhere did the modern face become more evident than at Baton Rouge. The high-rise buildings of the city proper marked its center. On either side of the river, loading terminals lined the banks with oceangoing ships of every description. Containers were being unloaded and giant cranes were loading others. Selena left her comfortable deck chair to walk to the railing for a better look.

"Baton Rouge is the farthest inland major port in the States," said Chance, appearing at her side.

Selena found the scene too fascinating to object to his presence. Besides, there was never a tour guide around when you needed one, and he could answer a few questions and make himself useful. "That's an impressive array of ships, but why are they all flying the American flag? They can't all be American ships."

"It's a courtesy to fly the flag of the port nation. The flag of the ship's country is on the stern," he explained.

"I see," she said, nodding. "There's one from Holland." She pointed.

"The next one is from Glasgow, Scotland, where the Delta Queen was made."

Selena faced him in surprise. "The Delta Queen was made in Scotland?" she repeated. "I didn't know that."

"Yes, the steelwork for her and the Delta King was fabricated in Glasgow and temporarily assembled on the River Clyde. The parts were all marked, then torn down and shipped to California, where she was re-assembled and finished. But she came from the same shipbuilding center in Scotland where the *Queen Mary* was fitted out."

"Amazing!" she breathed, and looked back at the freighter from Scotland.

Several crew members on the Scottish ship had gathered on the bridge of the freighter to watch the Delta Queen steam by, her paddlewheel churning out tan foam. One of the crew was taking pictures of the riverboat and Selena wondered if he knew of the Delta Queen's beginnings in his homeland. Or did she just seem an anachronism gliding slowly past the sleek, ultramodern tankers and freighters?

"When was she built?" Selena questioned absently.

"In the mid-1920s, I think. She carried passengers on the Sacramento River back and forth from San Francisco to Sacramento, California."

"Yes, I remember the couple at our dinner table last night mentioned that one of their older relations had been on the Delta Queen when she was in California many years ago."

The breeze had picked up, whipping around the stern. It tugged a strand of hair free of Selena's scarf and laid it across her cheek. Before she could push it aside, Chance's hand was there, smoothing it behind her ear and making her conscious of him.

He was tall and really built, his dark eyes glowing with an inner light. With the breeze ruffling the thick crispness of his black hair, he looked rugged, totally in command. His thick wool sweater was plastered to his chest by the wind, revealing his muscular physique despite the bulky knit.

He didn't seem to mind the brisk December air. The cuffs of his shirt sleeves were rolled up twice over the sweater to reveal a portion of the rippling muscles in his forearms. She glimpsed the unbuttoned collar of the shirt he wore underneath it, which exposed his throat and the tanned column of his neck. Chance Barkley was a handsome devil, as her mother would say, and the heady sight of him shook her senses.

She tore her gaze away from him, suddenly finding it very essential to speak and break the silence. "The Delta Queen has a very interesting history, doesn't she?" Her voice was much steadier than she had expected and she could feel her pulse settling into a more even rhythm.

"Yes, it has," Chance agreed.

Another couple moved to the railing near them, an older man and his wife. After several minutes, the man struck up a conversation with Chance and Selena drifted away to reclaim her deck chair and watch the outskirts of Baton Rouge slip by.

She hadn't been there long when Julia stopped by, saying, "Good morning, Selena. Are you going to take your 'eleven at eleven'?"

"I beg your pardon?" Selena blinked.

Julia laughed softly, "Eleven laps around the sundeck—which is a mile—at eleven o'clock, with the calliope providing the marching music."

"Sounds, um, aerobic. But I don't think so," she said, smiling wryly at her own lassitude. "I feel too lazy." Overhearing their conversation, Chance caught her eye, a mocking reminder in his that an Iowa girl should have more get-up-and-go. Selena ignored the look with an effort. "Are you going, Julia?"

"Oh yes. I have so much energy I must channel it somewhere," she declared, and moved toward the stairs. "See you at lunch."

Watching her leave, Selena knew that the bright sparkle in Julia's eyes came from more than just energy. She was sure it was born of excitement because the next day they would be arriving in Natchez, where Leslie was waiting for her.

Selena felt a pang of envy, hoping that someday she might have that special glow the older woman possessed. Almost of its own volition, her gaze swung to Chance, leaning backward against the railing, his arms crossed in front of him.

Something jolted through her as she found him watching her, but the emotion was fleeting and indefinable, and Chance's attention was soon claimed by the man standing beside him.

The sensation didn't return. In the afternoon Selena attended a lecture on the Delta Queen's history. Julia didn't go because she had heard it all before. Neither did Chance, and Selena guessed that he was equally well informed on the subject.

His sketchy outline had whetted her appetite to hear more, and, besides, she could always put the details into her daily travelogue for her parents, who **were great** believers in Educational Experiences.

She was not disappointed by the lecture. Mike, the cruise director, spoke of the Delta Queen's construction and the almost one million dollars that had been spent to build her, a phenomenal sum to pay for a riverboat in the 1920s. He told of her life on the Sacramento River in California and the years that she had been laid up when the Depression hit.

During World War II the U.S. Navy took over the grand riverboat, using her as a troop carrier in San Francisco Bay, ferrying soldiers to and from ocean vessels. With the navy's predilection for battleship gray, every inch of her was painted—including the stained-glass panels set with copper, which were set in the top of the windows in the lounges on both the cabin deck and the texas deck.

After the war the Delta Queen was auctioned off, sold to the Green Line, which was already operating overnight passenger trips on the Mississippi River. It was then that she was shored and crated like a huge piano in a box, and towed down the Pacific coast, through the Panama Canal into the Gulf of Mexico to the Mississippi River. The old riverboat was not designed for the ocean or its storms, yet she made it intact, to the stunned amazement of many an ocean seaman who had predicted her doom on the high seas.

The story of the congressional battle to keep her from being banned forever from traveling the western rivers was recounted, along with the tale of the ultimate success: she had been declared a National Historic Landmark, allowed to carry passengers by a special exemption of Congress. Finally, the cruise director told of the recent construction of her sister ship, the Mississippi Queen, a sleek, modern paddlewheel steamboat with a personality all her own.

Selena came away from the lecture with a new appreciation for the riverboat and the feeling that she had only heard the highlights, that there was much of the Delta Queen's rich history she didn't know.

At dinner that evening, their scheduled arrival at Natchez the following day was the main topic of conver-

sation between Julia and Selena. The older woman
talked about her anticipation of being with Leslie and
reminisced about their previous times together.

But Chance was almost grimly silent. As far as Selena
was concerned, his dislike of Leslie and his disapproval
of the coming marriage was inappropriate. No matter
what he thought of his aunt's decision, it was hers alone
to make. Selena considered his attitude autocratic and
insensitive.

"I've decided to buy a new dress in Natchez for my
wedding," Julia announced. "But I can't make up my
mind what color. I think it would be in bad taste for a
woman my age to wear white, even though I've never
been married before. I was thinking of something in
cream or beige or perhaps yellow. Leslie always said yellow was my color."

Selena was about to comment when Chance broke in
curtly, "Julia, you're boring Selena with all this non-
sense about your wedding."

"That's not true!" Selena said firmly, looking up
from her dessert to defend Julia, her spoon poised
above the peach melba. "What woman would find wedding plans boring? I think it's great that your aunt's in
love. It's incredibly romantic!"

His expression hardened at her quick and vehement
reply, and she turned away, fixing a determinedly interested look on her face as she glanced at the older
woman.

"With your hair, I think something in silver gray
might be just right," she suggested, noting the silver
wings at the temples of Julia's otherwise dark hair.

Julia hesitated for a second, glancing apprehensively
at her nephew before picking up the conversation
where Selena had left off, and Chance's disapproving silence was ignored. But a strained atmosphere remained.

It wasn't relieved until the three returned to the Orleans Room after dinner for the banjo concert. The room had been transformed into a nightclub with tables—minus their linen and silverware—chairs, the lights dimmed, and drinks being served from the Mark Twain Saloon. The bar waitress announced the arrival of the traditional eggnog by ringing a red-bowed bell, and specified that the bourbon would be served on the side in case anyone wanted to avoid the alcohol.

The bartender brought it forth in a gigantic cut-glass bowl, followed by two more waiters with trays of glasses and a member of the kitchen staff who sang "God Rest Ye, Merry Gentlemen" in an uncertain baritone and then promptly disappeared.

Holy cow, thought Selena. One of the worst hangovers of her young life had been after a Christmas party. Not guessing how potent the sweet stuff really was, she'd downed several cups and gotten, well, a little too eggnoggy. She settled for a Coke.

The banjo player sat on a stool in front of the band. Mustached, with brown, waving hair, he wore black pants, a white shirt and red vest with garters around his sleeves.

He introduced himself in a drawling voice and said, "Y'all have come here tonight to hear a banjo concert. That's good, 'cause that's what we got planned." He plunked a few strings and looked out at the audience. "Banjos and riverboats almost seem synonymous. You think of one, then the other." A shyly mischievous smile curved his mouth. "'Course, you all know that the banjo is the only musical instrument invented in America, and you are about to find out why we're the only country that had the nerve." With that, he immediately broke into a rousing version of "Waiting for the Robert E. Lee."

Before the song was over, everyone in the room was

clapping along, and Selena felt the tension leave her as if it had been zapped by the wild energy of the music.

After the concert and a few sing-along renditions of traditional carols, Julia left, insisting it was time for her to retire, what with everything happening the next day. Selena lingered to sample the late-night snacks, comfort food like cookies and hot chocolate and fresh fruit, as did Chance. Somewhere along the way, they were separated as Selena paused to chat with some of her fellow passengers.

When the band began playing some dance music, she saw Chance at the crew's table in the far corner of the room, talking to the chief purser. He seemed to have forgotten about her, and Selena was positive she was glad about it.

Sipping at her hot chocolate, she watched the older couples on the dance floor, marveling at their grace and ability. When the chocolate was gone, and with it her reason for staying, Selena walked to the stairs.

Before she reached the first step, Chance was at her side.

"I'll walk you to your cabin," he said.

She balked. "There's no need."

With typical arrogance, he ignored her protest and pressed a hand against the small of her back to guide her up the stairs. She submitted to his lead, however ungraciously, and they walked in silence up the stairs through the forward cabin lounge to the outer deck.

Ripples of moonlight danced over the river and the cobweb silhouettes of trees along the banks. A corner of the full moon was lopped off, making it look like a chipped silver dollar in a velvet sky. The stars were big and bright, so close Selena felt she could reach out and touch them. The night was quite cool, but there was a moist breeze stirring the air.

"Don't you think this charade has gone far enough?"

Chance issued the demanding question in a cold, hard voice that shattered the evening's mood.

Selena's eyes widened, partly in surprise and partly in annoyance that they were back to the question of her so-called profession. Just for the sheer stubborn pleasure of it, she wasn't going to enlighten him. Not that he would believe her. "What are you talking about?"

"I'm referring to the way you keep humoring Julia, of course," he snapped, impatient with her obtuseness.

"Oh, please," she snapped, her resentment at his attitude at dinner returning to fuel real anger. "I'm not humoring her! I'm glad she's found someone to love. And you should be, too, instead of trying to spoil her happiness. She's a warm, wonderful person. She doesn't deserve to have a family like yours!"

She didn't flinch under his piercing regard. His eyes narrowed to black slits as he seemed to mentally assess the sincerity of her words. Turning, he said nothing in his own defense but merely escorted her up the stairs to the texas deck and her cabin.

He left her at the door with a brusque good night, which, still simmering from their exchange, Selena didn't bother to return. As she closed her door she saw he had moved to the railing.

A lighter flamed in his hand. He cupped it to the slender cigar in his mouth, the lighter briefly illuminating his features and revealing an expression of grim thoughtfulness.

As Selena got ready for bed, the breeze carried the aromatic smoke from his cigar through her open cabin window. The scent lingered long after she had fallen asleep.

Chapter Seven

Selena awakened fairly early the next morning. The river was shrouded in fog when she stepped from her cabin. It seemed a white world with the sky paled to a pearl gray. Even the sun was a white glare in the east. The damp coolness seeped through her sweater to chill her skin, making her hurry down the stairs to the forward cabin lounge.

The first person she saw as she entered the lounge was Chance. He was standing at one of the windows and staring out, and, as if sensing her presence, he shot her a glance. An impassive mask had been drawn over his compelling features, making his thoughts unreadable.

Then Selena noticed Julia sitting in one of the chairs, looking dejected. Selena's mouth tightened; she was certain that in some way Chance was to blame for his aunt's expression. She walked directly to the older woman to offer moral support and perhaps undo whatever damage Chance had done.

"Good morning, Julia," she greeted the woman quietly.

Looking up in surprise, Julia recovered to respond,

"Oh, good morning, Selena." But it was an absent greeting, her thoughts were obviously far away.

"Is something wrong?" Selena asked.

"The chief purser just brought me this message," was the sighed answer.

Selena noticed the crumpled slip of paper between Julia's twisting fingers. "From Leslie?" she guessed.

"Yes, he won't be able to meet me in Natchez." Emotions, intense and painful, clouded her expression.

"Oh no!" Selena breathed out, feeling only compassion for Julia's disappointment.

"He said he'd meet me in Vicksburg instead." Julia attempted to fix a reassuring smile on her face, but she couldn't conceal her regret over the postponement.

"What happened?"

"His car broke down," Julia explained. "Something major, I guess, since he says it's going to take a couple of days to fix."

"I'm so sorry," Selena offered, knowing it was cold comfort.

"It's all right. We'll be in Vicksburg tomorrow, and the day after that Leslie will be there, so I don't have long to wait. It's you I feel bad about," she murmured apologetically.

"Me? Whatever for?" Selena exclaimed.

"My dear, I know you didn't book for the tour of Natchez because you expected to meet Leslie in the afternoon. Now it's too late and you're going to miss seeing it altogether," Julia sighed.

"I don't mind, really," Selena insisted.

"Of course you do," Julia dismissed Selena's protest. "You're on vacation. You should be going places and doing things instead of letting me interfere in your life, boring you with my troubles."

"You're not boring me and you aren't interfering,"

Selena stated flatly. "You've been listening to Chance too much." She flashed an angry glance in his direction, throwing invisible daggers at a point between his broad shoulders. "I enjoy your company, and I'm excited about your wedding. Don't pay any attention to what he says."

"You're such a good girl." Julia patted her hand, adding, "And you're so good for my ego."

"I'm glad." Selena smiled, her affection for the older woman steadily growing. Julia was a little eccentric, true, but Selena very much liked her that way. And why was it that whenever a woman didn't do exactly what everyone expected of her, she was criticized for it? Chance had no very good reason that Selena could see for his controlling behavior where his aunt was concerned.

"Before you came in the lounge, I was feeling so low. Now"—the older woman shrugged and smiled—"I even think I could eat some breakfast. Will you join me?"

Selena hesitated. "Not right away." There was something else she wanted to do first. "But I'll be down before you're through."

"Very well," Julia agreed, rising from her chair.

Selena waited until Julia had started down the steps to the Orleans Room before she walked to where Chance stood.

His glance and his voice were indifferent. "Good morning."

There were other passengers around the lounge helping themselves to coffee. Selena's mouth tightened into a hard line. She wasn't in the mood to exchange pleasantries.

"Would you come outside with me?" she requested stiffly. "I want to talk to you."

A brow lifted briefly at her request, his flat black gaze making an assessing sweep of her, noting the light of battle in her eyes, before he complied with her request.

The instant they were outside and out of earshot of their fellow passengers, Selena turned on him. "Was this your doing?" she demanded.

Chance tipped his head slightly to the side. "I'm afraid I don't follow you."

One of the deckhands was polishing the brass kick-boards of the stairs leading to the texas deck. Selena lowered her voice so she couldn't be overheard, but that didn't lessen the heat in her tone. "You follow my meaning all right," she retorted. "I'm talking about the message Julia supposedly received from Leslie, the one saying he wouldn't be able to meet her in Natchez."

"That message," he nodded in understanding, his bland expression not changing. "Yes, I know about it. What does it have to do with me?"

"That's what I want to know," Selena challenged. "What was your part in it?"

"As I recall it, Leslie had car trouble," Chance remarked with infuriating calm. "I've been on the boat with you ever since we left New Orleans, so I don't see how you could accuse me of possibly tampering with his car. That is what you're suggesting, isn't it? I guess you think I look like a member of the Future Felons of America. Add grand theft auto and attempted murder to that list when you get a chance. Did I mention those were my hobbies? Don't tell Julia."

"Spare me the sarcasm," Selena said tightly. "But I don't think Leslie sent the message."

"Meaning, you think I did and signed his name to it?" His gaze sharpened.

"It's possible," she said grimly. "I saw you talking to the chief purser last night. You could have paid him to deliver the message to Julia this morning. I wouldn't put it past you—you're so determined not to let them get married."

"It could happen that way," he admitted. "But your theory has a flaw."

"What's that?" Selena didn't hide her skepticism.

"If I sent the message and not Leslie, then he'll be waiting at the landing when the boat docks in Natchez, won't he?" Chance reasoned smoothly, causing Selena's doubt in her suspicions to flicker across her face. "Unless you're going to accuse me next of sending a message to Leslie from Julia calling off the wedding?"

She hadn't thought of that. "You could have."

"Perhaps. But I didn't. The message Julia received this morning wasn't sent by me," he said firmly. "Nor did I arrange to have it sent. I guess you'll have to assume it came from Leslie."

He sounded as if he was telling the truth, but Selena wasn't sure if she could believe him. "Maybe," she said grudgingly. "But if I ever have proof that you're lying, I'll—" She compressed her lips tightly, unable to think of the words to complete the threat.

"Yes?" Chance drawled the word, his eyes taunting her.

Pivoting, she stalked to the lounge door and jerked it open. She had her temper under control by the time she joined Julia for breakfast. Chance had already eaten, she learned, so she wasn't forced to endure his company for the morning meal.

Three whistle blasts signaled their arrival in Natchez shortly before noon. Along with many of the other passengers, Selena moved to the starboard railing to watch the tying-up process. There was no indication of a city, just scattered old buildings, mostly built of wood and a few of brick, with a sheer bluff rising behind them. A wide swath of trees and greenery stretched several hundred yards downstream.

The boom swung the landing platform to the ramp running down into the river. Deckhands jumped off to drag the heavy ropes to the tiepins. Selena glimpsed the historical plaque identifying the location as Natchez-under-the-Hill, once the most wicked hellhole on the river, peopled with thieves, murderers, gamblers, prostitutes and cutthroats. The river had carried away most of the old town, leaving a row of ramshackle buildings as a representative of the town's sordid past.

On top of the bluff was the city of Natchez, where the respectable citizens had lived. Selena knew the glory of its history was duly represented by the more than one hundred antebellum houses that had been restored to their previous grandeur. The Natchez Pilgrimage tours were famous, and she regretted that she wasn't going.

A few curious townspeople had driven to the waterfront to watch the Delta Queen's arrival. Some sat in their cars, while others, especially those with children, stood on the banks. The arrival of a steamboat was still an event in this river town.

But there was no middle-aged man alone on the landing, searching the faces of the passengers along the railing for a familiar one. Leslie was not there. Even though Selena didn't know what he looked like, she was sure he wasn't there. She sighed with relief, then wondered why. Because Chance hadn't lied to her? Selena shook her head. It couldn't be that.

When the boat was secured, she went ashore, strolling along the worn path in the parklike area. As the trail curved over a knoll, she stopped at the top to lean a shoulder against a tree and stare at the red paddlewheel of the Delta Queen, framed by two trees.

The flags circling the top deck ruffled in the breeze against an intense blue sky, which had been hiding behind the morning's fog, and a warm, golden sun. The farther they went up the Mississippi, the colder the days would be, she knew, but today was positively balmy. Two deckhands were in a rowboat at the bow, applying a fresh coat of paint to the hull.

The leaf of a twig tickled her cheek. Unconsciously she pulled it off and fingered the green leaf. She was in an oddly silent mood, and her mind seemed to be blank. Then she saw Chance coming toward her with slow, purposeful strides. She hesitated and finally stayed where she was.

"They're serving lunch. Aren't you coming?" he asked, stopping beside her.

"I'm not hungry." Her voice was low and flat.

"Watching your diet?" he returned with a teasing inflection. "Carbs or calories?"

"Neither. I'm just not hungry," Selena said, shrugging and looking away. She became aware of the leaf in her hand and released it, watching it spiral to the ground.

"What's bothering you, Red?" His voice changed to a serious tone.

"Nothing." She slipped her hands into her pants pockets, indifferent to his searching gaze.

"Something is," Chance insisted.

Irritation flashed at his persistence. "If there was something, would you really care?" she challenged.

He continued his quiet study of her without offering a reply. Finally her gaze fell from his, her annoyance burning itself out.

When Chance did speak, he asked, "Were you considering going into town?"

"I thought I would," admitted Selena.

"It's a long walk up that hill." She shrugged her indifference to his comment. "I've hired a cab. You could come along with me, if you'd like, and we'll have lunch and drive around to some of the plantations," he invited in a calm, unemotional tone.

She was surprised and more than a little wary. He must have some reason for asking her that he wasn't saying. A thought occurred to her.

"Is this your idea or Julia's?" she wanted to know.

"Do you really care?" Chance countered with mocking coolness.

With a painful jolt, Selena realized that she did. She didn't want Chance to be making this invitation out of a sense of duty prompted by his aunt.

"You haven't said whether you'd like to go," he reminded her.

Selena hesitated, then decided it didn't make any difference why he had asked her. This was her chance to see Natchez and she would be a fool to turn it down.

"I have to get my handbag," she said in the way of an answer.

"The cab is at the landing. I'll wait for you there."

"I won't be long," Selena promised, and started back to the boat.

After they lunched at Stanton Hall, Chance arranged with the cabdriver to take them by a few of the antebellum houses. They stopped at three that were open to the general public and not restricted to private tours, giving Selena an opportunity to see the interior of these gracious homes.

They returned to the boat half an hour before it was scheduled to leave. As they walked onto the gangplank, Chance asked, "How did you like Natchez?"

"I enjoyed it," Selena answered with genuine enthusiasm. "Thank you for taking me."

"Are you going to your cabin now?"

She nodded. "I thought I'd change for dinner."

"It isn't required, you know," he commented.

"Yes, I know, but I feel like it," she said, shrugging as they climbed the stairs to the cabin deck.

When they reached the top of the stairs, Selena

turned toward the double doors leading to the outer deck, but Chance stopped. "Meet me in the texas lounge in a half hour for a drink," he suggested.

"All right." Selena was surprised at how quickly she agreed.

When she left her cabin to meet Chance, the boat was just getting under way. As its stern swung away from the river bank so the boat could back away from the landing, the calliope played a farewell concert on the sundeck.

Its music was interrupted by an announcement over the public address system requesting the passengers to move to the stern of the steamboat. The Delta Queen's bow was temporarily stuck in the Mississippi mud, and the captain wanted as much weight as possible to the rear of the steamboat.

Obligingly, Selena waited by her cabin, smiling to herself at the simple remedy. Soon the bow was free and the steamboat was reversing into the channel, once again heading upstream.

Chance was waiting for her at a table in the lounge when she walked in, a drink already in front of him. Greg, the bartender she had met the first day aboard, was at the table almost before she sat down.

"What will you have, Selena?" he asked with familiar ease.

Selena felt the speculative look Chance gave her. "I'll have a margarita," she decided.

"Good choice," Greg said with a wink. "Lots of vitamin C. And I make the best margarita aboard this boat." And he moved away.

"Do you know him?" questioned Chance, in a bland and impersonal tone that was at odds with the look in his eyes.

"I met him the first day," Selena explained somewhat defensively. "It's a very friendly crew."

"Especially around passengers like you," he added dryly.

Her chin lifted as she had the impression of something derogatory in his remark. "What is that supposed to mean?"

"That you're a babe, as if you didn't already know," he answered.

As much as she tried, Selena couldn't interpret that as a compliment. Chance had been stating what he saw as a fact, not making a personal comment.

Greg returned with her drink. "The word is out that we'll be meeting the Mississippi Queen on her way downstream," he said.

"When?" Selena's interest was immediate.

"Sometime tonight. It will depend how fast we go upstream and how fast she comes downstream," he smiled. "The captain will be in contact with her by radio before we ever see her. He'll make an announcement ahead of time, letting you know when she'll pass. It'll be a sight to see," Greg declared.

"Where is she coming from?" Selena asked.

"Vicksburg, I think."

"That reminds me. What time will we get into Vicksburg tomorrow?"

"Haven't you heard?" Greg looked at her curiously. "We aren't going to stop at Vicksburg this trip."

"What?" She frowned and glanced at Chance, who was studying his drink. But she had understood that Julia was to meet Leslie in Vicksburg. "Why not?" she asked Greg.

"The river is still fairly high from the hurricane season, which ran well into November this year. And the runoffs mean the current is swifter, and it's going to take us longer to go up," he explained. "No one wants to risk getting into Louisville late and missing the steamboat race."

"The steamboat race?" Selena repeated. But what about Julia and Leslie?

"Yeah," he said eagerly, not seeming to notice that her thoughts were elsewhere. "The one between us and the Belle of Louisville. We won it last year, and nobody wants to give up the golden antlers, especially by default." A passenger at another table called to him for a round of drinks. Greg excused himself and returned to the bar.

Selena darted an accusing look at Chance. "Did you know we weren't stopping at Vicksburg?"

Impassively he met her gaze. "I heard about it the other day."

"And you didn't say anything to Julia? You know as well as I do that she's planning to meet Leslie in Vicksburg!" She was angered by his indifference.

"She'll find out about it soon enough, if she hasn't already."

"And you didn't see fit to warn her this morning when she was suppressing her disappointment with the knowledge she'd be meeting him in Vicksburg?"

"No, I didn't," Chance admitted without a flicker of remorse.

"I don't know whether you don't have a heart or if you're just naturally cruel," Selena declared, almost choking with the effort to keep her temper in check.

He seemed unmoved by her caustic description of him. Lifting his glass to his mouth, he said, "Memphis is our next scheduled stop. I imagine Julia will plan to meet him there."

"Unless you can find a way to prevent it," she added bitterly, and rose from her chair. "You can keep your drink. I'm not interested."

Chance made no attempt to stop her as she walked swiftly from the room. As she neared the grand staircase, she overheard a low comment from one of the passengers, "A lovers' quarrel." It only made her more anxious to leave the room.

At dinner that evening Selena pointedly ignored Chance, her dislike of his heartless ways feeding on itself. It made the meal miserable, turning delicious food into tasteless mush. Julia gave no indication that she was aware they wouldn't be stopping at Vicksburg. She didn't mention either Vicksburg or Leslie at the table. Her conversation was centered on Natchez and the sights that Selena had seen.

The gift shop in the forward cabin lounge was open when Selena left the dining room. She dawdled there for a while, looking over its items without buying anything, then wandered up the grand staircase and out through the double doors of the texas lounge to the outer deck.

A three-quarter moon was slipping out from behind a cloud. Selena leaned against the railing and gazed out at the shapeless black shadows darkening the banks, trying to convince herself that she was content with her own company.

At eight-thirty the announcement came that the Mississippi Queen would be passing them in fifteen minutes on the port side. Selena walked to the left side of the boat to sit in one of the wrought-iron chairs. She was soon joined on deck by other passengers, their obvious excitement building as the time approached.

Someone said, "There she is, dead ahead."

And a crew member groaned, "Don't put it that way!"

Selena leaned forward to look over the railing and saw the big steamboat coming around the river's bend. She caught her breath at the sight of it. All the decks were ablaze with light, like a tiered birthday cake with all the candles lit in a darkened room.

In the clear night air came the exuberant music of

the Mississippi Queen's calliope. A murmur ran through the passengers as they recognized the tune, "Cruising down the River."

A spotlight was shining—from the Delta Queen, playing over the water ahead of her. The rasping whistle was blown once to officially signal to the other boat that they would pass on the port side, and her whistle blasted once in agreement.

As the large paddlewheeler drew steadily closer, one of the bartenders crowded into the railing beside Selena, a flashlight in his hand. He smiled a quick apology, then began flashing the light at the approaching vessel. She caught the answering flash from the forward deck of the Mississippi Queen.

The bartender let out a short whoop of delight and began flashing in earnest. "That's my brother," he said, offering Selena a quick explanation. "He works on the Mississippi Queen. This is about the only time we see each other."

"Couldn't you guys just use cell phones?"

The bartender grinned. "This is a hell of a lot more fun. We used to do it when we were kids and snuck out at night."

Selena laughed, distracted from her preoccupied mood.

"Didn't you have a secret signaling system with your brothers and sisters?"

She shook her head. "I was an only child."

The bartender switched off his flashlight. "At least you got the bathroom to yourself once in a while."

"Gee, I didn't know boys fight over bathrooms. Most of the little boys I knew never took baths any oftener than they could help it."

It was his turn to laugh. The bows of the two boats were nearly even now, spotlights roaming over each other's decks. The passengers of the Mississippi Queen were all gathered on the outer decks, too, and they shouted in unison, "Hello!" Automatically, Selena heard herself and the others respond with the same greeting. Everyone was waving. It seemed the thing to do.

Slowly the two sister ships glided by each other, the Mississippi Queen floating along in the current, her red paddlewheel motionless to prolong the moment of meeting. Then she was past, and her paddlewheel reluctantly began churning the river water again.

Selena leaned back in her chair as the other passengers began leaving the railing. The night was once again ink black, the moon and stars unable to match the brilliant lights of the Mississippi Queen.

"Here." A white cloth was offered to her.

Selena glanced up at the giver in surprise. It was Chance, smiling gently as he looked down at her. She was about to protest that she had no need for a handkerchief when she realized that her throat was tight, gripped by the craziest mixture of nostalgia and happiness and the magical beauty of the event. What was more surprising were the welling tears in her eyes.

"Thank you," she muttered, and took the handkerchief to dab her eyes. Laughing, with an emotional catch in her voice, she declared, "I don't know what's the matter with me!"

"I'd say you're turning into a steamboater."

"What's that?" Selena asked, too unnerved by her reaction to remember that she was determined to dislike Chance actively.

"That's a person who loves steamboats," he answered, taking the handkerchief she returned to him and stuffing it back in his jacket pocket. "Do you feel like a stroll around deck?"

"Yes, I think so." The lump in her throat was beginning to ease as she rose to walk with Chance.

A companionable silence lay between them, his arm

curved lightly and impersonally along the back of her waist. Their circuitous route eventually brought them to the stern of the boat near Selena's cabin. In silent unison, they paused at the rear railing to gaze at the waterfall created by the spotlighted paddlewheel.

Other passengers, too, were strolling the decks, exchanging quiet greetings as they passed Selena and Chance. However, one man stopped when he saw them, smiling broadly. "I see the two of you finally made up after your little tiff this afternoon," he commented, and walked on just as Selena recognized him as being the man she had overheard remarking about their "lovers' quarrel."

Stiffening under the light pressure of Chance's hand, she gave him an odd look. "Why didn't you correct him?"

"What was the point?" he shrugged.

"He thinks we're . . ."

"Lovers?" supplied Chance, his mouth quirking a little at her hesitation over the word.

"Yes," Selena clipped out the answer.

"It's only natural. What do you expect the other passengers to think when they see us together almost constantly?"

"Maybe if you quit following me around all the time, they wouldn't get the wrong impression," she retorted. "And stop hanging around outside my cabin at night."

"Outside your cabin?" he repeated, a dark brow arching.

"That's what I said."

"It just so happens, Red, that I'm hanging around outside my own cabin."

"Your cabin? Where's your cabin?" She demanded in disbelief.

"Number two thirty-nine, the one right beside yours," he said with a complacent look in his eyes.

"You're lying," Selena accused.

Chance reached into his pocket. "Would you like to see my key?"

She believed him. "No, I wouldn't."

"Which bed do you sleep in?" he asked. "The one on the right as you walk into your cabin?"

"I don't see that it's any of your business, but, yes, that's the one," she retorted, still trying to recover from the shock of learning that he had the cabin next to hers.

"We're sleeping side by side with only a wall between us. It's a pity the wall isn't removable," Chance commented in a low voice. "Then I could start collecting on that promise you made in my hotel room."

"I didn't make any promise." She twisted away from the hand on her back. "I keep telling you that, but you refuse to listen. So, from now on, you can just stay away from me."

As she turned away, he caught at her hand. "Where are you going?"

"To my cabin." She slipped out of his grasp. "Good night."

"Selena, one word of caution," he followed her to the door. "Don't start sleeping in the other bed or the maid will get suspicious and think someone else is sleeping in your room. You wouldn't want to know how fast rumors spread on this boat."

Inserting the key in the lock, she jerked her cabin door open and slammed it in his face. But it didn't shut out his remark. When she crawled into bed that night, it was the one she had always slept in.

Chapter Eight

Shortly after sunrise Selena stepped out of her cabin, unable to sleep, and tiptoed by Chance's. The chill of the night was still in the strong breeze whipping around the stern. She buttoned the last two buttons of her jacket and tucked her hands in its pockets.

Streamers of scarlet-pink trailed across the eastern horizon, and the sun was a heavy orange ball. Bluffs rose high along the river banks, the water's course a twisting series of oxbows.

She wandered around the empty deck and descended the stairs near the bow to the cabin deck. A coffee urn was in the forward cabin lounge for early risers, and Selena helped herself, warming her hands around the steaming cup.

A figure was standing on the outer deck at the bow, wearing a suede jacket and a scarf tied around her head. It took Selena a few minutes to recognize Julia. Cup in hand, she walked back on deck to join her.

"Good morning, Julia."

The woman turned, smiling automatically yet with a

touch of absentness. "Good morning, Selena. You're up
early."

"I couldn't sleep."

There was silence as Julia gazed intently ahead. The
Delta Queen glided under a railroad bridge. Around
the bend, a highway bridge stretched high across the
river. There was a suggestion of activity concentrated
behind the river's tree-lined banks. It was this that held
Julia's attention.

As if sensing Selena's curious eyes on her, Julia explained, "That's Vicksburg ahead."

Selena hesitated an instant before saying, "You do
know we aren't stopping, don't you?"

"Yes." It was a quiet word, but it spoke volumes about
Julia's disappointment.

Again there was silence as the boat moved steadily
nearer. The wind gusted, tearing through Selena's uncovered hair. The sun was yellow, the streaks of dawn
gone from the sky.

"The chief purser used his laptop to help me send
Leslie a fax. I don't really understand this wireless business, but Doug assured me the fax would get there. I
told Leslie we wouldn't be stopping here," Julia said
softly. "It went to his office. I'm not sure where he is. I
hope he received it."

"I'm sure he did," Selena consoled her. She waited
with Julia while she maintained her silent vigil on the
bow until the Delta Queen followed the channel mark-
ers past the mouth of the Yazoo River. Only then did
the older woman suggest that they go inside. Vicksburg
was behind them and Memphis was ahead.

Later that afternoon Selena came up from the
Orleans Room after watching a navigation video.
Afternoon tea was being served in the aft cabin lounge.
Wanting some fresh air, she decided to walk along the

outer cabin deck to get to the aft section instead of using the wide passageway through the center of the deck.

At a leisurely pace, she began walking beside the railing to the stern. A cabin window was open, releasing familiar voices from within. Selena realized she was approaching Julia's stateroom. When she heard her name on Chance's lips, she stopped.

She didn't hear what Chance had said about her, but she heard Julia reply. "How can you say that? Selena is such a wonderful girl. You should know that by now from spending time with her on this cruise." Since her insistence last night that Chance leave her alone, he had been mostly absent all day. Selena didn't know how long it would last, but she realized that even Julia had noticed how much time he had been spending in her company.

There was a moment of ominous silence from the cabin. Selena was afraid that Chance was going to tell Julia the sordid circumstances of their first meeting.

Instead he offered an impatient, "You're entirely too trusting, Julia. Sooner or later—"

"You think she's going to hurt me, don't you?" was Julia's gentle response.

"In one way or another, I can practically guarantee it," he retorted.

A fellow passenger was walking toward Selena, and she realized she didn't dare dawdle any longer outside Julia's window or she would risk being discovered eavesdropping. She moved on, knowing Chance was still wrong about her. She certainly would never do anything that would hurt Julia.

She couldn't imagine what Chance had been saying, but it obviously wasn't anything good. The fact that he had been talking about her in such unflattering terms was unnerving. But what did she expect?

She had never set him straight about what had happened between them, thinking that the cruise would be over soon enough and they would all go on their merry way. Just the idea of really talking to him involved a degree of intimacy that she simply wasn't ready for. Every conversation they'd had so far had been no more than small talk—or bickering.

Yet it rankled her that he could be so suspicious still and talk about her behind her back, although she'd have to say that he had been a gentleman otherwise. It was a two-faced, creepozoid thing to do. *But he doesn't look like a creepozoid,* a part of her mind protested. Not the smart part, she thought immediately. The part that wrote articles for women's magazines—the part that was programmed to come up with a surefire, please-the-reader happy ending for everything from psoriasis to unrequited love.

Two mornings later the Delta Queen steamed into Memphis. The sky was slate gray with a steady drizzle of rain coming from the clouds and the weather, the outer edge of a winter storm front hammering the Midwest, hadn't changed much in the last forty-eight hours.

A group of passengers had begun a no-holds-barred penny poker tournament that moved from lounge to lounge, depending on whether they were in the crew's way and how raucous they got. Selena had joined in for a few hours, anteing up her handful of pennies with a flourish worthy of Gaylord Ravenal from *Showboat,* and getting cheers from the mostly male players.

Looking on, Chance had only smiled slightly, observing the play but not willing to participate, it seemed, while she was at the table. The bartender told Selena later that Chance, an expert bluffer, had won hand after hand once she went off to bed, and walked away from the last game a rich man, at least in penny-poker terms, his pockets bulging with coins.

That he was good at bluffing didn't surprise her. She wondered whether he had been bluffing her all along, but that was another question she just wasn't going to ask him. The best word for the way he acted toward her was *neutral*.

A word that was neither here nor there, not positive and not negative. Just sort of . . . gray. Like the gloom that surrounded them. Selena stood beside Julia on the outer cabin deck beneath the overhang of the deck above them as the boat maneuvered to tie up. Despite the miserable weather, spectators were on the riverfront to watch the boat's arrival.

It was these faces that Julia searched so anxiously. When the lines were tied and the gangplank was secure on the cobblestone ramp, she turned to Selena.

"Leslie isn't there," she announced, pain obvious in her expression.

"It's a little before nine, and we weren't scheduled to arrive until nine, so maybe he doesn't know the boat is in yet," Selena suggested. "He still might show up."

"I'll bet he didn't get the message to come to Memphis." Julia sighed.

As the minutes stretched into half an hour, Selena had to admit it was possible that Leslie had not received Julia's message. Silently she berated Chance for not being here to comfort his aunt.

"Listen," Selena said, refusing to give up, "why don't I go ashore and phone the different hotels to see if I can find out where he's staying? I mean, I have a cell phone, but I forgot the charger, and I haven't made a single call since I've been on the boat. You don't have a cell phone, do you, Julia?"

"No, alas," the older woman answered. "I did for a while. Chance gave me one, but I never did figure out how to use it. The buttons were so small and it did so many things. So I lost it . . . on purpose."

"We're two of a kind, aren't we?" Selena smiled.

"Yes, dear. I think that we are. But I do wish that I could reach Leslie."

"Maybe he overslept. I really can call the hotels, you know."

"Oh, thank you, but I can't ask you to do that."

"You aren't asking me. I'm volunteering." She opened her purse and took out a piece of paper and pencil. "What's Leslie's full name?"

"Leslie Reid." Julia spelled it for her.

Selena slid the paper into her purse. "Is there any chance he might he staying with family or friends here in Memphis?"

"I don't think so," Julia replied, shaking her head uncertainly. "When Leslie and I were on the autumn cruise, we stopped in Memphis. He didn't mention knowing anyone here, and I'm sure he would have."

"That just leaves the hotels and motels," Selena smiled, trying not to think about what a daunting list that would prove to be in a city the size of Memphis. "I'll be back as soon as I can. Wish me luck."

She was off, entering the forward cabin lounge and descending the stairs to the main deck and the gangplank. The light rain made the cobblestones slippery. It was tricky going until Selena reached the sidewalk.

The downtown shopping mall was only a few blocks from the dock. Every other building along the waterfront seemed to be occupied by cotton brokers or cotton warehouses. As she crossed the street, the clouds opened up, nearly drowning her in a downpour. No umbrella, bareheaded, wearing a cotton jacket that wasn't waterproofed, she was soon soaked to the skin before she could reach any kind of shelter.

Two hours later, after putting a pocketful of change

into the pay telephone in her fruitless search for Leslie's hotel, she made her way back through the driving rain, now being whipped by a cold north wind. Her feet slithered and slipped down the slanting cobblestones to the boat.

She was drenched by the rain, nearly frozen into an ice cube by the cold wind, and disheartened by the long list of calls she had made in vain. At the back of her mind, she kept hoping that Leslie would be aboard the boat when she got there.

Someone was walking up the cobblestones directly toward her. At the moment her footing was fairly solid. She didn't care who it was, she wasn't going to give ground. He could just go around her.

The person kept coming directly toward her, not altering his path an inch. She didn't dare take her eyes off the uneven ground for fear of slipping and landing ignominiously on her backside.

"I thought country girls like you were supposed to have enough sense to come in out of the rain," Chance declared in an exasperated tone.

Selena stopped at the sound of his voice, glaring at him through the strands of the hair plastered across her eyes. "That's what I'm trying to do, if you'd get out of my way." Her teeth chattered uncontrollably when she spoke.

His arm circled her waist, providing solid support as he half lifted and half carried her to the more secure footing of the gangplank. He didn't slow the pace until they were under the shelter of the main deck.

"Where were you during the first half of that descent?" Selena muttered between shivers.

"You look like a drowned rat," Chance observed.

"Thanks a lot!" She was shaking all over, frozen to the bone.

The arm around her waist pushed her to the stair-case.

"What was so urgent that you had to go out in the middle of a downpour?" he demanded.

"I had to make some calls," she answered, gritting her teeth to keep them from clattering together. "My cell phone died, and I didn't bring the charger."

"You could have borrowed mine."

"Ah, we're not compatible," she said hastily. She had no way of knowing if that was true or not, but she wouldn't have dreamed of asking him anyway. Using his charger would mean he would have to be in her room, or she would have to go to his, and she'd had a very good idea of what would happen then.

"How do you know that?" Chance inquired. "You've never seen my cell phone."

"I thought I did—in the hotel room," she lied.

"You have an excellent memory then."

"Oh, yes. I do. I really do."

He gave her a dubious look and shrugged. "So what was so urgent?"

"I wanted to see if I could find where Leslie was stay-ing. Did he show up here at the boat?"

"Of all the harebrained, wild-goose chases—" Abruptly he cut off his exclamation and snapped, "No, he didn't."

"Poor Julia." Selena sighed. "She'll be heartbroken. You should be with her."

"I'm going to talk to her, all right." There was an ominous note in his voice. "But first you're going up to your cabin and get out of these wet clothes."

"That's where I was going," she retorted with as much strength as her shivering voice could muster. "Or did you think I was going to wear them until they dried?"

"I wouldn't put it past you," Chance muttered,

forcibly ushering her through the forward cabin lounge, unmindful of the gawking passengers. "Any fool that would go out in a downpour without a raincoat or an umbrella"—he pushed open the door to the outer deck and shoved Selena through—"might not have enough brains to change into dry clothes."

"It was only drizzling when I left," she said defensively. "And I'm not made of sugar. I don't melt."

He gave her a cutting look and demanded, "Where's your room key?"

"In my bag."

Before Selena could open it, he was pulling the bag from her shaking hands and moving her up the stairs to the texas deck. Her reactions weren't as quick as they normally were.

Before she could stop her impetus forward and protest his taking over, Chance had found the key and was handing back her purse. He hustled her the rest of the way up the stairs to her cabin door, opening it and pushing her inside.

Now that she was out of the wind and the rain, she was shivering even more. She stopped short when she realized that Chance had followed her into the cabin.

"Get out of here," she said impatiently. "I want to change my clothes."

He gave her a raking glance that told her what a sorry sight she was. It didn't do much for her self-confidence. "I brought you here to change your clothes, so get undressed."

Her mouth opened to order him out, but he was already brushing past her into the bathroom. He emerged a second later with a bath towel in his hand. "Are you going to undress yourself, or am I going to do it for you?" he challenged.

The hard set of his jaw warned her that there was no use arguing. She would simply be wasting her time and expending energy in a useless effort. Shuddering from the bone-chilling wetness of her clothes, she gritted her teeth and lifted her numbed fingers to her blouse buttons. If they had been all thumbs, they couldn't have been more awkward.

"You could at least turn around," she snapped, blaming his intent gaze for her fumbling efforts.

Chance ignored her request. "The clothes will be dry before you ever get them off." He pushed her hands away and began unbuttoning the blouse.

"I can do it myself," Selena protested almost tearfully, angered and miserable to the point where she wanted to cry.

"There's a time for modesty, Red"—he stripped the blouse from her shoulders and gave it a toss into the bathroom—"and this isn't it."

He got her sitting down on the bed while he knelt to remove the soaked leather shoes from her feet. They followed her blouse into the bathroom, along with her socks. Impersonally, Chance reached up and unsnapped her pants. Grabbing the sodden material of the pants legs, he pulled those off, too. Then he rose and turned to pull down the covers of the other single bed.

"Wrap the towel around your head and get into bed, little Miss Prim and Proper," he ordered. "While you're hiding under the covers, you can take your underclothes off."

He waited until Selena had done as she was told. When the underclothes were lying in a wet heap on the floor, he turned and left the cabin. Continuing to shiver, Selena closed her eyes and snuggled deeper under the covers, certain she would never be warm again. But at least Chance was gone.

After fifteen minutes, she began to warm through and feel like a human being again. There was a warning rattle of metal, then the door opened and Chance walked through, carrying a tray.

"The door was locked!" she protested angrily.

"I took the key with me," he explained offhandedly, and slipped it into his pocket.

"Why don't you go away and leave me alone? You've had a pretty good laugh at my expense. I don't know why I seem to end up reinforcing your controlling behavior—"

"You sound like a goddamned talk show," he said. "Is it really that hard to let someone take care of you?"

"Now who's talking like a talk show?" Selena cried in frustration, in no position to enforce her demand. "I—"

"I brought you some soup from the kitchen," Chance interrupted as if he hadn't heard a word she'd said.

"Oh, thank you so much. With a side of humble pie, I'm sure. Leave it on the chest of drawers."

He sat down on the edge of the bed beside her, balancing the tray on his knees. As he removed the cover from the bowl, the mouthwatering smell of chicken soup filled the room. Picking up the soup-spoon, he dipped out some broth and carried the spoon to her lips. Selena couldn't believe it. He was actually going to feed her.

"Come on, eat up," Chance ordered calmly, touching the metal spoon to her lips.

She swallowed it, the liquid warming her throat as it went down. When he put the spoon in the bowl again, Selena couldn't help smiling.

"You look ridiculous," she said. He flicked an impassive glance in her direction and started to bring the spoon to her mouth. "Any minute I expect to hear you say, 'Open the hangar, here comes the airplane,' just as if you were feeding a child."

"Are you going to eat or talk?" he questioned.

The warmth of the soup seemed to dissolve her mistrust—and she had to admit the way he was jamming it into her with that serious expression, like she would come down with a raging case of double pneumonia if she didn't lap it up, was endearing.

That was one thing about men that she knew was true: in a crisis they had to *do* something. Fight bears. Lift giant boulders. Hunt for wild soup and bring it home.

Going on a pointless errand in pouring rain was not exactly a crisis, but maybe it looked like one to him. And she had felt pretty all-around awful by the time she was slipping and sliding on the cobblestone ramp, that was true enough.

"I'm going to eat." Selena pushed herself into more of a sitting position, taking her arms from beneath the covers while keeping the blankets tucked securely across her front. "But I'm going to feed myself."

With a shrug of acceptance, Chance shifted the tray so that it was on her lap and slid another pillow behind her head to prop her up.

"Have you seen Julia to tell her I couldn't find Leslie registered at any of the hotels?" Selena asked between spoonfuls.

"Not yet," he answered with a grim look.

"I feel so sorry for her," she sighed.

"My aunt doesn't need your pity."

"Well, she certainly doesn't get any from you!" she retorted, stung by his sudden rudeness. "You couldn't care less if Leslie ever shows up, and you know it."

Chance eyed her narrowly. "There's a great deal that you don't know about my aunt and me and my family. And you aren't in any position to condemn my behavior since you aren't in possession of all the facts."

"Then tell me the facts," she challenged.

"I don't discuss personal family matters with strangers.

And you, Red . . . despite all the intimate moments we've shared or almost shared"—there was a sexy glint in his steady look—"you're a stranger."

Selena's hunger for the soup ended with his words. She set the spoon on the tray and handed it to him. "I don't want any more," she said stiffly. Grudgingly, she added, "Thank you for bringing it."

"It was the least I could do," he said, accepting her thanks indifferently, "since it was at my aunt's instigation that you ended up half-drowned."

After Chance left with the tray, Selena pulled the covers around her neck and slid down into a horizontal position. All his concern had been prompted by a sense of duty and responsibility. Nothing more.

She felt let down somehow, cheated out of a feeling that could have been exceedingly pleasant. His protectiveness had surprised her—but it hadn't been more than a few minutes before he'd turned back into the Chance she knew, or sort of knew. Hell, she didn't want to know him. Selena closed her eyes, trying to shut out her mixed emotions. It wasn't long before she was asleep.

A hand touched her shoulder, and she rolled over in alarm. She had difficulty focusing her vision, which was fuzzy from sleep. Chance was sitting on the bed, watching her with those intent black eyes.

"How do you feel?" He pressed his palm across her forehead, then turned it to let the back of his hand rest against her cheek.

"I'm fine." Her insistent voice was thick and husky from the sleep. He took his hand away in apparent satisfaction, assured that she wasn't running a fever.

"What are you doing here again?"

"I wanted to see how you were and whether you were

going down to dinner tonight," he explained with a faintly amused twist of his mouth. "It's six o'clock."

"It can't be!" She frowned in protest.

"I'm sorry. Maybe it can't be, but it is." Chance shrugged. "So what's the decision? Are you coming down or do you want something sent up?"

"I'm coming down," Selena answered.

"Good. I'll wait for you outside." He straightened from the bed.

As he walked to the door, she said, "And leave my key on the chest of drawers."

There was a jangle of metal as the key was deposited on the wooden top before Chance walked out the door. She heard the click of the lock and slipped out of bed to dress hurriedly.

Most of the passengers were already in the dining room when Selena and Chance arrived at the staircase leading to the Orleans Room. Another couple approached the stairs at the same time. Both men gave way to permit the women to go first.

"How are you feeling?" the woman asked Selena.

"Fine," she said, blinking in surprise.

"That was quite a drenching you got today. It's a miracle you didn't catch your death of cold."

"I never get sick," Selena replied.

"A person can never be too careful at this time of year. I've had more colds in spring than any other time of year," the woman remarked. "It was probably a good thing that you stayed in your cabin and rested and kept warm this afternoon."

"Yes." Holy cow, Selena thought, how much more does this woman know about me?

At the bottom of the stairs, the woman paused and smiled. "It must have made you feel good the way Chance looked after you, bringing you hot soup and all. I couldn't think of anyone nicer to take care of me than him——unless of course it was my husband," she said with a laugh.

"Right," Selena said weakly before the couple separated from them to go to their own table. If every person in the dining room had turned to look at her with Chance, she couldn't have felt more self-conscious.

As Chance escorted her to their table where Julia waited, Selena asked in a low, accusing tone, "Does everyone on board know about my rain-soaked morning?"

"Probably," he conceded, amusement glinting in his downward glance at her rigidly set expression of composure.

"Did you have to tell them?" she muttered in an aside before greeting the woman at the table. "Hello, Julia."

"How are you feeling, Selena?" came the question of concern.

"Fine," she said, and wondered how many times she was going to have to repeat the answer before the evening was over.

She sat down in the chair Chance held out for her. As he helped her slide it closer to the table, he bent low to murmur a taunt near her ear. "Would you have preferred that I didn't explain what I was doing in your cabin in the middle of the day?" Her color rose briefly, giving him the answer that didn't need to be put into words.

Straightening, he took the chair opposite Selena while she attempted to concentrate her attention on Julia. "I'm sorry I—" She was about to apologize and offer her sympathy for not being able to find any trace of Leslie.

Julia broke in with a radiant smile, "Did Chance tell you the news? I've heard from Leslie!"

"No, he didn't." She flashed him a reproving glance, not understanding why he had omitted that when he knew how concerned she was for Julia. "That's wonderful!"

"Yes, it is." The older woman was bubbling over with happiness.

"Did he explain why he wasn't in Memphis to meet you?" Selena asked.

"Yes. There was some mix-up and he didn't receive my fax in time to get to Memphis before the boat left. He's driving to Louisville now," Julia told her.

Again Selena couldn't help noticing the profound silence surrounding Chance, just as it had other times when the subject of discussion was Leslie. She also noticed the way he changed the subject at the first opportunity, drawing Selena's attention to the menu choices so that the waiter could take their order.

When the main course was served, Julia asked, "Are you wearing a costume to the Christmas party tomorrow night, Selena?"

"Is it tomorrow night? I guess I forgot," she replied. "And my antlers are at home."

Chance gave her a quizzical look.

"You know. The felt kind, attached to a headband. Cheap costume, but they look cute, especially with a brown sweater."

"I bet you do look cute," he murmured.

"I had thought about buying another set in the gift shop when I heard about it. They have a lot of Christmas knickknacks, but . . ." She let the sentence trail off. Tomorrow night didn't give her much time to come up with anything. "Are you going to wear a costume, Chance?"

"I might. I hadn't thought about it."

"It doesn't have to be Christmassy, right? You could always go as a riverboat gambler," Selena suggested, half seriously, "with a string tie and brocade vest."

"That's an idea," Chance agreed smoothly. "And you could be a saloon girl."

"Except that I don't have the costume for that," she corrected, not liking his innuendo.

"Of course, you don't have to be in costume to attend the party," Julia pointed out. "The majority of the passengers probably won't, but it does make it so much more fun when you participate in the spirit of the event."

Selena started to make a comment, but Chance's low voice came first. "Your orange dress would be perfect."

She was about to remind him that she didn't have it anymore when she realized that he just might have kept it. A strange souvenir of an even stranger encounter. But he couldn't possibly have it with him.

"Perhaps," she agreed curtly, expecting any second for Julia to ask how Chance knew about a dress that Selena hadn't worn while on the boat. "I'll have to borrow something flouncy and tight."

Julia, whose wardrobe ran to tasteful tweeds in boxy cuts, pondered that in silence. "I could ask my new friend, Janet. She seems to be a very flouncy person."

"You'd need to wear your hair up, glue a black beauty spot on your cheek, and wear a black ribbon around your neck," Chance said. "I'm sure one of the boys in the band would lend you his garter."

"Oh, I know that Janet has a black boa you could borrow," Julia offered. "One of those silly feathery things. There's crepe paper you could use to make an ornament for your hair. And I should think one of Janet's dreadful ruffled things could be taken in at the waist temporarily. She wouldn't mind a bit."

"So long as you don't tell her she has dreadful taste," Chance said dryly.

"I would never," Julia said.

Selena had little room left for argument. "Okay, I'll go as a saloon girl—as long as you go as a riverboat gambler, Chance," she qualified.

"You have a deal, Red." His mouth twitched in amusement, his expression otherwise bland.

"By the way, Julia, what colors does Janet wear?" Selena inquired. "I don't think you've introduced me to her."

Julia waved a hand in the air. "Very bright colors, dear. Shades of orange, mostly. She really does have very bad taste, but she is the nicest person."

Orange. Selena had found out the hard way that that particular color was a great big Don't. And here she was, cornered into wearing it to a party—with Chance. She didn't understand how she talked herself into these situations. But it had been easy. She just hadn't had the sense to say she wasn't going to wear a costume, that was all.

Suppressing a sigh, she sliced a bite of stuffed pork chop. With her mouth full of food, she wouldn't have room for her foot.

CHAPTER NINE

Selena knew she wouldn't have missed the party the following night for anything. Not that a costume ball was a typical Christmas tradition, even by the anything-goes standards of New Orleans, but most of the passengers came in improvised costumes anyway, parading down the stairs and feeling festive.

She suspected that the bourbon served on the side with the inevitable eggnog had ended up inside quite a few revelers tonight. There was a highly imaginative assortment from sheeted ghosts to a Roman warrior, courtesy of the pots and pans from the kitchen. The range went from the ridiculous to the sublime.

Selena's own gown, made over in a few hours by Janet and Julia, had been slashed up to here to show a lot of leg and cut down to there on the bodice. The less of it, the better, Julia had said briskly, taking scissors to acres of ruffles while Janet safety-pinned what was left together.

The material was bright orangey-red, striking, to say the least, with black stockings and high heels. With the waist cinched to don't-you-dare-breathe narrowness,

Selena made a spectacular saloon girl, especially since no one was giving points for historical accuracy.

Janet added a black feather boa that made Selena sneeze when she first put it on, but she had to admit that it added even more flair to her already outrageous getup.

When Chance appeared, dressed as a riverboat gambler, her heart skipped a beat. Just where he had gotten his hands on a black brocade vest, stock tie, and high-collared shirt, she didn't know—probably borrowed from one of the musicians. But he looked dangerously delicious.

He refastened a loose cuff link while she watched from across the room, her mouth a little dry. He had *nice* hands. Strong. Ultra sexy. She could easily imagine hands like that doing a dazzling shuffle of the cards for a cutthroat game of poker—or tenderly caressing a woman he loved.

Selena put that thought out of her head fast. He didn't love *her*. She wasn't sure he even liked her, and vice versa. Anyway, if she was going to get through this cruise with her sanity intact, fantasies about hot sex with a riverboat gambler wouldn't help. She reminded herself that she hardly knew Chance, and she wasn't likely to see him again once they were back in New Orleans.

He finished fiddling with his cuffs, looked up, and gave her an appreciative once-over that took in every detail of her showy, revealing gown. Selena blushed. She turned away and made small talk with the older man next to her.

A total waste of time. Fascinated by her décolletage, the older man never even looked at her face, and all she got was a great view of his truly awful combover. When she turned back, Chance had moved away.

After the parade of costumes and entertainment by

the crew and passengers alike came the late-night snacks, followed by dance music from the band. Selena was too caught up in the party spirit to leave when the music began, nor did Chance suggest they should. Instead he turned to her and asked for a dance. "That's a hell of a dress for a minister's daughter. But you look great. Reminds of what you had on—maybe I should say took off—when we first met."

Selena was simply in too good a mood to take offense. "Thank you," she said, smiling, and let him lead her onto the floor.

As he turned her into his arms, she noted once again his sensual strength, the feeling of power kept contained, the firm arm around her waist. She remembered the other times Chance had held her in his arms to kiss and caress her, and immediately shied away from those memories.

Chance bent his head slightly to better see her face. "I liked the first dress better." He smiled wryly.

"Whatever happened to it?" Selena asked.

"I put it in my suitcase. Seemed easier to take it than leave it hanging in the hotel closet. A souvenir of a very interesting encounter."

"You mean you still have it?"

"Somewhere, yeah." He winked. "It's keeping my summer suits company."

She felt oddly pleased, inferring that he didn't have anyone in his life right now who would ask him questions about a sexy dress in his closet. He was dangerously charming tonight, flirting with her in his mocking way. The admiring light in those lazy black eyes made her feel very special. But maybe she was, maybe she wasn't. Any woman would like attention from a man like Chance.

With each dance, it became easier to match his steps,

to let her body sway with his in tempo with the music. Her senses came alive in his embrace. Whatever resistance she might have had melted under the warmth of his body heat and the intimate pressure of his thighs brushing against hers. With each breath, she caught the scent of expensive aftershave on his smooth cheeks, a heady mixture of spice and musk. And the steady rhythm of his heartbeat was hypnotic.

It was with regret that Selena left his arms when the last song ended. She shifted the feathery boa higher up around her shoulders as the hand at the small of her back guided her from the floor to the stairs.

"Shall we take the long way to our cabins?" Chance suggested.

Selena nodded, trying to steady the leap of her heart at his suggestion. At an unhurried pace, they wandered onto the outer cabin deck to slowly make their way around the bow to the texas stairs. A half moon was beaming a silvery light from the midnight sky. The air was briskly cool, invigorating to senses already sharply aware of everything around them.

Climbing the stairs, they made a circuitous route around the texas deck. Neither spoke, not wanting to break the spell that was somehow making the evening seem so special.

As they rounded the stern where the paddlewheel splashed rhythmically in its circle, a sudden breeze whipped the trailing end of the black boa, sending it across Selena's face before the gust of wind faded. The fluff tickled her nose and she sneezed.

"Are you catching cold?" Chance stopped, studying her intently.

"You sound like my dad," Selena said, shaking her head. "No. It was just these feathers."

"It's chilly, though, and your arms are bare." He took his hand away from her to slip off his jacket. "Therefore, I will do the gentlemanly thing and offer you my coat."

"I'm all right, really," Selena protested.

But he was already swinging his jacket behind her to drape it over her shoulders. As he drew the lapels together in front of her, his shadowy dark eyes focused on her lips. She held her breath, her heart beating a mile a minute. His fingers tightened on the material, pulling her toward him. And she realized this was what she had been waiting for all evening.

His head blacked out the half moon as he moved toward her. His mouth was hungry in its possession, its appetite insatiable, taking, devouring, and always demanding more. His hard length pushed her into the shadows of the overhang, pinning her against the wooden frame of the boat.

There was no pressure, no force to make her submit. No, the insidious seduction was taking place within her, making her hands weak and trembling as they spread across the solid muscles of his shoulders.

When he lifted his head, it was to bury his cheek in the flaming silk of her hair. "Selena . . . oh, Selena. Damn it." His demanding voice was rough, his breathing equally so. "Your dad would come after me with a shotgun if he knew what I wanted to do."

She laughed softly, but the unsatisfied ache she felt inside was anything but funny. "He's a pacifist," she said lightly. "Never shot anything but a rubber band, as far as I know. You're safe."

"You're not." Chance nipped at her earlobe. "I never felt more like saying to hell with propriety."

She shuddered against him, knowing how much she echoed his sentiments, and he gathered her close, pressing her face into his chest, his hands running caressingly over her spine.

"Still cold?"

"I wish I were," Selena murmured, and felt him smile against her hair.

"Now you know at least a little of the way I feel," he said softly. "I'm not used to playing these games, of being satisfied with kisses. I've always gotten what I wanted."

Selena made no response. It had been clear enough from the moment of their encounter in the hotel room that Chance was experienced in ways that she was not.

"But not anymore," he said.

"Why not?"

"Because you came along." He sighed. "With your red hair and hot green eyes and the way you walk—okay, I'll shut up."

Selena grinned. "You don't have to."

"Oh, but I do. Right now I can practically see the menacing specter of your father, the reverend with the rubber band. And I get the awful feeling I should re-form."

Selena drew her head away from his chest to look up at him. "Chance, I—"

He kissed her hard to silence the response, leaving her breathless when he was through. "Let's get to your cabin before my better judgment gets pushed aside."

But it was a gentle arm that encircled her shoulders and guided Selena to her cabin. Chance took the key from her hand and unlocked the door, but she didn't immediately enter. Flirting with danger, she looked up at him, her eyes still luminous with the emotions he had aroused.

"Chance, I—" She tried again to speak.

His mouth tightened as he pressed his hand across her lips. "Just say good night, Red," he ordered.

"Good night," Selena complied, and returned his jacket before slipping quietly inside the door.

In the room, she listened to him walk to the railing. She partly understood his reluctance to talk about what was happening between them. She was confused, too. At times, she disliked him intensely, distrusted him. She didn't know what her true feelings were. Possibly he didn't, either.

With a sigh, she began undressing. As she hung the bright orange gown up on a hanger, she wondered if it had been a good thing or a bad thing that it reminded him of the dress she'd worn in New Orleans. She would have to ask him about it tomorrow, she supposed.

Although he was outside, she knew he was right that the evening was at an end for them tonight. There were a few things they had to think about before they met each other in the morning.

The next morning Selena awakened to discover the boat was tied up at Paducah, Kentucky, to take on fresh water for the boilers. In the night the Mississippi River had been left and the Delta Queen had entered the Ohio River.

When she went down to breakfast, Julia was at their table but not Chance. There were indications at his place setting that he'd been there and gone.

"Good morning, Selena. Did you and Chance dance all night?" Julia had retired the past evening when the dancing had started.

"We tried," she admitted, taking her chair. Her gaze slid to the empty chair opposite hers. "He must have been up early this morning."

"Yes. He was leaving as I came down," Julia told her. "He seemed restless, as if he had something on his mind. He said he was going to walk into town."

Regret swept through Selena. She would have gladly

gone with him if he had asked. Subdued, she ordered her breakfast, discovering that she wasn't nearly as hungry as she had thought.

She was in the forward cabin lounge when Chance returned, within minutes of the boat's departure. A newspaper was tucked under his arm as he climbed the stairs from the main deck. He smiled and wished her good morning, then walked to the coffee urn to pour himself a cup before settling in one of the sofas to read the paper.

Expecting something more demonstrative, Selena managed to hide her disappointment and began chatting with some of the other passengers in the lounge. When the boat was well under way, she wandered outside.

After a week of viewing the levee-lined banks of the Mississippi and the flatlands stretching beyond them, the scenery along the Ohio River provided a startling contrast. Massive hills came right up to the water's edge on one side, their slopes thick with trees that permitted only occasional glimpses of rock faces.

The other side of the river was valley farmland with more hills in the distance. Selena noticed these features alternated. One time the hills would be on the right and the valley on the left. Around the bend, the positions would be reversed.

The buildings along the river ranged from farm homes to ramshackle huts to beautiful country homes. The wind turned brisk and blustery, forcing Selena to the lee side of the boat, where she watched the changing scenery alone.

Not until the afternoon did Chance seek her out. He was friendly and charming, but something was missing. She had the distinct impression that he had withdrawn behind that bronze mask he sometimes assumed to conceal his true feelings from the outside world.

It was as if the previous night had never happened. Selena wondered whether she had only imagined the difference in Chance's attitude last night. He had opened to her in a way he never had, enough to let her know that just being with her had aroused him, even if he'd joked about it—but she had sensed the seriousness underneath that and had been well aware of his physical desire for her.

The saloon girl get-up had been quite effective, though he'd been too much of a gentleman to look down the bodice that Julia had cut so daringly low. Or maybe he'd seized his chance when she'd relaxed in his arms and closed her eyes, just letting the music dissolve her reserve where he was concerned.

What would happen next, she had no way of knowing. Chance was an enigma to her in many ways—and now that it was the morning after, he seemed inclined to keep his distance.

Nothing she could do about that, Selena thought ruefully.

The next afternoon there was kite flying off the stern of the sundeck. Selena had assembled her kite in the aft cabin lounge and was carrying it up to the sundeck when she met Chance.

"Well, if it isn't Mrs. Benjamin Franklin!" he said, his eyes crinkling at the corners. "Ha ha. Lame joke. Sorry."

"Why don't you go fly a kite?" she suggested laughingly. "Yuck yuck."

"I certainly hope you don't intend to fly that one," Chance commented, eyeing her kite skeptically.

"Why not?" She looked at it, finding nothing wrong.

"Because it won't fly. Didn't you follow the instructions when you put it together?"

"I couldn't understand the directions." Selena gave a helpless little shrug. "But I thought it looked like a kite when I was through."

"Here." He reached for the kite. "The string is tied wrong, I'll fix it for you."

Obligingly Selena handed him the kite and its skein of nylon string. With quick, sure movements, he cut away her work and rethreaded the string properly through the kite before he gave it back to her.

"Have you ever flown a kite before?" he asked.

"No," she admitted with a dimpling smile.

"Then I'm coming along to view the launching. It's bound to be something to see." The grooves around his mouth were deepening in an effort to hold back a smile. It didn't matter, because his eyes were laughing at her.

"Okay," Selena agreed readily. "But don't make fun of me."

"Would I do something like that?" His voice was heavy with mock innocence.

"Yes."

There were quite a few fellow kite flyers on the sundeck when they reached it, but only two kites were actually in the air. The rest were still trying.

After Selena made four unsuccessful attempts to get her kite airborne, Chance stepped forward to offer some advice. Under his direction she succeeded on the next attempt.

"Give it a little more string." Chance stood close behind her, and her shoulder brushed against his chest as she obeyed his instructions. She gave a low whoop.

"More string," he said.

"It's flying! It's actually flying!" she breathed, her eyes sparkling. The words were barely out when the kite began looping crazily like a wild thing trying to free itself from its tether. "What's wrong?" she asked, frantically feeding out more line.

"I think it's caught in the downdrafts created by the paddlewheel's rotation," Chance answered, watching the erratic behavior of the kite. At that moment it swooped, diving for the red paddlewheel. "Look out! You're going to lose it."

Jointly they attempted to reel the string in to rescue the kite from the churning paddles. For a few seconds, it looked as if they were going to save it. Then it was gone.

"That red monster ate my kite!" Selena declared with a mock sigh.

"We'll see how everybody else fares," Chance smiled.

No longer participating in the flying, they stood to one side and watched the others. The "red monster" had a voracious appetite. It gobbled up more of the kites until there were only six left, soaring high out of reach of the paddlewheel. It became a contest to see which kite could fly the highest, and more skeins of string were added to each kite.

A practical joker in the spectators called out, "Bring them in. There's a bridge just around the bend!" There was a moment of panic until the kite flyers realized their legs were being pulled. There were numerous threats to throw the joker overboard, but all six kites remained on the boat.

Gradually the crowd of spectators thinned, and Chance and Selena wandered to an empty section of the port railing. Chance rested his elbows on the teak wood and leaned forward, clasping his hands in front of him.

The sun was warm and the breeze was cool, a freaky combination, considering it was December, but Selena wasn't going to complain. She laid her hands on the railing and lifted her face to the wind and sun.

With no advance warning of his topic, Chance said, "I had my assistant call the charity you said you sent the money to in New Orleans."

His announcement caught Selena completely off guard. Stunned, she could only look at him, unable to make any response for a moment. "Whoa," she said at last. "What happened to make you think of that? You were being the Friendly Kite Guy. I liked him. Bring him back."

He gave her a wry look. "Sorry about the timing. I wanted to be sure before I said anything and I wanted to apologize."

"Really."

"Really. Anyway, their office manager wasn't exactly eager to help. But she admitted that they had received that amount in a money order from an anonymous donor," he finished.

"Are you convinced now that I've been telling you the truth?"

"Yes." He straightened from the railing and turned to her, his gaze steady as it met hers. "Selena, I have to say I'm sorry. For my behavior in New Orleans and aboard this boat."

Her smile was a mixture of chagrin and regret. "It wasn't entirely your fault that you got the wrong impression about me." She had to admit it.

"Do you forgive me?"

"I guess so," Selena said slowly. "Well, while we're doing true confessions, I guess I should tell you what I really do. You never did ask."

"That's because I assumed— Okay, I don't want to be a total jerk a second time."

"Thanks." Her tone held a noticeable edge.

He looked at her curiously. "So what do you do?"

"I'm a freelance journalist."

"Really." He didn't seem to like the sound of that. "Taking notes on all this?"

"Now and then. There are some colorful characters on this old boat. And going up the Mississippi is a pretty amazing thing to do, even in this day and age."

"Yes, it is," Chance remarked dryly, turning away to study the valley farmland the boat was approaching. "But tell me something. Does my aunt Julia count as a colorful character?"

She was about to make a response when he distracted her attention. "Look!"

She followed the direction of his pointing finger and saw a small boy racing across a plowed field toward the river, running and stumbling over the clods of dirt. He wanted to reach the bank before the Delta Queen went by. Selena held her breath, afraid he wouldn't make it and knowing he was running his heart out.

"He's going to make it," Chance announced.

"Do you think so?" Selena asked doubtfully.

"This isn't exactly a speedboat."

Just as the bow of the steamboat glided past a grassy area on the bank, the boy reached the same spot. Winded, a sandy mop of hair tousled by his race, he began waving wildly, a broad grin on his freckled face. Selena waved back with equal enthusiasm, along with Chance.

When they had glided past and the red paddlewheel was churning its good-bye, Selena continued to watch the figure on the bank growing steadily smaller.

"How exciting it must be for a small boy to see a boat like the Delta Queen steaming up the river," she commented. "How exciting for anyone. I guess children can just better express it."

"True," Chance agreed absently, and moved away

from the railing, unexpectedly adding, "I'll see you at dinner."

After his apology, she had thought that his air of remoteness would leave. But there was a part of him that was still reserved and aloof. He was holding back and she didn't know why.

On Wednesday, the Delta Queen arrived in Louisville, Kentucky. For the third time, Selena stood on deck with Julia as the boat docked, unable to believe that Leslie would fail to appear again. Yet there was no one waiting on the waterfront except an obliging deckhand from the Belle of Louisville to help them tie up.

Cars and trucks whizzed by on the elevated interstate passing above the wharf, some honking at the Delta Queen as she docked. The crew members not involved in the tying up were busy decking out the boat in all her finery. Pennants streamed from her landing boom and bunting was draped on her railings, all in festive preparation for the great steamboat race later in the day.

Neither woman felt festive as they turned away from the railing. Selena was confused and concerned. The same expression was mirrored in Julia's face . . . and aching disappointment.

"What do you suppose happened this time?" Selena asked.

"I don't know." Julia shook her head bewilderedly. "Leslie said he was driving straight here. He should have arrived at least by Monday. I can't think why he's not here."

"Would you like me to go ashore and make some telephone calls?"

"Oh no, I can't let you do that—not after the last time," Julia refused hurriedly. "Chance would never forgive me."

"Chance doesn't have any say in what I do," Selena answered with a trace of irritation.

"Perhaps not." But Julia didn't exactly concede the point. "But I think I should make the calls. Would you stay on the boat in case Leslie comes while I'm gone?"

"Yes."

"He's a tall, rather strongly built man, plain-looking, with a mustache, and he always wears a hat." A smile touched the older woman's mouth as she described him.

"I'll watch for him," Selena promised.

Twenty minutes after Julia had left, Chance came by. He gave Selena one of those disarming smiles that reached his eyes. She felt her heart flutter at the sight of him. He was just too damned handsome and so, um, male.

"Want to do some sightseeing in Louisville?" he suggested. "Go out to Churchill Downs and see if we can pick next year's Derby winner on Saturday? There might not be a race, but we could watch the horses exercise, get something to eat, hang out for a while, whatever."

"I'm sorry." She hated to refuse, wanting very much to accept his invitation. "I promised Julia I'd wait here in case Leslie arrived while she was gone."

His mouth immediately thinned, his features setting into hard lines. "Leslie isn't—" he began impatiently, then abruptly cut off the rest of the sentence.

But Selena had heard enough to take a wild guess that it would have been, "Leslie isn't coming." Her look became wary and accusing.

"Leslie isn't coming?" She demanded that he finish it. "What do you know about this?"

The bland mask slipped into place. "I don't know anything about it," he returned smoothly. "I was simply going to say that this Julia-and-Leslie stuff is none of your business."

"I don't see it that way." Her reply was cold, although he didn't seem to be trying to be rude.

He seemed to shrug, although Selena detected no movement. Perhaps it was his attitude of indifference that gave her that impression.

He moved away, adding only, "I'll see you later," over his shoulder.

It was the middle of the afternoon before Julia returned, disheartened by her fruitless efforts to find or contact Leslie and upset by his unexplained absence. The state of her nerves wasn't improved by the influx of photographers and cameramen and various other members of the news media aboard to cover the race, as well as the hundred or so extra passengers who were coming on the Delta Queen just for the race.

"Why don't you lie down in your room for a while?" Selena suggested. "I'll tell the chief purser and the porters where you are. If a message comes from Leslie, then they'll know exactly where to find you."

"Yes, perhaps you're right," Julia agreed, her hands twisting in agitation. "I'll do that."

Selena spent some time in Julia's room, trying to calm her down and offer some words of reassurance, however meager. When she returned to the outer deck, the railing was crowded with passengers, the regular list and the newcomers.

The deep, rasping whistle of the Delta Queen blasted its long-and-two-shorts signal that it was leaving port. The Belle of Louisville was already in midstream along with the starter's boat. A crowd of spectators stood behind the barricades on the dock. The great steamboat race was about to get under way. Reversing into the channel, the Delta Queen moved upstream to draw level with the Belle.

"The railroad bridge overhead is the starting line."
Chance was at her elbow, holding a mint julep in each
hand.

"Thank you." As Selena took one of them, the paddlewheels on each boat stopped turning and they
floated toward the bridge.

When the bows of the boats reached the imaginary
line, the cannon on the starter's boat went off. Smoke
billowed from the stacks, and the paddlewheels began
rotating again, churning up the water.

Yet nothing seemed to be happening. They were
inching forward at a snail's pace, no explosive accelera-
tion, no leap forward. The passengers on each boat
were yelling, "Go! Go! Go!" Selena couldn't help laughing at the slow start, so very different from the beginning of any other race.

"I told you before, this isn't a speedboat," Chance
murmured dryly. "The Belle is shorter and lighter.
She'll get up steam and power first and move into the
lead. It takes the Delta Queen a little longer to get
going. Then we'll catch up—I hope."

As he predicted, the Belle of Louisville took the early
lead with the Delta Queen slowly closing the gap.
Selena sipped at the sweet drink in her hand. The race
was a novel experience and definitely something worth
writing up, whether she could sell it as a feature or not.

"How long is it?" she asked.

"Twelve miles. We go up to Six Mile Island and turn
around," he explained. "The starting line is the finishing line, too. The race takes about two hours."

Both sides of the bank as far as Selena could see were
lined with people, sometimes four and five rows deep,
family groups bundled up against the cold while they
watched the two old-time riverboats churning up the
Ohio. The helicopters carrying more members of the

news media followed the race's course, swooping low, sometimes hovering above the two boats.

A roar went through the passengers on the Delta Queen as they realized she was pulling ahead. The crowds on the bank saved their cheers to encourage the hometown favorite, the Belle of Louisville.

They had not reached the halfway point when Chance suggested, "They have a buffet set up in the Orleans Room. Want to eat before the rest of the passengers decide to crowd down there?"

Selena agreed, once he assured her that they would have plenty of time to eat and be back on deck for the finish of this unique race. Only a few other people had the same idea as Chance, so the room was fairly empty. They helped themselves to the buffet and sat down at their regular table. They were halfway through the meal when the Delta Queen was jolted.

"What was that?" Selena looked up in alarm.

"A towboat," Chance explained as they were jolted again. "We've reached Six Mile Island and are turning around. There are two towboats waiting, one for us and one for the Belle, to help us make a sharp, clean turnaround."

With the turn complete, the Delta Queen headed downstream, tooting her hoarse whistle twice. For a moment, Selena didn't understand the implication of the signal. Then it struck her. The pilot was signaling to the Belle that they would be passing on the starboard side.

The Belle of Louisville was still coming upstream, not having reached the turnaround point, and they were heading down, well in the lead. Suddenly the whistles carried the sweet ring of victory.

"We're going to win, aren't we?" She smiled at Chance.

"Barring a catastrophe," he agreed.

Her gaze slid to the empty chair Julia usually occupied, and some of the delight left her as she remembered that the older woman was in her room, heartsick and worried by Leslie's absence.

"I wonder why Leslie wasn't here to meet Julia," she mused aloud.

"I don't know," was the clipped response from Chance.

Her temper flared at his curt words. "What you mean is that you don't care."

"I don't know exactly what I mean." His voice was calm. "But I don't want to get into a discussion about it now."

"You never want to discuss it." She realized with alarm that she was close to tears and felt a flash of major annoyance with herself for getting emotional for no really good reason. Chalk it up to PMS, she thought miserably. Or maybe it was indigestion. Exactly when the subject of Julia's love life had become so charged, she didn't know. It really wasn't her business, just as Chance had said.

"Selena—" His voice was husky, stroking her like thick, rough velvet.

"You can save your charm. It isn't going to make me forget how you're treating her. Butt out, Chance. She could be happy with Leslie."

There was more she wanted to say, but this didn't seem like the time or place. There were more passengers at the buffet now, in hot pursuit of cold cuts and the pimento'ed egg salad she was already regretting, who might overhear. Selena pushed away from the table and walked stiffly from the room, ignoring his low command to come back.

It was easy to lose herself in the crowd on deck. If Chance searched for her in the milling throng, he didn't find her. As the Delta Queen crossed the finish line first, Selena cheered along with the rest, but hers rang hollow amidst the whistles of victory. She felt chilled and empty inside. Her heart was elsewhere.

A sense of failure troubled her. Where it had come from, she had no idea. Selena sighed and looked down into the churning water.

CHAPTER 10

The next day Selena stood on deck alone and watched the Delta Queen pulling away from Madison, Indiana, after their morning stop, a town renowned for its classic examples of fine architecture. Many of the houses she could see wore elegant swags of Christmas greenery and she could just glimpse a decorated tree here and there behind windows that sparkled in the sun. There was a light dusting of snow on the ground, and she felt a pang of regret, remembering how thrilled she had been by a white Christmas when she was a kid.

She missed her parents suddenly, even though she knew they were probably thrilled to be in Florida. She could imagine them whooping it up in their sedate way, sipping half-price, senior-strength daiquiris amidst a flock of pink plastic lawn flamingos.

She wondered what everyone was doing in her Iowa hometown. Everyone in Madison seemed to be indoors. And everything and everyone on the riverboat seemed quieter, the excitement of yesterday's race over and the realization that tomorrow morning they would be in Cincinnati, journey's end.

With a sigh, she turned from the railing and walked into the forward lounge. Just as she entered, she saw Julia walking toward the passageway leading to her stateroom. There was no spring to her step and no happiness in her expression. A surge of compassion swept through Selena at the uncertainty and confusion the older woman had to be experiencing.

"Good morning, Miss Merrick," a voice commented. "Or is it a good morning? You look downright glum. Aren't you enjoying the cruise?"

Selena turned to find Doug Spender, the chief purser, standing beside her. She forced a smile. "Yes, of course I am. Just not awake yet, I guess—" She broke off at his shrewd glance. "Okay, that's not true. I drank, like, three cups of coffee. And it was really good coffee."

The purser smiled. "Glad to hear it."

"But I was thinking about Julia," Selena began, glancing in the direction the older woman had taken, "and wishing there was something I could do. I feel so sorry for her."

"Yes, I know what you mean," he agreed. "All of us in the crew, especially the ones that have been with the Delta Queen for a while, are very fond of Miss Julia. It seems a shame that she keeps putting herself through this year after year."

Puzzled by his comment, Selena looked at him with a frown. "I beg your pardon?"

"Don't you know?" He looked at her with faint surprise.

"Know what?" she questioned.

"Leslie has been dead for fifteen years. He was killed in a car crash on his way to Louisville to meet Miss Julia," the chief purser explained.

"What?" Selena paled. "No, I didn't know that."

"It's true. Tragic but true," he concluded.

"Mr. Spender!" One of the other passengers approached to claim Spender's attention.

Shaken by the information, Selena left the room in a daze, unaware of where she was going until the briskness of fresh winter air touched her skin. She was on the outer deck. With a trembling hand, she groped for the support of the railing.

She couldn't take it all in. Leslie was dead. He had been for fifteen years. And Julia—sweet, eccentric Julia—was going through the whole sequence of events again, probably just as it had happened fifteen years ago. A sob rose in her throat, and she swallowed it back. Poor Julia, she thought.

"Selena, are you all right?" Chance was beside her, studying her with concern.

She looked at him, a fine mist of tears blurring her vision. "I've just found out . . . about Leslie," she explained tightly. "He's dead."

"Ah, yes." His features were suddenly grim, and there was a sardonic inflection in his voice. "Julia must have gotten the message about the accident now."

His response struck a raw nerve. "How can you be so cold?"

"Don't jump to conclusions, Selena—" he began.

"Why didn't you tell me?"

Chance didn't answer. Selena shook her head, thinking about the day she'd met Julia. The odd dinner. The impulsive decision to come along on the Christmas cruise. Remembering Julia's way of drifting off at times, and the sad vulnerability she'd seen in her eyes, Selena wondered why she hadn't realized just how fragile the older woman was.

Doug Spender's revelation had put together a lot of pieces, but that didn't make the situation any easier to comprehend. For some reason, Chance had chosen not to explain his aunt's behavior, and that, in Selena's opinion, was close to unforgivable.

"You don't have any compassion at all," Selena said bitterly.

Not that having the last word was any great satisfaction. She swept away from him to reenter the lounge. Inside the door, she hesitated for only a second before making her way to Julia's stateroom. It didn't matter that Leslie had been dead for so long. Julia still needed some comforting, and it was certain that Chance wouldn't provide it. Besides, Selena wanted to understand why Julia was doing this.

She knocked twice on the door, lightly, and heard Julia's muffled voice bid her enter. As Selena walked in, she saw the older woman tucking the message card back in its small envelope, the one that had accompanied the bouquet of roses delivered the first day of the cruise, the one that read, *I love you, May I always and forever be—your Leslie.* A flash of sympathy made Selena's throat tighten.

"Selena, my dear, come in and sit down," Julia welcomed her graciously. "I was just"—she fingered the small envelope in her hand and smiled wistfully—"rereading the note Leslie sent me with the roses."

Selena took a seat on the bed near Julia. "I don't know how to say this exactly," she began hesitantly. "But I just found out that Leslie is dead."

Julia frowned. "No, that isn't until tomorrow." Then she lifted a hand to her lips, discovery of Selena's meaning dawning in her eyes. "Oh, someone has told you that he's been dead for some time. You must think I'm crazy for pretending he's still alive."

"No." Selena shook her head and would have added more.

But Julia interrupted with a wry smile. "If not crazy, then just a little bit eccentric."

"I just don't understand why you put yourself through this."

"But don't you see? It was the happiest time of my life," she explained. "Oh, it did end tragically for me when Leslie died, but before that I felt warm and alive and wonderful, knowing I was going to marry him."

Selena still didn't understand. It was revealed in the confusion of her green eyes. Julia took her hand gently, as one would take a child's, and patted it.

"I was very lonely when I met Leslie sixteen years ago. My father always accused me of being too choosy, when the right word was shy. I'd always wanted to marry, if only to get away from my father. . . ." she trailed off. "Then when Leslie came into my life, I began feeling like a real woman for the first time in my life. Maybe our marriage wouldn't have worked, as my family said, but I'll always be grateful to him for the way he changed me. When I lost him, I was afraid I'd turn into a bitter old maid."

"Oh, Julia," Selena said, almost afraid to give advice—what did she know, after all, about real love? But she was determined to offer comfort. "He meant everything to you, didn't he?"

"Yes," Julia said simply. "I was shattered by his death—and terrified that I would shrivel up inside myself again. That's when I decided I had to keep taking this cruise."

"To renew the memories of how you felt." Selena was beginning to follow Julia's reasoning.

"It's a harmless game of make-believe I play in my mind. Until this trip, I've never involved anyone else in my pretending except a few members of the crew, whom I have known a long time."

"Yet this time you included me."

"Yes, I did," Julia admitted somewhat ruefully. "Perhaps I shouldn't have, but your reactions, your concern and interest made all the sensations so very real again. I hope you don't think badly of me. I truly meant no harm."

"I don't—I couldn't," Selena assured her. An instinctive understanding of the older woman's plight made her soften her tone. The last thing she wanted to do was sound judgmental, or angry. "It was just a shock to learn that Leslie was dead . . . has been dead for some time. I was worried that—" She hesitated, unsure of how to say what was on her mind.

"That I was trying to bring Leslie back from the grave?" Julia inserted in the blank.

The phrase was faintly macabre, but Julia spoke with such tenderness that Selena let it go. This trip was obviously a ritual, an eccentric way of cherishing some very precious memories. The holiday season must have made those memories almost unbearably poignant for Julia. "Something like that, yes," Selena said with a nod.

"No, I only want to keep the gift that he gave me," Julia explained. "*Joie de vivre*, as we say in New Orleans. The joy of life. I loved him, and I'm sorry I lost him. But it doesn't accomplish anything to forever mourn the loss of a loved one. You must learn to rejoice in the good things they left with you. That's all I'm trying to do."

"I understand." And she did.

"I was sure you would," Julia said, smiling. "After all, you know how it feels to be in love, how warm and deliciously alive it makes you feel inside."

"Me?" Selena echoed with a blank look.

"You've fallen in love with Chance, haven't you?" Julia tipped her head to the side on a questioning angle.

"I—" Selena started to deny it, then was jolted by the discovery that it was true. "I . . . think I have, yes."

"It's a wonderful feeling, isn't it?"

"It is," she agreed weakly, but the realization was too new for her to know exactly what her reaction to it was. Love. That great big sensation that the whole world seemed to be chasing after—had it really happened to her?

A few questions from a quiz in her favorite women's magazine floated through her mind. *Does he only have eyes for you?* Check. *Does he feed you chicken soup when you're sick?* Check. *Does he think you're sexy even in waist-high, baggy flowered underwear?* Check. *Does his kiss melt your willpower once and for all?* Check and double-check.

An announcement came over the public-address system, snapping her out of her reverie. Quizzes and questions like that were for teenagers—unless, Selena thought, she was as dotty as Julia and just didn't know it. On the other hand, maybe that was what love did to people.

"They're serving tea in the aft lounge. Shall we go have some?" Julia suggested.

"What?" For a moment the question didn't register, then Selena shook her head, copper-colored hair moving briefly against her shoulders. "I have some packing to finish yet, and I want to shower and change before the Captain's Dinner tonight." She rose from the bed, and Julia stood, too.

"I think I will have a cup," Julia decided, then smiled. "In a way, it's something of a relief that you know about Leslie. I knew I had to tell you the truth before the cruise was over. I do feel better now that you know and understand."

"So do I," Selena agreed, but her mind was elsewhere and she took her leave of Julia the instant she could.

The Captain's Dinner that evening was the only meal on the cruise where the passengers were required to wear formal dress. Selena dressed with elaborate care, her stomach feeling as if there was a convention of butterflies fluttering within its walls. She would be believing in love songs next.

Her gown was a special one, saved for this occasion, although at the time she hadn't known this last dinner of the cruise would be particularly significant in another way. It was most likely her last evening meal with Chance.

As she walked down the grand staircase, the busboy was going through the forward cabin lounge ringing the dinner chimes. Chance was near, standing at the base of the stairs with Julia. Selena hesitated for a split second when he glanced up, her heart pounding against her ribs. She felt the assessing sweep of his gaze and was reassured by the knowledge that her appearance was flawless.

Her dress was a filmy chiffon print, totally feminine, adorably retro and sexy, from an era when women were women and expected flat-out masculine worship when they dressed up. The pale blue was a perfect foil for the gleaming copper of her hair.

Her heart leaped into her throat when he stepped forward to meet her. Tall and devastatingly handsome, he wore a rich black suit that emphasized his dark looks and that aura of something dangerous. There was an admiring glint in his eyes, but he offered no compliment regarding her appearance.

"Shall we go down?" He addressed the question to both Selena and Julia.

"Yes," was all Selena managed.

Her heart was pounding. She felt awkward and unsure of herself, unable to behave naturally in his presence. She barely sipped the champagne, handed round courtesy of the captain, afraid it would loosen the knots inside her and let something slip.

Her silence went unnoticed, thanks to the numerous

toasts by the captain and crew before dinner and the entertainment afterward, which made conversation at their table almost unnecessary. At the close of the entertainment, before the dancing started, Julia made a discreet withdrawal to leave the two of them alone.

But Selena knew the older woman's thoughtfulness was wasted. She was too uncomfortable and self-conscious to be alone with Chance and much, much too aware of the way she truly felt toward him to behave as she had on previous evenings.

"Excuse me, I think I'll call it a night," she declared with a stiff smile and rose from the table.

"Aren't you going to stay for the dancing?" he questioned mildly.

"I still have some packing to do," Selena lied. "Good night."

"Good night," Chance returned.

At the stairs leading to the cabin deck, Selena paused to glance over her shoulder. Chance seemed not the least interested in her departure. It looked like a case of "out of sight, out of mind." Selena turned and walked slowly up the steps, trying to keep her head held high and not reveal how much his indifference hurt.

She woke up early the next morning, feeling cranky and out of sorts. She had barely slept all night. Once she was sure she'd caught a faint whiff of cigar smoke, light and not unpleasant, that she recognized as his brand. The thought of him being near was soothing, almost protective against the restlessness that kept her so edgy. But the most she had managed was fitful dozes. Rising, she dressed and did the last of her packing, setting her luggage outside the cabin door.

There was already a line at the purser's office in the

forward cabin lounge when she entered the room. Moving to the end of the line, she waited with the other passengers to settle what charges she had to pay.

The thought of returning to Iowa was far from thrilling. With her parents still in Florida and the holiday season drawing to a close, she was facing the dismal prospect of spending Christmas Eve and Christmas Day on her own.

Yes, she could go over to Robin's and teach her how to make decorative cross-cuts on a big, pink, slippery canned ham and stick on maraschino cherries and pineapple rings with toothpicks. Very *Ladies' Home Journal.* Very not exciting. They could slurp supermarket eggnog mixed with Jack Daniel's and get all choked up over scratchy videos of Frosty the Snowman and the Grinch. Selena felt faintly queasy just thinking about it.

Of course, going back meant she could help out her folks and check the water level in the boiler and make sure the houseplants hadn't withered from neglect. She was happy to do that. But the town handyman knew his way around their basement, and her parents had improvised a terrarium with cling wrap in the upstairs bathtub for the African violets.

She reminded herself, feeling a little guilty, that plants couldn't talk. She could always sneak in replacements if the high-maintenance African violets did shrivel up and die, and her mom would never know.

Taking her New Orleans guidebook from her tote bag, Selena flipped to the section on Christmas festivities and leafed through it. She studied a picture of the famous Angel Hair Lobby at the Fairmont Hotel, and the spectacular, block-long display of decorated trees, fairy lights, and twinkly stuff. Very pretty. She had always been a hopeless sucker for anything that twinkled.

She turned the page. She could check out Celebration at The Oaks, and its gorgeous outdoor show.

The five hundred thousand tourists who visited the elaborate display annually couldn't be wrong, could they? There were rides, too. Okay, she could skip the sleigh pulled by—yikes—real alligators. Selena peered at the photo. They couldn't possibly be real. Either way, their evil reptilian smiles were not exactly festive.

Well, she could commemorate her first Christmas on her own the Creole way, with a multicourse Reveillon meal after midnight mass somewhere. The traditional feast was served at the Fairmont and any number of fine restaurants. She could meet some new people if she went out, or she could end up . . .

Alone, she told herself sternly. And she really didn't want to be alone on Christmas Day. Even hanging out with a girlfriend and a canned ham was better than that. She closed the guidebook and stuck it back in her tote bag, craning her neck to see if the line had moved.

She saw Chance walk in and tried to ignore him as well as the crazy leaping of her heart.

His searching gaze found her in the line and he made straight for her. The boat's whistle blew the docking signal and she jumped a little. They had arrived at Cincinnati. Selena supposed Chance was coming to say good-bye, and she wished he wouldn't.

The trip was over—and nothing had happened between them. Had she wanted something to happen? She would have to think about that. But she fully intended to keep all that to herself. Picking it to pieces with Robin was not something she was going to do. She didn't expect to see Chance again, and that was that.

When he stopped beside her, she offered a tense, "Good morning, Chance."

He didn't bother with a greeting. "I want to talk to you, Selena." His dark gaze flickered to the other passengers covertly observing their exchange. "Privately, if you don't mind."

Her nerves tightened. She didn't want to speak to him alone. She was afraid she would blurt out something that she would regret and make a terrible fool of herself in the process.

"I'd lose my place in line," she protested lamely. "Can it wait until I'm through?" Maybe then she could slip away and avoid the meeting altogether.

"No, it can't," he insisted, eyeing her steadily.

She couldn't hold his gaze and glanced at her watch. "I don't have much time, Chance. I have a flight to catch back to Iowa."

"You can always catch a later flight." There was a hint of impatience in the line of his mouth.

"Maybe I can, but I'm not going to," she retorted.

Chance moved a step closer, his gaze narrowing. "We are going to have this talk," he said, lowering his voice to an I-mean-business tone. "It's important to Julia. And therefore it's important to you. Am I right?"

Compressing her lips tightly, Selena swept past him with a slightly angry toss of her head. His hand immediately clasped her elbow to guide her onto the outer deck, up the stairs to the texas deck and ultimately to his cabin.

"We can talk outside," Selena declared nervously as he inserted a key into his door lock.

"I said privately." He gently but firmly pushed her resisting figure into the cabin ahead of him, then closed the door.

Instantly she turned to face him, her pulse behaving erratically at the implied intimacy of his cabin. "All right, you got me to agree to this conversation," she attempted to challenge him. "What is it that you have to say that can only be said in your room?"

"I wanted a place where we couldn't be seen or overhead," he reasoned, that dark, enigmatic gaze of his studying her closely.

"What is it you want to say?" she demanded again, her breath not coming at all naturally.

"My aunt tells me that you've found out about her little pretense, as she puts it," he stated.

"That's true," she admitted.

"And?" A dark brow lifted with a touch of arrogance.

"What do you mean—*and?*" Selena asked, frowning.

Chance took a minute to study the cabin key in his hand. "Don't you find her behavior a little strange?" When the question was out, he glanced at her, his eyes shuttered by a black wall.

"By strange, I suppose you mean weird or crazy." An angry hurt began building, making her voice quiver slightly. "I expect you think I'm going to condemn her behavior the way you do. Well, the truth is, Mr. Chance Barkley, I find her little pretense unusually touching. So if you think for one minute that you've found a an ally in your attempts to end these trips—and I'm presuming that is what you've been doing, rather than trying to stop an imaginary elopement—then you're very sadly mistaken."

That was quite a speech, she thought anxiously. Self-righteousness mixed with a touch of indignation, served up with obvious annoyance. How would he take it?

He looked at her levelly and took a deep breath before replying. "Selena, if you think it's easy to keep an eye on an aunt who wanders around Louisiana like a character from a Tennessee Williams play, think again."

Selena gave him an outraged glare. "I applaud what Julia is doing, and I'm going to do everything I can to encourage her to keep right on doing it. If you had an ounce of feeling for her, you'd do the same."

"I protect her. Do you think everyone she meets is as understanding as you? Or as kind?"

Selena hesitated. That sounded a hell of a lot like a

compliment. But she wasn't sure exactly what he was getting at.

He didn't wait for her reply. "Listen up. Once I knew a little more about you, I decided to trust you. You seemed smart enough to figure out the truth eventually. So I kept out of it. She needs friends and she likes you. But it took me a while to get that you really are just about the most innocent damn girl that ever came out of Iowa."

"I'm not that innocent," she said indignantly.

A slow smile curved Chance's mouth. "Glad to hear it."

His arms were around Selena and his mouth was kissing hers into silence before she knew what was happening. For an instant, she was rigid in his embrace, then she melted, unwilling to deny her heart what it wanted. She was breathless and shaken when he finally lifted his head.

"Anyway, I only asked for an answer to my question. I didn't expect to receive a lecture."

"What question was that again?" She felt a little dazed by his kiss, and there was a peculiar glint in his eyes that puzzled her.

"The one about my aunt."

His arms were still locked around her, holding her close. Finding his mouth too compellingly close for her peace of mind, Selena stared at his shirt buttons.

"I'm not taking back anything I said. Stop treating your aunt the way you do and you won't be getting any lectures," she replied defensively.

"And just how do I treat my aunt?" Chance bent his head, tipping it slightly in an effort to see her face.

"You know how you treat her," she insisted weakly. "Every time she mentioned Leslie's name on the boat, you'd go all cold and hard, totally unsympathetic to her feelings. And look at how you tried to stop her from even taking this cruise—you and your high-and-mighty family. You did your best to persuade her not to come. Don't forget, I was there," she finished more strongly.

His mouth twitched. "That was part of the act, Red."

Warily, she met his gaze, dark and sparkling with an inner light. "Do you mean you were only pretending that you didn't want Julia to take this cruise?"

"That's right," he nodded.

"And you came on the boat with her as—"

"No," Chance quickly corrected her. "I came on the boat because of you. The first thing I thought when I saw your face was getting my money back."

"Oh!" Selena breathed.

"The second reason I came aboard," he continued, "was because I'd found you with Julia, and the two of you were very cozy and friendly. At the time I had every reason to suspect your motives for befriending an older and wealthy woman."

"I suppose so," she conceded.

"As far as my reaction to Leslie's name was concerned, I didn't like the idea that Julia was involving you in her little game of make-believe. At first I thought you knew it was only a game and were going along with it. When I realized you didn't, I knew eventually you would find it out, and I kept imagining what your reaction would be."

"It threw me for a loop," Selena admitted.

"Well, yeah. But Julia is very fond of you, and I didn't want to see her doubt her own sanity, as shaky as it is," he explained. "Look, she's not crazy, just eccentric. Nothing wrong with that, really."

"Seems like a grand old Louisiana tradition—being eccentric, I mean."

His answering grin was wry, and he nodded. "Julia

accuses me of being overly protective. Perhaps she's right. All I know is that I was irritated because I couldn't protect her from your ultimate discovery."

"But I don't think she's crazy for doing it," Selena protested.

"That's what she told me this morning. She said you understood her reasons, but being the cynical skeptic you've often described me as, I had to find out for myself."

"And that's why you brought me here," Selena concluded.

"That's it." His eyes smiled.

She struggled, trying to twist out of his arms. "Now that you have, you can let me go. I still have to go to the office and catch my flight." There was a catch in her voice, part of her desperate need to get away from him.

"Right. To Iowa. I take it you're not going sightseeing in Cincinnati first? Fair warning—it's a great old town but not exactly a pleasure palace. Not a patch on New Orleans. Take it from a native son."

"I'm sure you're right."

"Can I make you a proposition?"

Selena gulped, not sure she'd be able to resist.

He didn't wait for an answer. "I'd love to show you my city. My way." The strong circle of his arms tightened, keeping her in his embrace.

"I'd have to think about it." She didn't want to tell him that she'd been thinking about returning to New Orleans while she was waiting in line. He'd assume that meant yes.

"Okay. You have fifteen minutes before we disembark."

"That's not fair, Chance, and you know it."

He only shrugged. "It's a fact. And I don't set the

schedule." He brushed a straggling wisp of red hair out of her face with a tenderness that melted her. "Hey, there's one more thing."

"What's that?" she whispered.

"Julia also told me that you're in love with me. Is that right?" he asked calmly.

Selena froze in his arms. "She had no right to tell you that," she choked.

"Is it true?" Chance persisted.

"Yes, it's true," she retorted, "but she had no business telling you."

"How else would I have found out?" His voice was complacent and infuriatingly calm.

"I have no idea!" Selena tried desperately to sound self-assured. "But I can't just stroll off the boat arm in arm with you, like we're having a corny shipboard romance."

"You watch a lot of old movies, don't you?"

"Should I feel guilty about it?"

"No." Chance smiled. "I suppose the next step is for me to fly home with you to ask your dad's permission to marry you, wouldn't you say?" he suggested in the same composed tone.

"What?" Her head jerked up at his question, not believing she could have possibly heard correctly. "You're crazy."

"Runs in the family," he said cheerfully.

Those dark eyes were laughing silently into hers.

"Oh, shut up," Selena said, exasperated—and interested. Simultaneously.

"I hope he doesn't believe in long engagements. I don't think I could stand up under the strain."

Selena was still wary. "Chance, if this is your idea of a joke, I don't think it's very funny," she declared tightly.

"It's no joke. I was just trying to get your attention."

He stopped smiling, gazing at her so intently that she was certain he could see into her soul.

"You got it," Selena said wide-eyed.

"Guess what, beautiful. I love you, too. Kind of sudden, I have to agree, but it happens."

It had happened. Selena could not, would not argue with that inescapable and disconcerting fact.

"But it would probably help if we got to know each other. What do you say?"

"Um." She couldn't think of anything more intelligent to say at the moment.

"Um? Just um? What does that mean in Iowan?'" he inquired.

"It means you really are crazy!" Selena assured him, laughing and crying at the same time. "I can't possibly say yes to a proposal like that!"

Her arms wound around his neck as his mouth sought her lips.

"Then say yes to getting to know me. Take all the time you want. I know what I want—and I want you, Red."

"Why?"

"Because . . . oh, hell. This is hard to explain."

"Try," she said, enjoying having him on the spot.

"Because . . . I like the way you can morph into a long-legged saloon girl and dance the night away, and be just as happy flying a kite like a kid the next day. And you went out of your way to be kind to my aunt when you didn't have to be, and that means a lot to me."

"I see," she murmured. "Well, that's a start."

"We have to start somewhere. Why not now? Come back to New Orleans with me. We'll share Christmas . . . and ring in the New Year together. I'll be good."

Selena laughed. "Good? Hey, just be yourself. Let's see what happens. I'm ready for this. I mean, I think

I'm ready. Maybe what I am is willing—mmf!" He kissed her again, long and lovingly. Selena surrendered to the magic of the moment, body and soul.

"Can you imagine," Chance murmured against the pliant curve of her lips, "how we're going to explain to our children the way we met?"

Selena thought that over. "Very carefully."

Don't miss this romantic excerpt from
LONE CALDER STAR
by Janet Dailey,
available now from Kensington . . .

There is something about Saturday night that has always drawn a cowboy to the lights of town, and Quint was no exception. While drinking and carousing had never been part of his nature, a cold beer, a good meal, and a change of surroundings held a definite appeal for him.

Fort Worth with its array of nightspots sat northeast of the Cee Bar with other towns of varying sizes lying in between. Quint left the ranch with no particular destination in mind, but he turned in the direction of Loury. The Corner Café hadn't crossed his mind until he saw the fluorescent glare of its lighted windows. The sight summoned up an immediate image of Dallas with her pale copper hair and unusual light brown eyes.

Quint found himself wondering whether she was working tonight. At almost the same moment, he remembered all the times in the past when he had been a stranger in a strange town and experienced the loneliness that could be found in a crowd. A familiar face suddenly had more appeal than a beer and a good meal. In the blink of an eye, the decision was made and he swung the pickup into an empty parking slot in front of the café.

Dallas saw him when he walked through the door. One glimpse of his high cheekbones, the slight bronze cast of his skin, and the black gleam of his hair when he slipped off his hat, and she identified him instantly. Oddly, her spirits lifted. The night suddenly didn't seem to be as dull and ordinary to her as it had before he arrived.

The touch of his gaze was almost a tangible thing when he saw her crossing to a booth, a heavily laden serving tray balanced on one arm.

She nodded to the table he had occupied on his previous visit. "You can sit at your old table if you like," she told him.

"Thanks." His eyes smiled at her.

There was a warmth in their gray depths that Dallas didn't recall noticing before. Considering some of the things her grandfather had told her about him, she had a feeling she might have been too quick to dismiss him as an ordinary cowboy.

After she finished distributing the food orders on her tray, Dallas collected a glass of ice water and a cup of hot coffee from the counter and carried them to his table.

"I didn't expect to see you in here tonight." She set the water and coffee before him.

His eyes gleamed with amusement. "You didn't really think I'd leave town just because you told me I should."

"It was good advice." Dallas still believed that. "Or have you found that out? I heard you went to the Slash R."

"News travels fast," he replied, neither confirming nor denying.

Dallas realized that he had seldom given her a direct answer. "It's a small town. And anything to do with the Rutledges spreads like crazy. And the news that you bought hay from them went through this town like a category-four tornado."

"They were just doing the neighborly thing." He reached for the menu and flipped it open.

Dallas liked the way he played down the purchase. "Maybe, but the Slash R has never been known for making neighborly gestures."

"Maybe no one's given them a chance," he suggested, tongue-in-cheek.

Dallas reacted with a crooked smile that grooved a dimple in one cheek. "Yeah, right."

His smile widened into something dazzling and warm that snatched at her breath. "For a minute there I thought you were going to accuse me of being a fool again."

The remark was an instant reminder of the futility of one man attempting to stand against the Rutledges. It sobered her. "I don't think you realize how big the odds are against you."

An amused dryness entered his expression. "I imagine the odds were long that I'd get any hay, too." Without giving her a chance to reply, he asked, "Is it safe to order a steak?"

"Yes. It's just the meat loaf you need to avoid," she told him.

"In that case, I'll have a T-bone, medium rare, and a baked potato with all the trimmings."

"What kind of dressing on your salad?" Dallas pulled the order tablet from her apron pocket and flipped to a new sheet.

"Blue cheese, if you have it."

"Coming right up," she promised and moved away.

When she left, that lonely feeling closed around Quint again. Looking at the empty chairs pushed up to his table, he realized that it was her company and conversation he wanted.

There was a glimmer of rare annoyance in the glance he flicked at the scattering of other customers. Their presence forced Quint to put aside any hope he might have entertained of persuading Dallas to join him at the table. The knowledge left him with an edgy, irritated feeling, something that was new to him.

The sensation didn't fade until she returned to his table a few minutes later and placed a salad liberally drizzled with blue cheese dressing before him.

"I thought it would be busier than this on a Saturday night," Quint said to prevent her from walking away.

Her easy smile gave him the impression that she didn't mind being drawn into conversation, perhaps even welcomed it. "The supper crowd always comes early. By now the homebodies are back in front of their televisions and the rest are bending their elbows at Tillie's."

"Tillie's. That must be the local bar," Quint guessed. "Is it here in town? I don't remember driving by one."

"It's a block off the main drag, so it isn't a place that you would happen by," she explained. "Tubby's sister owns it. I keep telling him they should merge the two businesses. He'd have more customers if he sold beer and she'd have more if she sold food. But he just turns a deaf ear to the idea."

"Sounds like a good one to me. We have a place like that back in Montana," he said, thinking of the former roadhouse called Harry's in Blue Moon that had always sold both food and liquor. "Come Saturday night, it's packed to the rafters."

She tipped her head to one side, curiosity entering her expression. "Is that where you're from—Montana?"

"Born and raised there," Quint confirmed with a nod. "How about you? Are you a native Texan?"

"Of course." There was an impish light in her eyes. "Care to guess where I was born?"

Quint laughed softly in response. "Something tells me it might be Dallas."

"It's a little obvious, isn't it?" she agreed.

"I'd say you were lucky the hospital wasn't in Fort Worth."

"True. Although my mother told me that if she had gone to Fort Worth to deliver, she would have named me Gentry. But when I was born in Dallas, she thought it would be more original to name me after the city of my birth. Of course, you have to understand, she had an absolute aversion to commonplace names. Her own was Mary Alice, and she hated it."

Made sensitive by the recent loss of his father, Quint was quick to note her use of the past tense in referring to her mother. "How long has she been gone?"

"It was seven years ago this past spring."

"It's hard losing a parent," he said, speaking as much for himself as for her.

"Yes." But she seemed a little surprised that he understood that. After an instant's hesitation, Dallas glanced down at his untouched salad. "You'd better dig in," she told him. "Your steak will be up soon."

Left alone again, Quint picked up his fork and started on the salad with a renewed appetite, only distantly aware that his conversation with her, brief as it had been, had stimulated a male kind of hunger as well.

During the course of his meal, he had more occasions to talk to her, some exchanges longer than others. On a subconscious level, Quint knew it was all part of an age-old dance between a man and a woman. He had long ago become familiar with the steps to it, the advance and retreat, and the waiting and watching for that signal from the woman indicating her interest, or lack thereof.

With the only other remaining customer at the cash

register, Quint let his attention focus on Dallas, recalling the small, personal things he had learned about her tonight and the thousands more he still wanted to know— things like whether her hair felt as smooth as it looked, and the look of her light brown eyes when passion glazed them.

There was a natural grace to the relaxed, yet erect, posture of her body, long and slim and unmistakably feminine in its well-proportioned curves.

His bill paid, the man at the register headed out the door, and Dallas emerged from behind the counter and looked directly at Quint, her eyes bright and alive to him.

"Ready for more coffee?" Her warm smile was an encouragement to agree.

But Quint wasn't really interested in another cup of coffee. "What time do you close?"

And don't miss this exciting excerpt from
CALDER STORM
by Janet Dailey,
coming in June 2006 from Kensington . . .

Six-thirty on the dot Trey arrived at the door to Sloan's motel room. There was a dark sheen to his hair, still damp from his recent shower, and his face was shaved smooth of any end-of-the-day stubble. Blood ran hot and strong through his veins, part of the heady anticipation that put the dark and eager sparkle in his eyes.

A rap of his knuckles on the door drew an immediate and muffled response. "Be right there."

Yet for Trey, the seconds seemed interminable. At last there came the rattle and click of the security chain and deadbolt. Then the door swung inward.

"Come in." Sloan backed away from the opening in further invitation, a bath towel in her hand and a white terry-cloth robe swaddled around her slight frame. Her hair was a tousle of slick, wet strands that framed a face absent of any makeup, revealing a beauty that was absolutely natural. "I'm running a little late, I'm afraid," she said and turned away, reaching up to briskly towel her wet hair as she retreated into the room. "When I checked with my answering service, there were some calls I had to return, and they took longer than I planned."

"No problem," Trey told her and stepped into the room, closing the door behind him.

"Have a seat." Sloan waved a hand at the room's lone chair. "I promise I won't be long."

"You don't have to hurry on my account." But Trey made no move toward the chair, not with a king-sized bed dominating his view.

For a moment he stared at its smoothly made surface, the sight of it conjuring up images of the way he wanted the night to end. The rawness of all those desires made him restless and edgy. He took off his hat and turned it absently in his hand, while his glance scoured the rest of the room. Except for a black carry-on bag on the luggage rack and a smaller leather bag on the floor next to it, there was little evidence of the room's occupant.

"Are you always this neat?" he asked, thinking of his sister who would have had her stuff strewn all over.

Sloan moved back into his line of vision, flipping open the carry-on and retrieving a cosmetic bag from it. "It isn't so much a matter of neatness as it is organization. Keeping things put away eliminates the risk of leaving something behind and makes the packing process go much faster."

"Makes sense." It also made sense that she could leave at a moment's notice. It was a knowledge that reached down into his guts and churned them up.

"It does to me." Sloan disappeared into the bathroom.

But she didn't close the door. Trey gravitated to the opening, arriving as the loud hum of the hair dryer started up. Sloan stood facing the mirror, holding the dryer in one hand while she finger-combed and fluffed with the other. She turned her head to aim the dryer at the other side and caught sight of him in the doorway.

"This really won't take long," she told him, her voice lifting to make itself heard above the dryer's noisy hum. "I just want to get it damp-dry."

"No hurry. We've got all night," Trey replied, but his mind locked on the night thing.

Remnants of the shower's steam edged the bathroom mirror, beading into moisture droplets. Its presence prompted Trey to notice the bathroom's excessive warmth and heavy humidity. His glance strayed to the combination tub and shower and the wet sheen of its sides.

With no effort at all, he visualized Sloan standing beneath the spray, water sluicing down her shoulders onto her breasts and stomach. It was an easy leap to imagine himself showering with her, his hands gliding over her slick skin in an exploration of its rounded curves.

The blood started hammering so loudly in his head that he never heard the hair dryer click off. But the clear sound of Sloan's voice penetrated to shatter the images in his mind.

"Why don't you go watch some television while I finish getting ready?" The tone of suggestion was in her voice, but her hand was reaching for the bathroom door as if to close it on him when Trey jerked his gaze back to her. "The remote should be on the stand by the bed."

Not trusting his voice, Trey nodded and turned from the opening. He was conscious of the bathroom door swinging shut as he took his first steps away from it. That forward impetus carried him part way into the room. Then he halted at the foot of the bed.

Television held no appeal to him, not with all these fevered longings coursing through him. They left him raw and hungry for the feel of Sloan in his arms. With all his senses sharpened by it, he turned the instant he heard the releasing click of the bathroom door latch.